eSA

PLEASE RETURN TO THE ABOVE LIBRARY OR ANY OTHER ABERDEEN
CITY LIBRARY, ON OR BEFORE THE DUE DATE. TO RENEW, PLEASE
QUOTE THE DUE DATE AND THE BARCODE NUMBER.

 Aberdeen City Council
Library & Information Services

WITHDRAWN

CRITICAL

CRITICAL

ROBIN COOK

THORNDIKE
WINDSOR
PARAGON

This Large Print edition is published by Thorndike Press, Waterville, Maine USA and by BBC Audiobooks, Bath England

Thorndike Press, an imprint of the Gale Group.
Thomson and Star Logo and Thorndike are trademarks and Gale is a registered trademark used herein under license.

Thorndike Press® Large Print Basic.
The text of this Large Print edition is unabridged.
Other aspects of the book may vary from the original edition.
Set in 16 pt. Plantin.

LIBRARY OF CONGRESS CATALOGING-IN-PUBLICATION DATA

Cook, Robin, 1940-
 Critical / by Robin Cook.
  p. cm. — (Thorndike Press large print basic)
 ISBN-13: 978-0-7862-9446-6 (lg. print : alk. paper)
 ISBN-10: 0-7862-9446-9 (lg. print : alk. paper)
 1. Hospital administrators — Fiction. 2. Nosocomial infections — Fiction.
3. Staphylococcal infections — Fiction. 4. Drug resistance in microorganisms
 — Fiction. 5. Medical examiners (Law) — Fiction. 6. New York (N.Y.) —
Fiction. 7. Large type books. I. Title.
 PS3553.O5545C76 2007b
 813'.54—dc22
                                                            2007019410

BRITISH LIBRARY CATALOGUING-IN-PUBLICATION DATA AVAILABLE

Published in 2007 by arrangement with G.P. Putnam's Sons,
a member of Penguin Group (USA) Inc.
Published in the U.K. in 2008 by arrangement with Pan Macmillan Ltd.

U.K. Hardcover: 978 1 405 61918 9 (Windsor Large Print)
U.K. Softcover: 978 1 405 61919 6 (Paragon Large Print)

Printed in the United States of America on permanent paper
10 9 8 7 6 5 4 3 2 1

ACKNOWLEDGMENTS

Dominique Borse, MBA,
entertainment venture capitalist

Jean E. R. Cook, MSW, CAGS,
psychologist

Joe Cox, J.D., LLM,
superb tax and estate planning attorney

Rose Doherty, A.M.,
academician

Mark Flomenbaum, M.D., Ph.D.,
Chief Medical Examiner, Commonwealth
of Massachusetts

Angelo MacDonald, J.D.,
criminal law attorney

To Cameron and the joy he brings

PROLOGUE

Within the course of a week spanning March and April 2007, a serious, untoward event in the health of three strangers, two of whom lost their lives, was destined to impact the lives of hundreds, even thousands of people in a complicated web of causality. The victims had no premonition of their individual tragedies. Though they were all generally healthy married men of similar ages, they were engaged in totally different occupations, and each had absolutely no knowledge of the others, either socially or through business. One was a Caucasian physician who experienced a painful and debilitating athletic injury; the second an African-American computer programmer who contracted a fulminant, and rapidly fatal, nosocomial postoperative infection; and the third was an Asian-American accountant who suffered a ruthless, execution-style death.

■ ■ ■ ■

Like most people, Dr. Jack Stapleton never truly appreciated the anatomical and physiological marvel of his knees until they gave out, on the evening of March 26, 2007. He'd been at work as a forensic pathologist at the Office of the Chief Medical Examiner, or OCME, since early that morning. He'd commuted to and from the OCME on his beloved Cannondale mountain bike without once acknowledging the contributions of his knees. During the rest of the morning, he'd done three autopsies, one of which was a complicated affair involving painstaking dissection of the tracks of multiple gunshot wounds. In total, he'd been on his feet in the autopsy room, colloquially referred to as "the pit," more than four hours, moving by reflex to aid him in his work. Never once did he think about his knees and the effort expended by their various ligaments, which faithfully maintained the integrity of the joints despite the considerable stresses placed on them, and by the menisci, which cushioned the substantial pressure exerted by the distal ends of the femurs, or thighbones, on the tops of the tibias, or shinbones.

It was later, toward the end of one of Jack's almost nightly runs on the illuminated neighborhood basketball court, that disaster struck. To Jack's chagrin, he and several of the best players with whom he'd teamed up for the evening, including his friends Warren and Flash, had not won a single game, requiring them to sit out for frustratingly long periods of time before getting back in the action.

As the evening dragged on, Jack didn't need Warren to remind him that he had been responsible for several of the losses by either missing easy shots or losing the ball, yet Warren ragged on him mercilessly. Jack couldn't say it wasn't deserved; at the end of one game, with the score tied, Jack had utterly embarrassed himself, losing the ball and ultimately the game by dribbling off his own foot.

The real calamity occurred toward the end of the final game when Jack took a long inbounds pass from Warren. With the final game again tied and the next basket to determine the outcome, Jack was intent on redeeming himself. To his delight on what he hoped would be the final play, there was only one person between him and the basket. His name was Spit, in reference to one of his less endearing habits, but more important, from Jack's perspective, he was tall and lanky and hard put to keep up with Jack's quickness.

"Money!" Warren called out from the opponent's end of the court, fully expecting Jack to leave Spit in the dust for an easy layup.

After a convincing head fake to the left augmented by a rapid cross-dribble, Jack initiated a drive to his right. It began with his right leg lifting from the pavement, and the right knee rapidly flexing and then extending. As soon as his foot slammed down and planted itself on the macadam, Jack twisted his torso to the left to go around Spit, who was still recovering from the head fake and the cross-dribble. With Jack's left foot now off the pavement, his entire weight was transferred to his partially flexed right knee, which also had to deal with the sudden counterclockwise torsion.

If Jack had stopped to calculate the forces acting on his fifty-two-year-old knee, he might have thought twice about what he was asking his heretofore-faithful anatomy to withstand. Although his lateral ligaments held, since they effectively distributed the forces along their comparatively sizable width, the situation was different for the anterior cruciate ligament, which had lengthened slightly over the years as Jack had aged. Vainly, the relatively narrow band of tissue, which most people referred to as gristle when encountered in a leg of lamb but which Jack knew as collagen, tried to keep the femur from dislocating backward from the tibia. Unfortunately, the involved forces overwhelmed the ligament, and with a popping sound, it literally ripped apart and briefly allowed Jack's femur to dislocate out of its socket, tearing the delicate leading edges of both menisci in the process.

Jack's right leg crumbled, hurling him onto the rough-surfaced pavement, where he skidded forward a few feet, leaving a significant amount of skin behind. One instant he was a coordinated mass of goal-directed muscle and bone, the next a bruised and abraded heap prostrate on the ground, wincing in pain while clutching his knee. Jack wasn't one hundred percent certain of what had happened, but he had an idea. All he could do was hope he was wrong.

"Man, you're going from bad to worse," Warren said after he'd sprinted over and assured himself that Jack was basically okay. Warren's tone reflected half sympathy, half disgust. He straightened up and thrust his hands on his hips, glaring down at his injured friend. "Maybe you're getting too old for this, doc, you know what I'm saying?"

"Sorry," Jack managed. He felt embarrassed, since everyone was looking at him.

"Are you done tonight or what?" Warren questioned.

Jack shrugged. The pain had peaked, then lessened considerably, giving him a false sense of hope. Gingerly, he got to his feet and gradually put weight on the injured joint. He shrugged again and took a few tentative steps. "It doesn't feel that bad," he announced as he assessed the abrasions on his left elbow and knee. Then he tried yet another couple of steps, which seemed okay until he twisted himself to the left. At that point, the joint again briefly dislocated, causing Jack to revisit the pavement. For a second time, he struggled to his feet. "I'm done," he remarked with equal resignation and regret. "I'm really done. Clearly, this isn't a simple sprain."

Like most people, David Jeffries had never truly appreciated the molecular marvel that bacteria represented, nor the fact that whether an infection, once started, would be contained or spread depended on the outcome of an epic molecular battle waged between the bacteria's virulence factors and the human body's defense mechanisms. He also had never truly appreciated the threat that bacteria continued to pose, despite the extensive pharmacopoeia of antibiotics available to the modern physician. He had been aware that bacteria were responsible for terrible scourges in the past, including the black plague, but that had been in the past. He certainly hadn't worried about bacteria the way he worried about viruses such as H5N1 (bird flu), Ebola, or the virus that causes AIDS, whose threat was continually hyped by the media. Besides, David had been vaguely aware there were so-called good bacteria that helped to make things like cheese and yogurt. So when he had entered Angels Orthopedic Hospital early one Monday morning in 2007 to have his anterior cruciate ligament repaired with a cadaver graft, bacteria weren't one of his concerns. What he had worried about was the anesthesia and not waking up after the operation was over. He had also worried about the possibility he'd go through the whole ordeal, which a buddy had confided was painful, and it wouldn't work, meaning he wouldn't be able to get back to the tennis he loved.

As a computer programmer for a high-flying Manhattan-based software company, David had spent, as he put it, a lot of hours on his butt, shackled to his monitor. Being an athletically inclined individual from as early as he could remember, he needed competitive exercise, and tennis was his thing.

Up until his injury a month prior to his surgery, he'd played at least four times a week. He'd even vainly tried to interest his two preteen sons in the game.

As for his injury, he had no idea how it had happened. He'd always kept himself in good shape. All he had remembered about the event was charging the net after making what he thought had been a good lead shot. Unfortunately, his shot had not been as good as he had hoped, and his opponent had followed up with a well-placed return to David's left. On the run, David had planted his leading foot and twisted left to try to get to the ball. But he never got near it. Instead, he had found himself on the ground, clutching a painful knee that had immediately begun to swell dramatically.

Considering David's fulminant postoperative course, one certainly could say that he should have been more respectful of bacteria. Within hours of his surgery, relatively small numbers of staphylococci, which had found their way into David's knee and the distal bronchioles of his lungs, began their molecular magic.

Staphylococcus is a common type of bacterium. At any given time, two billion people, a third of the world's population, have them commensally residing inside their nares and/or in moist locations on their skin. Indeed, David was so colonized. But the species that had gotten inside David's body was not from his flora, but was rather a particular strain of staphylococcus aureus that had taken advantage of the ease with which staphylococci exchange genetic information to enhance their virulence and hence competitive advantage. Not only did this particular subspecies resist penicillinlike antibiotics, it also carried the genes for a host of nasty molecules, some of which helped the invading bacteria adhere to the cells that lined David's smallest capillaries while others actually destroyed the defensive cells that David's body sent to deal with the developing infection. With David's cellular defenses crippled, the invading bacteria's growth rapidly became exponential, reaching in hours a secretory stage. At this point, a group of other genes in this particular staphylococcus genome switched on, allowing the microorganisms to spew out a library of even more vicious molecules called toxins. These toxins began to wreak havoc inside David's body, including causing what is commonly referred to as the "flesh-eating effect," as well as the symptoms and signs referred to as toxic shock syndrome.

David was first made aware of the gathering storm by a slight fever, which developed six hours after his surgery, well before the invading bacteria reached the secretory stage. David didn't give the rise in temperature much thought, nor did the nurse's aide, who duly recorded it in his digital record. Next, he noticed what he described as tightness in his chest. With his narcotic pain medicine onboard, the administration of which he was able to adjust himself, he didn't complain. He thought these early symptoms were par for the course until his breathing became labored and he coughed up blood-tinged mucus. Suddenly, it was as if he couldn't quite catch his breath. At that point, he became truly concerned. His anxieties ratcheted up when he called attention to his worsening condition and the nurses responded by erupting in a flurry of anxious activity. As blood cultures were drawn, antibiotics were added to his IV, and frantic calls were made about a possible emergency transfer to the University Hospital, David hesitantly questioned if he was going to be all right.

"You'll be fine," one of the nurses said reflexively. But that reassurance notwithstanding, David died several hours later of overwhelming sepsis and multiorgan failure while en route to a full-service general hospital.

■ ■ ■ ■

Like most people, Paul Yang never truly worried about his ultimate fate, yet he should have, particularly around the time that David Jeffries was losing his molecular battle with bacteria. Similar to other fellow human beings cursed by the knowledge of their mortality, Paul didn't dwell on the harsh reality of death, even with the nagging reminder of progressively aging at a gradually quickening pace. At age fifty-one, he had too many more immediate concerns, such as his family, which included a spendthrift wife who was never materially satisfied, two children in college and another soon to follow, and a large suburban house with a commensurate mortgage and the constant need of major repair. As if all that wasn't enough, over the last three months his job had been driving him to distraction.

Five years previously, Paul had given up a comfortable yet predictable and somewhat boring job at an established Fortune 500 firm to be the chief and only accountant for a promising new start-up company proposing to build and run private, for-profit specialty hospitals. He had been aggressively recruited by his former boss, who had earlier been recruited to be the start-up's CFO by a brilliant woman doctor named Angela Dawson, who was just finishing her MBA at Columbia University. The decision to switch jobs had been agonizing for Paul, since he was not a gambler by nature, but his growing need for disposable income and the chance to make it big in the rapidly growing, trillion-dollar healthcare industry trumped the uncertainties and the associated risks.

Remarkably, everything had gone according to plan for Angels Healthcare LCC, thanks to Dr. Angela Dawson's innate business acumen. With the stock, warrants, and options Paul controlled, he was within weeks of becoming rich along with the other founders, the angel investors, and to a lesser extent the more than five hundred physician equity owners. The closing of an IPO was just around the corner, and due to a terrifically successful recent road show that had institutional investors drooling, the stock price was just about set at the upper limits of everyone's expectations.

With an anticipated five hundred million dollars to be raised on the first go-round, Paul should have been on cloud nine. But he wasn't. He was more anxious than he'd been in his entire life, because he was ensnared in an epic ethical dilemma exacerbated by the series of recent corporate accounting scandals, including that at Enron, which had rocked the financial world during the previous six or seven years. The fact that he had not cooked the books was not a consolation. He religiously adhered to GAAP — Generally Accepted Accounting Procedures — and was confident that his books were accurate to the penny. The problem was that he didn't want anyone outside of the founders to see the books, specifically because they were accurate and therefore clearly reflected a major negative-cash-flow situation. The problem had started three and a half months previously, just after the independent audit had been completed for the IPO prospectus. It began as a mere trickle but rapidly mushroomed into a torrent. Paul's dilemma was that he was supposed to report the shortfall, not just to his CFO, which he certainly did, but also to the Securities and Exchange Commission. The trouble was, as the CFO quickly pointed out, such reporting would undoubtedly kill the IPO, which would mean that all their strenuous effort over almost a year would go down the drain, perhaps along with the future of the company. The CFO and even Dr. Dawson herself had reminded Paul that the unexpected burn rate was a mere quirk and obviously temporary, since the cause was being adequately redressed.

Although Paul acknowledged that everything he was being told was probably true, he knew his not reporting definitely violated the law. Forced to choose between his innate sense of ethics and a combination of personal ambition and his family's insatiable need for cash, the conflict was driving him crazy. In fact, it had driven him back to drink, a problem he'd overcome years ago but that the current situation had reawakened. Yet he was confident the drinking wasn't completely out of control since it was restricted to having several cocktails prior to boarding the commuter train on his way home to New Jersey. There had been no all-night binges and partying with ladies of the night, which had been a problem in the past.

On the evening of April 2, 2007, he stopped into his designated watering hole en route to the train station, and while sipping his third vodka martini and staring at himself in the smoky mirror behind the bar, he suddenly decided he would file the required report the following day. He'd been flip-flopping for days, but all at once he thought maybe he could have his cake and eat it too. In his mildly inebriated state, he reasoned that it was now so close to the IPO closing that maybe the report would sit around at the bureaucratic SEC and not get to the investors in time. That way, he'd have assuaged his conscience and, he hoped, not killed the IPO. Feeling a sudden euphoria at having made a decision even if he would change his mind overnight, Paul rewarded himself with a fourth cocktail.

Paul's final vodka seemed more pleasurable than the previous, but it might have been the reason he did something an hour later that he normally would not have done. Weaving slightly while walking home from the train station, he allowed himself to be approached a few doors away from his house and to be engaged in conversation with two nattily dressed yet vaguely unnerving men who had emerged from a large, vintage black Cadillac.

"Mr. Paul Yang?" one of the men had questioned in a raspy voice.

Paul stopped, which was his first mistake. "Yes," he responded, which was his second mistake. He should have just kept walking. Coming to such a sudden halt, he had to sway slightly to maintain his balance, and he blinked a few times to try to sharpen his mildly blurry vision. The two men appeared about the same age and height, with hatchetlike faces, deeply set eyes, and dark hair carefully slicked back from their foreheads.

One of the men had considerable facial scarring. It was the other man who spoke.

"Would you be so kind as to afford us a moment of your time?" the man asked.

"I suppose," Paul responded, surprised by the disconnect between the gracious syntax of the request and the heavy New York accent.

"Sorry to delay you," the man continued. "I'm certain you are eager to get home."

Paul turned his head and glanced at his front door. He was mildly discomfited that the strangers knew where he lived.

"My name is Franco Ponti," the man added, "and this gentleman's name is Angelo Facciolo."

Paul looked briefly at the man with the unfortunate scarring. It appeared as if he didn't have eyebrows, which gave him an other-worldly appearance in the half-light.

"We work for Mr. Vinnie Dominick. I don't believe you are acquainted with this individual."

Paul nodded. He had never met a Mr. Vinnie Dominick, as far as he knew.

"I have been given permission by Mr. Dominick to tell you something financially significant about Angels Healthcare that no one at the company knows," Franco continued. "In return for this information, which Mr.

Dominick is certain will be interesting to you, he only asks that you respect his privacy and not tell anyone else. Is that a deal?"

Paul tried to think, but under the circumstances it was difficult. Yet as Angels Healthcare's chief accountant, he was curious about any so-called significant financial information. "Okay," Paul said finally.

"Now, I have to warn you that Mr. Dominick takes people at their word, and it would be serious if you don't honor your pledge. Do you understand?"

"I suppose," Paul said. He had to take a sudden step back to maintain his balance.

"Mr. Vinnie Dominick is Angels Healthcare's angel investor."

"Wow!" Paul said. In his position as accountant, he knew that there was an angel investor to the tune of fifteen million dollars, whose name no one knew. On top of that, the same individual recently provided a quarter-of-a-million-dollar bridge loan to cover the current shortfall. From the company's perspective, and Paul's, Mr. Dominick was a hero.

"Now, Mr. Dominick has a favor to ask. He would like to meet with you for a few moments without the knowledge of the principals of Angels Healthcare. He told me to say that he is concerned the principals of the company are not following the letter of the law. Now, I'm not sure what that means, but he said you would."

Paul nodded again as he tried to clear his alcohol-addled brain. Here was the issue he'd been struggling with solo for weeks, and suddenly he was being offered unexpected support. He cleared his throat and asked, "When would he like to meet?" Paul bent down to try to see into the interior of the black sedan, but he couldn't.

"Right now," Franco said. "Mr. Dominick has a yacht moored in Hoboken. We can have you there in fifteen minutes, you can have your talk, and then we'll bring you back to your door. It will be an hour at most."

"Hoboken?" Paul questioned, wishing he had skipped the cocktails. It seemed to be getting harder and harder to think. For a second, he couldn't even remember where Hoboken was.

"We'll be there in fifteen minutes," Franco repeated.

Paul wasn't wild about the idea, and hated being put on the spot. He was a bean counter who liked to deal with numbers, not hasty value judgments, particularly when suffering a buzz. Under normal circumstances, Paul would have never gotten into a car at night with total strangers for an evening meeting on a yacht with a man he'd never met. But in his current muddle and with the prospect of being abetted in his business decision-making by such an important player as Vinnie Dominick, he couldn't resist. With a final nod, he took a wobbly step toward the open car door. Angelo helped by taking Paul's laptop and handing it back to him when Paul was settled.

There was no conversation as they drove back in the direction of New York. Franco and Angelo sat in the front seat, and from Paul's vantage point in the back, their heads were dark, motionless, two-dimensional cutouts against the glare of the oncoming traffic. Paul glanced out the side window and wondered if he should have at least gone into his house to let his wife know what he was doing. He sighed and tried to look on the bright side. Although the interior of the car reeked of cigarettes, neither Franco nor Angelo lit up. Paul was at least thankful for that.

The marina was dark and deserted. Franco drove directly to the base of the main pier, and all three got out. Since it was off-season, most of the boats were out of the water, standing on blocks, and covered with white, shroudlike vinyl covers.

There was no conversation as the group

walked down the pier. The cold air revived Paul to a degree. He took in the nighttime beauty of the New York City skyline, marred by the fact that in the foreground, the Hudson River looked more like crude oil than water. The gentle waves made soft, lapping sounds against the pilings and the refuse-strewn shoreline. A slight odor of dead fish wafted in the breeze. Paul questioned the rationality of what he was doing but felt it was too late to change his mind.

Halfway out the pier they stopped at the mahogany stern of an impressive yacht with the name *Full Speed Ahead* stenciled in gold letters across it. The lights were ablaze in the main saloon, but no one could be seen. A row of fishing rods stuck out of cylindrical holders along the afterdeck's gunwales like bristles on the back of a giant insect.

Franco boarded and immediately scampered up a starboard ship's ladder and disappeared from view.

"Where's Mr. Dominick?" Paul asked Angelo. Paul's unease ticked upward without seeing the investor.

"You'll be chatting with him in two minutes," Angelo reassured him while gesturing for Paul to follow Franco across the narrow gangplank. With resignation, Paul did as he was told. Once on board, Paul had to steady himself as the large craft moved up and down with the gentle swells.

The next surprise was that Franco started the engines, which let out a deep, powerful, throaty roar. At the same time, Angelo quickly dealt with the mooring lines and pulled in the gangway. It was obvious that the two men were accustomed to running the craft.

Paul's unease again ratcheted upward. He had assumed his supposedly short meeting with Mr. Dominick would take place while the boat was moored. As the craft eased out of its slip, Paul briefly contemplated leaping off the moving boat onto the dock, but his natural indecision allowed the opportunity to pass. After four martinis, he doubted he could have managed it even if he had decided to try, especially clutching his laptop case.

Paul peered through the windows into the main saloon in hopes of seeing his missing host. He made his way over to the door and turned the handle. It opened. He glanced back at Angelo, who was busy coiling the heavy mooring lines next to several stacked cinder blocks. Angelo gestured for him to go inside. The gradually increasing roar of the diesels made conversation difficult.

Once the door was closed behind him,

Paul was relieved that most of the engine noise vanished, although not the vibration. The décor of the yacht was tastelessly glitzy. There was a large, flat-screen TV with La-Z-Boy recliners grouped in front, a gaming table with chairs, a large L-shaped couch, and an impressively stocked bar. He walked across the room and glanced down a few steps into the galley area, beyond which was a passageway with several closed doors. Paul presumed they were staterooms.

"Mr. Dominick," Paul called out. There was no answer.

Paul steadied himself as he felt the engines accelerate and the boat's angle of elevation increase before quickly flattening out. He glanced out the window. The boat had picked up speed. A sudden roar turned Paul's attention back to the door leading to the afterdeck. Angelo had come inside, and he approached Paul after pulling the door closed behind him. In full light, Paul was taken aback by the extent of the man's facial scarring. Not only didn't he have eyebrows, he didn't even have eyelashes. Even more startling, his abnormally thin lips were retracted back to the extent that they gave the impression they could not completely close over his yellowed teeth.

"Mr. Dominick," Angelo announced, extending Paul a cell phone flipped open.

Suppressing a sudden flash of resentment with the absurdity of the situation, Paul snatched the phone from Angelo. He plopped his laptop case onto the game table, sat down, and put the phone to his ear while watching Angelo drape himself sideways across the arms of one of the La-Z-Boys.

"Mr. Dominick," Paul snapped with the intention of expressing his irritation and frustration of having been tricked into talking on a cell phone, something that could have been done just as well from the backseat of the car. He also intended to say that he wasn't happy about having a confidential conversation within earshot of Angelo, who made no motion to leave.

"Listen, my good friend," Vinnie interrupted. "Why don't you call me Vinnie, seeing as though you and me might have to work together to straighten things out at Angels Healthcare. And before I say anything else about that, I want to apologize for not being there in person. That had been the plan, but I had an urgent business problem that needed my immediate attention. I hope you will forgive me."

"I suppose . . ." Paul began, but Vinnie again interrupted.

"I trust that Franco and Angelo have been

treating you with appropriate hospitality, since I'm not there to do it myself. The plan was for them to pick me up at the pier at the Jacob Javits Center, but I'm stuck here in Queens. Tell me! Have they offered you a drink?"

"No, but I don't need a drink," Paul lied. He was dying for a stiff drink. "What I would like is to be brought back to the marina. You and I can talk on the way."

"I've already told Franco and Angelo to bring you back," Vinnie said. "Meantime, let's you and I get down to business. I trust that you are now aware of the extent of my interest in Angels Healthcare."

"I am indeed, and thank you. Angels Heathcare wouldn't be where it is without your generosity."

"Generosity has nothing to do with my involvement. It is strictly business — serious business, I might add."

"Of course," Paul said quickly.

"As a director through a proxy, I've heard rumors there is a serious problem with short-term cash flow. Is there truth to these rumors?"

"Before I answer," Paul said, looking over at Angelo as he nonchalantly picked at his fingernails, "one of your men is sitting here within earshot. Is that appropriate?"

"Absolutely," Vinnie said without hesitation. "Franco and Angelo are like family."

"In that case, I have to admit the rumors are true. There is a very serious cash-flow problem." Paul's voice had an uncharacteristic lisp, as if his tongue was swollen.

"And I've also been told that SEC rules require that such a material change in the company's fiscal situation must be reported within a stipulated time frame."

"That is also true," Paul admitted guiltily. "The required form is called an eight-K, and should be filed within four days."

"And I've been further informed that this required form has not been filed."

"Once again, you are correct," Paul confessed. "The form has been composed but not filed. I was told not to file it by my boss, the CFO."

"How is it normally filed?"

"Electronically, online," Paul said. He glanced out the window, wondering why they had not changed course. He felt slightly dizzy, and his stomach was doing flip-flops.

"Just so I understand: Since this report has not been filed, we are in violation of SEC rules."

"Yes," Paul said reluctantly. The fact that he had been told not to file it did not resolve him of responsibility. The new Sarbanes-

Oxley rules made that very clear. He glanced at Angelo, whose presence still bothered him, considering the nature of the conversation and despite Mr. Dominick's assurances.

"It has also been pointed out to me that not filing in a timely fashion could be considered a felony, which leads me to ask if you plan to file so that neither of us are considered accessories."

"I'm going to have one more talk with my boss tomorrow. No matter what, I'm going to take it upon myself to file. So the answer is yes."

"Well, that's a relief," Vinnie said. "Where exactly is the file?"

"It's here, in my laptop."

"Anyplace else?"

"It's on a USB drive. My secretary has it," Paul said. He felt the engine vibrations slacken. Looking back out the window, he could see they had slowed down.

"Is there some particular reason for her having it?"

"Just for a backup. Obviously, my boss and I have not seen eye to eye on this issue, and the laptop actually belongs to the company."

"I'm certainly glad we had this talk," Vinnie said, "because it appears that you and me see eye to eye. I want to thank you for having a moral compass. We got to do the right thing, even if it means temporarily delaying the IPO. By the way, what's your secretary's name?"

"Amy Lucas."

"Is she loyal?"

"Absolutely."

"Where does Amy live?"

"Someplace in New Jersey."

"What does she look like?"

Paul rolled his eyes. He had to think. "She's very petite, with pixielike features. She looks much younger than she is. I suppose the most notable thing about her is her hair. Right now it is blond with lime-green highlights."

"I'd say that is unique. Does she know what is on the digital storage device?"

"She does," Paul said, aware the engines had come to a near stop. Through the window, he could see from the distant lights along the shore that they had essentially come to a stop. Looking out the other direction, he could see the illuminated Statue of Liberty.

"Was there anyone else involved in either preparing the eight-K or just knowledge of its existence? I don't want to worry about some would-be whistle-blower who might be in the process of filing the damn thing before you do in order to get a few bucks, claiming it wasn't going to be filed."

"No one that I know," Paul said. "The CFO could have told somebody, but I doubt it. He was very clear he didn't want the information to get out."

"Terrific," Vinnie said.

"Mr. Dominick," Paul said, "I think you will have to talk to your men again about getting me back to the marina."

"What?" Vinnie questioned with exaggerated disbelief. "Let me talk to one of those lumpheads."

Paul was about to call out to Angelo and give him the phone when Franco noisily descended, as if on cue, from the bridge deck and approached Paul with his hand outstretched. Paul was surprised at the timing. It seemed that Franco might have been listening in on the conversation.

While Franco stepped away to talk, Angelo stood up. He couldn't have been happier about the prospect of heading back to the marina. Even though he had to make frequent trips on the *Full Speed Ahead,* he had never become accustomed to being on the boat. It was always at night and usually to pick up drugs from ships coming from Mexico or South America. The problem was that he couldn't swim, and being out on the water, particularly in the darkness, made him more than uneasy. What he needed at the moment was a stiff drink.

At the bar, Angelo took out an old-fashioned glass and poured himself a knuckle of scotch. In the background, he could hear Franco on the phone repeating over and over "yeah" and "okay" and "sure," as though he was talking to his mother. Angelo tossed down the drink and faced back around into the room at the moment Franco said, "Consider it done," and flipped the cell phone closed.

"Time to get you home," Franco said to Paul.

"It's about time," Paul grumbled.

"Finally," Angelo silently mouthed as he slipped his hand under his jacket's lapel and allowed his fingers to close around the butt of his shoulder-holstered Walther TPH .22 semiautomatic.

1
APRIL 2, 2007
7:20 P.M.

At age thirty-seven, Angela Dawson was no stranger to adversity and anguish, despite having grown up in an upper-middle-class family in the affluent suburb of Englewood, New Jersey, where she had enjoyed all the associated material advantages, including the benefit of an extensive Ivy League education. Armed with both M.D. and MBA degrees as well as excellent health, her life on this early April night in the middle of New York City should have been relatively carefree, especially considering that she had every advantage of a wealthy lifestyle at her fingertips, including a fabulous city apartment and a stunning seaside house on Martha's Vineyard. But such was not the case. Instead, Angela was facing the biggest challenge of her life and suffering significant anxiety and distress in the process. Angels Healthcare LLC, which she had founded and nurtured during the previous five years, was teetering on the edge of either mind-numbing success or utter failure, and its outcome was to be decided in the next few weeks. The outcome rested squarely on her shoulders.

As if such an enormous challenge was not enough, Angela's ten-year-old daughter, Michelle Calabrese, was having a crisis of her own. And while Angela's CFO and COO, the presidents of Angels Healthcare's three hospitals, and the recently hired infection-control specialist waited impatiently in the boardroom down the hall, Angela had to deal with Michelle, with whom she'd been talking on the phone for more than fifteen minutes.

"I'm sorry, honey," Angela said, struggling to keep her voice calm yet firm. "The answer is no! We have discussed it, I've thought about it, but the answer is no. That's spelled n-o."

"But Mom," Michelle whined. "All the girls have them."

"That's hard to believe. You and your friends are only ten years old and in the fifth grade. I'm sure many parents feel the same as I do."

"Dad said I could. You are so mean. Maybe I should go live with him."

Angela gritted her teeth and resisted the

temptation to respond to her daughter's hurtful comment. Instead, she swiveled in her chair and glanced out the window of her corner office. Angels Healthcare was located on the twenty-second floor of the Trump Tower on Fifth Avenue. Her private office faced both south and west, with her desk oriented to the north. At the moment she was looking south, down the length of Fifth Avenue, chockablock with traffic. The receding red taillights appeared like a thousand radiant rubies. She knew her daughter was responding to her own anger about life with divorced parents and was trying to use Angela to get her way. Unfortunately, such hurtful comments about her ex-husband had worked several times in the past and had gotten Angela furious, but Angela was determined to try to keep it from happening. Especially under the strain she was, she had to keep herself calm for her upcoming meeting. Parenting and running a multimillion-dollar business were often at odds, and she had to keep them separate.

"Mom, are you still there?" Michelle questioned. She knew she'd crossed the line and already regretted her comment. There was no way she wanted to live with her father and all his crazy girlfriends.

"I'm still here," Angela said. She swung

41

back around to face her sparsely furnished, modern office. "But I did not like your last comment one bit."

"But you are being unfair. I mean, you let me pierce my ears."

"Ears are one thing, but belly-button rings are something else entirely. But I don't want to talk about it anymore, at least at the moment. Have you had supper?"

"Yeah," Michelle said dejectedly. "Haydee made paella."

Thank God for Haydee, Angela thought. Haydee Figueredo was a gracious Colombian woman Angela had hired as a live-in nanny right after Angela had separated from her husband, Michael Calabrese. Michelle was only three at the time, and Angela was six months away from finishing her internal medicine residency. Haydee had been like a gift from heaven.

"When are you coming home?" Michelle asked.

"Not for a couple of hours," Angela said. "I'm going into an important meeting."

"You always say that about meetings."

"Maybe I do, but this one is more important than most. Do you have homework?"

"Is the sky blue?" Michelle said superciliously.

Angela wasn't happy about the disrespect

42

Michelle's comment and tone suggested, but she let it go.

"If you need any help with any of your subjects, I'll help you when I get home."

"I think I'll be asleep."

"Really! Why so early?"

"I have to get up early for the field trip to the Cloisters."

"Oh, yes, I forgot," Angela said with an exaggerated grimace. She hated to forget events that were important to her daughter. "If you are asleep when I get home, I'll sneak in, give you a kiss, and then I'll see you in the morning."

"Okay, Mom."

Despite the conversation's earlier tone, mother and daughter exchanged heartfelt endearments before disconnecting. For a few moments, Angela sat at her desk. But the phone conversation with her daughter had reminded her of a time and an episode that had been equally as challenging and distressing as the current situation. It had been when she had to deal with both divorce proceedings and the bankruptcy of her inner-city primary-care practice, and the fact that she had survived them gave her confidence in her current circumstance.

With slightly more optimism than she had had earlier that afternoon, Angela pushed back from her desk, picked up her notes, and emerged from her office. She was surprised to see her secretary, Loren Stasin, sitting dutifully at her desk. Angela had not given the woman a thought over the previous three hours.

"Why are you still here?" Angela questioned with a touch of guilt.

Loren shrugged her narrow shoulders. "I thought you might need me."

"Heavens, no. Go on home! I'll see you in the morning."

"Do I need to remind you of your meeting tomorrow morning at the Manhattan Bank and Trust, followed by your meeting with Mr. Calabrese at his office?"

"Hardly," Angela said. "But thank you anyway. Now, you get out of here!"

"Thank you, Dr. Dawson," Loren said while surreptitiously putting away a novel.

Angela continued down the stark interior hallway. For a multitude of reasons, she wasn't looking forward to tomorrow's meetings. She always found it somewhat demeaning to try to raise money, and now, in such a desperate situation, it would be that much more humiliating. Even worse was that one of the people she would be asking for money was her ex-husband. Whenever she met with him, regardless of the reason, it almost never failed to evoke all the emotional turmoil of the divorce, not to mention the vexation she felt toward herself for having married him in the first place. She should have known better. There had been too many subtle suggestions that he would turn out like her father, challenged by her success to the point of encouraging bad behavior.

At the closed door to the boardroom, Angela paused, took a fortifying breath, then entered. Similar to her private office, the interior was aseptically modern, and dominated by a striking central table composed of a two-inch-thick piece of glass placed on the top of a white marble Ionic capital. The floor was white marble tile. Each of the side walls to the right and left had imbedded flat-screen television monitors for PowerPoint presentations. The far wall was glass, overlooking Fifth Avenue. The gilded and illuminated top of the landmark Crown Building immediately across the street filled the starkly modern room with a reflected warm glow.

The round table had been Angela's idea. Her management style emphasized teamwork rather than hierarchy, and the round table was more egalitarian than the usual boardroom fare. Although there were chairs for sixteen people, only six were occupied at the moment. The CFO was by himself at the opposite end, his back to the window. The three hospital presidents were to Angela's left. The COO was a few chairs away from the CFO, to Angela's right. The infection-control professional was next to the COO.

Purposefully, none of the department heads of Angels Healthcare, such as those from supply, laundry, engineering, housekeeping, public relations, personnel, laboratory services, and nursing, medical staff, or outside members of the board, were present. In fact, none had even been notified that the meeting was scheduled, much less invited.

Angela smiled cordially as she quickly glanced around at individual faces and acknowledged each person. The expressions were mildly apprehensive, except for CFO Bob Frampton, whose fleshy face had an ever-present sleep-deprived appearance, and for COO Carl Palanco, who looked to be in a state of continual surprise.

"Good evening, everyone," Angela said as she sat down. She again glanced around the room. "First, let me apologize for keeping you waiting. I know it is late and you are eager to get home to your families, so we will make this short. The good news is that we are still in business." Angela glanced at the three presidents, all of whom nodded in a restrained fashion. "The bad news is that our cash-flow problem has gone from concerning to critical. Of course, we felt the situation was critical a month ago, but it has gotten worse."

Angela gestured toward Bob Frampton, who shook his head slightly as if to wake himself. He leaned forward, putting his elbows on the table with his beefy hands together and fingers interlocked. "We are rapidly approaching, if not violating, our eighty percent margin on our loans with the Manhattan Bank and Trust. We had to sell some bonds to make a payment to our cardiac stent provider. They were threatening to cut off our supply."

"Considering how tight finances are, I want to personally thank you for doing that," Dr. Niesha Patrick said. She was a young African-American woman with light skin and a scattering of freckles in a butterfly pattern across her nose and cheeks. Like Angela, she had an MBA in addition to an M.D. Angela had recruited her from a large West Coast managed-care company to run Angels Heart Hospital. "With our ORs intermittently closed, our only dependable source of income has been from invasive angiography and cardioplasty. Without stents, even that revenue would be severely impacted."

"Invasive angiography and Lasik have probably been responsible for keeping us afloat," Angela said. She nodded in appreciation toward both Niesha and Dr. Stewart Sullivan. Stewart was the president of Angels Cosmetic Surgery and Eye Hospital.

"We are all doing what we can," Stewart said.

"As much of a gold mine specialty hospitals are in the current reimbursement milieu," Angela said, "they are at a particular disadvantage when their operating rooms close."

"But the operating rooms are now all open," Dr. Cynthia Sarpoulus said defensively. Cynthia was a medical-school classmate of Angela's who'd gone on to specialize in infectious disease and epidemiology. Angela had hired her when the current nosocomial infection problem started three and a half months previously. Cynthia was a dark-complected, raven-haired woman with a bit of a temper. Angela had been willing to put up with her thin-skinned and often caustic style because of her training, dedication, intelligence, and reputation. She'd been the reputed savior of several institutions with infection-control problems.

"They might be open, but they aren't

48

being utilized except by a fraction of our medical staff," Dr. Herman Straus said. Angela had recruited Herman from a Boston community hospital, where he'd been a well-respected assistant administrator. A big, athletic man with an outgoing personality, he had a particular affinity for dealing with orthopedic surgeons. That quality combined with his Cornell Hospital administration training made him an ideal president of Angels Orthopedic Hospital, and his record was proof of it.

"And why is that?" Angela asked. "Surely they know we have been on top of this problem right from the beginning. Cynthia, remind everyone what has been done."

"Just about everything possible," Cynthia snapped, as if she was being challenged. "Every OR has been cleaned with sodium hypochlorite and fumigated at least once with a product called NAV-CO$_2$. It's a nonflammable alcohol vapor in carbon dioxide."

"And not without considerable expense," Bob interjected.

"And why that particular agent?" Carl questioned.

"Because methicillin-resistant staphylococcus aureus, or its more common designation, MRSA, is highly sensitive to that particular preparation," Cynthia shot back, as if it were a fact everyone should know.

"Let's not get testy," Angela said. She wanted to keep the meeting friendly and, she hoped, productive. "We are all on the same page here. No one is casting aspersions. What else has been done?"

"Every hospital room that has seen an infection has also been similarly treated," Cynthia said. "More important, perhaps, as you all know, every member of the medical staff and every employee of the hospitals are cultured on a recurrent basis, and those who test positive as a carrier are treated with mupirocin until they test negative."

"Also at great expense," Bob added.

"Please, Bob," Angela said. "We are all aware of the expense side to this disaster. Cynthia, continue! Do you think culturing and treating the staff and employees is critical?"

"Absolutely," Cynthia said. "And we might consider the same for patients as a prelude to admission. Both Holland and Finland had a particularly bad problem with MRSA, and the way that they brought their problem under control was by treating both staff and patients: anyone who tested positive as a carrier. I'm beginning to wonder if we might have to do the same thing. Yet my real concern is that the MRSA is occurring at all three of our hospitals. What does that say? It says that if a carrier is responsible, then that carrier must routinely visit all three hospitals. Consequently, I have as of today ordered the testing and treating of all employees from even here at the home office who regularly visit all three hospitals, whether they have actual patient contact or not."

"Anything else?" Angela asked.

"We have mandated aggressive handwashing after each patient contact," Cynthia said, "particularly with the medical staff and nursing personnel. We've also instituted strict isolation for all MRSA patients, and more frequent changing of medical staff clothing, such as white coats and scrub outfits. We also require more alcohol cleaning after each use of routine equipment, like blood pressure cuffs. We've even cultured all the condensate pans of all the HVAC air handlers in all three hospitals. All have tested negative for pathogens, especially the strain of staph that has been plaguing us. In short, we are doing everything possible."

"Then why haven't the doctors been admitting patients?" Bob questioned. "As they are all owners, they have to be aware they are taking money from their own pockets by not doing so, especially if we go bankrupt."

"I don't want to hear that word," Angela

said, having already been through that demeaning experience.

"It's clear why they are not admitting," Stewart said. "They are terrified of their patients getting a postoperative infection despite all the infection-control strategies. With reimbursement solely based on DRGs, or diagnostically related groups, patients getting a postoperative infection directly cuts down on their productivity, and it is productivity that determines their income. Besides, there's the malpractice worry. Several of our plastic surgeons and even two of our ophthalmologists are being sued over these recent staph infections. So it's pretty simple. Despite being equity owners, it makes economic sense for them to go back to University or the Manhattan General, at least in the short run."

"But all hospitals are having trouble with staph," Carl said, "particularly methicillin-resistant staph. And that includes both the University and the General."

"Yeah, but not over the last three months, nor at the rate we have been seeing it," Herman said. "And despite all these efforts that Dr. Sarpoulus has been spearheading, the problem has not run its course, given that we at Angels Orthopedic had another case late today. It's a patient by the name of

52

David Jeffries."

"Oh, no!" Angela lamented. "I hadn't heard. I'm crushed. We'd been spared for more than a week."

"Like all the previous cases, we're trying to keep it quiet," Herman said. "As I said, it unfolded late this afternoon."

For a few moments, silence reigned.

All eyes switched to Cynthia. The expressions ranged from anger to dismay to inquisitiveness: How could this happen after all that Cynthia had just told them was being done, with considerable funds that they did not have?

"It hasn't been confirmed it was methicillin-resistant staph," Cynthia snapped defensively. She'd been called by the hospital's infection-control committee chair and briefed on the case just prior to coming to the current meeting.

"If you mean it hasn't been cultured, you're right," Herman said. "But it was positive by our VITEK system, and my lab supervisor says she's never had a false positive: false negatives yes, but not false positives."

"Good Lord," Angela said, trying to keep her composure. "Was the patient operated on today?"

"This morning," Herman said. "Anterior cruciate ligament repair."

"How is he doing, or shouldn't I ask?"

"He died while being transferred to the University Hospital. For obvious reasons, once it was clear he had septic shock, he would have been far better treated over there."

"Good Lord," Angela repeated. She was devastated. "I hope you realize that was a bad decision. Sending two patients in as many days to a regular, full-service hospital raises the risk the media might get ahold of the story. I can just see the headlines: *Specialty Hospital Outsources Critical Patient.* That would be a PR nightmare for us and do what we are trying desperately to avoid: negatively affect the IPO."

Herman shrugged. "It wasn't my decision. It was a medical decision. It was out of my hands."

"How has the Jeffries family taken it?" Angela asked.

"About the way you would expect," Herman responded.

"Have you spoken with them personally?"

"I have."

"What is your sense; are they going to sue?" Angela asked. At this point, damage control had to be a priority.

"It's too early to tell, but I did what I was supposed to do. I took responsibility on behalf of the hospital, apologized profusely, and told all the things we have been doing and will do to avoid a similar tragedy."

"Okay, that's all you can do," Angela said, more to reassure herself than Herman. She made a quick note. "I'll inform our general counsel. The sooner they get on it, the better."

Bob spoke up: "If there had to be another postoperative infection, as tragic for everyone as it is, it's best the patient passed quickly. The cost to us is considerably less, which could be critical under the circumstances."

Angela turned to Cynthia. "Find out if the procedure was in one of the operating rooms that had just been cleaned. In any case, see that it is again taken care of, but don't shut the whole OR. And find out when all the involved personnel had been cultured and if any of them had been a carrier."

Cynthia nodded.

"Isn't there some way we can get our physician owners to up the census?" Bob asked. "It would be enormously helpful. We have to have revenue. I don't mind billing Medicare in advance if it is only for a couple of weeks."

The three hospital presidents looked at one another to see who would speak. It was

Herman who spoke up: "I don't think there's any way to increase census, especially with this new MRSA case today. I don't know how my colleagues feel, but orthopods are very infection-adverse, because bone and joint infections have a tendency to stay around for a long time and eat up a lot of the surgeon's time, even in the best of circumstances. I've spoken about this issue with my chief of the medical staff. He's the one who clued me in."

"I've spoken with my chief of the medical staff," Niesha said. "I got essentially the same response."

"Ditto for me," Stewart added. "All surgeons are risk-averse when it comes to infections."

"It's probably too late, in any case," Angela said, trying to recover from this new blast of bad news. "But Bob's question gets to the heart of the reason I called this meeting. First, I wanted you all to hear about everything Dr. Sarpoulus has done concerning our MRSA problem. Of course, I wasn't aware there had been a new case. I'd truly hoped we were in the clear. Be that as it may, we have to somehow weather the next few weeks."

Angela then turned to Cynthia. "Angels Healthcare thanks you for your continued efforts, today's events notwithstanding. Now, would you mind leaving us for our boring financial discussion?"

Cynthia didn't respond at first. Her coal-dark eyes regarded Angela briefly, then swept around at the others. Without a word, she pushed back from the table and left the room. The door closed with a definitive thump.

For a moment, no one spoke.

"Rather headstrong," Bob commented finally, breaking the silence.

"Headstrong but dedicated," Carl said. "She's taken this whole problem and its persistence personally. I bet she thinks we are going to talk about her negatively, especially with this new case."

"I'll assure her tomorrow," Angela said. "But now let's get to the crux of the matter. As you all know, the closing of our IPO is two weeks away. The trick is how we are going to get there without any would-be investor or SEC official finding out about our ongoing cash-flow disaster. We've been lucky so far, despite the malpractice suits. We're also lucky that the problem with the staph occurred after the external audit, so its impact is not reflected in our IPO prospectus. I know you have all made enormous personal sacrifices. No one in the top echelon has taken any salary over the last two months, and that includes me. We've all maxed out our personal credit. I thank you for that. I can assure you we have begged and borrowed from all our investors to the maximum, including a quarter of a million from our lead angel investor syndicate.

"The irony of this desperate situation is that if the IPO goes as planned, the underwriters have recently guaranteed us five hundred million dollars, meaning we all will be rich and the company will be swimming in cash. Equally as important, our three hospitals proposed for Miami and our three hospitals proposed for Los Angeles will start construction. We are poised to be the first specialty hospital company to go public after the lifting of the United States Senate moratorium on specialty hospital construction, and we are involved in all the most lucrative specialties. The timing could not be more perfect. The sky is the limit. We just have to get there."

Angela paused and engaged the eyes of each of the people in the room to make sure there was no dissent. No one moved or spoke. Angela briefly glanced down at her notes.

"There is no blame in this situation," Angela asserted. "None of our spreadsheets that we used for forecasting even worst-case scenarios predicted such a catastrophe, where all our ORs would shut down essentially simultaneously. With revenue at near zero and fixed costs high, the burn rate on our emergency capital was enough to leave us here in the home office breathless. But you know all this, and with your help, we have survived. We've limped along, withholding payment to our suppliers until it was critical. We're continuing to do that, but still, it might not be enough. Bob, tell everyone how much capital we would need to get us through the IPO."

"I'd be very confident with two hundred thousand dollars," Bob said. "As the amount drops to zero, so does my confidence."

"Two hundred thousand," Angela repeated with a sigh. "Unfortunately, that's a lot of money, and I'm fresh out of ideas. What it comes down to is whether any of you smart people have any suggestions. From your perspective, the main problem, of course, is that all of you will have to meet payroll, and with a negative cash flow continuing, that is getting more and more difficult unless we help you. The trouble is, all our cash accounts are drawn down."

"What about withholding paying taxes?" Stewart suggested. "It's just two weeks."

"Bad idea," Bob said with hesitation. "Payroll tax and withholding tax are paid by wire transfer. If any of you or we hold it up, the bank will know, because we would have to instruct them to do so. Instructing the bank to not pay taxes would be an enormous red flag."

"What about going back to our lead angel investor?" Niesha suggested.

"I'm going to try tomorrow," Angela said. "I'm not optimistic. Our placement agent, who found the angel investor initially, has already squeezed out a quarter of a million a month ago, and at the time led me to believe that well was dry. Yet I'm still going to try."

"What about a bridge loan from the bank?" Stewart said. "They know about the IPO. Hell, it will only be two weeks. With the interest we've been paying on our loans, they've been making a fortune from us."

"You are forgetting what I said at the outset," Bob said. "I got a call Friday from our healthcare relationship manager at the bank. He was disturbed that we'd drawn down on facility by selling the bonds to pay our stent provider. They are not all that happy with us at the moment. If he called even part of our loan, the game would be over."

Angela looked from one person to another at that point. Everybody was looking down at their feet through the glass table. "All right," she said, when it was apparent no one had any other ideas. "I'm off to the bank and then our placement agent tomorrow. I'll do my best. If anyone has any additional ideas, I'll have my cell phone at all times. Thank you all for coming."

There was a scraping sound as all the chairs save for Angela's were pushed back on their Teflon-tipped legs. Everyone filed out, with most giving Angela's shoulder a reassuring squeeze in the process. For a few moments she stayed where she was, staring out at the gilded conical roof of the Crown Building across the street, while thinking about her company's predicament. It didn't seem fair that after all her work and anxiety, she and her nascent Angels Healthcare empire might be brought down by some lowly bacteria. At the same time, she wasn't surprised. In the financial world, whether it involved manufacturing lightbulbs or delivering healthcare, fairness was at best an afterthought. Money was king, and she'd learned that lesson the hard way, vainly trying to keep afloat her primary-care practice, which saw more than its share of Medicaid patients. It was that wrenching experience of bankruptcy more than anything else that had driven her to business school, where she had excelled as a kind of revenge and where she came to realize that medical care, if approached correctly, could make one not just financially comfortable but truly rich.

With a renewed sense of resolve, Angela pushed back her own chair and stood up. She retrieved her coat and umbrella from her office but purposefully left the notes she was holding and her briefcase on her desk. She planned to retrieve them in the morning before heading over to her first meeting of the day at the Manhattan Bank and Trust. She knew that in order to get a good night's sleep and be in top form on the morrow when she'd need all her wits, she had to make an active effort to clear her mind. By doing so under similar stressful circumstances in the past, she not only felt better the following day but often viewed problems from a different perspective and had new ideas. It was as if her subconscious was an active participant in her decision-making.

On the corner of Fifth Avenue and 56th Street, Angela stood a step away from the curb and raised her hand in an attempt to hail a cab, well aware that cabs were hard to come by at eight-twenty-five in the evening, especially on a drizzly early-April night. Since many of the city's taxi drivers were ending their shift, most of the cabs she saw had their off-duty lights on. The others were occupied. Until the previous month, Angela had regularly used a car service, but with the account seriously in arrears, she'd been reduced to taking cabs. Just when she was about to start walking to her 70th Street apartment, a taxi pulled up to discharge a passenger. The moment the man paid and jumped out, Angela climbed in.

As the cab sped toward Angela's destination, she took a deep breath and let it out with a huff. It was only then that she became conscious of her tenseness. With her arms crossed in front of her, she massaged the tips of her shoulders, then did the same with her temples. Slowly, she could feel her abdominal muscles and thigh muscles relax. Opening her eyes, she took in the lights of the city reflected in the slick, wet streets. There were plenty of pedestrians out, many arm in arm, sharing umbrellas. It was at such moments, between the demands of the workday and the domestic concerns involving her daughter, that Angela was aware of the fact that she had no social life, specifically with members of the opposite sex. Interacting with men was restricted to work-related encounters, the rare parents' night at her daughter's school, or, sadly enough, with someone in the checkout line at the grocery store. The fact that it was her choice, both as a driven woman and as a woman whose experiences with men caused her to question their monogamous ability, didn't lessen the occasional desire.

Refusing to give the issue more thought, she pulled out her cell phone and pressed the speed-dial button for home. Expecting to hear her daughter's voice since she usually answered before the completion of the first ring, Angela found herself talking with Haydee, the nanny-cum-majordomo. As busy as Angela's life was, she allowed Haydee to fill multiple roles.

"Where's the terror?" Angela questioned. The appellation "the terror" was the way Angela and Haydee humorously referred to Michelle behind the girl's back. It was humorous because it was the opposite of what they felt. Both women thought Michelle mildly and age-appropriately willful and occasionally argumentative, as evidenced by the belly-button-piercing issue, but otherwise near perfect.

"She's in bed, and I believe already asleep. Should I wake her?"

"Heavens, no!" Angela said, feeling a mild pang of loneliness. "Surely not."

After a short conversation about various domestic issues, Angela made an impromptu decision. She concluded the conversation by telling Haydee not to wait up for her, as she wouldn't be home for several more hours.

Sliding forward on the seat, Angela spoke to the driver through the Plexiglas partition. Instead of going home to a sleeping daughter, she'd decided to go to her health club. With all that was going on, she'd not been there for months and certainly could use a workout for mental as much as physical reasons. Besides, she reasoned, there would be people around, and on top of that, she could get a bite to eat in the club's surprisingly good restaurant/bar.

Angela's athletic club was close to her apartment, a block over and a few blocks down Columbus Avenue. She found her underused membership card without much difficulty in her overstuffed wallet. In short order, she changed into her workout clothes and took a turn on one of the stationary bikes while watching CNN. She was dismayed at how out of shape she was. Within five minutes, she was out of breath. After ten minutes, she was sweating to the extent that she feared she looked like a glass of iced tea in the tropics. Yet she persisted on sheer willpower until she had reached her twenty-minute goal.

Dismounting from the bike, Angela put

her hands on her hips and stood with her chest heaving, trying to catch her breath. For a moment, it took all her concentration. On top of that, she was drenched. Her hairband, which in the past had been more of an affectation than a necessity, was completely soaked. She imagined she looked like a wreck with her face flushed, her workout gear clinging to her body, and her hair a veritable mop. What was so embarrassing was that the people on the neighboring bikes were all riding with such apparent ease. No one seemed to be perspiring, and many were able to concentrate on reading as they pedaled. Angela knew there was no way she could have read anything during her workout, especially toward the end.

She picked up her towel and dried her face. Feeling self-conscious about her lack of endurance and bedraggled appearance, she quickly scanned the faces of the other riders as she set off toward the weight room. Luckily for her self-esteem, no one paid her any heed until she briefly locked eyes with a blond man who was pedaling furiously yet hadn't broken a sweat. The rapidity with which he looked away confirmed Angela's concerns about her appearance. As she passed behind him, she had to smile at her paranoia; in point of fact, she didn't care what the stranger thought.

Angela wandered around the weight room with no particular plan, using the machines randomly. She was careful not to use too much weight or do too many repetitions. The last thing she wanted to do was pull a muscle or sprain a joint. Despite the hour, the room was reasonably crowded. She noticed how a number of the men were checking out the women while pretending they weren't, reminding her how shallow some men could be.

Taking a pair of very light free weights, she positioned herself in front of a mirror and began stretching more than exercising the muscles of her upper body. While she continued, she appraised herself and tried to be objective. Her figure was still quite good and hadn't significantly changed from how it had looked in her mid-twenties. Obviously, that was due far more to genes than to effort, considering how seldom she'd made it to the gym while she'd nurtured Angels Healthcare. Her belly was flat, despite her pregnancy. Her legs had good definition, and her tush was firmer than she deserved. All in all, she was content with her appearance, except for her hair.

Angels Healthcare had been embroiled in the current MRSA-induced catastrophe only a month when she found a few stray gray hairs. Her mother had gone gray early so she shouldn't have been so surprised, but it had bothered her to the extent that she'd secretly gotten a rinse at the local pharmacy and used it several times. Although the gray had disappeared, she'd worried that some of her natural sheen had gone with it. And now, as she looked at it in the health-club weight room mirror, she was convinced.

Angela suddenly made a brief but exaggerated expression of utter horror in the mirror as a way of mocking herself. In the final analysis, she was not a vain person. Accomplishment was what interested her, not appearances.

"Are you all right?" a voice asked.

Angela turned and looked up into the face of the blond man with whom she'd briefly locked eyes in the room with the stationary bikes. He was somewhere in his mid-forties, reasonably handsome, and probably equivalently intelligent. He had bright blue eyes, cropped hair, and an insouciant, engaging smile. He was wearing a T-shirt that said *Make my day.*

"I'm quite okay," Angela said after her brief assessment of the stranger. "Why do you ask?"

"I thought there for a minute you were

about to cry."

Angela laughed heartily. When she'd made her mocking expression in the mirror, she'd momentarily forgotten she was in a room with a bunch of secretly attentive males.

"Why are you laughing? Really! A minute ago, while you were doing your curls, you looked like you were about to break down in tears."

"It would take too long to explain."

"Time is not a problem for me. How about a drink after we finish our workouts and you can explain? After that, who knows?"

With a wry smile, Angela regarded the man standing next to her. It had been a while since she had experienced such a rapid, unabashed come-on. Under normal circumstances, she would have merely smiled and walked away. In her current mood, some repartee and companionship had an uncharacteristic appeal, at least for an hour or so. After all, she was trying to clear her mind.

"I don't know your name," Angela said, knowing full well she was opening the proverbial door.

"Chet McGovern. And yours?"

"Angela Dawson. Tell me, do you pick up women frequently here at the club?"

"All the time," Chet said. "Actually, it is

the reason I come as often as I do. The exercise itself is too much like work."

Angela laughed again. She appreciated both honesty and a sense of humor. It seemed that Chet McGovern had both.

"You can drink while I eat," Angela said. "I'm famished."

"You've got a deal, lady."

Forty minutes later, after the two had showered, they sat across from each other in the combination bar/restaurant. The bar was packed. Behind the bar was a flat-screen TV televising a baseball game that everyone ignored. The level of the background chatter was like a bunch of feeding seabirds. Angela was sensitive to the noise, since she hadn't been in such an environment for years. She had to lean forward over her grilled salmon salad to hear.

"I asked what kind of work you do," Chet repeated. "You look like a model."

"Oh, sure," Angela scoffed. With comments like that, she knew for certain she was with an individual who thought of himself as a pickup specialist.

"Really!" Chet persisted. "What are you, twenty-four or twenty-five?"

"Thirty-seven, actually," Angela said, resisting the temptation to be sarcastic.

"Never would have guessed it. Not with a

figure like you have."

Angela merely smiled. Such comments were fun to hear, even if less than sincere.

"If not a model, what kind of work do you do?"

"I'm a businesswoman," Angela said without elaborating, and to turn the conversation away from herself, she quickly added, "And how about you? Movie star?"

It was Chet's turn to laugh. Then he leaned forward and said, "I'm a doctor." Then he sat back. From Angela's perspective, he'd assumed a decidedly self-satisfied smile, as if she was supposed to be impressed.

"What kind of a doctor?" Angela asked after a pause. "M.D. or Ph.D.?"

"M.D. and board-certified."

Whoop-de-do! Angela thought sarcastically but didn't communicate.

"As a businesswoman, what do you actually do?"

"I suppose I'd have to admit I mostly spend my time trying to raise money, as unpleasant as that is. Start-up companies are like plants: They constantly need water, and sometimes it takes a lot of water before they bear fruit."

"That's quite poetic. How close is the company you work for away from bearing fruit?"

"Very close, actually. We're two weeks away

from going public."

"Two weeks! That must be very exciting."

"Right now, it's more anxiety-producing than exciting. I need to raise about two hundred thousand dollars to shore up our liquidity to get to the IPO."

Chet whistled through his teeth. He was impressed, and gathered that Angela had to be a rather high-level executive. "Is the company going to be able to do it?"

"I try to be optimistic, especially since the investment-banking gurus promise the IPO will be a sellout. Maybe you, as a board-certified physician, would like to invest. We can certainly make it worth your while with interest or equity or both. We do have a lot of physician investors: more than five hundred, to be exact."

"Really?" Chet questioned. "What kind of company is it?"

"It's called Angels Healthcare. We build and run specialty hospitals."

"I suppose that means you know something about doctors."

"You could say that," Angela agreed.

"Sadly, I'm not as liquid as I'd like at the moment," Chet said. "Sorry."

"No problem. If you change your mind, give us a call."

"Well," Chet voiced, obviously wanting to

change the subject. "Are you single or married, or somewhere in between?"

Back to the come-on, Angela thought. All at once, she didn't care to keep up her side of the conversation. She'd been amused, but suddenly she felt tired, which had been the goal. She wanted to go home. "Divorced," she said, and then added what she thought would be a turn-off. "I'm divorced, and I live with my ten-year-old daughter, who is home sleeping."

"I guess that rules out your apartment," Chet said. "I'm single — very single, actually — and I have a terrific apartment just around the corner. How about a nightcap?"

"And see your etchings, I suppose. Sorry. I've got both my daughter and the two hundred thousand dollars to think about." Angela waved to one of the waiters and motioned for the check.

"I'll take care of the check," Chet said magnanimously.

"No, you won't!" Angela said with a voice that brooked no disagreement. "I'm afraid I used you, in a way. As penance I insist."

"Used me?" Chet questioned with a confused expression. "What do you mean?"

"It would take much too long to explain, and I've got to get home."

Chet acted a tad desperate as Angela

signed the check to her house account. "How about dinner tomorrow night?" he suggested when she'd finished.

"That's very generous of you, but I'm afraid I can't take the time. I'm not sure what to expect at the office tomorrow."

"But it would give you a chance to explain how you, quote, 'used me,'" Chet said. "I certainly don't feel used, and I've truly enjoyed meeting you. If I've offended you, I apologize. I promise I won't be so flippant. It's just an act."

Mildly surprised at Chet's willingness to reveal what seemed to be vulnerability, Angela stuck out her hand as she got to her feet. While shaking hands, she said, "I've enjoyed your company. I mean that. Maybe after the IPO we can have another drink or even a dinner."

"I'd like that," Chet said, regaining his aplomb. "And it will be my treat."

"It's a deal," Angela said, knowing that now it was her turn to be the one less sincere.

2
APRIL 3, 2007
7:15 A.M.

"Listen," Dr. Jack Stapleton said with un-camouflaged irritation, "I'm lucky to have gotten on Dr. Wendell Anderson's schedule. Hell, he does all the knees for all the high-priced athletes in the city. There has to be a reason, and the reason is he's obviously the best. If I cancel for this Thursday, I might not get back on the schedule for months. The man is that busy."

"But you only tore your ACL a week ago," Dr. Laurie Montgomery said with equal emotion. "Obviously, I'm not an orthopedic surgeon, but it stands to reason that operating on your knee, which has been so recently traumatized, is taking added risk. For God's sake, your knee is still twice its normal size, and your abrasions haven't completely healed."

"The swelling has come down a lot," Jack said.

"Did the doctor suggest you have the surgery this quickly?"

"Not exactly. I told him I want it ASAP, and he turned me over to his scheduling secretary."

"Oh, great!" Laurie said mockingly. "The date was set by a secretary."

"She must know what she's doing," Jack contended. "She's been working with Anderson for decades."

"Now, that's an intelligent assumption!" Laurie said with equal sarcasm.

"Another reason I don't want to cancel is that I was lucky enough to be assigned as Anderson's first case. If I have to have surgery, I want to be scheduled as the first case. The surgeon is fresh, the nurses are fresh, everybody's fresh. I remember when I was doing surgery back when I was practicing ophthalmology, I would have wanted to be my own first case."

"And where is this Angels Orthopedic Hospital?" Laurie questioned irritably. She ignored Jack's attempt at humor. "I've never even heard of it."

"It's north and not too far away from the University Hospital on the Upper East Side. It's relatively new — I don't know exactly when it opened, but less than five years ago. Anderson told me for the patients it's like checking in to the Ritz, which you can hardly say about either University or Manhattan General. He likes it because the doctors run the show, not some bureaucratic administrator. In the same amount of time, they can do twice the number of cases."

"Damn it, Jack!" Laurie complained. She turned away and glanced out the side window of the taxi at the rain-swept New York City streets. To say that Jack could be stubborn was putting it mildly, and when she was irritated, she considered "bullheaded" to be much closer to the truth. When they'd first started working together as forensic pathologists at the Office of the Chief Medical Examiner for the City of New York, she'd thought his wild bike riding to and from work and his brutish outdoor basketball playing with kids half his age were somehow charming. But now, twelve years later and married to the man for less than a year, she considered such risk-taking behavior by a fifty-two-year-old to be juvenile and even irresponsible now that he had a wife and a hoped-for child to consider. If truth be told, she wanted to delay his surgery not only to reduce surgical risk but also because she couldn't help believe the longer he stayed away from commuting on his bike and street basketball, the more chance he'd give it up altogether.

"I want to have my surgery Thursday," Jack said, as if reading her mind. "I need to get back to my normal exercise routine."

"And I want an intact husband. You could be killed carrying on the way you do."

"There's lots of ways to be killed," Jack responded. "As medical examiners, we both know that better than most."

"Put it off for a month," Laurie pleaded.

"I'm having the surgery," Jack said. "It's my knee."

"It's your knee, but we are supposed to be a team now."

"We are a team," Jack agreed. "Let's drop the subject. We can talk about it tonight if you insist."

Jack gave Laurie's hand a squeeze, and she squeezed back. Knowing Jack as well as she did, she took his willingness to suggest that they could bring the subject up again as a small victory.

When the traffic light changed at the corner of 30th Street and First Avenue, the cabbie made a wide left-hand turn and pulled to the curb in front of a dated six-story, blue-glazed brick building with aluminum-mullioned windows wedged between NYU Medical Center on one side and the Bellevue Complex on the other. They had arrived at the Office of the Chief Medical Examiner, or OCME, where Laurie had worked for sixteen years and Jack twelve. Although Jack was older, forensic pathology had been a second medical career for him after a large HMO had gobbled up his private practice back when HMOs were in their heyday.

"Something's brewing," Jack commented. Ahead of them were several TV news vans parked at the curb. "Interesting deaths attract reporters like honey attracts flies. I wonder what's up."

"I think of reporters more like vultures," Laurie commented as she got out curbside, then reached back into the taxi to extract Jack's lengthy and awkward crutches. "They feed on carrion, are more destructive of evidence, and can be a hell of a nuisance."

Jack paid the driver while he gave Laurie credit for a more apropos and clever simile. Out on the street, he took the crutches, got them poked into his armpits, and started toward the stairs. "I hate taxis," he murmured under his breath. "They make me feel so vulnerable."

"That's a strong statement," Laurie scoffed, "coming from a person who thinks commuting on a bike and challenging the city traffic is appropriate."

As expected, there were a half-dozen reporters in the OCME reception area busily chatting and feasting on takeout coffee and doughnuts. Several TV cameras were perched on the aged magazines on the coffee table. The reporters briefly glanced at Laurie and Jack as they traversed the room. Jack could move quickly on the crutches. Since he could put weight on the injured knee without a lot of pain, he could have done without the crutches, but he didn't want to take any chance of reinjury. Marlene Wilson, the receptionist, buzzed Laurie and Jack into the ID room before any of the reporters recognized them.

Within the ID room were two groups of people occupying separate sides. One group was six Hispanic-appearing individuals of widely mixed ages. They looked enough alike to be members of the same family. Two were children, and were wide-eyed in the spooky alien environment. Three youngish adults were whispering to an elderly matronly-appearing woman who intermittently dabbed a tissue against her eyes.

The second group was a couple who could have been husband and wife and who, like the Hispanic children, appeared like deer caught in headlights.

Laurie and Jack passed through a third door into a separate room that housed the OCME's communal coffeepot. It was here that the medical examiner on call for the week went through the cases that had come in overnight and decided which cases needed to be autopsied and who out of the eleven doctors on staff would do the case. Laurie and Jack almost always arrived early, mostly at Jack's insistence, since Laurie was a night person and more often than not had trouble getting up in the morning. Jack liked to get in early to cherry-pick through the cases, requesting the most interesting. The other doctors didn't mind, because Jack always did more than his share as compensation.

Dr. Riva Mehta, Laurie's office mate, who had started at the OCME the same year as Laurie, was sitting at the ID room desk behind various stacks of large manila envelopes, each representing a different case. She nodded and smiled a greeting at Jack and Laurie. There were two other individuals in the room, both sitting in vinyl club chairs and concealed behind newspapers, with steaming mugs of coffee within arm's reach. Laurie and Jack knew who was behind the *Daily News.* It had to be Vinnie Amendola, the mortuary tech who had to come in prior to the other techs to help in the transition from the night shift to the day shift. Frequently, he worked with Jack because Jack also liked to get a jump on the day down in the pit.

Neither Jack or Laurie knew who was hiding behind *The New York Times,* but they soon learned, when Jack's crutches clattered to the bare wooden floor as he tried to lean them up against one of the other two club chairs in the room. The noise was sharp, not too dissimilar from the sound of a gunshot. *The New York Times* dropped and exposed the surprised, tense, and chronically sleep-deprived face of Detective Lieutenant Lou Soldano. By reflex, the detective's right hand shot inside the lapel of his rumpled jacket. With his gravy-stained tie loosened and the top button of his wrinkled shirt unbuttoned, he had a decidedly disheveled appearance.

"Don't shoot!" Jack said, holding up his hand in mock surrender.

"Jesus," Lou complained as he visually relaxed. As was often the case, he sported a heavy five-o'clock shadow. It was apparent he'd not been to bed that night.

"Considering the reporters out in reception, I suppose we shouldn't be surprised to see you," Jack said. "How the hell are you, Lou?"

"As good as can be expected after spending most of the night out in the harbor. It's not something I'd recommend."

Lou had been Laurie's friend initially. Laurie and Lou had even dated after solving a case together, but their brief romance hadn't worked out. When Jack had come on the scene and ended up dating Laurie, Lou had been a strong advocate of their relationship. He'd even been part of their wedding the previous June. They were all good friends.

Laurie went to Lou and briefly touched cheeks before heading to the coffeepot.

Jack sat in a club chair next to Lou's and elevated his bum leg on the corner of the desk. Laurie called out to ask if Jack wanted any coffee. Jack gave her a thumbs-up sign.

"What's up?" Jack asked Lou. Since Lou had become a strong advocate of the contribution medical forensics played in homicide cases, he was a frequent visitor to the morgue, although he hadn't been there for more than a month. From experience, Jack knew that when he did come, there was a high probability it would be an interesting case. The previous day, Jack had had three routine autopsies, two natural deaths and one accidental. There'd been little challenge. Lou's presence augured that things might be different.

"It's been a busy night," Lou said. "There are three homicides I need help with. From my perspective, the most important one is a

83

floater that we hauled out of the Hudson River."

"Do you have an ID on the victim?" Jack asked. Laurie came over and put Jack's coffee mug down. He mouthed a thank-you.

"Nope, not a clue, at least so far."

"Are you sure it was a homicide?"

"Absolutely. He was shot in the back of the head at close range with a small-caliber bullet."

"Sounds straightforward from a medical forensics point of view," Jack said with some disappointment.

"But not from mine," Lou said. "The body is that of a well-dressed Asian man, not some street person. What scares me is that this might be an organized crime-related hit. We know there's been some friction between the established crime syndicates and some up-and-coming Asian, Russian, and Hispanic gangs, particularly in regard to recreational drugs. If some kind of crime war over territory breaks out, a lot of innocent people get killed. I'm hoping you or Laurie could find something, some kind of break so we can nip this in the bud, before all hell breaks loose."

"I'll do my best," Jack said. "What else?"

"The next one's a sad story. A detective sergeant in Special Fraud, and a good guy, has a daughter who has been arrested for killing her good-for-nothing boyfriend with a baseball bat last night. His name is Satan Thomas, if you can believe it. She's been a disaster for the detective since she was a pre-teen, always hooking up with the dregs for boyfriends and into drugs and you name it. Anyhow, she denies killing the guy and says the boyfriend was using the baseball bat to trash the apartment. She even claims he came after her, which he'd done in the past. By the way, Satan's delightful family is camped out in the waiting room."

"You mean he'd been physically abusive to her."

"Apparently. She claims that when she fled, he was still busting up the place."

"Did it look like he died of blunt trauma?"

"Oh, yeah! I'm afraid it looks like he got bashed in the forehead with the bat."

Jack rolled his eyes. "Sounds bad for your detective friend, and even more so for the daughter." Jack felt depressed. Two out of three autopsies were going to be straightforward. Reluctantly, he asked for the details on the third case.

"This one is similar to the last, but it's the girl who got whacked. She, too, was in an abusive relationship, according to her parents, the Barlows, who are also still in the waiting room. Apparently, Sara Barlow and her boyfriend got into a row over the fact she didn't clean the apartment to his liking. He admits he slapped her around but claims that when he left to calm down, she was fine, just bawling and saying she'd do better. When he gets back, he claimed she was lying across the bed with her face and hands purple."

"Purple blotches or her whole face?"

"One of the patrolmen who responded to the scene insisted the boyfriend said the whole face, but when the patrolman viewed the body, all he saw was what he described as purple bruises."

"What about the hands?"

"He didn't say."

"Did you see the body?"

"I did. I happened to be in the area because of the detective's daughter's case, so I went over."

"And?" Jack questioned.

"Just looked like bruises to me, too. I was convinced he beat her up good."

"What about the hands?"

"I guess they could have been somewhat blue. What are you thinking?"

"I'm thinking this case might be interesting," Jack said, as he reached for his crutches and got to his feet. "How about we do it first."

"I'm more interested in the floater," Lou called after him. "I might not be able to stay awake for all three, so I'd appreciate the floater first."

Jack approached the desk. Riva was still going through the cases, suggesting it was going to be a busy day. Laurie had a couple of envelopes on her lap. She was sitting in the club chair next to Vinnie, who was still behind his paper.

Remembering the reporters in reception, Jack called back to Lou, asking which of the three cases had brought the reporters to the OCME so bright and early. Short of possibly the floater, Jack had a hard time imagining any of the three being particularly newsworthy. In a city the size of New York, sad, violent events were all too common.

"None of the ones I've talked about," Lou called back. "The media is salivating about a death in police custody in the Bronx of a man called Concepcion Lopez. It's going to be one of those excessive-force brouhahas, I'm afraid. What I was told was that the guy went ballistic with an overdose of cocaine."

Jack merely nodded, thankful Lou wasn't encouraging Jack to do it. Police custody cases invariably were political disasters, which Jack found trying. No one was ever satisfied with the report, always claiming a cover-up.

"I'll see you downstairs," Lou said, getting up out of his chair with some effort. "I want to stop in Sergeant Murphy's cubbyhole and see if a missing-person complaint has been filed for John Doe."

"Have you come across Lou's John Doe floater?" Jack asked Riva.

Riva was immediately able to put her finger on the case file, since it was on top of the pile of apparent homicides. She handed it to him.

"How about two blunt-injury cases?" Jack asked. "The names are Thomas and Barlow."

Riva had to hunt for these cases in the stack, which was uncharacteristically high.

"Ugly night in the Big Apple," Jack commented. "You'd think people could solve their differences more amicably."

Riva smiled politely at Jack's weak attempt at humor. It was too early in the morning to respond verbally. She found the folders, and handed them over as well.

"Mind if I do these cases?" Jack asked.

"Not at all," Riva said in her soft, silky voice. She was a petite, gentle Indian American with dark skin and even darker eyes.

"Who is going to do the police custody case?" Jack asked.

"The chief called and said he wanted to do it," Riva said. "Since I was on call, I guess I'll have to be the one to assist him."

"My condolences," Jack said. Although Dr. Harold Bingham had an encyclopedic knowledge of forensics, helping him on a case was always an exercise in frustration control. No matter what you did as the assistant, it was never right, and the case invariably dragged on interminably.

Jack was about to wake Vinnie up from his sports statistics-induced trance when Laurie looked up from her reading. In contrast to Jack, who was content to skim-read the case material prior to the autopsy, she liked to go over it in exquisite detail. Jack felt that too much attention to detail initially prejudiced his ability to keep an open mind, while Laurie felt that not going over the history increased the chances she'd miss something. They'd argued over the issue but had finally agreed to disagree.

"I think you should read this," Laurie said in a serious tone, extending a case toward Jack. "I think you will find it personally disturbing."

"Oh?" Jack questioned. He read the victim's name, David Jeffries, which he did not recognize. His brows knitted in confusion over Laurie's comment and tone as he slid out the contents of the envelope. "What do you mean, 'personally disturbing'?"

"Just read the PA's investigator's note," Laurie suggested. PAs were physician assistants who worked as forensic investigators. It was the OCME's policy that PAs visited the scenes when indicated rather than forensic pathologists. The Chief Medical Examiner, Dr. Harold Bingham, felt strongly that it wasn't an efficient use of the M.D.'s time, despite his recognition that in some cases a site visit was crucial to determine the mechanism and manner of death.

It took only a few sentences for Jack to understand. David Jeffries had died of a fulminant postoperative staphylococcus infection following an anterior cruciate ligament repair, due to a particularly nasty type of staph called methicillin-resistant staphylococcus aureus, or MRSA. Considering the argument he and Laurie were having over Jack's upcoming surgery, it seemed coincidentally relevant, even if it involved another hospital. "I know what is going through your mind," Jack said, "but it ain't going to change my mind. I've already taken into consideration the risk of postoperative infection. Fearmongering is not going to work."

"But this coincidence has to give you pause," Laurie said. She knew it would certainly give her more than pause if the situation were reversed and she was slated to have the surgery.

"Frankly, it doesn't," Jack said. "First, I'm not superstitious, and second, I specifically asked Dr. Anderson what his postsurgical infection rate was. He told me that the only postoperative infections he'd had over his entire career involved compound-fracture repairs, which are a totally different situation. Besides, this case you're showing me involved University Hospital." Jack tried to return the file to Laurie, but she wouldn't take it.

"If you'd read further, you'd see that's not the case."

"What do you mean?" Jack asked. He felt himself getting irritated about the surgery issue all over again. Laurie could be like a dog with a bone, which he found frustrating at times, although he knew people often accused him of having the same trait.

"The patient had had his surgery eleven hours earlier at Angels Orthopedic Hospital, not University Hospital. The reason he ended up at the University Hospital was to treat his septic shock and fulminant staphylococcal pneumonia."

"Really?" Jack's eyes went back to the PA's note. Although he trusted that Laurie would never make such a thing up, he had to read it himself.

"This has to worry you," Laurie said. "The fact that they had to transfer a critically ill patient at all doesn't speak very highly for the Angels Orthopedic Hospital. What kind of hospital outsources its dirty laundry? The patient apparently died in the ambulance. That's crazy!"

"New treatments for septic shock require specialized personnel," Jack said. He was distracted by what he was reading. The rapidity with which the patient's infection progressed was shocking. Jack, as the OCME's putative infectious-disease guru, from having made several — what he called lucky — diagnoses on cases of infectious disease ten years ago, couldn't help but be impressed. In fact, he started to wonder if Mr. Jeffries had had a more truly infectious disease like Rocky Mountain spotted fever.

"Was the infectious agent unequivocally proved to be staph aureus?" Jack asked. He tried to remember what other known diseases caused such a rapidly fulminant course.

"Not by culture but by a monoclonal-based automate diagnostic system. Both the incision site and the lungs tested positive for methicillin-resistant staph, and interestingly enough, it was a strain associated with what they call 'community-acquired staph,' not the kind of antibiotic-resistant staph that has been plaguing hospitals over the last ten or fifteen years."

"Which means the patient probably brought the bug in with him rather than acquired it in the hospital."

"Could be," Laurie agreed. "But there's no way to know. Doesn't this bother you at all? I mean, the victim was roughly your age, had suffered the same injury, and was going to have the same operation at the same hospital. It would sure make me think twice. That's all I can say."

"To be honest, a postoperative infection had been one of my concerns," Jack said. "Maybe even the biggest, which is why I asked Dr. Anderson about his record and why I have been using antibacterial soap ever since the accident. I'm going to be damn sure I'll not be bringing any bacterial hitch-hikers into the hospital if I can help it."

Jack flicked the back of Vinnie's newspaper hard enough to startle the man.

"Quit it!" Vinnie groused when he'd recovered from his shock and saw who was the culprit. "Please, God, don't let the self-proclaimed super forensic sleuth insist on breaking the rules by starting early," Vinnie added sarcastically and with seeming disrespect. In point of fact, there was enough mutual respect between Vinnie and Jack to allow for such teasing banter, and technically they were breaking the rules. By decree from Chief Bingham, autopsies were supposed to start at seven-thirty sharp, although they never did. Jack was always early, thanks in part to Vinnie's willingness to cut short his coffee break while all the other medical examiners, including Laurie, were always late because Bingham or the deputy chief, Calvin Washington, were rarely there to enforce the edict.

"The supersleuth wants the super mortuary tech down in the pit," Jack said to the back of Vinnie's paper. Defiantly, Vinnie had gone back to his reading.

Laurie asked Riva if she could do David Jeffries's autopsy.

"Of course," Riva said. "But it's going to be a busy day. You'll have to take at least one more. Do you have a preference?"

"Sure," Laurie said absently. She was back to rereading David Jeffries's history.

"Come on, Vinnie," Jack called, leaning on his crutches at the doorway leading into the communications room. Vinnie had become reabsorbed in his paper.

"I'm here!" a voice called out. "The day

94

can now officially begin."

All eyes turned to the door leading out to the main part of the ID room. Even Vinnie, who was passive-aggressively avoiding Jack, lowered his paper to see who had arrived. It was Chet McGovern, Jack's office mate. "Have you guys left anything mildly interesting? Hell, I'd have to camp here overnight to avoid getting your rejects." After ditching his coat on an empty chair, he stepped behind Riva to paw through some of the folders. Jokingly, as if a schoolmarm, Riva hit his hand using a foot-long wooden ruler.

"You're in a good mood, sport," Jack said. "What's the occasion? How come you're here so early?"

"I couldn't sleep. I met a woman last night at my health club who's an impressive businesswoman. I had the feeling she's a CEO or something. I woke up this morning early, trying to figure out how to get her to go out with me."

"Ask her," Laurie suggested.

"Oh, sure, in case I hadn't thought of that."

"And she said no?"

"Sort of," Chet said.

"Well, ask her again," Laurie said. "And be direct. Sometimes you men can be rather vague to protect your fragile egos."

Chet saluted, as if Laurie were his superior officer.

"Come on! You lazy good-for-nothing," Jack said after returning to where Vinnie was sitting and snatching his paper out of his hands. Vinnie scrambled after Jack, who managed to keep the newspaper away from Vinnie until they reached the clerical room beyond communication. There was a brief tug-of-war amid laughter.

The battle for the newspaper over, Jack gave Vinnie the John Doe case file and asked him to put up the body, meaning prepare the body for the autopsy. Meanwhile, Jack stuck his head into Sergeant Murphy's closetlike NYPD office. The aging, amiable cop looked up from his computer screen. He'd been assigned to the OCME forever. Jack was fond of the man, as was everyone else. Murphy was one of those rare individuals who managed to get along with everyone. Jack admired the trait and wished some of it could rub off on him. Over the years, he'd become progressively intolerant of perfunctory bureaucrats with mediocre administrative or professional skills, and he was unable to hide his feelings, as much as he tried. In his mind, there were too many such tenured people hiding out in the OCME.

"Have you seen Detective Soldano?"

Jack asked.

"He was here earlier but left to go down to the morgue," Sergeant Murphy said.

"Did he ask you about the unidentified floater that came in last night?"

"He did, and I told him the only missing-person report filed overnight was for a woman."

Jack thanked the sergeant and managed to catch up to Vinnie, who'd summoned the back elevator. Downstairs, Jack found Lou in the locker room, already suited up in a Tyvek coverall, which had replaced the far more bulky protective moon suits except for known exceptionally infectious cases.

As Jack quickly changed into scrubs, Lou couldn't help but notice the swelling and discoloration of Jack's injured knee.

"That doesn't look so good," Lou commented. "Are you sure you should be doing these posts?"

"Actually, it's gotten better," Jack said. "I just have to baby it until Thursday, when it's scheduled to be repaired. That's what the crutches are for. I could do without them, but using them is a constant reminder."

"You're having it operated on so soon?" Lou questioned. "My ex-brother-in-law had an ACL tear, and he had to wait six months before having it fixed."

"The sooner I have it, the better, as far as I am concerned," Jack said as he climbed into a Tyvek coverall. "The quicker I get back to my bike and, hopefully, my b-ball, the saner I'll be. The competition and the physical exercise keep my demons at bay."

"Now that you remarried, are you still tormented by what happened to your family?"

Jack stopped and stared at Lou as if he couldn't believe Lou had asked such a question. "I'm always going to be tormented. It's just a matter of degree." Jack had lost his wife of ten years and two daughters, aged ten and eleven, to a commuter plane crash fifteen years earlier.

"What does Laurie think of you having surgery so soon?"

Jack's lower jaw slowly dropped open. "What is this?" he questioned with obvious irritation. "Is this some kind of conspiracy? Has Laurie been talking to you about this behind my back?"

"Hey!" Lou voiced, raising his hands as if to fend off an attack. "Calm down! Don't be so paranoid! I'm just asking, trying to be a friend."

Jack went back to finishing his suiting up. "I'm sorry to jump on you. It's just that Laurie has been on my case to postpone my surgery since it was scheduled. I'm a little touchy about it because I want the damn thing fixed."

"Understood," Lou said.

With hoods in place and tiny, battery-powered fans recirculating the air through high-efficiency particulate air, or HEPA, filters, the two men entered the windowless autopsy room, which had not been upgraded for almost fifty years. The eight stainless-steel autopsy tables bore witness to the approximately five hundred thousand bodies that had been painstakingly disassembled to reveal their forensic secrets. Over each table hung an old-fashioned spring-loaded scale and a microphone for dictation. Along one wall were Formica countertops and soapstone sinks for washing out intestines, and along another wall were floor-to-ceiling glass-enclosed instrument cabinets, the contents of which looked like something that should have been in a house of horrors. Next to them were backlit x-ray view boxes. The whole scene was awash in a stark blue-white light coming from banks of ceiling-mounted fluorescent fixtures. The illumination appeared to suck the color out of everything in the room, especially the ghostly pale corpse on the nearest table.

While Vinnie continued the preparations by getting out instruments, specimen bottles, preservatives, labels, syringes, and evidence custody tags, Jack and Lou went to the view box to look at the whole-body X-rays that Vinnie had put up. One was anterior-posterior; the other was lateral.

After checking the accession number, Jack gazed at the films. Then he said, "I think you are right."

"Right about what?" Lou asked.

"It being small-caliber," Jack said. He pointed to a cylindrical, half-centimeter-long translucent defect within the lower part of the skull's image. Composed of metal, bullets totally absorb X-rays, and since X-rays are viewed as negatives, the image appears in the color of the background illumination.

"Twenty-two-caliber would be my guess," Lou said, moving his face close to the film.

"I think you're also right about it being execution-style," Jack said. "From its position in the films, it's undoubtedly lodged in the brain stem, where a professional killer would aim. Let's take a look at the entrance wound."

With Vinnie's help, Jack rolled the corpse on its side. First, Jack took a digital photo. Then, with his gloved hand, he separated the hair covering the point where the bullet entered the victim's head. Since the victim had bobbed around in the Hudson River, most of the blood had been washed away.

"It's a near-contact wound," Jack said. "But certainly not contact, since it's a circular, not a stellate defect." He took another photo.

"How far away?" Lou questioned.

Jack shrugged. "By the looks of the stippling, I'd say somewhere around twelve inches. Noticing the position of the entrance wound in relation to the bullet's position on the X-ray, I'd guess the perpetrator was behind and above the victim, maybe with the victim seated. That's seemingly confirmed by slightly more stippling below the entrance wound than above."

"More weight to it being execution-style."

"I'd have to agree."

Jack took some measurements of the position of the wound, and another photo with a ruler in close proximity. Then, with a scalpel, he dislodged some of the embedded soot from within points of stippling. He put the material in a specimen tube. Finally, he took additional photos before motioning for Vinnie to allow the body to roll back into a supine position.

"What do you make of these deep slices across the thigh?" Lou asked, pointing to two parallel sharp cuts in the anterior aspect of the right thigh.

Jack took a photo before inspecting the wounds and palpating them. "They were certainly made by a sharp object," he said, looking at the clean edges. "There's no skin bridges. I'd guess they are propeller injuries, and I'd be willing to bet they were post-mortem. I don't see any extravasated blood within the tissues."

"Do you think the victim could have been run over after being thrown from a boat?"

Jack nodded, but something more subtle caught his attention. Moving down to the ankles, he pointed out some oddly shaped abrasions.

"What is it?" Lou asked.

"I'm not sure," Jack said. He went over to the counter and hefted a dissecting micro-scope detached from its base. Bracing his el-bows on the edge of the table, he studied the subtle abrasions.

"Well?" Lou questioned.

"I'm going out on a limb," Jack admitted, "but it looks as if his legs might have been tied with chains. There's not only abrasions but also suspiciously shaped indentations."

"Occurring after he was dead or before?"

"Whatever it was, it was after he was dead. I don't see any blood in the tissues here, either."

"It could have been he was chained to a weight and supposed to sink and stay sunk. Somebody could have screwed up."

"Could be," Jack said. "I'll take a photo, even though it probably won't show up."

"If this was a screwup, it could be important to keep it quiet," Lou said.

"How come?"

"If it is an organized-crime war, there will be more bodies. I'd want them to all come to the surface."

"Our lips will be sealed," Jack said.

"Hey, can't we move this along?" Vinnie complained. "At this rate, with you two long-winded old farts carrying on, we're going to be here all day."

Jack let his arms go limp at his sides and stared at Vinnie as if shocked. "Are we keeping the super mortuary tech from something more important?" he questioned.

"Yeah, a coffee break."

Jack switched his gaze to Lou and said, "See what I have to put up with around here? The place is going to the dogs." He then reached up, adjusted the overhead microphone, and began dictating the external examination.

Laurie slipped David Jeffries's file back into its envelope. It included a case worksheet, his partially filled-out death certificate, his inventory of medicolegal case records, two sheets for the autopsy notes, a telephone notice of his death as received by communications, his completed identification sheet, the PA's investigative report, his lab slip for an HIV test, and the slips indicating that the body had been weighed, fingerprinted, photographed, and x-rayed. She had read the material over several times, as she had done with her second assigned case, Juan Rodriguez, but it was Jeffries she was more interested in.

Feeling appropriately prepared, she pushed back from her desk and headed toward the back elevator. Fifteen minutes earlier, she'd called down to the mortuary office and had had the good fortune to get Marvin Fletcher. She was pleased and recognized his voice instantly, as he was her favorite mortuary tech. He was efficient, intelligent, experienced, eager, and always in a good mood. Laurie had an aversion for those techs who were moody, such as Miguel Sanchez, or those who always seemed to be moving at half-speed, such as Sal D'Ambrosio. She also was not fond of the sarcastic, black-humor repartee in which some of the other techs indulged. When she briefly described David Jeffries's case, warning that it involved an infection and asking for the body to be put up for an autopsy, Marvin's response had been simply: "No problem. Give me fifteen minutes, and it's a go."

As Laurie rode down from the fifth floor to the basement morgue level, she thought of what she was going to find on Jeffries. According to the PA's report, the man had had all the symptoms of a toxic shock-like syndrome: high fever, an obvious wound infection at both incision sites, diarrhea with abdominal pain, vomiting, severe prostration, low blood pressure, unresponsive to medication, low urinary output, rapid heart rate, and respiratory distress with some blood-tinged mucus. Laurie shuddered at the thought of how quickly the man had succumbed and how virulent the bacteria had to be. She also couldn't keep herself from worrying about the case being a negative omen, involving, as it did, the exact same surgery Jack was facing, even the same knee. Jack had blithely dismissed the coincidence, but she couldn't. It made her more committed than ever to talk Jack into at least delaying his surgery. She even saw a bright side to David Jeffries's tragedy. Maybe if she found something different or unexpected at the post, it could help her change Jack's mind, which was why she had requested the case.

Generally, she tried to avoid cases involving fatal infection. She'd never admitted it to anyone, but they made her uneasy. Yet as she approached the locker room, she acknowledged that she felt more eager and keyed up about doing the case than she had ever felt about doing another.

Laurie changed quickly, first into scrubs and then putting on her disposable protective gear. Although the newer gear was less burdensome and limiting than the old moon suits, she occasionally groused about the equipment like everyone else, but, on this occasion, dealing with a fatal infection, she was pleased to have it. She carefully cleaned off the plastic face mask — even slight smudges bothered her — and turned on the fan before pulling the contraption over her head. Then, prepared, she pushed into the pit.

Stopping just inside the door, she surveyed the scene. Four tables were in use. The nearest supported the corpse of an extremely pale Asian-American male. Three people were grouped around the head, the scalp of which had been reflected forward and the skullcap of which had been removed. The bloody brain glistened in the raw light. Although Laurie couldn't see any faces through the plastic face masks, she guessed it was Jack, Lou, and Vinnie, since they had started first.

The next table also had three people working, and as Laurie viewed them, her face flushed. She'd forgotten that the chief, Dr. Harold Bingham, was expected. He rarely came to the autopsy room, as most of his time was spent in administrative duties or testifying at high-profile trials. It was easy to pick him out, not only because of his almost square silhouette but because of his harsh baritone voice that suddenly reverberated throughout the tiled room. He was giving one of his impromptu lectures about how his current case reminded him of one of his innumerable previous cases. As he was carrying on, a slight figure standing on a stool opposite him, who Laurie surmised was her office mate, Riva, was actually doing the work. For her reward, Bingham intermittently interrupted his monologue to offer negative comments about her technique.

The next two tables had a pair of people working at each. Laurie had no idea who they were. The fifth table contained the corpse of an African-American male. Standing at the head of the table, a figure she assumed was Marvin waved toward her, and over the sound of Bingham's raucous voice, he called out, "We're set to go on table five,

Dr. Montgomery!"

Bingham's head snapped around toward Laurie, making her wish she could disappear. The overhead light glinted off his plastic face screen, blocking a view of his face, so she could not anticipate his frame of mind. "Dr. Montgomery, you are a half-hour late!"

"I've been going over my cases for this morning, sir," Laurie said quickly, and as deferentially as possible. She could feel her heart rate bump up. Laurie had struggled with authority figures since childhood. "I also needed to speak with Cheryl Myers to get some missing data." Cheryl Myers was a PA whom Laurie had slipped into the investigator's office to see after leaving the ID room. Although Cheryl had written a generally good note for the construction death, Laurie's second case, Laurie had noticed that the distance from the building the corpse had ended up after the fatal ten-story fall was not included. As Laurie had assumed, Cheryl had obtained the figure but had mistakenly left it out of the report.

"All that is supposed to be done before seven-thirty," Bingham snapped.

"Yes, sir," Laurie said, not interested in arguing. Unlike Jack, Laurie generally followed rules reflexively. However, the one mandating that autopsies start at seven-thirty sharp she generally ignored, since it conflicted with her belief that it was more important to know the case prior to doing the post. In an attempt to preclude any more conversation with Bingham about the issue, Laurie stepped directly up to Jack's table and asked loudly how his case was going.

"Stellarly," Jack quipped, "except the inconvenient fact that the patient died. The only bad side is that it has been dragging on. We'd have made significantly more progress if there was any decent help around here."

"Screw you!" Vinnie said. "If you two old windbags hadn't carried on like you've been doing, we could be up having coffee by now."

"Gentlemen," Bingham's voice called out. "I'll have no disrespect, nor profanity, in the autopsy room."

Lest she incite any further comments from Jack and subsequent retorts from Bingham, Laurie quickly headed toward Marvin and her own case. As she passed Bingham's table, she cringed for fear of being called over, but luckily Bingham had been distracted by what he called a "catastrophic mistake" on Riva's part as she dissected the neck.

"Are you going to need anything special?" Marvin asked as Laurie came up abreast of the fifth table. As prepared as Laurie was, she generally knew in advance when special needs were required for a case.

"A good supply of culture tubes," Laurie said as she surveyed David Jeffries's corpse. For fifty-one years of age, the man appeared to have been in good physical condition. There was no excess fat. In fact, his muscles, particularly the pectorals and quadriceps, had the definition of a much younger man.

Laurie grimaced behind her plastic face screen. Besides the obvious infection at the surgical sites on either side of the right knee, there was a sprinkling of small pustules all over his body, which given the time would have turned into abscesses or boils. Even more striking were areas of desquamation, particularly on his pelvis, with the skin sloughing in relatively large sheets.

"Are you looking at his hands?" Marvin asked.

Laurie nodded.

"What caused his skin to peel off like that?"

"Staph makes a lot of toxins. One of them causes skin cells to separate from their neighbors."

"Ugh," Marvin said.

Laurie nodded again. She'd seen staph infection before, but this was the worst.

"Anyway, to answer your question about culture tubes," Marvin said, "I got plenty."

"Did you get a good supply of syringes as well?"

"Yup."

"All right, let's do it," Laurie said, as she pulled down the suspended microphone.

"Want to check out the X-ray? I put it up just in case."

Laurie stepped over to the view box and gazed at the film. Marvin followed and looked over her shoulder.

"Our X-rays are mainly for foreign bodies and fractures," Laurie said. "Even so, you can certainly appreciate the pneumonia and how diffuse it is. It looks like the lungs are filled with fluid."

"Hmmm," Marvin said. X-rays were a mystery to him. He couldn't understand how doctors could see what they did in the foggy image.

Laurie went back to the body and completed the external examination. After making sure the endotracheal tube was where it was supposed to be in the trachea, she pulled it out. It had been placed by the doctors to ventilate him when he had begun to have trouble breathing. She cultured the bloody mucus adhered to it. Turning to the multiple IV lines, she made sure they were also properly placed and, after doing so, pulled them out and cultured them as well. Medical examiners insisted such tubes be left in place to be sure that they played no role in the patient's death. She also cultured the pus issuing from the surgical site.

Once the external exam had been finished and dictated, Laurie began the internal with the standard Y-shaped incision starting at both shoulders, meeting at the midline, and then extending down to the pubis. She worked quietly, shunning the usual banter she normally exchanged with Marvin, who was an eager learner.

For a time, Marvin stayed quiet as well, correctly sensing Laurie's awe at the virulence of the microbe that had played such havoc throughout David Jeffries's body. It wasn't until Laurie lifted out the heart and lungs and put them in the pan he was holding that he broke the silence. "Shit, man," he commented. "This baby weighs a ton."

"I noticed," Laurie said. "I think we'll find both lungs full of fluid." After she removed the lungs and weighed each separately, she made multiple slices into them. Like fully soaked sponges, a mixture of edema fluid, blood, necrotic tissue, and pus emerged.

"Ye gods!" Marvin said. "That's ugly."

"Have you heard of the term *flesh-*

eating bacteria?"

"Yeah, but I thought people only got that in their muscles."

"This is a similar process, but in the lungs and much more lethal. Its official name is necrotizing pneumonia. You can even see beginning abscesses." Laurie pointed to minute cavities with the tip of the knife.

"You guys look like you are having way too much fun," Jack said, after silently coming up along Laurie's right side.

Laurie let out a short, sarcastic laugh that was enough to briefly fog her face screen. She gave a quick glance at Jack before holding up the exposed cut surface of the lung for him to see. "If you call seeing the worst case of necrotizing pneumonia fun, then Marvin and I are having a blast."

Jack used his gloved index finger to assess the turgidity of the lung section. "Pretty bad, I'd have to admit. Shows you what can happen if you smoke too many Cuban cigars."

"Jack," Laurie said, ignoring his attempt at humor, "why don't you stay with us for a few minutes? I think you should see the full extent of this postoperative infection. This poor individual was being literally and rapidly digested from the inside out. This might be the worst or best advertisement for not having elective surgery I've ever seen."

"Thanks for the invite, but I've got two more cases to do before Lou conks out," Jack said. "Besides, I know how your mind works, especially with your not-so-subtle reminder the victim had surgery, meaning I know you have an ulterior motive for your kind invitation vis-à-vis my Thursday plans. So I'll let you two have all the fun." With a little wave, he started to leave.

"What about your first case?" Laurie asked, mindful of Lou's interest. "What did you find?"

"Not a whole bunch. We recovered the twenty-two-caliber slug, for whatever that's worth. Lou says it's a Remington high-velocity hollow-point, but he could just be trying to impress me. The thing's a bit mangled from penetrating the guy's skull. There were also some abrasions and indentations on his legs, suggesting he'd been chained, perhaps attached to a weight. I think he was supposed to sink, which suggests he was thrown overboard out of a boat, not dumped into the water on shore. Lou thinks that's important. Otherwise, the guy was healthy except for a slight cirrhosis of the liver."

After Jack limped off, Marvin asked what Jack had meant about her having an ulterior motive.

"We're having a disagreement about when

he gets his knee repaired," Laurie said without elaborating. "Now, let's get back to work."

"What have you got?" Arnold Besserman asked. Working at the next table, he'd overheard Laurie and Jack's conversation. Arnold had been at the OCME longer than any of the other medical examiners. Although Jack dismissed him as long in the tooth, outdated, and haphazard, Laurie was friendly with him, as she was with most everyone else.

"Do you mind me interrupting?"

"Certainly not," Laurie said sincerely. His stepping over to her table was what made working in the communal autopsy room enjoyable and stimulating for her.

"Quite an amazing case," Laurie said. "Take a peek at this lung. I've never seen such dramatic nosocomial necrotizing pneumonia, and it apparently developed over less than twelve hours."

"Impressive," Arnold agreed as he looked at the cut surface of David Jeffries's lung. "Let me guess: It's a staph infection. Am I right?"

"You hit it on the nose." Laurie was impressed.

"I've had three similar nosocomial cases over as many months, with the last one about two weeks ago," Arnold said. "Maybe not quite as bad, at least not all of them, but bad enough. Mine were from a methicillin-resistant strain coming from outside the hospital but which apparently had hybridized with bacteria coming from within the hospital."

"That's exactly what my case apparently is," Laurie said, even more impressed.

"The strain is called community-acquired MRSA, or CA-MRSA, to distinguish it from the usual nosocomial, hospital-acquired MRSA, or HA-MRSA."

"I remember reading about it," Laurie said. "Someone had a case five or six months ago, of a football player who picked it up in the locker room and had an infection that ate away a lot of his thigh."

"That was Kevin's case," Arnold said. Kevin Southgate was another senior ME who'd joined the OCME only a year after Arnold had. As the old guard, Arnold and Kevin stuck together like a team, although opposites in their politics. Both were infamous around the office for constantly conspiring to take as few cases as possible. It was like they were working half-time full-time.

"I remember when he presented the case at Thursday conference," Laurie said. Other than the informal but effective give-and-take

116

in the autopsy room, the formal Thursday conference with its required attendance was the only other opportunity for all of the city's nineteen MEs to share their experiences. Laurie, for one, lamented this situation because it hampered the OCME's ability to recognize trends. She had complained about it, but without coming up with a solution, the issue had died. With the OCME doing more than ten thousand cases a year, there wasn't time for more interaction, and there were no funds to hire more forensic pathologists than the one they had hired that year.

"The CA-MRSA bug is scary, as this case of yours aptly demonstrates," Arnold said. "It's been a mini-epidemic outside the hospital, like Kevin's football player and even, tragically enough, some young, healthy children getting scrapes on the playground. Now it seems to be going back into the hospital. That's the bad side. The good side is that it is sensitive to more antibiotics, but the antibiotics have to be started immediately because, believe it or not, being more sensitive to antibiotics has given the strain added virulence. Not making the complete line of defensive molecules for antibiotics like the HA-MRSA strains, these community-acquired strains are able to spend more time and effort making a soup of powerful toxins to enhance their virulence. One of them is called PVL, which I'm sure has played a role in your case here. PVL toxin chews up the patient's cellular defenses, particularly in the lungs, and initiates an overwhelming and perverse release of cytokines, which normally help the body fight infection. Do you realize that as much as one-half of the destruction you are seeing in the lung sections you are holding comes from the victim's own completely overstimulated immune system?"

"You mean like the cytokine storm they are seeing with people dying from H5N1 bird flu?" Laurie asked. The thought went through her mind that she would have to suggest to Jack that he might need to adjust the opinion he had of Besserman. He was embarrassing her by how much more he knew about MRSA than she.

"Exactly," Arnold said.

"I'm afraid I'm going to have to do some serious reading about all this," Laurie admitted. "Thanks for all the information. How is it that you are such an expert?"

Arnold laughed. "You're giving me too much credit. But a month or so ago, Kevin and I got interested in the issue because of several cases we each had. We kinda challenged each other to learn about it. It's a good example of the genetic versatility of bacteria and how quickly they can evolve."

Laurie struggled to rein in her mind, which was bouncing from one topic to another. She looked down at the turgid, nearly solid slice of lung she was holding. She knew pathological bacteria were making a comeback, but what she was facing in terms of pathogenicity seemed beyond the pale.

"So the cases you mentioned earlier were necrotizing pneumonia?" she asked. "Just like this case appears to be."

"That would be my guess, but I'd be even more certain if I looked at the microscope section of your case. I'd be glad to take a peek."

Laurie nodded. "And Kevin's cases were the same as yours?"

"Very much so."

"Were his nosocomial also?"

"Of course. They were nosocomial but also involved the community-acquired strain, the same as mine."

"Why didn't you bring this up at Thursday conference?"

"Well, frankly, it was not that many cases, and everyone is aware of the burgeoning problem of staph, particularly antibiotic-resistant staph."

"Were the involved hospitals fairly evenly

distributed around the city?"

"No, they were all here in midtown Manhattan. I mean, there could have been cases in Queens or Brooklyn, since they would be sent to their respective borough morgues."

"What hospitals here in Manhattan?"

"I can't remember the exact breakdown from individual institutions, but all six came from three specialty hospitals: Angels Heart Hospital, Angels Cosmetic Surgery and Eye Hospital, and Angels Orthopedic Hospital."

Laurie stiffened. It was as if Arnold had slapped her. "None from Manhattan General or University or any of the other big city hospitals?"

"Nope. Does that surprise you?"

"Yes and no," Laurie said, taken aback by such a coincidence. There were a lot of hospitals in New York City. It begged the question: Why just three?

"Did you contact the hospitals, or look into the situation at all? I mean, why just those three hospitals?"

"Kevin and I thought it coincidental, so yes, we looked into it to a degree. I also asked for Cheryl Myers's help as well. I called the Angels Orthopedic Hospital and spoke to a very nice woman whose name escapes me at the moment. I'd gotten the name from the hospital administrator. The individual I spoke with chaired the interdepartmental infection-control committee."

"Was she helpful?"

"Absolutely. She said the hospital was well aware of the problem and had hired an infection-control professional, or at least the company that owned the hospital did. So I called this individual whose name I can't forget was Dr. Cynthia Sarpoulus."

"Was she helpful?"

"Well, I suppose, at least to an extent."

"What do you mean?"

"She wasn't terribly cooperative, although I suppose she was stressed and defensive under the circumstances. My assumption was that her employer, Angels Healthcare, which is the name of the company, had put the burden on her. Anyway, she essentially told me to butt out, and that the situation was well under control, thank you very much. You know the attitude, I'm sure. To her credit, it sounded to me that she was on top of the problem. Against management's objections, according to her, she had insisted all the ORs in all three hospitals be closed, which also according to her had everybody on her back. She then had all the ORs fumigated by an alcohol-based agent, which is what is recommended. She'd also instigated a rigorous hand-washing regimen. On top of that, she'd had the entire staff tested as potential carriers, and those who tested positive treated. I have to say I was impressed. They surely weren't sitting around, wringing their hands."

"Thanks for the information. Sorry to take so much of your time," Laurie said.

"My pleasure," Arnold said.

"Would you mind if I came up to your office later and got the names of the cases you've mentioned?"

"Not at all! I might still have a couple of the case files. You can also borrow the notes I made about CA-MRSA if you'd like. And you can talk with Kevin. Back when we were working on this, I think he also called over to one of the involved hospitals, but I don't remember if he told me what he learned."

After Arnold had stepped back to his table, Laurie looked over at Marvin, who had patiently waited through the whole conversation. "That was incredible," she said.

"What, that he's sweet on you?"

"No, silly! What he said. He's not sweet on me!"

"That's not the chatter around the morgue. It's generally accepted both Southgate and Besserman would throw themselves in front of a subway train for you."

"Nonsense," Laurie said, although hearing

she was even remotely the source of gossip made her uneasy. She never liked being the center of attention, which was why she had such trouble talking in front of a group.

By the time Laurie had finished with Jeffries, she'd found far more pathology than she had expected. Every organ was grossly involved with obvious destructive infection or at least inflammatory swelling. Within the heart, she found beginning infectious vegetations on the valves. In the liver, there were incipient abscesses, as well as in the brain and kidneys, suggesting the victim had had a massive bacteremia. There were even ulcers in the gut, attesting to the ease with which the bacteria spread.

"How long to the next case?" Laurie asked, as she and Marvin finished suturing the giant autopsy incision encompassing both David Jeffries's chest and abdomen.

"As little time or as much time as you'd like," Marvin said. "If you want a coffee break, I'll stretch it out."

"Actually, if you don't mind, I'll call you when I want to do it. Among other things, I want to see if Cheryl Myers is here and catch her before she goes out on a case."

"Then I'll take my time," Marvin said. "Give me a call when you want to start."

"Make sure you leave a note for whoever

releases Jeffries's body to inform the funeral home that a serious infection is involved and precautions should be taken."

On her way out of the autopsy room, Laurie briefly stopped at Jack's table.

"Ah! The doomsayer!" Jacked quipped at recognizing her. "Forsooth, Vinnie! Take heed! She's surely here to terrify us with the grisly horrors of her nosocomial surgical-site infection case."

Despite Vinnie's reflective face mask, she could see him roll his eyes. She felt similarly. On occasion his creative but oft irreverent black humor was not amusing. After being married to him for almost a year, she now saw such behavior as defensive and a way to avoid what he was really thinking.

"I do have to talk with you about my case," Laurie admitted. "There are some additional facts you should know."

"How could I have guessed?" Jack questioned mockingly.

"But it can wait until you are more receptive."

"Praise be to the Lord."

"Where's Lou?"

"He literally fell into a deep sleep leaning against the autopsy table between cases. I thought it best he head home, lest one of the mortuary techs mistake him for a corpse."

"Which case are you doing now?" Laurie asked, to change the subject.

"Sara Barlow, and it's a hell of a lot more interesting than the John Doe floater."

"How so?"

"See the obvious bruises on the face and the upper arms. Obviously, she'd been beat up a lot over time, but do you think any of them could have been fatal, as the police assumed?"

"Probably not, but were there any on the anterior chest?" Laurie asked. She couldn't see because the chest walls were butterflied open. From a case she had when she'd first started at the OCME, she knew that blunt injuries that one would not expect to be lethal could be if they occurred on the chest. "Any reason to suspect commotio cordis?"

"Nope! Chest was clean. What if I tell you there was extensive pinkish pulmonary edema, injected eyes, and sloughing of the tracheal epithelium."

"What's your presumptive diagnosis?" Laurie asked with a sigh. Sometimes she found Jack's forensic guessing games tedious, and this was one of them.

"What if I told you our clever PA, Janice Jaeger, found a mixture of rather strong, open cleaning products in a glass-enclosed shower stall with a bucket of water and a damp cloth? Earlier, when she had viewed the body, she noticed the knees of the woman's jeans were wet, and the victim was not wearing any socks or shoes."

"I'd have to know if the cleaning products contained hypochlorite, which many do, and if others contained acid, which a lot do, and if she had ignored the warning not to mix them, and did."

"Bingo!" Jack said. "Chlorine gas, the first chemical-warfare agent used in World War One, did her in, not her boyfriend. It's amazing to me how many people blithely ignore product warnings. Anyway, Lou will be pleased it is not another homicide he has to worry about."

"Not unless the boyfriend was the one who insisted she use the deadly products, and use them together."

"Now that's a twist I hadn't even thought of," Jack admitted.

"Well, you boys enjoy yourselves," Laurie said, as she headed toward the exit. She felt no pleasure at having guessed the right answer to Jack's quiz. She would have been much happier if he were not in such a distractingly playful mood, whether real or feigned. It amazed and irritated her that he didn't see or was purposely ignoring the corollary between her case and his proposed surgery.

Instead of leaving Jeffries's specimens for the staff to bring up to the appropriate labs, as was the normal routine, Laurie took them herself. She wanted to talk to both the head of microbiology, Agnes Finn, and the head of histology, Maureen O'Connor, to try to move things along. But first she stopped on the first floor and went into the PA's office. Knowing they were often out in the field, Laurie was pleased to find Cheryl Myers still at her desk.

"Can I help you with something else?" Cheryl questioned. She was a striking African-American woman who wore her hair in tight, bead-encrusted cornrows. She was part of the old school at the OCME. In fact, she'd been working there long enough to put her two boys through college.

"I hope so," Laurie said. "Earlier, I was speaking with Dr. Besserman about some infection cases at three hospitals run by a company called Angels Healthcare. He said he asked you to look into it. Do you recall?"

"Are you talking about the MRSA pulmonary cases?"

"Those are the ones! Did you make a site visit?"

"No! What he asked me specifically was to obtain hospital records, so I merely called and spoke to the medical records department in each hospital. It was easy to get the charts, because Angels hospitals have their medical records computerized. The material was e-mailed over. I didn't need to make a visit."

"Were the hospitals cooperative?"

"Very cooperative. I even got an unsolicited call back from a very helpful woman by the name of Loraine Newman."

"Who is she?"

"She is the chairperson of the orthopedic hospital's infection-control committee."

"Dr. Besserman mentioned her," Laurie said. "He commented on how genial she was as well. Why did she call back?"

"Just to leave her name and direct-dial number in case I needed anything else. She said she was very concerned about the problem. She told me that prior to the MRSA outbreak, they'd had no nosocomial problems to speak of. She said the situation was keeping her awake at night. To tell you the truth, she sounded a little desperate."

"Did she mention a Cynthia Sarpoulus?"

"Not that I can recall. Who is she?"

"I've just posted another case of MRSA that came in from Angels Orthopedic Hospital," Laurie said, ignoring Cheryl's question. "I'd like Loraine Newman's phone number."

"Not a problem," Cheryl said. With a few clicks of her computer mouse, she had it on her screen.

"I need some other numbers," Laurie said. "The CDC in Atlanta has an MRSA program as part of its National Healthcare Safety Network. I'd like you to get me a name and phone number of one of its epidemiologists. I'd also like you to call the Joint Commission for Accreditation of Healthcare Organizations and get me a name and number for someone in surveillance of mandated hospital infectious-control programs."

"I'll do my best," Cheryl said.

"The name of my case is David Jeffries," Laurie continued. "I'd like his hospital record."

"That will be easy," Cheryl said. "But I'm not sure I understand who it is you want to talk to at the joint commission. Could you give me a better idea?"

"The joint commission requires hospitals to have infection-control committees for accreditation. What I want to find out is whether there is any policing of these committees and whether any reporting of outbreaks is required between formal inspections. I know this is a bit unusual," Laurie said, "but I'm pressed for time."

"I'm happy to help," Cheryl said good-naturedly.

Laurie left the forensic investigator's office and went to the stairs, avoiding the back elevator. She'd started the day with a selfish desire to talk Jack out of his imminent surgery. Now she was worried about his well-being, maybe even his life. Among herself, Besserman, and Southgate, there were seven cases of fatal MRSA necrotizing pneumonia within three months at three hospitals, one of which Jack was scheduled to enter, and all run by the same company. And worse yet, these cases were occurring despite what Besserman had described as aggressive infection-control measures. Although Laurie was the first to admit that she didn't know too much about epidemiology, she knew enough to wonder if there might be a lethal, unknowing MRSA carrier, like a kind of Typhoid Mary, in the Angels Healthcare organization who was inadvertently spreading MRSA as he or she went from hospital to hospital in the course of his or her job. Laurie wanted a lot of information, and as stubborn as Jack was, she wanted it fast if she hoped to influence his mind-set.

The next stop was microbiology, which was part of the laboratory complex on the fourth floor. Laurie found the taciturn, sinewy microbiologist Agnes Finn in her small, windowless office. Of all the employees of the OCME, Agnes's appearance was the most stereotypic for working in a morgue from central casting's point of view. Her grayish-yellow coloring contributed; it was as if she never saw the light of day. Yet, of all the supervisors, Laurie found Agnes to be the most helpful by far, always willing to go out of her way. It was as if she had no life outside the OCME.

Laurie sat down and explained the situation, which elicited from Agnes a mini-lecture on MRSA, including everything Besserman had to say and then some. She explained in detail how staphylococcus was such a pluripotent microbe, and perhaps the most adaptive and successful human pathogen.

"When you think about it from the bacteria's point of view," Agnes said, "it is truly a superbug, capable of killing someone in a frightfully short time while the same strain is able to merely colonize an individual, usually just within the nares. This is a convenient location for the bacteria, because every time the carrier puts his or her finger in their nose, their fingers are contaminated from where it can be spread to the next person."

"Is there an estimate as to how many people are so colonized?"

"Absolutely. At any given time, a third of the world's population carries staph; that's about two billion people."

"Good Lord," Laurie said. "Are there many strains of MRSA besides the hospital-acquired and the community-acquired?"

"Very many," Agnes said. "And they are evolving all the time in people's noses and elsewhere, like moist skin surfaces, where they exchange genetic material."

"How are the strains differentiated in the laboratory?"

"Many ways," Agnes said. "Antibiotic resistance is one."

"But that's not particularly sensitive, considering everything you've said."

"That's correct. The more sensitive methods are all genetics-based: the simplest and most commonly employed being pulse-field gel electrophoresis, and the most complete being full genotyping. In between, there are a number of other sequence typing techniques all based on PCR."

"What can you do here in microbiology?"

"Only the simplest: antibiotic resistance."

"If needed, where can the more complicated be done?"

"The state reference lab can do the pulse-field gel electrophoresis. As for more specific typing, the CDC is the best bet. They are actually building a national library of MRSA strains, so they can give you a lot of information. They encourage submissions of isolates, and they can do it all. Of course Dr. Lynch in our DNA lab over in the new highrise can do the various genetic typing, but we won't be able to tell you much about the specific strain."

"Which of the genetic tests is the fastest? I'm up against a time constraint."

"Truthfully, I don't know. What I do know is that our standard culture and antibiotic sensitives take twenty-four to forty-eight hours. Hospitals can do it much faster using monoclonal antibody-based methods. Interesting enough, such machines came out of work for NASA."

Laurie shook her head. She was humbled. "Before today I thought I knew a reasonable amount about staph. But I was sorely mistaken."

"We all have to keep learning," Agnes said philosophically. "What do you want to do about these specimens you've brought in?"

"I'll take one over to Ted Lynch in the DNA lab. I'd like one for you to culture, and the rest can go to the reference lab. I'm also going to want to get some frozen samples from some of Dr. Besserman's and Dr.

Southgate's cases to compare. I'd like to know if they are from the same strain. I'm concerned about an unsuspecting carrier, particularly after what you've told me."

"Let me know the cases you are interested in. I'll try to expedite the process. As for Ted Lynch, you'll have to leave it to me to provide him with a pure culture for his DNA analysis."

With her head in whirl, Laurie hurried out of the lab and headed toward the faster front elevator. As she hit the up button repeatedly, in vain hope of speeding up the elevator's arrival, she tried to plot the course of the rest of her morning. The first stop was going to be Maureen O'Connor in the histology lab, where Laurie intended to beg for David Jeffries's lung sections to be processed into slides as quickly as possible; Laurie didn't care about the rest of the slides at the moment, just the lung, since she had in mind to make some large photomicrographs if the pathology appeared as bad as she fully expected it would. She thought they would make terrific PowerPoints for the argument she intended to wage against Jack to get him to cancel his ACL repair.

Laurie boarded the elevator and pushed the button for the fifth floor. She looked at her watch. It was close to ten. Exiting, she literally ran down the hall into histology and arrived mildly out of breath.

"Uh-oh! Ladies," Maureen scoffed in her heavy brogue, "I seem to sense another acute emergency from Miss Montgomery. Errr . . . that's Mrs. Montgomery-Stapleton. Who'll volunteer to tell her this time, her patient is already dead?"

There was general laughter from the women who worked in histology. Thanks to Maureen's good humor, it was a happy environment. Even Laurie found herself smiling despite her anxiousness. Like most humor, there was truth in Maureen's comment. Laurie and Jack were the only pathologists on the ME staff who, on occasion, felt they needed a rapid turnover with their microscope slides. All the others were content to have them in due course.

Maureen listened to Laurie's request and explanation, and promised to do them herself. Within minutes, Laurie was back in the hall. She hurried down to Arnold Besserman and Kevin Southgate's office. As she knocked, the door swung open on its own, and Laurie leaned inside.

The interior of the office reminded Laurie of the two men's polar political leanings. As the archconservative, Arnold had a desk that was the picture of neatness, with a single cardboard tray of slides on one side of his microscope and a new yellow legal pad on the other. Both were aligned perfectly parallel to each other along with a precisely sharpened pencil. Southgate's side of the room was the opposite, with slide trays, unfinished case files, lab reports, and all manner of other documents piled on both his desk and file cabinet, leaving only a small arc of cleared horizontal space directly in front of his chair. A vast clutter of Post-it notes hung from the shade of his desk lamp like so much Spanish moss. It was a wonder to Laurie how the two men got along so well and for so long.

After leaving a note on the door for either man to call her, Laurie went down the hall, knocking at the other medical examiners' doors to do a quick survey of their recent MRSA experience. No one was in his office, which was entirely understandable, since the morning was the busy time in the pit, although she'd not seen George Fontworth, Paul Plodget, or his newly hired office mate, Edward Gonzales. Edward was a gifted forensic pathologist who was a product of OCME's own program and New York University.

Momentarily thwarted in scaring up more MRSA cases at the OCME, Laurie retreated to her own office. Suddenly, remembering Arnold Besserman's comment about Queens, Brooklyn, and Staten Island, all of which had their own ME offices, she realized her conclusion that there had been no fatal MRSA cases in any of the other city hospitals during the last three months or so was premature.

With her Rolodex open, Laurie first called Dick Katzenburg, the chief of the Queens office. He'd helped Laurie in the past by coming up with cases that matched the two series of cases she had become deeply involved with. As the call went through, Laurie recalled that both those previous series of hers had surprisingly turned out to be homicides, which no one suspected, even she. The remembrance briefly stimulated the thought that the manner of death of her current series might not be accidental, especially considering that a third of the world's population was colonized with staph organisms at any given time.

The Queens ME office answered, and Laurie asked for Dick. While she waited, she tapped her fingers nervously. She hoped he'd be available, which she thought was a reasonable expectation. In his role as chief of the satellite office, administrative duties often kept him at his desk and out of the autopsy room. As the time dragged on, she got out a fresh legal pad, and with the phone in the crook of her neck, she drew multiple vertical parallel lines, creating a checkerboard matrix in which she planned to add information about the MRSA cases as she learned it. With her two previous series, it had been the matrixes that had given her the insight she'd needed. Hoping for a similar outcome, she wrote *David Jeffries* on the top row, to the left of the indent line.

Dick came on the line apologetic for keeping her waiting. After a bit of social chatter, Laurie asked if they had seen in the Queens office any MRSA nosocomial infections over the last three or even four months.

"We have indeed!" Dick said without hesitation. "They weren't my cases; they were Thomas Asher's. I remember them because they were fairly ugly."

"Meaning?"

"Necrotizing pneumonia. The victims, who were all healthy people, didn't have a chance. Their histories reminded me of the stories of the influenza epidemic in 1918."

On the spur of the moment, Laurie felt a pang of selfish disappointment. The fact that other hospitals in the city were experiencing the same problem as the Angels Healthcare institutions would undoubtedly dilute the cases' impact on Jack.

"Do you know if they occurred at one hospital or at a number of hospitals?" Laurie inquired.

"Just one. It was an orthopedic hospital. Why do you ask?"

Laurie sat up straighter in her chair. "What was the name of the hospital?"

"Angels something. I think Angels Orthopedic Hospital. They were all orthopedic cases."

A slight crooked smile turned up the corners of Laurie's mouth. Instead of losing strength, the potential success of her argument with Jack notched upward.

"There have been some cases here as well," Laurie said, "including one I autopsied today. I'm going to look into it, even though I was told the hospital has been aggressively proactive in dealing with the problem."

"Let me know if I can help."

"Can you give me the names?"

Laurie could hear the familiar sound of Dick's keyboard. A minute later, he said, "Philip Moore, Jonathan Knox, and Eileen Dimalanta."

Laurie quickly added them to her matrix. "Have all three been signed out?"

"Yup, so you can access them in the database."

"I'd still like to see the case files; hospital records, if you have them; and also a tissue sample, so I can have the strain accurately typed, if it hasn't already been done."

"I'll bring what I have over for Thursday conference."

"I'd prefer you messenger them over today. I'm under a time constraint."

"How so?"

"A personal commitment," Laurie said, not wishing to elaborate.

Next, Laurie called Jim Bennett in Brooklyn and Margaret Hauptman in Staten Island. Although Margaret had had no MRSA cases, Jim had had three, like Dick. Two were necrotizing pneumonias like the others and were from the same hospital, but another one was fatal MRSA toxic shock syndrome secondary to a fulminant endophthalmitis, a massive infection inside the victim's right eye, which had quickly followed a routine cataract extraction. Hanging up the phone, Laurie added Carlos Suarez, Matt Collord, and Kayla Westover to her rapidly growing matrix. Laurie was now convinced that something was wrong — something was very wrong.

3
APRIL 3, 2007
10:20 A.M.

"Rodger Naughton will be with you shortly," the priggish secretary said. "Would you mind taking a seat?" From Angela's perspective, the woman seemed more like an automaton than a real person. As many times as Angela had been to Rodger's office, she expected some small gesture of familiarity rather than cool indifference, and although Angela had anticipated the reception from having experienced it so often in the past, it still added to her discomfort.

For as long as Angela could remember, she had been an independent person, loath to ask people for favors, always determined to do whatever it was herself. As she grew older, this characteristic extended to asking for money. Yet there she was, sitting in the columned splendor of the Manhattan Bank and Trust with her metaphorical tin cup, forced to beg for a loan.

The only bright side was that Rodger's

personality was quite the opposite of Miss Darton's. From their first encounter, Angela had found him to be friendly, helpful, and all around remarkably simpatico. Under different circumstances she would have looked forward to seeing him, but not today. From the moment she'd awakened, through getting Michelle off to school amid the continuing belly-button-piercing debate, through talking with the lead counsel about the previous day's MRSA death, and through reassuring Cynthia Sarpoulus that no one blamed her for the continuing infection problem, Angela had tried to come up with a strategy to talk Rodger into giving her a sizable personal loan or giving Angels Healthcare a commercial loan.

Unfortunately, she'd been unsuccessful in coming up with any ideas short of getting down on her knees and begging. As dire as the situation was, she'd do it if she thought it would help.

"Mr. Naughton will see you now," Miss Darton said. The only change in her expression was a slight lift to her eyebrows and a flutter of her eyelids.

Feeling like she was headed to the principal's office after having been nabbed committing an infraction such as smoking a cigarette in the girls' room, Angela headed into

Rodger's office.

"Angela!" Rodger called out with alacrity as he bounded out from behind his desk with his hand outstretched. "So glad to see you. This is a treat. Normally, I have to deal with your CFO, not that I dislike Bob Frampton. He is very much a gentleman, but if I had my druthers, I'd prefer to deal with you directly. Now, don't you tell him that!" He laughed as he shook Angela's hand vigorously and guided her toward a seat facing his desk.

Angela sat and observed Rodger as he returned to his tufted leather high-backed desk chair. He was a handsome, boyish man with a carefully groomed appearance. He had fine, closely trimmed blond hair and pale blue eyes. His position at the bank was one of several healthcare relationship managers. As a business with no discernible ceiling to its growth, healthcare was of great interest to banks in general and to the Manhattan Bank and Trust in particular. When Angela had come to the bank five years previously to arrange for Angels Healthcare's first construction loan, she had been assigned to Rodger. Over the ensuing years, Rodger had worked with the company as its liaison with the bank, earning considerable money for the bank in the process. During this time, Angels

Healthcare had built three multimillion-dollar hospitals, which had been veritable cash cows until the recent MRSA outbreak. It was this reality that Angela planned to emphasize and hopefully exploit.

"How is your daughter?" Rodger asked with sincerity rather than merely to make conversation.

"Other than some preteen angst, she's okay," Angela said, while her mind struggled with how to begin the quest for yet another loan. "And yours?" She knew Rodger had a girl a year older than Michelle, but that was the extent of her knowledge of the man's private life.

"She's struggling with the same issues. I'm learning that teenage daughters can be a handful."

Angela remembered her own teenage struggles all too clearly. It was during that stressful middle-school interval that her problems with her father had come to a head, never to be truly resolved.

"Angela," Rodger said. "I'm assuming you are here today about the call I made to Bob, your CFO. I want to reassure you it was pro forma bank policy. The margin on Angels Healthcare loans comes to my attention automatically when it nears a specific point. The problem, of course, is the bridge loan we arranged a little over a month ago, combined with the recent sale of bonds from your company's management account. It is bank policy that I, as your relationship manager, make the call. Rest assured, I am not calling any of the company's loans."

"I appreciate that," Angela said, groaning inwardly. His comments, although solicitous in trying to put her at ease, had the opposite effect. Rodger was, in effect, telling her that Angels Healthcare had no more credit. Regardless, Angela cleared her throat and added, "But your call to Bob was not the reason for my visit."

"Oh," Rodger said. He leaned back in his chair. "How can I help you?"

"I know you are aware of our upcoming IPO," Angela began. "Its scheduled closing is just a little more than two weeks away, so we are in the quiet period, meaning I cannot divulge any specifics. Let me just say that we have been assured the IPO will be successful."

"I'm happy for you," Rodger said. "An underwriting guarantee! Wow!"

"Congratulations may be a little premature. The short-term problem which prompted our need for a bridge loan a month ago has cost considerably more to fix than we had predicted. We need another bridge loan, but only for three weeks. The interest doesn't matter, and we can pay it up front."

Rodger leaned forward. His chair squeaked. He rubbed his forehead and breathed out through puffed-up cheeks. Then he looked across at Angela. He suddenly looked tired, and even a little sad. "What kind of money are you talking about?"

"Two hundred thousand is what we'd like, but we'll settle for what you could arrange."

"You are asking for the impossible," Rodger said. He took a deep breath. "When I said your company's loans were nearing the margin, I was not completely forthright. They are at the margin. I'm afraid you are fully drawn down on facility."

"Can't you make an exception?" Angela asked. She hated to plead but had no other choice. "You have been working with us for almost five years. You understand current medical economics. You know how well we are positioned. We will be the first specialty hospital company to go public after the senatorial moratorium was lifted this past October. You know that we will be tapping into an almost limitless amount of guaranteed revenue because of the way healthcare reimbursement favors procedures. You also know

146

Angels Healthcare is going to mushroom into a very big company, and you know Manhattan Bank and Trust will continue to be our bankers, with you as our relationship manager. I give my word. I'll even put it in writing."

"What about your personal assets?" Rodger asked. "I can get you a home equity loan. I'll facilitate it myself. I can have the money for you — "

"That will not work," Angela said, interrupting. "I've already maxed out the equity in all my personal assets, including my jewelry. Everything!"

For a few minutes, silence reigned in Rodger's office. The only sound was a ticking Tiffany desk clock. A narrow beam of sunlight streamed into the room. A million motes of dust danced silently in its glare.

Rodger sat back and spread his hands in the air. He shook his head. "I'm sorry. I cannot authorize a loan with no collateral. It's not that I don't want to: It's just not in my power to do so. I'm sorry, Angela. I admire you greatly as a doctor, a businesswoman, and a fine human being. I just can't do it."

"What about someone higher in the bank's hierarchy? Surely someone can authorize such a loan, especially considering the money the bank has made in the short run and will be made over the long haul."

"I'll try," Rodger said, without a lot of enthusiasm. "I'll send the request up the ladder to my superiors."

"Will you recommend it?" Angela asked.

"I will recommend they consider it," Rodger said, skirting the question.

"Thank you," Angela said. She stood, managed a half-smile, and shook hands with Rodger across his immaculate desk. It was then that she noticed the sole framed photograph on the desk was of a young girl. There was no family shot, nor a wife.

"I should tell you that even if the powers that be were to approve the loan, it would surely take several weeks to go through the process. I'm sorry, Angela. Please don't take it personally. If it were my prerogative, I would do it in a second."

Angela headed for the door. Five minutes later, she was on the street trying to hail a cab to ride downtown. Even though the outcome of the meeting was as she had anticipated, it still depressed her. Of the two meetings she'd scheduled that morning, the one she'd just had with Rodger had at least been cordial. The next one with her ex-husband, Michael Calabrese, probably wouldn't be; they almost never were. Although Angela truly loved and treasured her daughter, often she was regretful that the child tied her inexorably to continued and sustained contact with a man she wished she'd never met, much less married. Of course, she'd made the situation worse by allowing him, against her better judgment, to act as her fledgling company's placement agent back when she was initially founding Angels Healthcare.

The collaboration did not happen by forethought. Sharing custody required continual contact, and Michael had used the opportunity to quiz Angela about her experiences getting her MBA. Although Michael had been in the securities business with Morgan Stanley since graduating from Columbia, where he'd first met Angela, he never got a graduate degree. His curiosity about Angela's MBA experience had been a combination of genuine interest and also a kind of jealousy. Like her father, Michael had been challenged by Angela's medical degree, especially when his friends would tease him that she was the brains and he was the brawn. Even though they were divorced, Angela's getting an advanced degree in business, the arena he claimed as his area of expertise, had reawakened the negative feelings of insecurity that her scholarship engendered. Discussions would invariably turn into mutual irritation until the day Angela described a business plan she was creating as an exercise for one of her courses. When she finished the description, Michael had been so impressed that he'd encouraged her to actually do it as a real company. He told her he could get seed capital from what he called his "unique" clients. He never explained what he had meant by "unique clients," but Angela had reason to believe he was not merely bragging. Michael, by that time, had left Morgan Stanley to form his own boutique placement firm. In that capacity, he often worked with his former employer, Morgan Stanley, on IPOs, and was doing very well for himself.

Encouraged by Michael's urging, Angela had gone to several of her professors, who were also intrigued by her business plan, and she used their contacts to found Angels Healthcare. True to his word, Michael raised a portion of the seed capital from his clients, and even found the eventual "angel investor" as a syndicate of the same clients, which ultimately committed fifteen million plus a recent bridge loan convertible into stock at their discretion. However, the true success came from Angela's efforts, which raised the rest of the seed capital. During her MBA, she had moonlighted at University Hospital and, like a born saleswoman, had culled a group of eager university physician investors, who interested a number of colleagues, who interested more doctors from other institutions in a rapidly self-fulfilling process. Not only did all these physician investors contribute money, but once the hospitals were built, they also brought in the patients in droves, which was in essence the critical factor in the business plan and the source of the company's success.

Angela climbed out of the cab in front of a large marble-and-glass office building not too far from Ground Zero. Michael shared office space with a number of other independent financial wheeler-dealers. Each had their own private offices but shared common areas and secretarial services. It was a convenient relationship for all, since they got better quarters and services than they would if they were on their own.

Michael's office had an impressive view of the Hudson, with the Statue of Liberty standing midriver on her postage stamp-sized island. Across the river loomed apartment buildings in New Jersey.

Michael's door was ajar, and since the shared secretary was at a considerable distance, Angela merely walked in. Her ex was on the phone, leaning back in his chair with legs crossed and his feet perched on the corner of the desk. His jacket was hung over the back of his chair, his tie was loosened, and the top button of his shirt was undone. He was the picture of casual ease. Without interrupting his conversation, he motioned for Angela to sit on the couch.

Angela took off her coat, laid it across the arm of the couch, stashed her briefcase on the floor, and sat down. On the coffee table directly in front of her were the usual masculine appurtenances, including a decanter filled with an amber fluid, several cut-crystal old-fashioned glasses, and a polished mahogany humidor with a flush, inset humidity gauge. On the wall was a flat-screen TV with stock prices trailing along the lower part of the screen and silent talking heads above.

Just seeing her former spouse made her heart speed up, but certainly not due to attraction, although she had to admit he was darkly handsome. His features were angular and rugged, and his anthracite-colored hair was slicked back. One hand held the phone; the other gestured wildly in the air as his conversation progressed. He was obviously trying to convince someone of something.

Angela had met him when she was a junior and he a senior at Columbia University, and he had swept her off her feet. She thought he was exactly what she was looking for. He was undeniably masculine, a good student, somewhat of a rebel, outspoken, seemingly honest, popular with and patriotic to his buddies new and old, passionate and outspoken about his attraction to her, romantic with little gestures like special-occasion flowers, and, particularly importantly to her, not afraid of showing emotion. In short, he was the opposite of her father, a personality profile Angela demanded in anyone she might consider for a long-term relationship. She even appreciated his blue-collar background and his confirmed allegiance to his high-school friends, few of whom had gone to college. It suggested he had good values. The only chink in the picture was that one night Michael had admitted that his domineering father had not spared the belt in his maniacal goal that his sons attend an Ivy League university. Since the modus operandi had worked for Michael, although not for Michael's older brother, Angela didn't pay heed to the old proverb "the ends do not justify the means," although she should have. In a big, ugly way, it would prove to be prophetic.

"All right, all right!" Michael said finally, while waving his free hand in the air as if batting away a pesky insect. "Get back to me!" He positioned the phone receiver several inches over its cradle and let it drop. "God, some people are such assholes."

Angela wisely held her tongue.

"So," Michael said, rising up to his full six-foot-three stature. "What's up?" He came around the desk, grabbed a side chair, swung it over to the coffee table, and mounted it backward. With his arms crossed and resting on the chair's back, he regarded Angela with a wry, challenging smile that unfortunately evoked enough unpleasant memories that Angela scrapped her initial plan of restricting the conversation to her company's desperate need for cash and then leaving. Instead, she said, "First, let's clear the air about some minor issues."

"Okay. What's your idea of minor issues?"

"Why on earth would you give permission to our ten-year-old daughter to get her belly button pierced before talking to me about it?"

"The kid wants it. Why not?"

"And that's enough of a reason for her to do it?" Angela asked with uncamouflaged disbelief. "Just because she wants it?"

"She told me all her friends have them."

"And you believed her?"

"Why shouldn't I? It's kinda a fad."

Angela instinctively knew it was a waste of everyone's time to continue the conversation. Michael had never been much of a parent — nor much of a husband. Only after they had gotten married did Angela learn that Michael had a "very blue-collar" idea of matrimonial duties. In his mind, his role was to come home from work, sit in front of the TV, and keep the family updated on current events, particularly in the sports world. And that was on those nights when he didn't have to meet his friends, supposedly for work-related dinners in lower Manhattan. Gone were the romantic gestures and compliments. Angela became pregnant and put up with their failing relationship, vainly hoping the birth of the supposedly longed-for child would turn Michael back into the person he'd been during the courtship. But Michelle's arrival only made Angela's life more difficult, as she desperately tried to balance graduate medical training in internal medicine with the rigors of parenting a newborn. Michael had refused to help except in very superficial ways. He even openly prided himself for never having changed a diaper. Such duties were simply below the dignity of a young, hotshot, rapidly rising investment banker.

"Listen," Angela said, trying to keep herself as calm as possible, "let's not argue, but I assure you all her friends do not have them.

And there's always the risk of infection."

"They can have problems with infection?"

"Yes, indeed! But the point is that when something like this comes up and you think there is any chance I might feel strongly about it, talk to me before making a decision."

"Fine," Michael said, with a roll of his eyes. "Okay, you made your point about the piercing issue. What else? You implied there was more."

"Yes, there is," Angela said, trying to think of the right words. "I want to let you know under no uncertain terms that your telling Michelle that it is my fault you and I are divorced is unacceptable. Trying to get Michelle to take sides in a problem that is between you and me is not okay. You have to stop."

"Hey, I didn't file for divorce, you did," Michael said. "I didn't want to get divorced."

"Who files for divorce has nothing to do with cause," Angela snapped. "It was your behavior that got us divorced."

"So I got drunk and hit you. I said I was sorry. What are you, perfect?"

"I wasn't the one having affairs. And you got drunk and hit me more than once."

"I wasn't having affairs. I was just blowing

off steam. A lot of the guys do it, especially when their wives are off to the Hamptons in the summer. It doesn't mean anything. It's just booze and entertainment."

"We live on different planets," Angela said. "But I didn't come here to argue. The past is the past for us, except for Michelle and Angels Healthcare. For Michelle's sake, don't talk about whose fault the divorce was. You can think one way, and I another. Just don't mess up her head pointing fingers. All I say to her is that it just didn't work out. I don't try to influence her relationship with you. That's totally between you and her."

"All right," Michael said, with another roll of his eyes. Ultimately, he didn't care. From his perspective, his current life was far better than his life when they were married. But at the time it had bothered him that Angela had the gall to file and embarrass him. He'd never expected it. None of the other guys got divorced. Hell, some of them had known, steady girlfriends and even allowed themselves to be seen in public with them.

"What we really need to talk about is Angels Healthcare," Angela said.

"I hope you're not here to tell me that accountant of yours filed the damn eight-K."

"No, that's not why I'm here," Angela said with a shake of her head. "I haven't seen him yet today. I was in the office only briefly before going to the bank, then coming down here. But why are you asking me if he filed? You assured me you knew someone who could talk to Paul Yang, and there wouldn't be a problem."

"True," Michael said simply. "So what is it that you want to talk about?"

"I need to raise more money. If I don't, I'm not certain we are going to make it through the IPO with our current cash flow. You have to help!"

"You're not serious."

"I'm very serious."

"What the hell happened to the quarter of a million I raised for you a month ago?"

"It was more than a month."

"That's one hell of a burn rate."

"It's not all gone, but yes, it is a rapid burn rate. A sizable portion went out to suppliers. But the real draw is keeping three hospitals open with very little revenue."

"But you told me last time you were here that you were dealing with an infection problem, which was soon to be under control. You said that your revenue stream would quickly recover."

"It hasn't happened."

"Why the hell not?" Michael demanded.

"When I was here last, our ORs were

closed. Apart from loss of revenue, the cost of containing the infection was four times our estimate, but things are looking up. The ORs are now open, but our census is low. Except for a few stalwart individuals, our doctors are still gun-shy. Things will turn around rather quickly but not soon enough."

Michael ran a nervous hand across his forehead and gazed out at the placid expanse of the Hudson River.

Angela watched him and knew him well enough to recognize true anxiety. He did not like what he was hearing. He was upset a month ago when she'd come with her woes, and he was more upset now. Not only had he committed a lot of his client's money to Angels Healthcare, he'd committed a lot of his own, not to mention his working relationship with Morgan Stanley, who he'd convinced to be the underwriter for the IPO.

Michael looked back at Angela. He nervously licked his lips. "What kind of money are we talking about here?"

"My CFO says we'd be confident with two hundred thousand."

"Holy shit!" Michael exclaimed, leaping off his chair to pace his office. "Tell me you are joking," he said, suddenly stopping and staring at Angela with an expectant expression. "Tell me. You're highballing me as a psychological ploy."

"I'm telling you straight. This is too serious a situation to be joking or playing games."

"What the hell is your crackpot CFO doing with all the cash?"

"Michael, it is expensive to run three hospitals. You've seen our books. Salaries alone are enormous, and the costs don't stop just because the revenue does. The eye hospital and the heart hospital are producing some cash, but the ortho hospital is producing almost none. We've let a few people go, but we are limited unless we want to call attention to our cash-flow problem, which we don't. Many of us haven't taken any salary for months."

"I'm getting more than a bad feeling here. Yesterday, you call me about the problem with the accountant. Today you pop in, asking me to raise another two hundred grand! What's it going to be tomorrow?"

"Wait a minute!" Angela said. "You're the one who offered to help with the accountant when the issue arose a week ago. You said you had people who could convince him that filing the eight-K wasn't necessary."

Angela waited for a moment before continuing. "We only need the money for three weeks, tops. Angels Healthcare will then be swimming in cash, even taking into account the obscene amount we have to pay Morgan Stanley."

"Don't begrudge Morgan Stanley's take. They are the ones assuming the most risk here, and from what you are saying, it's even more than they think."

"Go back to your clients! Offer them whatever you need to. I tried the bank, and I pleaded with Rodger, but it's a no go."

"I can't go back to my client," Michael said, decisively suggesting that there was no room for discussion.

" 'Client'? I thought it was clients?" Angela said. She was confused. He'd always said *clients* and used the word *syndicate.* She was certain.

"It's really one client," Michael said reluctantly.

"Why can't you go back to him? Surely he doesn't want to risk his generous payoff, with as much stock and options as he controls."

"That's what I said when I went back for the quarter of a million."

"Tell him again. I assume he's a smart man. Tell him exactly what I told you, that the ORs are open."

"He is a smart man, especially about money. If I go back to him at this point, he'll know we are desperate."

"We are desperate."

"Whether it is true or not, it is a bad negotiating position. He might demand to take controlling interest."

It was now Angela's turn to stare out the window at the river. The idea of losing control of her company was anathema after all her effort. Yet what other options did she have? For a brief moment, she thought about going back to the practice of medicine and giving up the entrepreneurial lifestyle. But the thought was short-lived. She was realistic enough to know that the freedom her current lifestyle afforded her, at least prior to the current cash-flow problem, had become addictive. She couldn't help but recall her disastrous experience with her primary-care practice and the realities of the current healthcare reimbursement, which was totally out of her control. Also, she reminded herself that if nothing else, she was persistent. She wasn't going to give up now that she was fifty yards from the finish line after a ten-mile race.

"Let me talk to your client directly," Angela said, breaking the silence. She had suddenly redirected her attention to Michael, who'd sat back in his chair. A few dots of perspiration had appeared along his hairline.

"Oh, yeah, sure!" Michael mocked, as if it

was the most ridiculous suggestion she could possibly make.

"Why not? If he has any questions, he can ask them directly instead of through you. I can reassure him. With all the experience I've been having, I'm getting good at convincing investors."

"My client has made it abundantly clear he only wants to talk to me about investment issues."

"Oh, come on, Michael. I'm not going to steal your client. Don't be so paranoid."

"It's not me who is paranoid, it's him. Just so you understand the situation, there's several shell companies between him and his position in Angels Healthcare, as well as with several other pending deals."

"Why so much secrecy? Is there something here you're not telling me?"

"I'm only following his orders."

"Is he your major client in most of your placement deals?"

"Let's just say he's a big player. I can't be more specific."

Angela eyed her ex. This need for secrecy added to her general unease. Although she truly didn't know why, it was apparent that Michael had no intention of enlightening her further. Instead of pressing him, she said, "Why don't you raise the money from some-

163

one else? Make it a sweet deal to one of your other clients."

"It's too short a time frame for that. There's no one I know whom I could approach."

"Then what about yourself? I've already maxed out all my equity."

"Me, too."

"What about your jet?"

"It's pledged to the hilt. Hell, it's been on one hundred percent charter as well."

Angela threw up her hands and stood. "Well, there's not much more I can say or do. I'm afraid all our fates are in your hands, Michael. You are our placement agent, for better or worse."

Michael breathed out noisily. "Maybe I can come up with fifty grand," he said reluctantly. After everything he'd all but promised people, if this IPO stalled, he knew he'd be in deep trouble, and not just financially.

"That's a start," Angela said. "I can't say it will guarantee success, but it will be much appreciated. What do you want as compensation?"

"Twelve percent as a loan, but convertible at my discretion to one hundred thousand dollars of preferred stock."

"Jesus Christ!" Angela murmured, then, in a normal voice, added, "I'll have Bob

Frampton call you as soon as I get back to the office. When can we expect to have access to the cash?"

"In a day or so," Michael said distractedly. He was already trying to think of how he'd manage to cobble together the funds. He had not been joking when he told Angela he was maxed out, although he did have some gold futures he'd kept out of the mix for a disaster. He reasoned that this might be the disaster.

"I'll be at the office putting out fires if you have any bright ideas," Angela said as she got her coat and briefcase. She looked back at Michael before leaving. He'd gone back to staring out the window.

As she walked to the elevator, she vaguely thought that Michael was his own worst enemy. She also thought of the proverb that you can take the boy out of the country, or in this case his old neighborhood, but often you could not take the country out of the boy, especially since Michael had moved back to his old neighborhood after the divorce. To Angela, Michael's story smacked of a Greek tragedy. Michael was a smart, well-educated, handsome, and often charming individual who had the potential to be successful on many fronts, yet he had a tragic flaw: He was a prisoner of his past, when he had unknowingly absorbed indelible and ultimately harmful allegiances, attitudes, and values.

Thinking in this vein about Michael, Angela couldn't help but reflect for a moment about herself. As a realist, she knew that she too carried some emotional baggage from her past, and her current life was far from serene. As she boarded the elevator, she wondered if she too had a tragic flaw that could explain how she had gone from a very idealistic first-year medical student to where she currently was: begging for money from a man she despised to prop up a nascent financial empire.

4

APRIL 3, 2007
11:25 A.M.

Laurie couldn't remember the last time she
had been so keyed up. Moving quickly, she
left Paul Plodget's office after speaking with
him and Edward Gonzales. She'd again hit
pay dirt. The first time had been a half-hour
earlier with George Fontworth, an ME
who'd been with the OCME for almost as
long as Arnold and Kevin. He'd provided
her with four MRSA cases he'd had over the
last three months. And now she'd learned
Paul had also seen four MRSA cases over
the same time period, and Edward one. Although one of Paul's cases was from Manhattan General, a tragic case of a previously
well five-year-old girl who'd developed rapidly fatal necrotizing pneumonia from a boil-
like lesion obtained at a local playground, all
the others were from an Angels Healthcare
hospital. First, there was a Jonathan Wilkin-
son, who'd died of necrotizing pneumonia
after a triple coronary bypass; second was

Judith Astor, who died of toxic shock–like syndrome after a facelift; and third was Gordon Stanek, who died of necrotizing pneumonia after a rotator-cuff repair. Edward's case was Leroy Robinson, who passed away from necrotizing pneumonia after the repair of an open wrist fracture.

Walking quickly enough to briefly skid on the highly waxed vinyl floor, Laurie stormed into her office. After sitting down, she pulled herself toward her desk and reached for her rapidly expanding matrix to add Paul's and Edward's cases.

"Remind me, if asked, never to do another case with our beloved chief," Riva said, turning around toward Laurie. It was a common joke around the OCME to express such sentiments after working with Bingham. Riva had come up to the office between cases to make a few work-related calls. For a moment, she watched Laurie diligently work, wondering why her office mate hadn't even greeted her. It was so unlike Laurie.

"Hey!" Riva called out after several minutes had ticked by. "What are you doing?"

Laurie's head bobbed up. She apologized, belatedly realizing her rudeness. "I've stumbled onto something quite extraordinary."

"Like what?" Riva asked dubiously. She knew Laurie to be a passionate woman who loved her work and who frequently became excited over problematic cases. Sometimes it was appropriate, and sometimes not.

"There has been a mini-epidemic of noso-comial MRSA that's gone essentially unno-ticed."

"I wouldn't say it's gone unnoticed," Riva said. "It's been happening for a decade or more, not only in this country but interna-tionally as well. Didn't it start in Britain?"

"Let me phrase it differently. Within the last three and a half months or so, there's been a number of very severe MRSA inpa-tient infections resulting in rapid death, all occurring at three hospitals owned by An-gels Healthcare."

"Just those three hospitals?"

"That's it! Except for one I uncovered five minutes ago that happened at Manhattan General, all the others have been at the three hospitals."

"How many cases are you talking about?"

Laurie looked back to her ballooning ma-trix and silently counted what she had recorded. "I've got twenty-one so far, but I have yet to talk with Chet, our deputy chief, or Jack, for that matter."

"Are these cases of necrotizing pneumo-nia involving this newer, community-acquired MRSA?"

"Most of them," Laurie said. "A few of the others are described as toxic shock syndrome. In those cases, there is extensive lung inflammatory damage from the bacterial toxins and from the overproduction of cytokines by the deceased, but the infection itself is elsewhere. As for the involved strain, it's been the community-acquired MRSA in those cases where I've seen the case files. The problem is I have yet to see too many case files."

"Then you have twenty-three, not twenty-one."

"How so?" Laurie asked. She looked back at her matrix and started to recount.

"Because I have had two," Riva explained. "It was three months ago and maybe a week or two apart." Swiveling around in her chair, Riva took down a small, bound notebook from her bookshelf above her desk. Unlike any of the other medical examiners, Riva kept a longhand chronological journal of all her cases. On several occasions Laurie wished she had thought of doing the same. In it, Riva added personal observations and feelings that were inappropriate for the official report. It was more like a diary than a mere case-by-case compendium. After rapidly flipping the pages, Riva came to the respective entries. She quickly read them before raising her eyes to meet Laurie's. "You definitely have twenty-three: One of mine was from Angels Orthopedic Hospital, and the other from Angels Cosmetic Surgery and Eye Hospital."

"Can I see?" Laurie asked eagerly.

Riva handed over the journal and pointed to the two entries.

Laurie read rapidly. As an exceptionally thorough pathologist, Riva had recorded the name of the hospital and even the specific strain of MRSA involved in both cases. She had written it as: CA-MRSA, USA400, MW2, SCCmecIV, PVL.

Laurie looked at Riva. "In the few case files I've seen, the bacteria wasn't so specifically typed. Was there some reason it was in your cases?"

"I had it subtyped," Riva explained. "Like you, I was impressed with the pathology in the lung. More for general interest, I sent an isolate of each case to the CDC because I'd read they were looking to obtain MRSA samples for their MRSA library."

"Do you have any idea what all the alphanumeric acronyms mean?"

"Not a clue," Riva admitted. "If you read further, you'd see I'd promised myself I'd look it up, but unfortunately, like a lot of good intentions, I never did it."

171

"Was the CDC surprised that the strains were the same despite coming from different hospitals?"

"I don't believe I mentioned there were two hospitals involved."

Laurie nodded, but the fact that the two strains were exactly the same bothered her, considering what Agnes had told her about how easily staphylococcus exchanged genetic material. She felt pleased that she'd asked Cheryl to get an appropriate contact with someone involved with MRSA at the CDC, as it would give her an opportunity to ask the question directly to someone particularly competent.

"You wrote in your journal that you obtained hospital records," Laurie said. "Do you still have them?"

"Probably," Riva said. "They came in as e-mail attachments. I usually save those just for this kind of situation."

Riva turned to her computer keyboard and began typing.

Laurie picked up her own phone and called down to Cheryl Myers. Luckily, she was still at her desk rather than out on a site visit. Laurie apologized in advance before telling her she needed quite a number of additional hospital records from the Angels Healthcare hospitals.

"Not a problem," Cheryl said. "Just e-mail me the names."

"I did save the hospital records," Riva said when Laurie hung up her phone.

Laurie got up and looked over Riva's shoulder. "Fantastic!" Laurie said. "I guess I can access that from my computer. What's the file name?"

Within a few minutes, Laurie had Longstrome and Lucente's hospital medical records on her screen. Of all the MRSA cases that had come in to be autopsied over the last four months, these were the first hospital records she had. Arnold Besserman had provided her with several of the OCME case files he still had in his office, but he couldn't put his finger on the hospital records.

"Well, I've got to get downstairs and do my next case," Riva said.

Laurie waved over her shoulder, preoccupied by printing out the documents.

"Don't you have another case as well?" Riva asked.

"Oh! Shit!" Laurie said. With her burgeoning interest in the MRSA cases, she'd forgotten. It was embarrassing to think that Marvin was patiently waiting.

"You're preoccupied," Riva said. "I'm sure I can get someone else to do it."

"I'll do it," Laurie said. While she didn't

want to take time away from her current project, she felt guilty about not doing her share. "If you see Marvin down there, tell him I'll be calling him shortly."

With a final nod, Riva disappeared, leaving the door ajar.

Laurie went back to her computer and made the final click to load the second document into the printer queue. Knowing she'd have to wait five or ten minutes for the two documents, she went back to her matrix, adding Riva's cases. When she was finished, she leaned back. It was a sizable list, certainly bigger than the two matrixes she'd made in the past. Now she had to decide how to label the columns. Some of the information she thought appropriate was intuitive, such as: age, sex, race, doctor, date, hospital, diagnosis, type of surgery, predisposing factors, anesthesia, and staph type. Laurie then drew more vertical lines next to the ones she'd already drawn. She knew she needed little space for things like age and sex, and more for predisposing factors and diagnosis. When she was finished, she made sure there was room for more columns. And it was for that reason she was pleased to have the hospital records. She knew that by going over them, she'd come up with more categories.

Satisfied with her progress, Laurie leaped

up from her desk with the intention of dashing to the computer room, only to collide into Jack as he appeared in the doorway. Both were surprised, but more so for Laurie, who let out an involuntary yelp. In the process of grabbing Laurie's upper arms, Jacked dropped the case files he was carrying, as well as his crutches.

"My God!" Jack joked. "What is there, a fire in here?"

Laurie pressed a hand to her chest. It took a few breaths before she could talk. "I'm sorry," she managed. "I guess I'm preoccupied and in a hurry."

"I heard as much about the preoccupied part," Jack said. "I ran into Riva getting off the elevator. She said you'd come across something that you found particularly interesting but didn't elaborate. What's up?"

"Have you had any MRSA cases in the last three months or so with pulmonary involvement?"

"You have to give me more of a clue what you are asking. You know I'm not good with acronyms."

"Methicillin-resistant staphylococcus aureus," Laurie said.

"Uh-oh. Is this a setup? Isn't MRSA what your ACL case had this morning?"

"It is," Laurie admitted. She started to

bend down to retrieve Jack's case files and crutches.

Jack, who was still holding onto Laurie's upper arms, restrained her and then bent down to gather his belongings. "I can't recall having any MRSA ever," he said, while straightening up.

"How about Chet?"

"Now, he might have. It seems to me I heard him talking on the phone about staph with Miss Smiles, Agnes Finn. Whether it was MRSA or not, I have no idea."

"Thanks for the tip. I'll have to ask him."

"So it's obviously MRSA that has you so preoccupied and in a hurry."

"It's certainly the preoccupied part, but the reason I'm in a hurry is because I forgot I've got another case to post. Poor Marvin's been waiting for several hours."

"Riva mentioned the case as well. She said she offered to have someone else do it. She said you didn't take her up on the offer, although she sensed that you wanted to."

Laurie let out a small laugh. "That's sensitive enough on her part to be almost scary."

"Then let me do it," Jack said. "I'm done with all my cases, and from what Riva said, the post itself should be straightforward. I mean, it's going to be plain blunt trauma with the poor guy falling ten stories onto concrete."

"You don't mind?" Laurie questioned. "Maybe you should give it another thought. Riva mentioned to me earlier that there are three stakeholders who are very interested in the case. All three want a different manner of death. No matter what you come up with, two other people are going to be disappointed. That's not your favorite kind of case."

"I think I can handle it."

"Well, then I'll take you up on the offer. But there's one important fact that didn't get in the PA's report, which I got from Cheryl, and which might be important. It was the distance from the building that the body landed. It was twenty-one feet."

"Sounds like I might have to dust off my high-school physics," Jack said. "Now that we have that settled, why are you preoccupied about MRSA? It's not that it is new; it's been a big problem in hospitals for some time. Or shouldn't I ask?"

"You shouldn't ask!" Laurie agreed. "Not until I get more information. Then I'll sit you down for a convincing PowerPoint presentation."

"Why do I have a bad feeling about the goal of this supposed presentation?"

"Because you are worried I'm going to

change your mind."

"Fat chance, Laurie, I'm having my knee fixed come Thursday."

"We'll see," Laurie said confidently. "Come on! I'll ride down in the elevator with you. I need to pick up some material I just had printed."

As they walked down the hall toward the elevator, Laurie asked Jack about his previous case, the last of the three homicides Lou was interested in. She'd heard Lou's description that morning about the detective sergeant's daughter and the baseball bat.

"It's a good one," Jack said, manipulating the crutches like a pro. "It was another opportunity for our PAs to shine. Steve Mariott noticed there were no footprints in the copious amount of blood on the floor. I mean, in and of itself, it doesn't mean a whole lot, but it made him look at the scene a little closer than he might have otherwise, which turned out to be key. The victim's forehead was bashed in, with even a bit of brain tissue extruding, but the overall shape of the wound wasn't concave like you'd expect a bat to cause. I made a mold of the injury, and its tramline."

"You mean it's more like having been caused by a sharp edge?" Laurie questioned as they boarded the elevator.

"Exactly," Jack said, grabbing both crutches in one hand so he could press the button for the basement. Laurie leaned over and hit the button for the first floor. The OCME printer was in the computer room, which was part of the administration area.

"Steve had noticed a bit of blood on the cast-iron edge of a granite coffee table. He'd even taken a picture of it, as well as the bat. I think Satan Thomas, in a drunken, drug-addled stupor, fell while trashing the apartment and hit his forehead on the edge of the coffee table. To prove it, I've sent one of the daytime PAs back to the scene to get a mold of the table's edge."

"That's terrific," Laurie said. "Lou is going to be pleased."

"I think the girlfriend is going to be the most pleased."

The door to the elevator opened. Laurie gave Jack a quick hug and thanked him for volunteering to do her case.

"I'll think of a way you can pay me back," Jack said with a wink and a smile.

After the elevator door closed, Laurie hustled down the main corridor toward the office printer in the computer room. She was determined to take advantage of this unexpected free time. With the hospital records of Riva's two cases, she planned on working

179

more on her matrix by creating more categories and filling in the boxes she could. What Laurie was interested in was finding some hidden commonality among the cases, which could explain the sudden cluster.

Laurie also wanted to get in touch with Cheryl Myers, if Cheryl hadn't called her already, and get the phone contacts Laurie had asked for. She wanted to call the CDC and the joint commission, but mostly she wanted to call Loraine Newman. In the back of her mind, Laurie had begun to believe that a visit to the Angels Orthopedic Hospital and perhaps even Angels Healthcare was in order, even though such excursions were discouraged by the chief. Ten years earlier, Laurie had been called into the chief's office and chastised for making a similar site visit; Bingham felt strongly that visiting scenes was the province of the PAs, not the MEs. But under the circumstances she felt justified, even impelled, and not just to bolster her argument against Jack's surgery. Her intuition was telling her that there was something vaguely unsettling about this series of MRSA cases that went beyond the Typhoid Mary theory.

Adding to her unease were the results of Jack's two cases that morning, the manners of death of which turned out to be the opposite of what was expected — accidental rather than homicidal. Such surprises reminded her that it was always important to keep an open mind about the manner of death. Even the most talented forensic pathologist could be fooled.

Laurie now began to question if the current series of MRSA cases involved something more sinister than the assumed manner of death, therapeutic complication, a relatively new death designation championed by Bingham to replace "accidental" in a hospital setting. Keeping in mind her two previous series, one fifteen years ago and the second two years ago, whose manners of death had been assumed to be accidental and natural, respectively, but whose ultimate determination shockingly turned out to be homicidal, Laurie could not dismiss the possibility that the current series could be the same. Knowing that she'd be ridiculed if she gave voice to her intuitions, Laurie was aware that she had to see if there was any real evidence to bolster her suspicions, and she had to do it quickly.

5
APRIL 3, 2007
11:55 A.M.

Angela removed her coat and draped it over her arm as she exited the elevator on the twenty-second floor of the Trump Tower and briskly walked down toward Angels Health-care. During the ride uptown from Michael's office, she'd been able to use her BlackBerry to respond to all her e-mails and was reasonably confident she wouldn't be overwhelmed when she got to her office. She wondered how people had functioned pre-Internet.

She acknowledged her secretary, Loren, who was on the phone as Angela passed by. Inside her office, she was about to hang up her coat when she stopped, doing a double take. There was a large clear-glass vase of luxurious red roses perched on the corner of her desk. They stood out in bold relief in the sparse, white décor. After finishing with her coat, and curious who could have sent the flowers and why, she looked for a note. There was none to be found. Now even more curious about the flowers, she leaned out her doorway. She had to wave to get Loren's attention.

"What's with the flowers?" Angela mouthed silently. Loren was still on the phone. From overhearing bits and pieces of the conversation, Angela could tell it was the union representative who'd been persistently trying to organize the Angels Healthcare hospitals. There was no way Angela wanted unionization, but with everything else going on, she didn't have the time or the patience to deal with him, so it fell to Loren to hold him off.

Loren put her hand over the receiver. "I'm sorry. They came with a card. It's here on the corner of my desk." She nodded toward the envelope.

Angela picked up the envelope and got a finger under the flap. Once it was open, she slid out the card. It said simply: *Regards from the used one.*

"What the hell?" Angela murmured. She turned the card over, but the back was blank. Curious but overwhelmed with all she had to do, she simply slid the card back into the envelope. She'd think about it later.

Tapping Loren's shoulder, Angela motioned for her to again cover the receiver with her hand, and then said, "Tell him I'll meet with him in three weeks. Go ahead and schedule an actual appointment. That should satisfy him. Then call Bob Frampton and Carl Palanco. Tell them to come into my office ASAP. And where's the afternoon schedule?"

Loren pulled out the schedule for the afternoon meetings and handed it over.

Angela retreated back into her office, closing her door. Seated at her desk, she looked at the schedule. Most of the everyday issues of running each of the hospitals was delegated to the department supervisors, but they reported to their respective hospital presidents as well as to a department head in the Angels Healthcare home office, and those individuals in turn reported to Carl Palanco as the COO, and ultimately to Angela as the CEO. By perusing the schedule, Angela could gauge what the rest of the day would be like. She'd been booked to see the general counsel, most likely about the previous day's MRSA death and how to stave off a lawsuit; the risk-management committee chair for the same reason; and the patient safety committee chair. After that, she was to travel over to the Angels Orthopedic Hospital to attend the hospital medical staff meeting. The final scheduled meeting would be back at her office with Cynthia Sarpoulus, so that the infectious-disease professional could give Angela a briefing of what she had learned and what she had planned to do about the previous day's MRSA death.

Of all the meetings, the medical staff meeting was the most important. It would afford Angela a chance, at least at the orthopedic hospital, to impress on the doctors the vital importance of upping their patient census, despite the minor setback the Jeffries case represented. The only way the revenue stream would turn around is if the surgeons did surgery. Angela was aware more than anyone that the success of the specialty hospital depended exclusively on the doctor owners admitting their paying patients, meaning those patients with insurance, either private or Medicare, or those patients with adequate wealth. The specialty-hospital business as per Angela's business plan was not interested in Medicaid or charity cases, or, for that matter, any cases where cost might exceed revenue.

Angela's phone jangled under her arm. It was Loren, informing the boss that the CFO and COO had arrived.

"Send them in," Angela said, putting aside the afternoon schedule.

The two men, dramatic opposites in outward appearance and mannerism, came into the room. Carl Palanco bounded in, snatched one of the four modern straight-backed chairs from where it stood against the far wall, positioned it in front of Angela's desk, and sat himself down. His expression and constant motion suggested he'd had eight cups of coffee. In contrast, Bob Frampton moved as if in oil, and everything about his face suggested a desperate need for a good night's sleep. Yet despite their contrasting miens, Laurie knew them both to be equivalently clever and resourceful, which was why she had strenuously recruited them at the outset to be her key employees.

It took Bob long enough to move a chair next to Carl's that Angela had been tempted to leap up and do it for him. But she stayed in her seat, and the thought gave her insight into her own hyper state. She wondered if she appeared as high-strung as Carl.

"Anything happen this morning that I should know about, apart from the e-mails you men have sent me?" Angela asked, to start things off.

Carl looked at Bob. Both men shook their heads.

"I've met with the heads of supply, nursing, laundry, engineering, housekeeping, and laboratory services to talk about a deeper cut in expenses over the next few weeks," Carl said. "I've gotten some creative ideas."

"I applaud the initiative," Bob said, "but at this point, any efforts in that regard are too little too late, as far as the IPO is concerned."

"I'm afraid Bob is right," Angela said.

"I had to do something," Carl explained. "I couldn't just sit in my office and do nothing. And come what may, an emphasis on cost-consciousness is a good mind-set for our central department heads to have for the future. I mean, it's hardly wasted effort."

Angela nodded. Keeping a rein on expenses was particularly key for hospital profitability, as holding companies of hospital chains had learned to great advantage over the last few decades. A large part of Angels Healthcare's profitability, at least prior to the MRSA problem, was due to Angela's business plan of building three specialty hospitals at the same time and centralizing things like laundry, supplies, housekeeping, engineering, laboratory services, and even anesthesia. Each hospital had a head, or chief, of these various services, but they all answered to the department head in the company's home office.

"How about your morning?" Bob asked Angela. "Any luck?"

"Marginal," Angela admitted. "As you mentioned last night, we're seriously drawn down on our credit at the bank after selling the bonds. The good news is that Rodger Naughton assured me he was not going to call any of our loans. The bad news is that he cannot authorize a loan without collateral, which I expected. On the other hand, he's sent the additional loan request up the ladder, but from his attitude, I think we have to assume it's a lost cause."

"What about your ex-husband?" Bob asked. As was the case with all the key employees, Bob was aware that their placement agent had been married to Angela but divorced a year before she founded Angels Healthcare. Although initially hesitant about the relationship, Bob had accepted it. He'd expressed a preference for a more direct relationship with a blue-ribbon investment bank, but had been won over by Michael Calabrese's ability to come up with an outstanding angel investor during their mezzanine round of raising capital.

"I was able to get him to commit another fifty thousand of his own money," Angela said. She did not mention how demeaning the meeting was.

"Bravo!" Carl said.

"It's a bit short of what I would feel comfortable with," Bob said.

"I did my best. Getting him to put in the extra money was like squeezing water from a rock."

"Did you discuss the terms?" Bob asked.

"Oh, yeah! You don't think Michael Calabrese would offer that kind of money without rewarding himself."

"What did you offer?"

"I didn't offer; he told me," Angela said, and went on to explain the terms.

"Whoa!" Bob commented. "He's being rather generous with himself."

"It can't be helped under the circumstances," Angela said. "Call him and draw up the documents. I want that money in our account before he changes his mind. I happen to know how fickle he can be."

"Will do," Bob said, typing himself a note on his BlackBerry.

"Okay, that's it," Angela said, placing her palms on her desk as if she were about to stand up. "Except I want to make sure everyone who knows about the MRSA death yesterday understands that the less said about it, the better. I'd like to keep it away from the medical staff as much as possible."

"I've reminded all the hospital CEOs," Carl said. "I also spoke to Pamela Carson in public relations."

"Good," Angela said. "Anything else?"

"There is one thing I just remembered," Bob said. He straightened himself in his chair. "Paul Yang hasn't come into the office today."

"Has he called in sick?" Angela asked. She felt her general anxiety rise another notch.

"No. I left a message on his cell and also e-mailed him, but he hasn't gotten back to me. I don't know where he is."

"Is that odd for him?" Angela asked, while she debated mentioning Michael's possible role.

"Of course it's odd! He's usually so methodical. I even called his wife. She said he didn't come home last night or even call."

"Good God!" Angela said. "Has she called the police?"

"No, she hasn't. He's done this before, although not for a number of years. He'd had a drinking problem, which had led to some odd behavior. His wife told me he'd been out of sorts of late and had gone back to having a cocktail or two on his way home."

"I never knew he had a drinking problem," Angela said. She did not like to be blindsided about any Angels Healthcare employees, particularly key employees.

"I kept it out of his record," Bob said. "I should have told you when I recruited him, but he and I had worked together for something like six years, and he'd been clean."

"Good God!" Angela repeated, raising her eyes to the ceiling for a moment. "Now we have to worry about a drunken binge by our accountant, who's been threatening us all with filing an eight-K. What else can go wrong?" She took a deep breath before looking back at Bob.

"I know he was struggling with his conscience," Bob said. "That's why I called you about him yesterday, to keep you in the loop. Up until then, he hadn't mentioned the problem for over a week. I'd thought it was a nonissue. Apparently, he'd read an article about the sentencing of the Enron and WorldCom people. I told him what I'd told him before, namely that our not filing the eight-K is justifiable. We're not trying to perpetrate a fraud by bilking people out of their savings or retirement funds, which is what the SEC rule is about. In fact, just the opposite! We're creating capital for people."

"After you called me yesterday about him, I called Michael because when you had originally brought the issue to my attention, I had discussed it with him. I thought with his IPO experience he would have a suggestion of how to handle the problem, and he did. He said he knew someone who could talk to him and put his mind at ease by convincing him that filing the eight-K wasn't necessary in our situation."

"Was it a corporate attorney?"

"I have no idea. I didn't ask, but I find myself wondering if talking with Michael's acquaintance could have had anything to do with Paul's not coming to work today."

"It's possible, but I bet the reason for his being incommunicado is more prosaic, like he got himself blotto and is currently sleeping it off in a fleabag hotel."

"Is there any way we could find out if he filed the eight-K?" Angela asked hesitantly.

"Not that I know of," Bob responded. "We'll just have to wait and see if the shit hits the fan." He laughed humorlessly.

"If you think of a way, let me know," Angela said. "It would be best if we know sooner rather than later, so we can prep our general counsel. We'll be forced to come up with a rational explanation of why we didn't file earlier. Maybe you should start giving it some thought, Bob."

Bob nodded.

"What about Paul's secretary?" Carl asked. "Has she heard from him?"

"Not that I know of," Bob said.

"Maybe we should ask her," Angela said, reaching for the phone. "What's her name?"

"Amy Lucas," Carl said.

Angela asked Loren to call Amy Lucas and have her come by ASAP. Angela glanced at her watch. It was twenty after twelve, meaning there was a chance Amy Lucas would be at lunch.

"What's the occasion for the flowers?" Carl asked. "When I saw them, I hoped it had something to do with your morning attempt at raising capital."

"I wish," Angela said. "To tell you the truth, I have no idea who sent them or why."

"Wasn't there a card?" Bob asked.

"There was a card," Angela said, "but it wasn't helpful." She reached for the envelope, slipped out the card, and handed it across the desk. Carl took it, and both men glanced at it.

"What does 'the used one' refer to?" Carl asked.

"Not a clue," Angela admitted. "You don't think it could have anything to do with Paul Yang, do you?"

Both men shook their heads. Carl handed the card back. Angela puzzled over it for a second, and then her phone rang. It was Loren saying Miss Lucas had arrived.

"Send her in," Angela said, tossing the mysterious card to the side.

Loren opened the door, allowed the secretary to enter, then pulled the door shut.

Amy Lucas was a waiflike woman in her mid-twenties. Her features were delicate and her complexion was pale, marred by a sprinkling of acne across her cheeks. Her frizzy blond hair with its lime-green highlights was pulled back from her face and held with a large tortoiseshell clip. Adding to her youthful, almost preteen mien was a simple shirtdress buttoned all the way to her neck. Her hands were clasped in front of her, evincing her nervousness.

Angela introduced herself, since she'd never before met the young woman, and thanked her for coming so quickly.

"No problem," Amy said. "I know who you are."

"Good. And of course you know these gentlemen."

Amy nodded but didn't respond verbally.

"To put you at ease, we called you in here to ask you a couple of questions about your boss, Paul Yang."

In her own hyper state, Angela wasn't certain, but it seemed to her that her attempt at putting Amy at ease had failed. The woman's hands, previously clasped, were now working at each other. The question of whether Paul and Amy might have had or were having an affair popped unbidden into her mind from

Bob's statement about Paul's past.

"What kind of questions?" Amy asked. Her eyes quickly jumped back and forth to all three individuals in the room.

"Have you seen him today?"

"No!" Amy said, inordinately quickly in Angela's estimation.

"Has he called or contacted you in any way?"

Amy shook her head.

"Did he say anything last evening about not coming in this morning?"

"No."

Angela looked at Bob and Carl and paused in case they had a question. When they didn't respond, Angela redirected her attention to Amy.

"Do you know what a Securities and Exchange Commission form eight-K is?"

"I think so."

"Has Paul Yang had you fill one out recently?"

"Yes, about ten days ago."

"Was it filed?"

"I don't know. I didn't file it. He told me specifically not to file it."

"Did you type it on your workstation monitor?"

"No, he wanted it on his laptop only."

"I see," Angela said. "Is the laptop in

his office?"

"No, he always takes it with him."

"So he took it last night in particular."

"Yes, like every night."

Angela glanced at the men again, but they didn't ask any questions.

"Thank you for coming by, Amy," Angela said.

"You're welcome," Amy responded. After a moment's hesitation, she turned and headed for the door.

"Amy!" Angela called out. "When you hear from Paul Yang, please let one of us know."

"Of course," Amy said, and then disappeared.

"Well," Angela said. "That was a little strange."

"How so?" Carl asked.

"She seemed overly nervous."

"I'd be, too, getting a summons to the corner office," Carl said.

"Maybe so," Angela said. "My main concern is that there is a completed eight-K resting in Paul's laptop, which the missing man presumably has with him."

"It doesn't surprise me," Bob said. "It speaks to his methodicalness. Just because it's in his laptop doesn't mean he's going to file it."

"Well, I hope he turns up soon," Angela

said. "I suppose that's it for now."

Both men got up and returned the chairs to their original positions against the wall.

"Remember to call our fearless placement agent to get the loan ASAP," Angela said as they filed out.

Bob waved over his shoulder to indicate he'd heard.

"And let me know the instant either of you sees or gets in touch with Paul Yang!"

"Will do," the two men voiced as the door closed behind them.

Angela sighed and looked out the window. She wished she'd not had any coffee that morning. With everything else that was going on, her usually pleasant buzz was magnified a hundred times over. Her phone rang suddenly, and she literally jumped. She took a deep breath to calm herself. When she picked up the phone, Loren told her that Rodger Naughton was on the line. Angela's pulse quickened. This call from Rodger was either very good news or very bad, meaning he was either letting them know that the bank would give them the desperately needed bridge loan, which would be terrific, or informing them that the bank was calling in one or more of their current loans, which would be an unmitigated disaster. Angela thought the chances were higher that it was the latter. With significant trepidation, she pressed the button below the blinking light and said hello as optimistically as she could manage.

"Sorry to bother you," Rodger said.

"No bother," Angela assured him. She had to restrain herself from demanding straight off whether he was calling with good news or bad.

"I just wanted to call and say it was terrific to see you this morning."

"Well, it was nice seeing you," Angela said with confusion. It seemed a strange way for the conversation to begin.

"I also wanted to convey how sorry I am that I cannot be more receptive to your short-term cash needs."

"I understand," Angela said, her confusion deepening.

"I have, as promised, passed it up through the channels."

"It's all that I can ask."

There was a pause. Angela gritted her teeth, expecting the worst.

"I have a request," Rodger said. "This might be out of bounds, so I apologize in advance. But I wonder if you'd be willing to meet with me for a drink after work. We could go to the Modern, which I find particularly pleasant."

"Is this business or social?" Angela asked with surprise.

"Purely social," Rodger said.

The unexpectedness of the request took Angela completely by surprise. Except for the brief and uncharacteristic reflection on her lack of a social life the previous evening, Angela was too busy to think such thoughts.

"That's very flattering," Angela said at length, coming from the credulous side of her personality. But then from the more powerful, experience-based cynical side, she added, "But what would your wife think of such a meeting?"

"I'm not married."

"Oh?" Angela responded, feeling somewhat guilty. The image came to mind of the single photo of his daughter on his desk.

"My former wife decided that having a boring banker husband and a demanding child was a burden on her preferred lifestyle, so she departed to greener pastures with half my assets. I've been divorced with full custody about five years now."

Angela instantly related personally to Rodger's situation and felt even more guilty about her reflex cynicism concerning his motives. His matrimonial history seemed uncannily similar to her own, barring the custody issue. Angela could only wish that

199

she had full custody.

"I'm sorry I was so flippant," Angela said. "I assumed you were just another male in a midlife crisis."

"That's understandable. I'm sure you are hit on on a regular basis."

"That's hardly the case, but I have learned to be skeptical."

"So, can I look forward to seeing you when you might be free? It could even be tonight and at your convenience."

"As you can guess from my visit to your office this morning, this is not a good time, so I'm afraid I must decline. But I appreciate your thinking of me, and perhaps after the IPO, if you are still inclined, I'd love to have a drink, and the Modern would be fine. I haven't been many places over the years. I suppose I fall into that sad and narrow category of the hyper, narrow-minded, workaholic businessperson chasing and being chased by the almighty dollar."

"I hardly think that's the case," Rodger said. "Having a preteen daughter and you not having a spouse obviates that. But we'll stay in touch, and good luck to Angels Healthcare."

"Thank you. A bit of luck would certainly help."

Angela replaced the receiver. She could

hear disappointment in Rodger's voice, which flattered her on one hand and saddened her on the other, especially hearing her own description of herself. For a brief moment, she lamented how she'd morphed from the person she was when she'd entered medical school to the person she was now, having abandoned committed altruism for equally committed but far less noble entrepreneurialism.

Angela's fleeting reverie was cut short by her insistent phone. Its discordant jangle rudely yanked her back to the exigencies of her company's plight. With more than a tinge of resentment, she snatched up the phone. Loren told her there was a Dr. Chet McGovern on the line who wanted to speak to her.

"What's it about?" Angela demanded, while she tried to place the doctor in one of the three Angels hospitals.

"He wouldn't tell me," Loren said.

For a second, Angela flirted with the idea of telling Loren to ask the man again what he wanted and if he refused, to tell him to . . . Angela caught herself and refused to even finish the thought. Profanity had been part of her rebellion in college, but she'd grown out of it, mainly because Michael had used it to such irritating excess.

With more than five hundred physician investors, there was no way for Angela to remember all their names. That reality, and the need for the doctors to be encouraged to admit more patients, meant Angela swallowed her pique and took the call. She assumed it would be about the MRSA death the previous day, and prepared herself mentally to describe everything being done to avoid any more infection in the future.

"First, I want to make sure the flowers arrived," the caller said.

Angela's gaze shifted to the roses and their mystery. All at once it dawned on her. She was speaking with the Chet McGovern she'd had the casual drink with the previous night at the club and had "used" to clear her mind and perhaps satisfy her transitory need for some sort of social contact, especially with a member of the opposite sex.

"The flowers arrived," Angela said. "Thank you. It was most unexpected. I hope they mean you have forgiven me."

"That goes without saying," Chet responded, "which brings me to the reason for the call. I thought it over, and after finding a spare two hundred thousand in my night table, I've decided to invest in Angels Healthcare."

There was a slight pause. "Really?" Angela

questioned, with her mind momentarily stalled between what she knew was reality and what she wished to be reality.

Chet laughed. "Hey! I'm making a joke. I wish I had a spare two hundred G's, but such is not the case."

"Oh," Angela said. She wasn't laughing.

"I have a sneaking sense you didn't find that so funny."

"What is the real reason for the call?" Angela asked. There was a new edge to her tone.

"I was speaking with a couple of my colleagues, one of whom is a very savvy woman. I told them about meeting you last night and being turned down for dinner tonight. She told me to ask you again and to be direct, even if it meant putting my fragile ego on the line."

Angela smiled in spite of herself. "So you're admitting you have a fragile ego?"

"Absolutely. Sometimes it takes me days to recover. With that said, I'm re-asking you to dinner tonight to stave off a depression."

Angela couldn't help but laugh. "You are persistent."

"I'm not sure that's accurate. Calling up like this and asking for more abuse is not my style."

"Well, your honesty and humor have intrigued me, though I didn't like the joke about the two hundred thousand. It was like you were mocking me."

"Absolutely not," Chet said.

"I wasn't joking about the need for short-term capital, and that is honestly why I cannot accept your gracious offer. I truly am distractedly busy. I wouldn't be good company even if I had the time."

"Well, I'm disappointed, but my ego is still intact, thanks to your diplomacy. I tell you what, if you are suddenly successful with your money-raising or depressed you are not, call me. I'll be available at a moment's notice."

When the call ended, Angela spun around in her chair, looking down the length of Fifth Avenue clogged with traffic. The unexpected dinner invites from two seemingly charming but different men, one obviously social and the other an apparent homebody, were remarkably unusual. And unsettling, in the way they made her question her choices and her lifestyle, causing her to wonder again about how she'd gotten sidetracked in her life. In a moment of insight, she sensed that the combination of the government reimbursement rules that caused her inner-city primary-care practice to go bankrupt and the demoralizing experience of divorce from

Michael had worked to undermine her value system. She'd become jaded. Success from business, as measured by wealth and its trappings, had trumped notions of altruism, charity, and, apart from her daughter, the pleasures of interpersonal intimacy.

Angela swung back around to face her desk and the problems besieging Angels Healthcare. Pushing the flowers away from her work area, Angela moved the afternoon schedule to center stage. A moment later, Loren brought in a sandwich and a Coke. While she ate, Angela's mind switched back to the new problem about Paul Yang's whereabouts and the laptop with the 8-K file. It was like missing a loaded grenade with its pin half out.

With that thought in mind, Angela reached for her BlackBerry to e-mail Michael about what he might know of Paul's failure to show up for work. As her thumbs danced across the miniature keyboard, she applauded the ability the instrument gave her to communicate without having to talk to the man. It meant she could get the information she wanted without the aggravation she'd otherwise have to endure.

Once the message had been composed, she was about to send it when she had a second thought. She was well aware of Michael's background and childhood, and at times had had unsettling questions about some of his friends and their current lifestyles, including his so-called clients, but she'd never asked because at the time she didn't want to know. Now, as she was about to send the message to Michael, she had a similar feeling and wondered if she wanted to know the answer to what she was asking. Vaguely sensing she might not, she saved the message as a draft and put the BlackBerry aside. She'd deal with the issue later.

6
APRIL 3, 2007
1:05 P.M.

Michael Calabrese was in a foul mood from an amalgam of fear and anxiety as he pulled his black Mercedes SUV alongside a row of parked cars and then backed into an empty spot. From where he was parked, he could see the entrance to the Neapolitan Restaurant on Corona Avenue in Corona, Queens. Corona was the next town over from Rego Park, where he'd grown up in a largely Italian neighborhood. A lot of people thought all the Italians in New York lived in Little Italy in Manhattan, but it wasn't true. They had all moved out, many to Long Island, including Michael's grandfather Ziggy, who'd started the family masonry-and-tile business in Rego Park.

Michael eyed the restaurant's entrance and tried to think of a strategy for his upcoming meeting. The restaurant's fame extended as far back as the 1930s when it was the favorite nighttime hangout of the Lucia organization. It had continued with the dubious association over the years with some ups and downs, but mostly downs, until Mayor Rudolph Giuliani managed to discourage a lot of mid-level mafioso bosses from schmoozing at night in Manhattan, and at that point, it had enjoyed a remarkable resurgence. Its revival had continued with Vinnie Dominick having chosen the joint to be his haunt when he was selected as the local Lucia capo.

As a sign of the times, the competing Vaccarro crime family had chosen a considerably newer establishment two blocks down the street, the Vesuvio, as their rendezvous. Both organizations believed it made sense to open a handy avenue of communication with the Asians, Russians, and Hispanics coming in and jockeying for some of the action. The only problem, of course, was that Paulie Cerino, the titular Vaccarro head, was still in the slammer, so communication wasn't what it should have been.

In a fit of unbridled rage, Michael pounded his steering wheel repeatedly while yelling "shit" over and over again. He'd experienced temper tantrums since he was a child, and back then they'd gotten him into more than his share of fights and a number of beatings from his father. Yet there was a positive side. Once the energy was expended, he'd calm down, and could deal with the bothersome issue at hand. As he'd matured, he'd learned to control his outbursts until he was alone, except when he'd been married to Angela.

As suddenly as he had started pounding the steering wheel, he stopped. "Spoiled bitch," he grumbled, thinking about Angela. She'd been his bane from the moment they'd gotten married. Up until then she'd been a doll, but within weeks of the big ceremony at Saint Mary's Church, he was no longer good enough the way he was. She wanted him to do this, and she demanded he do that, and she resented his going out, even for business dinners. In short, she wanted him to change, and he had no intention of changing for a spoiled, upper-middle-class Jersey girl who'd gotten everything she'd ever wanted by snapping her fingers. As far as the divorce settlement was concerned, he didn't want to go there in his current state of mind. Whenever he thought about it, it made him furious. For nothing but causing him grief, she walked away with the West Side triplex apartment and a ridiculous amount of child support.

And now, as the final twist of the knife, she'd sucked him into this business with Angels Healthcare that might be putting his life at risk. Of course, he couldn't fault himself. As a business plan, it was terrific. As she had explained to him, the government, in its infinite wisdom, had created a system via Medicare and essentially adopted by all health insurance companies that paid doctors vastly more money for doing procedures than they paid for taking care of people in general. The trick, then, was to recruit a host of physician investors to fund the construction of private hospitals, which did only procedures and avoided all the money-losing ventures, such as running emergency rooms and taking care of the uninsured or the chronically ill. Such a scenario took advantage of a loophole in the law that generally prevented doctors from referring patients to their own facilities, such as laboratories or imaging facilities, because it was thought that when physicians owned a share in a whole hospital, they were very small cogs in a very large wheel. What it all meant was that for the doctors, it was like a kickback, which encouraged them to admit their paying patients, since they got paid for doing the procedure and then got paid again from the hospital according to their small percentage ownership. For the real owners, who held the majority of stock, it was an unbelievable cash cow. This was why Michael had committed so damn much of his own assets and so much of his client's capital, and how he'd talked Morgan Stanley into underwriting the IPO.

Everything had gone according to plan to such an extent that Michael had pooled most of his remaining personal assets just six months ago and committed the capital to Angels Healthcare to strengthen his position before the IPO process started. As any financial analyst knows, diversification is key as an investment strategy, yet Michael was so certain about Angels Healthcare that he'd allowed himself to violate the cardinal rule, and now he was paying big-time in terms of anxiety. His problem was that he hadn't understood the scientific details or the potential economic consequences of the infection problem that had started three and a half months ago in the Angels hospitals. Now he did. He also knew all too well how Vinnie Dominick hated losing money.

Michael glanced back at the entrance to the Neapolitan. It was deceivingly serene, with plastic flowers stuck in the fake window boxes. Even the brick façade was fake. It was fiberglass sheets. There was no coming and going of patrons, because the restaurant wasn't open for lunch except for Vinnie and his close minions. For the owner, it was a small price to pay for the right to do business, and in the evenings he did a land office business, except for Sunday when it was closed and all the wiseguys spent the mandatory day with wives and family.

Michael checked himself in the rearview mirror and smoothed his hair, which he purposefully wore in the same style as did Vinnie Dominick. They'd known each other since elementary school, where Vinnie had been one year ahead of Michael. As far back as the fourth grade, Vinnie had dominated the playground of P.S. 157 by dint of his father's position in the Lucia organization. Even the sixth-graders gave way. From that time on, Michael had tried to copy Vinnie, even during their high-school years at Saint Mary's.

Since no particular strategy had come to mind as to how to handle the conversation with Vinnie, Michael reluctantly decided he'd just have to wing it, because ultimately everything depended on Vinnie's mood. If he was in a good mood, the ordeal might be a piece of cake. If he wasn't, anything could happen.

Climbing from his SUV, Michael had to wait for the traffic before crossing Corona Avenue. When Angela had left his office more than an hour earlier after delivering her depressing news about Angels Health-care's bleak liquidity, Michael had reluctantly decided that he had to talk with Vinnie. If worse came to worse, and Vinnie was blindsided by the potential loss of the organization's money, Michael would have to literally disappear, and without money of his own, that would not be easy. Although he knew Vinnie was not going to like what Michael had to say today, he was confident the worst case would be having to suffer a lambasting followed by a threat of some kind. With that mildly reassuring thought in mind, Michael had phoned Vinnie to ask for a meeting, and Vinnie had invited him to the restaurant.

Entering the restaurant, Michael had to push aside a heavy drape that protected nearby tables from the draft of the open door. Then he had to let his eyes adjust to the dim interior. To the left was a long bar and a lounge area with a fake fireplace. In the middle of the room was a sea of various-sized tables. All the chairs were upside down on the tables to facilitate the cleaning crew's activities. To the right were a series of six red velvet–upholstered booths, which were considered the most desirable tables. Two of them were occupied. At the first were Franco Ponti, Angelo Facciolo, Freddie Capuso, and Richie Herns. Michael knew them all from Saint Mary's. Of all of them, Franco Ponti was the one who scared Michael the most. It was common knowledge that he was Vinnie's main enforcer. Angelo wasn't as well known to Michael, as he had socialized in another group in high school, but his appearance was enough to make Michael shiver. Freddie was the most familiar and Richie the least, though both were essentially lackeys.

Vinnie, at the next table, waved Michael over. Sitting with him was Carol Cirone, Vinnie's girlfriend for years. With her bleached-blond bouffant, skintight white sweater, and string of pearls, she looked like a caricature from *West Side Story,* but no one kidded her about it, at least not in front of Vinnie.

"Mikey," Vinnie called. "Get over here! Have you eaten?"

Michael passed the table with the hired hands. "Hey, guys," he said to be respectful. They all nodded but didn't speak.

Vinnie took his napkin from his shirt collar, pushed out of his side of the banquette, stood up, and gave Michael a hug. Michael hugged back but felt awkward, knowing the news he was bringing was not going to make Vinnie happy.

With one hand resting on Michael's shoulder, Vinnie gestured toward his lunch companions. "You know Carol, of course."

"Of course," Michael said. Michael took the demurely extended hand and gave it an equally demure shake.

"Sit down, sit down," Vinnie repeated as he regained his seat. In contrast to his diction, his voice was more cultured than one would expect considering his line of work, and when he lost his temper, which was not infrequent, it didn't change, a characteristic Michael found unnerving.

Michael slid in on the opposite side, pinning Carol between himself and Vinnie.

"How about some spaghetti Bolognese?" Vinnie suggested. "And a glass of Barolo? It's 'ninety-seven and out of this world."

Michael agreed to everything rather than start out on the wrong foot. Vinnie hadn't changed much since high school, where he'd always wowed the girls. His nickname was "The Prince." His features were full and well sculpted. Like Michael, he favored the tailored look and dressed in a suit and tie every day. Also like Michael, he prided himself that he weighed the same as he did in high school, and worked out regularly to maintain his physique.

"So, how are our investments going?" Vinnie asked. When it came to business, Vinnie didn't waste a lot of time. Michael had been doing business with Vinnie for more than a decade. It had started small when Michael had joined Morgan Stanley and come to Vinnie with the idea of laundering the Lucia organization's take from drugs, loan-sharking, gambling clubs, fencing, extortion rings, hot-car rings, and hijacking, mostly from Kennedy Airport. Michael had proposed to use the money as venture capital for IPOs through a series of shell companies, and the relationship had proved remarkably beneficial to both parties. Michael not only laundered the money but often doubled it, whereas previously Vinnie had to pay for such a service. With ever-increasing capital available as Vinnie had become more and more comfortable, Michael had been able, on amicable terms, to leave Morgan Stanley and establish his own boutique investment-banking firm.

"To be truthful," Michael said, in response to Vinnie's direct question, "there's a problem I need to talk to you about."

"Oh, really?" Vinnie questioned with the deliberately calm, soft voice that made Michael's hackles rise.

"I'm afraid so," Michael said. His voice had a quavering quality that he hoped only he could hear.

"Carol, honey," Vinnie said. "Could you excuse us? Mikey and I need to talk."

"I'm not finished with my spaghetti," she whined.

"Carol!" Vinnie said in a slightly lower tone and looking at her askance.

"Oh, all right," Carol responded, throwing her napkin on top of her plate. "But where am I supposed to go?"

"Wherever you like, doll. Freddie or Richie can drive you."

After watching Carol depart, Michael regained his seat and again faced Vinnie, who stared him down. Michael inwardly squirmed.

"I hope this trouble isn't about Angels Healthcare, because if it is, I'm getting a bad feeling," Vinnie said at length.

Michael cleared his throat and was about to speak when the waiter appeared tableside with a steaming plate of spaghetti, a glass, and flatware. Sensing the tension, the waiter quickly laid out the place setting, poured wine into the glass, and disappeared.

"It is about Angels Healthcare," Michael admitted. "Angels Healthcare needs more money to keep the doors open. The problem has been getting rid of the bacteria. The bacteria required shutting the ORs, which turned off the revenue spigot."

"That's the same story I heard a month ago," Vinnie said. Although his voice stayed calm, his eyes reflected his rising ire. "My recent loan was supposed to cover expenses until the IPO."

"That was my understanding as well, until my ex told me differently an hour ago," Michael said, with the idea of transferring responsibility to her.

"Why didn't it happen?"

"The ORs stayed closed longer than expected, keeping revenue down, and the disinfecting process cost more than expected."

"Are the ORs open now?"

"Yes, but it will take a few weeks for the doctors to trust that the problem is over."

"Is it over?"

"Yes, that's my understanding."

"Your understanding about how much money was needed missed the mark. What makes you think your understanding about the infection problem is any more accurate?"

"I don't know," Michael said with a shrug. "I can only relate what I'm told."

"How much money is needed to get through the IPO?"

"I was told two hundred thousand."

Vinnie went back to drilling Michael with his eyes. Michael flinched first and glanced down at his food. Under the circumstances, he didn't know which was more disrespectful: eating or not eating. The last thing he wanted to do was irritate Vinnie over manners. Vinnie could be touchy about such issues.

"Eat!" Vinnie said, breaking the silence.

Michael wasn't hungry, but he picked up a fork and struggled to twirl a mouthful of spaghetti.

"I'm not at all happy about all this," Vinnie said. He leaned forward menacingly. "I'm starting to feel like your lackey. First you come to me for money, next it's about an accountant who wants to blab to the Feds about the negative cash flow, and now it's more money. When does this end?"

"I never expected any of this," Michael said in his defense. "But it's still a great investment. Trust me! I wouldn't have committed your money if it wasn't. I've even hocked just about everything I own to maximize my own position."

"In all honesty, I don't care about your money," Vinnie said. "I care about the money I'm responsible for. I don't want it to be lost. I'd have a lot of explaining to do."

"The money is not going to be lost," Michael said decisively, even though he wasn't as sure as he sounded. "Worst case is the IPO is postponed."

"I don't want that to happen, and I'm doing my part. I've already kicked in an extra quarter of a mil. I'm also dealing with the accountant issue."

"You haven't spoken to him?" Michael asked with alarm.

"Oh, I've spoken with him. Even Franco and Angelo have spoken with him."

"He's not being cooperative?"

"I wouldn't say that. I'm absolutely sure he's not going to file. It's just his secretary is an unknown quantity who, unfortunately, has a copy of the potentially troublesome report. It seems we have to talk with her as well."

"I'd never thought of that," Michael admitted. "Good idea!" He was relieved. The last thing he needed was the resurgence of a problem he'd thought had been solved. Although Michael liked doing business with Vinnie, he didn't want to know where the money came from or any of the details of Vinnie's operations. Michael's imagination was enough, which was why he was as nervous as he was in the current imbroglio.

"The point is, Mikey, I'm certainly doing my part," Vinnie continued, "and I'd like you to do yours. If more money is needed to get Angels Healthcare though the IPO, it comes from you."

"But —" Michael started.

"No buts, Mikey," Vinnie said calmly, interrupting Michael. "We've known each other for a long time, but this is business. I want this IPO to go through. You've been a good salesman and have raised my expectations. If the IPO doesn't happen as you've described, I'm going to blame you, and we'll no longer be friends. At that point, you'll be dealing exclusively with Franco."

Michael tried to swallow but couldn't. His throat had gone dry. Instead, he reached for his untouched glass of wine and took a sizable swig.

Detective Lieutenant Lou Soldano looked at his watch. It was almost one-thirty in the afternoon, which explained why his stomach was growling. After leaving the medical examiner's office that morning sometime after eight, he'd driven home to his apartment on Prince Street in SoHo and passed out on his couch. He'd been so exhausted that he didn't even make it into his bedroom.

When he'd awakened at noon, all he'd had was coffee while he shaved and showered. At that point, he'd called the OCME. He was curious about what Jack had found on the two homicides whose autopsies Lou had skipped. Jack was still in the pit and unavailable, so Lou asked to be connected to the NYPD liaison, Sergeant Murphy. Lou's biggest concern was the apparently gangland-executed, unidentified floater. What he wanted to know was whether Murphy had any leads as to the identity through Missing Persons. There hadn't been any calls about a missing Asian-American male, which made Lou even more curious. One way or another, Lou was becoming progressively interested in the case, in hopes of trying to prevent more bodies from popping up. In addition to the way the individual was shot, the fact that he had been tossed far out in the harbor strengthened Lou's conviction that the homicide was organized crime–related. In the spring, summer, and fall, such bodies were invariably buried in the woods upstate. In the winter, when the ground was frozen, they were tossed into the river or, if the perpetrators were more resourceful, into the harbor or even out beyond the Verrazano Bridge.

With his stomach growling, Lou began to look for a fast-food outlet. He was in his old PD-issued Chevy Caprice. He had a sentimental attachment to the car as the only connection to his previous life, since he was divorced and both his kids were in college.

"My God! Johnny's Sub is still here!" Lou said out loud, catching sight of the joint on his left. He snapped on his turn signal and quickly slowed, only to be blasted by a car horn six inches from his vehicle's rear. Lou rolled his window down and motioned for the irate driver to pass him, all the time trying to maintain his composure. Eventually, the guy took the hint and, still leaning on his horn, passed Lou. As he did so, he gave Lou the finger.

"Some things don't change," Lou murmured philosophically. He was in the familiar environment of Corona in the borough of Queens. Not only had he grown up in the immediately neighboring Rego Park, but when he'd been assigned to the Organized Crime unit of the NYPD, after having been a patrolman for three years, he'd spent a lot of time in Queens, both becasue he knew the area and because there was a lot of organized crime going on. During the six years he'd spent in the unit, he'd been promoted to sergeant and then to lieutenant when he switched to Homicide.

Lou made the turn into the restaurant's parking area. The establishment itself was a mere stand in the middle of an expanse of macadam. Patrons had to park, go up to the window, and order. When the appropriate number popped up, the patron had to hike back to the window and then eat the foot-long sub in his car. Lou could remember patronizing the place in high school when he got his first jalopy.

Fifteen minutes later, Lou couldn't have been happier as he indulged both his appetite with his old favorite sub called Johnny's Meatball Extravaganza and his nostalgia. It warmed his heart to remember coming to Johnny's late at night with Gina Pantanella during his senior year of high school. He'd parked way in the back, had the same sub, and then got laid.

The other reason Lou was content was that Johnny's was directly across the street from the Neapolitan. From his years in Organized Crime, he knew the restaurant was the de facto office of Vinnie Dominick, who ran the Queens arm for the Lucia family. Lou knew that the fragile equilibrium between the traditionally competing crime powers in the area — namely, the Lucias and Vaccarros — was being challenged, mainly by new Asian gangs in Flushing and Woodside. Lou had it in his mind to find out if this situation had anything to do with the floater, and he zeroed in on Vinnie Dominick because Vinnie's counterpart in the Vaccarro organization, Paulie Cerino, was in the slammer. But it wasn't Vinnie who Lou was going to approach but rather one of his flunkies, Freddie Capuso. Back when Lou was still working Organized Crime, he'd recruited Freddie as an informer, and Lou still had something to hold over the kid. Serendipitously, Lou had discovered the boy was living a dangerous, duplicitous life as a kind of double agent. Although ostensibly working for Vinnie, he was passing information to Paulie, sometimes real, sometimes misinformation. At the time, Lou had wondered how the kid could sleep at night, because if either side had known what he was up to, he would have simply disappeared, probably feeding the fish out beyond the Verrazano Bridge.

Lou wasn't certain Freddie still worked for Vinnie or if he was still alive, but he intended to find out. He guessed Vinnie was around, because there was a black Cadillac double-parked in front of the restaurant. The only trouble was that it was a vintage model, which Lou doubted was Vinnie's style.

All at once, Lou stopped chewing. Someone emerged alone from the restaurant. For a second, Lou thought it was Vinnie because of the hairstyle and the clothes. Lou was confused because Vinnie would never come out by himself. But then, as the man ran across the street directly at Lou, Lou saw

225

that it wasn't Vinnie. It was someone Lou didn't recognize but who was acting suspicious. He was either nervous or afraid as he fumbled with his remote while repeatedly glancing up and down the street and back at the restaurant. A second later, he was in the car, then pulling out into the street, where he made an illegal U-turn before accelerating with screeching tires in the direction of Manhattan. Lou tried to get the tag number, but he wasn't fast enough. All he'd managed was 5V and the fact that it was a New York plate.

Lou looked back at the restaurant, half expecting one of Vinnie's men to come bursting out the door in hot pursuit, but it didn't happen. All was serene. Lou relaxed back into his seat and took another bite of his sub. While he chewed, he pondered what the meeting was between Vinnie and the Vinnie lookalike that had made the stranger as nervous as he'd seemed to be. Lou guessed it was about money, and considering the guy's clothes and the fact that he drove an SUV, Lou suspected it had to do with gambling. And if it did, and the guy owed Vinnie big money, he was in a lot of trouble. Vinnie and his counterparts didn't tolerate people owing them money for very long. If they did, the whole house of cards would collapse.

Thinking such thoughts made Lou wonder if that was the story with the floater. Maybe it wasn't indicative of an incipient syndicate war but merely the elimination of a dead-beat.

All of a sudden, Lou again stopped chewing. A new black Cadillac sedan with heavily tinted windows appeared stage right and proceeded to pull up behind the older model. In the next instant, Lou tossed his sub to the side, scattering bite-sized meat-balls on his car's front passenger seat. He was out of the door in a flash and across the street as the driver of the Cadillac was rounding the car's rear. For once, luck was on Lou's side, since the driver was Freddie Capuso, and he was alone.

"Freddie, my friend," Lou called out.

Freddie stopped and turned as Lou came up to him. As soon as he recognized Lou, his face blanched. Nervously, he looked around, especially over to the nearby restaurant door.

"Gosh!" Lou effused. "How long has it been, Freddie, old boy?" The last time Lou had seen Freddie, he was a scrawny kid who artificially held his arms out from his body as if he were muscle-bound. Now he was a man: well, sort of.

"Holy shit, Lieutenant! What the hell are you doing here?"

"Just having a sub across the street for old time's sake. I used to go there when I was in high school, and then I see you pull up. What a coincidence."

"Nice to see you," Freddie said quickly. "But I gotta go."

"Not so fast," Lou said. He wrapped a restraining hand around Freddie's upper arm while Lou's other hand was holding on to his holstered gun. Lou knew these people were nasty and unpredictable.

"You could get me killed if I'm seen with you!" Freddie blurted.

"I could have you killed with a single phone call, my friend. I just want to talk to you for two minutes. My car is across the street in Johnny's parking lot. Let's hightail it over there, and we can talk out of sight."

Freddie looked around Lou over toward Johnny's, as if he didn't believe Lou, and then back at the Neapolitan's door.

"The longer you put this off, the more chance you're taking," Lou said. He gave Freddie's arm a tug in the direction of Lou's Caprice.

It didn't take long for Freddie to realize that he didn't have a choice. He nodded and quickly crossed the street. Lou followed Freddie all the way to the front passenger-side door. Freddie opened it quickly but took one look at the tiny meatballs, tomato slices, and onion rings fanned out on the seat and said, "I'm not sitting in that mess!"

Lou glanced around Freddie to see what he was referring to. "I can understand your reluctance," Lou said. He closed the door and opened the back. He motioned to Freddie to enter, then climbed in after him.

"Make this fast," Freddie commanded, as if he had a say in the matter.

"I'll try," Lou said, ignoring Freddie's bravado. "First up, who's the current local capo for the Vaccarros? I've been out of the loop."

"His name is Louie Barbera, but he's only a temp, because Paulie Cerino's supposedly getting out on parole."

"Really?" Lou commented. He'd not heard the rumor about Cerino.

"What the hell are you bothering me for with that kind of question?" Freddie grumbled. "You could learn that from any number of people."

"How do Vinnie and Louie get along?"

Freddie merely laughed.

"Is it that bad?" Lou asked.

"Vinnie made hay right after Paulie got sent up, especially with drugs. The Vaccarros want their old territory back."

"What about the Asians, Hispanics,

and Russians?"

"They are getting to be a pain in the ass for everyone."

"All three groups."

"Mainly the Asians bringing in drugs from the East rather than South America."

"It was rumored there was an apparent hit last night," Lou said, finally getting around to the point. "Do you know anything about it?" He purposefully didn't want to give any of the details.

Freddie's eyes flicked over toward the restaurant door in a nervous fashion, which for Lou was a giveaway. From his years of experience, he guessed skinny Freddie knew something.

"I don't know anything about no hit," Freddie said unconvincingly.

"Come on! Don't make me threaten, and don't make me call Vinnie for old times' sake."

"Okay, I know there was a hit last night, but that's all I know about it."

"Please! Don't drag this out."

"I don't know who it was, honest. All I know, it was some guy who was going to rat."

"What was the victim going to rat about and to whom?"

"Who knows?"

"Are you pulling my chain here or what?"

"Honest, I'm telling you all I know, which is close to zilch. Vinnie's upset about something, but I have no clue. He doesn't talk about such things, except to Franco Ponti."

Lou eyed the hopeless kid-turned-man. In one sense, he felt sorry for him, because Lou was sure he was going to end up in a Dumpster some night. He'd been playing two ends against the middle but wasn't intelligent enough to carry it off over the long haul. In another sense, Lou was angry with him because like all these other misfits, the shithead was abetting a tiny group of people who made all Italian Americans look bad.

"All right," Lou said after a pause. "I want you to find out who this guy was who got whacked. I don't want a war breaking out between the Lucia and Vaccarro factions, which is what I'm worrying about."

"There's no way for me to find out any such thing. Vinnie is tight-mouthed. If I asked him anything, he'd know something was screwy."

"Don't ask him, ask Franco."

"That would be worse than asking Vinnie. You know the guy's crazy."

"Figure out a way," Lou said. He reached across Freddie and opened the door.

Laurie's eyes were glazed over as she stared blankly out of the taxi's side window as it raced northward on Second Avenue. She was totally preoccupied with her MRSA series, which had started out as a possible way of convincing Jack to postpone his knee surgery but which had morphed into something else entirely. She still intended to use the issue with Jack, but now she sensed there was a wider significance, and the possibility electrified her. Her conception of the role of the medical examiner was to speak for the dead to help the living. Suddenly, she saw her current series as a means to do just that. If she could figure out why these MRSA deaths were occurring in such a cluster, she could presumably save potential victims.

Thinking in such a vein had a disheartening aspect. Why hadn't the OCME picked up on the problem sooner? Laurie pondered the question for a moment before guessing the reason: a low index of suspicion, which Laurie assumed would have influenced her, too, concerning David Jeffries, had the personal aspect not intervened. Laurie knew that as many as ten percent of all patients entering the hospital come away with a hospital-acquired infection, meaning about two million patients a year, resulting in nearly ninety thousand deaths in the United States alone. Of these infections, about thirty-five percent were staph, many of which were MRSA. In short, the problem was just too common to cause much of a stir, especially with bacteria on the rise.

A sudden crash jolted Laurie from her reflections. Had she not had her seat belt on, her head would have hit the ceiling.

"Sorry!" the cabbie said, glancing at Laurie in his rearview mirror to see if she was okay. "Potholes from the winter."

Laurie nodded. She appreciated the apology, as unexpected as it was, but not the driving style.

"Maybe you could slow down," she suggested.

"Time is money," the turbaned driver answered.

Knowing the futility of trying to influence the taxi driver's mind-set, Laurie went back to her musing. She was on her way to the

Angels Orthopedic Hospital, which was sited on Fifth Avenue on the Upper East Side, and surprisingly enough, approximately directly across Central Park from where she and Jack lived. Over the previous two hours she'd been frantically busy, and, despite a mild fear for her life in the cab, she appreciated the forced respite and time to organize her thoughts that the ride offered. She'd finally been able to meet with Arnold Besserman and Kevin Southgate, and had gotten the names of their six cases and four of the six case files and hospital records. Arnold had even given her the personal monograph he'd written on MRSA, which Laurie had quickly read.

Laurie now knew more about the bacterium than she'd ever known, even more than she had just before taking her forensic pathology boards, for which she had crammed in her old collegiate style, with all sorts of esoteric facts, including some about MRSA and other staph organisms. As Agnes had said, staphylococcus aureus was an extraordinary and versatile pathogen.

With the accession numbers of Arnold's and Kevin's cases plus those of George Fontworth, Laurie had relayed them all to Agnes Finn. Laurie wanted Agnes to retrieve their frozen samples for culture and subtyping just as she was already doing with Laurie's case that morning and Riva's cases. Laurie thought it was important to see how closely they all matched.

Laurie had then made some important phone calls with the numbers Cheryl had gotten for her. First, she called Loraine Newman at the Angels Orthopedic Hospital. Laurie found her as accommodating as both Arnold and Cheryl had described. The woman graciously agreed to a meeting that very afternoon at two-thirty.

Next, Laurie had called a woman at the CDC by the name of Dr. Silvia Salerno, who was associated with the CDC's national library of MRSA strains that had been formed to identify genetic patterns in the subtype, in hopes of influencing prevention and control strategies. In addition, she was part of the CDC's Web-based National Healthcare Safety Network and had been the person to whom Riva had been referred. It was she who had had Riva's isolates subtyped.

"If I am not mistaken, they were a community-acquired MRSA, or what we call CA-MRSA," Silvia had said when Laurie had asked if she remembered the cases. "Let me look it up. Okay, here it is. CA-MRSA, USA four hundred, MWtwo, SCCmecIV, PVL. Now I remember it very clearly. That is a particularly virulent organism, maybe one of the most virulent we've seen, particularly with the PVL toxin."

"Do you recall Dr. Mehta mentioning that her two cases came from two separate hospitals?"

"I don't. I assumed it was the same institution."

"It was definitely two hospitals. Does that surprise you?"

"It suggests the two individuals knew each other or they each knew a third person."

"Meaning you believe these were not nosocomial infection?"

"Technically, for an infection to be considered nosocomial, the patient has to have been in the hospital for more than forty-eight hours."

"But that's only a technical definition. I mean, the patients could have gotten them from the hospital."

"Of course. The definition is more for statistical reasons than scientific, but getting such an infection within twenty-four hours of admission would suggest to me that they were part of the patient's own flora."

Laurie described her series, all of whose victims had died of MRSA within twenty-four hours and, of those whose subtyping was available, had died of community-acquired MRSA, which Silvia said backed up her contention that the bacteria were most likely brought in by the patients. Regardless, Silvia had specifically said she was interested in the cases and had been surprised not to have heard of the cluster. Offering to help in any way she could, she took Laurie's direct-dial office number, and promised to get back to her after she'd asked around to see if anybody at the CDC had heard about the outbreak. She'd also promised to have a second look at Riva's samples to determine if they were the exact same strain or merely close.

Finally Laurie had called the Joint Commission on Accreditation of Healthcare Organizations. Cheryl had not been able to get her a specific person to talk with, and after Laurie had been switched around numerous times, each time being given the name of someone else who could supposedly help her, she had given up, defeated for the moment by the bureaucratic mind-set.

Arriving at her destination, the taxi pulled up to the curb and stopped, and Laurie handed over the fare and the tip. As she climbed from the cab, she looked up at an impressive, modern high-rise of green-tinted glass held in place by vertical ribs of green granite. The name, Angels Orthopedic Hospital, was inscribed into a pediment-shaped marble lintel over the front doors. A liveried doorman stood on the sidewalk. A sloping driveway led to a receiving dock, a service entrance, and a multistory parking garage in the rear.

The interior was even more impressive. It was more like walking into a Ritz-Carlton than a hospital, exactly as Jack described that morning. The floor was a mixture of hardwood and marble, and the information booth looked like a concierge desk, with two uniformed men sitting side by side in suits and ties. But what caught Laurie's eye more than the décor was the lack of people. There was no hustle and bustle like a normal hospital. Other than the two men at the information booth, there were only two people in the large lounge area sitting opposite each other on opposing, elegantly upholstered couches.

Laurie went up to the information booth and received the full attention of both gentlemen. She asked for Loraine Newman, mentioning her name and that she had an appointment.

"Certainly, ma'am," one of the men said. He picked up the phone, and after a brief conversation directed Laurie to a pair of interior doors to the left of the bank of elevators. "Miss Newman is waiting for you in administration."

Laurie followed the directions and pushed through the designated doors. The administration area was more utilitarian than the lounge area but still sumptuous compared to any hospital Laurie had ever been in. It was a wide, long room with glass-enclosed offices on either side, each fronted by individual secretarial desks. Most all the desks were occupied, but it didn't appear that much work was being done. Only a few of the secretaries were typing into their monitors, while most were chatting in subdued tones.

One of the secretaries caught sight of Laurie and asked if she could help her, but before Laurie could respond, a glass door to an office opened and an energetic woman wearing a white coat over a brown turtleneck sweater and skirt called out to her. She introduced herself as Loraine Newman before ushering her inside.

"Let me have your coat!" Loraine said. She was Laurie's height and build and even approximate age but had different coloring compared to Laurie's blond complexion. "Please take a seat," she said, as she placed Laurie's coat on a hanger and hung it inside a small closet.

Laurie sat down, and Loraine went behind

her desk and did the same.

"I've never met a medical examiner," Loraine said with a smile. "I'm awed by what you guys do."

"We don't get out much," Laurie said. "Most of our scene work is done by our forensic investigators." She inwardly winced, recognizing Bingham would surely not appreciate what she was doing.

"How can I help you?" Loraine asked. "I suppose you are here because of yesterday's unfortunate MRSA death."

"That and more," Laurie answered. "I did the autopsy on Mr. Jeffries this morning. The extent of his infection was dramatic, to say the least, especially how quickly it consumed him."

"You have no idea how upset we are, and not only about the tragic loss of a life of an otherwise healthy man but also because it has occurred despite our making maximum effort to prevent it."

"I heard from one of my colleagues the efforts that you have been making. I imagine it must be discouraging, especially since you have apparently had eleven such cases."

"*Discouraging* is not a strong enough word. Did you find out anything at autopsy that might help us? When you called, I was hoping that was going to be the case."

"I'm afraid not," Laurie admitted.

"Then why did you come over?"

Laurie squirmed in her chair. Although the tone of the question was far from hostile, Laurie found herself questioning exactly why she was compelled to make the visit, and for a moment felt foolish.

"I didn't mean to put you on the spot," Loraine said, sensing Laurie's discomfiture.

"It's okay," Laurie said. "After I did the autopsy this morning, I found out essentially by accident about all the other cases occurring over the last three and a half months. I just felt I had to do something. I'm afraid the OCME has let you and the rest of the city down by not being aware of the outbreak. It's part of our job not to let something like this fall through the cracks."

"I appreciate your sense of responsibility, but in this case I don't think it matters. We certainly have been aware, and believe me, we have done everything possible. And when I say everything, I mean everything, including the hiring of a full-time infection-control professional. And as the chairperson of this hospital's interdepartmental infection-control committee, I personally jumped on the problem from day one. We've had input from everyone, including our medical staff, nursing, engineering, laboratory, you name it. Our committee has met just about every other week since the first MRSA case. We even shut down our ORs for a time and halted all surgery and invasive procedures."

"So I heard," Laurie said. "I don't have much training in epidemiology, but there are several things about this outbreak that bother me."

"Such as?"

Laurie took a moment to organize her thoughts. She was afraid she might sound naïve, since she truly only had the basics in epidemiology. "For one thing, it has continued despite all your efforts at control; secondly, many of them are, like Jeffries, primary pneumonias, which I believe is unique for staph; third, they have apparently been occurring in only Angels Healthcare facilities. You do know that your sister hospitals are experiencing cases as well?"

"Of course. I've had multiple meetings and frequent communication with my counterparts at our heart hospital and at our cosmetic surgery and eye hospital. I was also the one who strongly encouraged Angels Healthcare's CEO, Dr. Angela Dawson, to hire the M.D./Ph.D. infection-control professional to coordinate our efforts, specifically because the problem was happening in all three of our institutions."

"Is that Dr. Cynthia Sarpoulus?"

"That's correct. Why do you ask?"

"I recall one of my ME colleagues mentioning her name. He spoke to her a month or so ago."

"She's one of the leaders in our specialty, and coauthored a major text on hospital-infection control programs. I was sure that, when I heard she'd been hired, we'd be out of the woods."

"But it hasn't happened."

"It hasn't happened," Loraine agreed.

"Well, back to my amateur concerns," Laurie said.

"I'd hardly call you an amateur, doctor," Loraine said with a smile. "Please, continue!"

"An hour or so earlier, I talked with a doctor at the CDC. She'd had the opportunity to subtype the staph from two of your cases that occurred more than a month ago at different hospitals. Using rather sophisticated genetic typing, they proved to be the same. She promised to confirm that with tests of even higher specificity and get back to me. To my informally trained epidemiological brain and contrary to what she thinks, it suggests to me a carrier is involved: a carrier who visits both hospitals. Do any of the Angels Healthcare personnel regularly visit all your hospitals?"

"Wow," Loraine remarked. She laughed in a fashion that indicated she was impressed. "Are you teasing me about not having epidemiologic training?"

"Just the required exposure for my pathology residency," Laurie said.

"We have definitely considered a carrier to be the source of the problem. In fact, so much so that we have repeatedly cultured everyone: medical staff, service personnel, and particularly those individuals who regularly visit all three of our hospitals. One of the ways that our CEO founder conceived of keeping expenses down was to have centralized services like laundry, engineering, laboratory, nursing, and food service. Each service has a department head whose office is at Angels Healthcare's central office but who travels on a regular schedule to all three hospitals. These people have been tested repeatedly for the exact reason you've suggested."

"Has anybody tested positive?"

"Absolutely. About twenty percent positive, which is what one would expect in the normal population. In fact, slightly more on the medical staff. And everybody who tested positive has been treated with mupirocin until they tested negative."

"Did any of them test positive for the

community-acquired MRSA?"

"Oh, yeah. Quite a few."

"Do you know if the subtype was the same as what killed your patients?"

"Our subtyping was by a VITEK system and only for antibiotic resistance, and yes, some were the same."

"Antibiotic resistance is not particularly sensitive in terms of differentiating substrains."

"I'm aware of that, but since we treated anyone positive for staph, we didn't think it mattered."

"Maybe so," Laurie said. "Did you have any of the isolates typed by the CDC?"

"No, we didn't."

"Why?"

"That was a decision made by the home office. I suppose because we were treating everyone who was positive, as I said, so that characterizing it more served no purpose. Also, we were already instituting every known infection-control procedure."

"Did you let the CDC know you were experiencing this MRSA outbreak?"

"We did not."

"How about the Joint Commission on Accreditation of Healthcare Organizations? Did you notify them?"

"No, we didn't. The JCAHO only needs to

be notified if our overall infection rate goes above four percent over our designated surveillance period."

"Which is what?"

Laurie watched Loraine hesitate as if Laurie had asked a state secret. "You don't have to tell me if you feel uncomfortable," Laurie added. "I don't even know why I'm asking."

"And I don't know why I'm hesitating. Anyway, it is a year interval."

"But your rate could be above four percent if you considered the last three months."

"It's possible," Loraine agreed. "But I've not stopped to figure it out."

"How about the New York City Board of Health?" Laurie asked. "I presume you let them know."

"Of course," Loraine said. "And the city epidemiologist, Dr. Clint Abelard, has made several site visits. He was impressed with everything we were doing and didn't have any suggestions, which is not surprising, since we had tried everything."

"Very interesting," Laurie commented. She felt better about coming for her visit, since Loraine hadn't ridiculed her about any of her thoughts. At the same time, she was reluctant to mention any of her more outlandish ideas. "How about a tour. Your hospital is truly elegant, and not like any other

I've ever seen."

"Sure," Loraine said without hesitation. "We all are quite proud of it, especially since we are all owners."

"Really?" Laurie questioned. "How so?"

"Our CEO, Dr. Dawson, gave all the employees a little stock when we signed on. It's not much, but there is a certain symbolic value. Actually, that might change for the better in the near future. The company is scheduled to go public in a few weeks. If all goes well, our tiny amounts of stock could actually be worth something."

"Well, I'll say a little prayer for the IPO."

"Thanks," Loraine said. "The rumor is that it is going to do very well."

"Can we do the tour now?" Laurie asked.

"Certainly," Loraine said. She stood and opened the door leading to the area occupied by the secretaries. Laurie followed.

"What is it you'd like to see?" Loraine questioned as they left the admin area and emerged into the main lounge. "It's fancier than other hospitals but otherwise basically the same."

"But no emergency room."

"Right, no emergency room. We're a surgical hospital. We don't want beds taken up with medical patients."

"How about an intensive-care unit?"

"Not an intensive-care unit per se. If that kind of care is needed, we can isolate part of the PACU, or post-anesthesia unit. If the PACU is too full, we send patients to the University Hospital. It saves a lot of money."

"I'm sure it does," Laurie agreed, but the idea of a surgical hospital not having a full-fledged ICU bothered her.

They paused out in the main lobby area, standing in front of the elevators.

"I cannot help but notice how quiet it seems to be," Laurie said. "There are so few people."

"That's because our census is very low, which has been progressive since the MRSA problem began. Of course, the worst was when the ORs were completely shut down. During that period we had the entire hospital staff, including the president, disinfecting everything."

"But the ORs are open now?"

"Yes, they are open now except for the OR where Mr. Jeffries was operated on."

"Was he the only case done in the room yesterday?"

"No, he wasn't. There were two others after Mr. Jeffries."

"And they are well."

"Perfectly fine," Loraine said. "I know

what you are thinking. It has us baffled as well."

"Since your census is low, does that mean some of your staff doctors are choosing to do their surgery elsewhere?"

"I'm afraid so."

"What about Dr. Wendell Anderson?"

"He's one of the brave ones, or should I say loyal. He's still operating here on a regular basis."

Laurie nodded while fantasizing about tying Jack to the bed during his sleep Wednesday night. More than ever, she did not want him to have his operation.

"What is it you'd like to see?" Loraine repeated.

"How about starting out with your HVAC system?"

Loraine did the equivalent of a double take. "Are you joking?"

"I'm serious," Laurie said. "Are the operating rooms and the PACU on a separate system from the main part of the hospital?"

"Absolutely," Loraine said. "This is a state-of-the-art facility. The HVAC for the operating rooms is designed to change each OR's air every six minutes. There would be no need to do that for the whole hospital. Even the laboratory area has its own system, although not with that kind of flow."

"I'd still like to see it," Laurie said. "Particularly the OR system."

"Well, I don't see why not." They boarded a waiting elevator. Loraine pressed the button for the fourth floor. She explained that the second floor was for outpatient services, the third was the OR and PACU as well as central supply, and the fourth was for the laboratory and engineering. Engineering included HVAC and the supply of various gases for the ORs and bedside. All the floors higher than the fourth were for patient rooms. The very top floor was a special VIP section, which had slightly larger rooms and more expensive décor. The service, she insisted, was the same.

"Are all the Angels Healthcare hospitals similar?" Laurie asked.

"Essentially identical, as will be the six hospitals slated soon to be constructed: three each in Miami and Los Angeles."

"My word," Laurie said simply. She was impressed with the edifice but bemoaned that its luxury represented the enormous amount of money essentially being stolen on an ongoing basis from full-service hospitals like University or even General, which were already struggling to make ends meet. Angels Healthcare, like other specialty hospitals, was interested only in the paying patients with acute problems, not the uninsured or the chronically ill. Not only that, the fortunes being made by the businessmen owners were also being sucked out of the healthcare system and unavailable for patient care.

"Here we are," Loraine said as the elevator door opened. "Engineering is to the left."

In contrast to the elegant five-star hotel décor of the lobby, the fourth floor was the epitome of high-tech minimalist design. Everything was gleaming, high-gloss white, and the hallway was spotless. The women's shoes clicked on the composite flooring, and the sound echoed off the bare walls. There were no pictures, no bulletin boards, only closed white doors. The only color came from city-mandated institutional exit signs with red letters at either end of the lengthy corridor.

"I think I know why you are interested in seeing our HVAC system," Loraine said as they walked.

"Really?" Laurie questioned. She wasn't entirely sure herself. What she knew of HVAC was the little she'd absorbed while the renovation of her and Jack's brownstone had been under way.

"You are thinking of airborne route of infection, which is another suggestion, as far as

I am concerned, you are not the epidemiological amateur you profess to be. But let me
reassure you, we have considered it also, and
we have tested the water in the condensate
pans for staph aureus on multiple occasions,
including just this morning after yesterday's tragedy."

"Have any of the tests been positive?"

"No, none!" Loraine said emphatically.
"Staph is not considered an airborne
pathogen, but that did not stop us from considering it, and even though the tests were
negative, we've drained all the pans and
treated them."

"I didn't think staph was spread by the airborne route, either," Laurie said. "But the
fact that a number of the cases seemed to
have been primary pneumonias suggested
the route of infection had to be airborne."

"I can't argue with that," Loraine said, "at
least not from an academic perspective, but
I can from a practical one. I chair an interdepartmental infection-control committee,
which is just as its name suggests: interdepartmental. We have people from all de-
partments, such as nursing, food service, engineering, and so forth. Currently, our
representative from the medical staff is a surgeon, and when we were discussing the possibility of the staph being spread via the air-

borne route and believing the HVAC would be involved, he set us straight on an important fact. Patients undergoing endotracheal or laryngeal-mask-airway anesthesia, which all do in our hospitals when they have general anesthesia, never breathe operating-room air. The air they breathe always comes from the piped-in source."

"They never breathe ambient air?" Laurie questioned. There went her only theory as to how the MRSA victims were getting sick.

"Never!" Loraine confirmed.

Loraine stopped at one of the closed doors. An eye-level white plaque with incised black letters said: *Engineering.* "It's going to be a little loud in here," she warned.

Laurie nodded as Loraine pushed open the heavy, insulated door. Once inside, Laurie scanned the large utilitarian high-ceilinged room. The walls and ceiling were concrete. A tangled web of piping, some insulated and some not, snaked out of various multicolored tanks and hung from the ceiling. Much larger ducts did the same after exiting or entering air handlers the size of small cars, each of which was mounted on rubber shocks.

"Anything in particular you'd like to see?" Loraine shouted.

"Which handlers service the ORs?" Laurie

shouted back.

Loraine led Laurie down the relatively narrow walkway between the meticulously maintained equipment. Halfway to the opposite wall, Loraine stopped and patted the side of one of the air handlers. "This is the one. The coolant comes from the condensers on the roof, and the hot water comes from the furnaces in the basement."

"How do you access the condensate pan?"

"This access door," Loraine yelled. She grabbed the handle and had to pull hard to break the suction. When the door opened, they heard a whistling noise.

Laurie stuck her head into the opening and the wind wildly tossed her hair in all different directions. She had to grasp it to keep it out of her face.

"That's the condensate pan down there," Loraine shouted, while pointing over Laurie's shoulder to the base of the machine's innards.

Laurie nodded. She was interested because she knew air-conditioning condensate pans were a frequent source of airborne outbreaks, such as Legionnaires' disease. She turned her head downstream into the mouth of the efferent duct, where she could see a mesh screen. "Is that a filter?" Laurie yelled.

"There are two," Loraine answered. She

closed the door to the coils, and it snapped shut. She took several steps forward. There were two vertical slitlike openings. She pointed to the two of them with both index fingers. "The first is a standard filter for relatively large-sized particles. The second is a HEPA filter for particles down to the size of viruses. And to anticipate a question, we have on multiple occasions tested the HEPA filters for staph. Only twice did we get a positive result."

"Was it CA-MRSA?" Laurie questioned.

"It was, but it was not meaningful."

"Why?"

"Because the HEPA filter stopped it."

"What's that access door beyond the HEPA filter?"

"That's the clean-out port of the efferent duct. We have all the ducting cleaned once a year."

After about six feet, the efferent duct split like the tentacles of a squid into multiple smaller ducts, each going to a separate OR, the PACU, and surgical lounge. Laurie could tell because each was labeled with an incised Formica plaque. Same as the main duct, each had a clean-out port. "When were the ducts cleaned last?"

"When the ORs were shut down."

Laurie nodded. Looking down toward the

end of the walkway between the equipment, she saw another door. "Where does that door lead?"

"Another HVAC room, pretty much the same as this one except that it also houses our electrical generators. Beyond that is a doorway into a vestibule with a pair of service elevators and a back stairwell."

Laurie nodded again, and then walked back to the other side of the air handler that served the ORs. Similar to the efferent side, there was a clean-out port for cleaning the return duct. She then looked back at Loraine and shrugged her shoulders. "I can't think of any more questions. It's a very impressive system. And thanks for the lecture on air handlers. You seem to know your stuff."

"Part of our training in hospital infection control included learning more than we wanted to know about heating and ventilation," Loraine yelled. She then pointed back the way they'd come.

As soon as the heavy insulated door closed behind the women, the silence of the seemingly empty hospital enveloped them like an invisible blanket. Laurie tried to fix her hair, which at the moment gave her the appearance she'd been out riding in a convertible.

"I'd like to see a patient room," Laurie

said. "Provided you have the time. I don't want to monopolize your afternoon."

"With as few patients as we have currently, I certainly have the time."

"How about David Jeffries's room."

"I think it's being thoroughly cleaned. We can look in, but I'm sure housekeeping will be there."

"Then another room will be fine."

Five minutes later, Laurie stood in one of the standard rooms. In keeping with the five-star hotel décor in the lounge area, the room was equivalently decorated and furnished. The bed and the rest of the furniture were hardly the usual hospital issue. The television was a flat-screen model, which was set up without extra charge to have blue-ribbon cable service as well as Internet access. There was even an upholstered couch that unfolded into a bed in case a family member wanted to stay over. But what impressed Laurie the most was the bathroom. "Oh, my goodness," she said as she glanced in. It was done in marble and had a second flat-screen TV. "Do you have trouble getting some patients to leave?"

"It's far better than my bathroom. I can assure you of that."

With no specific reason to visit the room, Laurie made a mild show of inspecting the position of the vents in the room for the HVAC system. There were several high near the ceiling and several low near the baseboard. It was the same in the bathroom.

"I guess that's it," Laurie said.

"Any other part of the hospital you'd like to see?"

"Well . . ." Laurie said hesitantly. Having had her rather vague but pet theory that the MRSA victims were being infected in the OR trashed by a combination of the presence of the HEPA filter and even more so by learning the patients undergoing general anesthesia never breathed ambient air, Laurie was convinced her site visit was a complete bust from the standpoint of solving the mystery of the MRSA outbreak. She certainly hated wasting any more of Loraine's time, even though the woman was graciously accommodating, even to the point of seeming to enjoy giving the tour. Laurie could tell she was proud of the institution.

"You are not keeping me from anything," Loraine said, guessing the reason for Laurie's hesitation.

"If that's the case, then I suppose I wouldn't mind seeing the OR area, particularly one of the ORs itself."

"We'll have to change into scrubs."

"I do it every day."

As they retraced their steps back toward the elevators, Laurie noticed the paintings lining the walls were real oils and not prints. While they waited for an elevator, Laurie glanced at the nearby nursing station. Behind it was a bank of high-tech flat-screen monitors, enough to serve every room. All were dark. Four nurses and an orderly were relaxing at the station: Three were in desk chairs, the other two sitting on the desk itself. There was intermittent laughter.

"They are acting as if there are no patients on this floor," Laurie said.

"There aren't," Loraine responded. "That's why I brought you here."

"Knowing how expensive it is to run hospitals, I'd hazard that the CFO, whoever he or she is, must be sweating bullets."

"That I don't know. Luckily, it is not my responsibility, and I don't often talk with the bigwigs."

"Has anyone lost their job?"

"I don't believe so. A number of people have taken a voluntary leave of absence, but the administration is counting on the low census turning around immediately. Our ORs are all back online."

"Except the OR David Jeffries was operated on in."

"It wasn't open for today while it's being

thoroughly cleaned, but it will be open to-morrow."

Laurie was tempted to ask if the morrow's patients scheduled for that particular OR would be told of David Jeffries's fatal experience, but she didn't. It would have been a provocative question, to which Laurie already knew the answer. Too often, patients were denied information that they had the right to know if the concept of informed consent was to be truly honest.

The décor of the OR floor and the OR suite itself, except for the doctors' lounge, looked to Laurie as she expected a NASA building to look: aseptically functional. It was also like the hall above: all white, with the same composite floor. The walls, however, were tile. In contrast, the doctors' lounge was mostly soothing green, and also in contrast to the rest of the hospital, there was a lot of activity in the OR area, because the day shift was leaving and the evening shift arriving.

The women's locker room was equally lively. Loraine gave Laurie a set of scrubs and directed her to a locker. While both women changed, Laurie overheard a short conversation Loraine had with an acquaintance who was going off duty. Loraine asked her if there'd been many cases that morning.

"It was slim pickings," the woman said. "I'm afraid everyone is getting a bit bored with all the sitting around. We were only running two out of the five rooms."

Five minutes later, Laurie and Loraine pushed into the OR and the double doors swung closed behind them, cutting off the chatter from the surgical lounge.

To Laurie's left was a blank OR scheduling blackboard, which suggested there were no cases under way. To Laurie's right was the OR desk, fronted by a chest-high countertop, behind which Laurie could see just the tops of two hooded heads. Beyond the OR desk was the open doorway into the PACU. The central corridor stretched out approximately eighty feet to a far wall.

Loraine advanced to the desk, and the two women seated behind looked up. "Dr. Sarpoulus!" Loraine said. She was surprised to see her infection-control superior. "I didn't know you were here."

"Is there some reason you should know?" Cynthia questioned, with an edge to her voice.

"Well, no, I suppose not," Loraine responded. She switched her attention to the other woman, whose nametag read: *Mrs. Fran Gonzales, OR Supervisor.* "Fran, I have a guest here who wanted to take a peek at our

OR." Loraine motioned for Laurie to step up to the counter, and Loraine introduced her as a New York City medical examiner.

Before Fran could respond, Cynthia's head popped back up. She'd returned to studying the OR scheduling log, which she and Fran had been busily doing before Laurie and Loraine had appeared. "You are a medical examiner?" she questioned, with even more edge to her voice than when she'd spoken with Loraine.

"I am," Laurie confirmed.

"What the hell are you doing here?"

"I'm ah . . ." Laurie began, but hesitated. She was taken aback by Cynthia's tone and challenging glare. Laurie couldn't help but remember Arnold's description of the woman as not being terribly cooperative, as well as defensive, and essentially telling him to butt out. The last thing Laurie wanted was some sort of a confrontation, knowing she was, to a certain extent, overstepping her bounds by making the site visit. Steve Mariott, the evening PA, had visited the hospital the night before, after Jeffries's death had been called into the OCME.

"Well?" Cynthia questioned impatiently.

"I autopsied a case this morning of a patient who'd been operated on yesterday here at Angels Orthopedic Hospital and who had died of an exceptionally aggressive MRSA infection."

"We are well aware of that, thank you very much," Cynthia snapped.

Laurie glanced briefly at Loraine, who appeared as surprised as Laurie. "When I canvassed my colleagues, I discovered you'd had a number of similar cases. I thought it was appropriate to come over here, and see if I could help."

Cynthia laughed cynically. "And just how did you think you could help? Have you been trained in epidemiology, infection control, or even in infectious diseases?"

"My training is in forensic pathology," Laurie said defensively. "My exposure to epidemiology has not been extensive, but my understanding is that in an outbreak of this sort, one of the first things that should be done is to accurately subtype the organisms."

"I'm board-certified in internal medicine with a subspecialty in infectious diseases and have a Ph.D. in epidemiology. As far as your comment about subtyping, you are correct but only if such information is needed to decide on a targeted method of control. In our situation, it wasn't needed, since our CEO insisted that we use a global control strategy. Our interest was not in saving money by restricting ourselves to a target approach. I spoke with one of your colleagues a number of weeks ago after he'd autopsied one of our MRSA cases. I assured him we were well aware of the problem and aggressively engaged in solving it, and thanked him for the call."

"That's all well and good," Laurie said, with her own dander rising. "Having had the dubious honor to autopsy the unfortunate individual this morning, I can say with some conviction that you have been unsuccessful in your control efforts."

"That might be the case, but we surely don't need interference. Your job is to tell us cause of death and anything else we might not know pathologically. The fact of the matter is that we are well aware of both the cause and mechanism of death, and we are doing everything humanly possible to control this unfortunate outbreak. What is it you wish to accomplish by visiting the operating room? What do you want to see?"

"To be totally honest, I don't know," Laurie said. "But I can assure you that there have been thousands of times that site visits have either helped or been crucial in a forensic investigation. Mr. Jeffries is officially a medical examiner's case, and I am duty-bound to investigate it fully, which in this case means viewing the scene of his proximate cause of death. Odds are, he was exposed to the bacteria that led to his demise in the operating room where he'd had his surgery."

"We'll see about that," Cynthia said, getting to her feet. "I'll have you talk with someone with considerably more authority than I. I insist you wait outside in the surgical lounge. I will be right back."

Without another word or even a glance over her shoulder, Cynthia walked quickly to the double doors and departed.

Laurie and Loraine exchanged another surprised and confused glance.

"I'm sorry," Loraine said. "I don't know what's come over her."

"It's certainly not your fault."

"She is under a lot of pressure," Fran, the OR supervisor, said. "She's been intense from the first, and it's only gotten worse. She's taking the whole problem very personally, so try not to do so yourself, Dr. Montgomery. She's even been at my throat on occasion."

"Who is she going to fetch?" Loraine questioned. "Mr. Straus, the hospital president?"

"I have no idea," Fran said.

"Let's go back to the lounge," Loraine suggested to Laurie.

"I think that might be a good idea," Laurie said. She felt anxious from an adrenaline surge engendered by the unexpected confrontation and its potential consequences.

As they walked, Loraine added, "Dr. Sarpoulus has always been uptight, as Fran suggested. Are you sure you want to stay? She was very rude."

"I'll stay," Laurie said, with some misgivings. What motivated her was the hope of being able to smooth things over with someone more rational than Cynthia Sarpoulus. Leaving on an unpleasant note certainly would not be helpful if she had additional questions, and there might even be a complaint made about her visit. Laurie specifically wanted to avoid such a possibility.

Back in the surgical lounge, Laurie accepted some coffee and crackers from Loraine. As busy as she'd been, she'd skipped lunch and was famished.

"So it was the CEO's decision not to characterize more fully the staph strains involved in the outbreak?"

"I guess," Loraine said. "I thought it had been Cynthia's decision, but I guess not."

Laurie had more questions, but her thoughts were interrupted by Cynthia's reappearance. By her expression, her mood had not mollified. Her sharply defined, full lips were pressed firmly together, and she walked with obvious determination. Behind her came a man and a woman. The woman was of medium height, with blemish-free pale skin, aristocratic features, and a helmet of short, thick hair. She was dressed in an elegant business suit and walked with a decidedly commanding resoluteness while still managing to exude classic femininity.

The man was her antithesis, not only in gender but in his general appearance and the way he moved. He wore a rumpled plaid wool jacket with leather elbows, the kind that Laurie had always associated with academia. Instead of resoluteness, he projected an air of wariness, with his pale eyes constantly on the move as if he were in a potentially hostile environment.

"Dr. Montgomery," Cynthia said triumphantly. "May I present Dr. Angela Dawson, the CEO of Angels Healthcare, and Dr. Walter Osgood, department head of clinical pathology. I believe you should direct your comments to them."

"What seems to be the trouble?" Angela demanded. From her tone, it was obvious Laurie's presence was not to her liking.

"I'm afraid I have no idea," Laurie said, as she got to her feet. Since they were nearly the same height, she and Angela literally saw eye to eye.

Loraine scrambled to her feet. "If there is any fault concerning Dr. Montgomery's presence, surely it is mine," she said. "Dr. Montgomery called me after she had autopsied Mr. David Jeffries. She asked to come to the hospital for a visit as part of her investigation. I invited her. She only asked to see our OR HVAC system in the engineering spaces, a typical patient room, and the OR itself. I didn't see any problem in that. I suppose I should have run it by Mr. Straus beforehand."

"As president of the hospital, that would have been wise," Angela agreed. "It would have saved us this embarrassment." Then, turning to Laurie, she said, "You do understand that this is private property."

"I understand," Laurie said. "But David Jeffries is a medical examiner case, and by law, I have subpoena power for documents and whatnot, and to visit the scene in order to investigate fully the cause and manner of death."

"There is no doubt legal recourse for you to carry out your duty, but barging in here is not one of them. Someone has already visited us from your office the previous evening and was shown appropriate hospitality. I will be very happy to discuss this with the chief of the OCME, Dr. Harold Bingham, whom I have had the pleasure of meeting on several occasions."

Laurie felt a chill descending her spine. Despite knowing she ultimately had the legal right to make the visit, the very last thing she wanted was for Bingham to be dragged into this ridiculous brouhaha over nothing, especially since she knew from past experience he'd probably side with the hospital.

"Thank you for your industriousness," Angela continued. "I'm sure your motivation was to help us, but as you can imagine, this problem has taken a terrible toll not only on some of our patients but on our institution, and, frankly, we are inordinately sensitive to the crisis. When I call Dr. Bingham, I will mention that we are not averse to you or anyone from the OCME visiting our OR, but we will require a warrant and that whoever is designated be tested as a carrier for MRSA. As part of our attempt to deal with this horrible problem, we insist that everyone entering the OR suite be clean."

"I had not thought of that," Laurie said, with a touch of guilt. Never once did it cross her mind that she could be a carrier herself, especially from having autopsied an individual just that morning who was chock-full of the bacteria.

"We, on the other hand, are extremely aware of it. But the point is we are not trying to limit your investigation. At the same time, we are certain your visiting our OR would not be enlightening in the slightest. The epidemiologist for the New York City Board of Health, Dr. Clint Abelard, who is a public servant like yourself, has inspected our OR on two occasions and found nothing. Of course, he wasn't allowed in until it was assured that he was not an MRSA carrier."

"I wasn't aware an epidemiologist had been involved until I got here," Laurie said. "Obviously, he's much more qualified than I. I'm sorry to have caused any misunderstanding. I hope I haven't inconvenienced you too much."

"You haven't. Dr. Sarpoulus, Dr. Osgood, and I were here attending the monthly medical staff meeting. It's not as if we had to come all the way from our home office."

"I'm pleased."

"There's one other point I wanted to make. You have questioned our decision not to accurately subtype the particular strains of the involved MRSA causing us such havoc. To explain, I've asked Dr. Osgood to accompany me to meet you. I know Dr. Sarpoulus has alluded to the reasons, but Dr. Osgood can explain it better, as he is boarded in both clinical pathology and microbiology. It's important for you to understand we have done every possible thing in our power to rid ourselves of this problem. Anything else would be irresponsible."

Fifteen minutes later, Angela and Cynthia were in a cab heading south on Fifth Avenue. Walter had stayed behind to meet with the orthopedic hospital's laboratory supervisor. Angela and Cynthia had ridden in silence, with Angela staring out the side window of the taxi and noticing that the trees of Central Park had the very first suggestion that spring was around the corner.

But Angela was thinking less about nature and more about her problems with Angels Healthcare, which seemed to grow with each passing day. The last thing she expected at this late date was a problem with the medical examiner's office. The concern was publicity, which had been a worry from the start. Back when the MRSA cases first occurred, she'd made it a point to contact the chief medical examiner, to convince him that they were on top of the problem to the extent of having reported it to the New York City Department of Health and encouraging the epidemiologist to come to the hospital.

Angela turned to Cynthia. "What was your

take on that medical examiner? Did she strike you as an independent sort?"

"Absolutely. Why else would she come out and visit our hospital when there was no mystery about the cause of death. I didn't like her there while we're trying to keep a lid on this affair. That's why I came down to get you. I thought it was something you should handle."

"I'm glad you did. I considered her a threat the moment I laid eyes on her. I don't know exactly why, but she struck me as very focused and driven, and, to compound it, very intelligent. Did you see how she made eye contact? Most people caught in a similar circumstance would have been cowed to some degree."

"She did the same to me," Cynthia said. "I definitely challenged her the moment I heard she was a medical examiner."

"She worries me," Angela admitted. "If she manages to get any of this MRSA problem into the press, it will certainly come to the attention of institutional investors as part of their due diligence. If that happens, more than likely the IPO will have to be postponed, or if it's not, it certainly won't be successful."

"I think you did a terrific job talking to her."

"You think so? Really?"

"I do. First, you mixed just enough condemnation and commendation, threat and praise, to put her off balance. Second, your warning about calling her boss definitely affected her negatively; I don't think she will be making any more visits, whether announced or not. And finally you made her understand that there are a number of people working on solving the problem who have much more epidemiological training than she has. I'm sure she feels she'd fulfilled her responsibility."

"I hope you are right," Angela said, not fully convinced.

"I'm sure I am. I was impressed. You were brilliant. You really played her like a violin."

Angela shrugged. She wasn't so sure. Her intuition was telling her the opposite, and that Dr. Laurie Montgomery was going to be a problem. Angela wondered if she should talk to Michael about her. But then, after another short session staring out the taxi's window, Angela suddenly pulled her cell phone from her Louis Vuitton bag, slipped it open, and speed-dialed her secretary.

"Loren? Get me Dr. Harold Bingham's number."

To Cynthia, she said, "I want to be totally certain Dr. Laurie Montgomery behaves."

Dr. Walter Osgood was nervous. The whole time he'd been talking with his supervisor of the Angels Orthopedic Hospital's clinical laboratory, Simon Friedlander, he kept thinking about the surprise visit from the woman medical examiner. He'd explained to her why he'd advised not to bother testing the MRSA to determine their explicit sub-type. The woman had nodded repeatedly as if she'd understood, yet he sensed she hadn't agreed. It was subtle but definite, and it worried him.

When he'd finished the meeting with Simon, which had been stressful because of his nervous preoccupation with Dr. Laurie Montgomery's visit, Walter asked if he could use Simon's office to make a private phone call. Sitting at the man's desk, he noticed a family photo. One of Simon's sons was the same age as Walter's only child. Before making his call, Walter picked up the framed photo so he could see the boy's image more clearly. He was an obviously healthy child, with a shock of unruly blond hair and a pur-posefully silly but happy expression. Walter fought off a sudden surge of sadness, anger, and envy. He put the photo back down, closed his eyes, and took a deep breath to rein in his emotions involving the unfairness of life. At the moment, his son was far from healthy, having been diagnosed with a rare, severe form of Hodgkin's disease requiring what his health insurer deemed "experimental" treatment. At the moment, Walter's son had no hair and had lost a quarter of his former weight.

Opening his eyes, Walter took out his wallet and extracted a small piece of paper with a single phone number with a Washington, D.C., area code. It was supposed to be for emergencies only, and he debated if this qualified. Making a sudden decision, he picked up the receiver and dialed.

On the other end, the phone rang a number of times, and Walter wondered what he'd say if he got voice mail. Just when he thought the phone wouldn't be answered, it was. A deep, wary voice said, "What is it?" There was no hello.

"This is Walter Osgood," Walter began, but he was immediately cut off.

"Are you on a landline?"

"I am."

"Hang up and call this number," the voice said. He rattled off a phone number and hung up.

Walter rapidly wrote the number on the edge of an envelope addressed to Simon. He then dialed the number. The same voice immediately answered. "You were not supposed to call me unless there is an emergency. Is that the case?"

"How do I know what constitutes an emergency?" Walter snapped. "As far as I'm concerned, if it isn't now, it will be."

"What is it?"

"A New York City medical examiner by the name of Laurie Montgomery came to the Angels Orthopedic Hospital asking questions."

"Why is that an emergency?"

"She'd autopsied a patient who'd died yesterday from MRSA. She wanted to go into the OR, and had even been up in the engineering spaces."

"So what?"

"That's easy for you to say. I don't like it. The next thing, it could be in the papers."

"What's her name again?"

"Dr. Laurie Montgomery from the Office of the Chief Medical Examiner. What are you going to do?"

"I don't know. But I'll keep you informed, and you do the same."

The line disconnected. Walter glanced at the receiver as if it could answer his question. Then he lowered it into its cradle. The strangest part was that he didn't even know the man's name.

Walter carefully erased the phone number he'd written on the envelope on Simon's desk before walking out into the lab.

Laurie's taxi was now speeding south on Second Avenue toward the OCME and running the lights. But instead of concern about her safety, other than being certain her seat belt was secure, Laurie was obsessed with her surprising visit to Angels Orthopedic Hospital. Nothing had been as she'd expected.

The edifice was far more luxurious than she'd imagined. And the cast of characters had run the gamut from congenial to rude, and the CEO of Angels Healthcare, whom she never expected to meet, was definitely in the latter category. Laurie wondered if the woman would act on her thinly disguised threat to call Bingham. Under New York City law, a medical examiner definitely has the right, while investigating a case, to do what is needed to protect the public, and visiting an OR where there had been eleven infectious deaths over three months would certainly fall into that category.

If anything, the visit had only intensified her urge to talk Jack out of his surgery, at least until the MRSA mystery had been solved. Although Angela Dawson had expressed a remorse for the toll the outbreak had taken on their patients, she seemed just as concerned about the institution itself. It was as if the two were equivalent, which shocked Laurie. She could not believe that under the circumstances, the hospital was continuing to do surgery, that the reduced revenues were on a par with lost lives. The CEO had been introduced to Laurie as a doctor, which Laurie had assumed to be medical doctor, but now she thought it must be Ph.D., not M.D. It just didn't seem possible for her to be otherwise.

She tried to focus on the outbreak, but the contradictions were confusing. Although she knew the airborne spread of staphylococcus was possible, it wasn't common, mainly because staph cannot be aerosolized like anthrax or other airborne bacterial threats. Staphylococcus remains viable for a very short time outside a warm, moist, nutrient-rich environment, and when a few errant molecules did land within someone's nose or mouth, it behaved itself admirably and almost never caused problems. Yet in her series of mostly primary pneumonia, it had to have been airborne, and it had to have been a large dose. But that meant the patients had to have been exposed in the operating room to a relatively large amount of the pathogen. The trouble with that scenario was that the HVAC system was outfitted with HEPA filters that caught viruses a hundred times smaller than bacteria, and even if a few got through, the air in the OR changed every six minutes. On top of that, the patients undergoing general anesthesia never breathed the ambient air. In short, Laurie told herself it was impossible. Her series could not happen either naturally or purposefully.

"We are here at your destination, ma'am," the cabbie said through the Plexiglas divider.

Laurie paid the fare and, still in a semi-trance from the staphylococcus conundrum, climbed from the cab and mounted the steps of the OCME. Once inside, she was surprised to see Marlene, still at her post.

"Aren't you supposed to be off duty at three?" Laurie questioned.

"My relief called in to say she was going to be a few minutes late," Marlene said in her soft southern accent.

Laurie nodded and headed toward the ID room door.

"Excuse me, Dr. Montgomery. I'm supposed to tell you when you come in that Dr. Bingham wants to see you in his office ASAP."

Laurie felt her face flush. Intuitively, she

knew that Angela Dawson had to have already called and complained about her visit. With Laurie's long-standing aversion to confrontations with superiors, she was not looking forward to being called on the carpet, if that was what was about to happen. It wasn't that she felt guilty in any way, it was her fear of losing control of her emotions. Such a reflex response had started when she was a preteen and had never entirely gone away. At that time, she had suffered a horrific confrontation with her autocratic father, who had unjustly blamed her for her older brother's death from a drug overdose. Since that awful episode, it was as if her response to confrontation was hardwired and beyond her control. As she approached Bingham's secretary, Mrs. Sanford, she could feel the involved synapses firing and setting herself up for the fall.

"You are to go right in," Mrs. Sanford said.

Laurie glimpsed the secretary's face as she passed by the woman's desk in hopes of getting a hint of what to expect, but Mrs. Sanford seemed to avoid eye contact.

"Shut the door, Dr. Montgomery!" Bingham bellowed from behind his massive and cluttered desk. Laurie did as she was told. The chief's use of such formality suggested the worst.

"Sit down!" he said, equally forcibly.

Laurie sat. She could tell her face was flushed, but she had no idea how obvious it was. She hoped it wasn't. What bothered her the most about her reflex emotionalism was the concern that people would interpret it as a sign of weakness. Laurie knew she was not a weak person. It had taken a while for her to be sure of it, but now that she was sure, it rankled her that she couldn't control behavior that suggested otherwise.

"I'm disappointed in you, Laurie," Bingham said, with a slightly more mellow tone.

"I'm sorry to hear that," Laurie said. Although there was a slight quaver to her voice, she felt encouraged. She'd managed to hold back any embarrassing tears.

"You have been so dependable of late. What's happened?"

"I'm not sure I understand your question."

"I just got off the phone with a Dr. Angela Dawson. She was furious that you showed up unannounced at one of her private hospitals, demanding entry into unauthorized areas. She even threatened to call the mayor's office."

Having overcome her emotions for the time being, Laurie allowed a more appropriate irritation to emerge. In her mind, Bingham should have been commending her re-

281

sourcefulness and supporting her rather than siding with a businessperson who was obviously more concerned about her institution than her patients.

"Well?" Bingham demanded impatiently.

Understanding that it was as important to control her anger as her tears, Laurie calmly explained why she had gone to the hospital and what she had learned about the MRSA deaths that were occurring at Angels Healthcare hospitals despite commendable infection-control efforts. She told Bingham that she hadn't arrived unannounced but had been invited by the chairperson of the infection-control committee, who had been hospitable and happy to give Laurie a tour.

Bingham harrumphed into a partially closed fist. He studied Laurie with his rheumy eyes. He was, Laurie thought, partially mollified by hearing the other side of the story.

"How many times have I or Dr. Washington told you that it is OCME policy that the PAs do the footwork and that you, as a medical examiner, stay here and do the cases?"

"Several times," Laurie admitted.

"Ha!" Bingham barked. "Without exaggeration, it has to be more like a half a dozen times. We have world-class forensic investigators. You are to utilize them! Let them slog through city hospitals and crime scenes. We need you here. If you are not busy enough, I can rectify that."

"I'm busy enough," Laurie averred, thinking about all the cases she had outstanding, waiting for additional information to come in.

"Then get back to work and get more cases signed out!" Bingham said, with a ring of finality. "And stay away from Angels Healthcare hospitals." With the matter taken care of, he reached into his in box and pulled out a handful of letters that needed his signature.

Laurie stayed in her seat. Bingham ignored her as he began to read the first letter.

"Sir," Laurie began. "May I ask you a few questions?"

Bingham looked up. His face registered surprise that Laurie was still seated in front of him. "Make it fast!"

"I couldn't help but be surprised you weren't more taken by the number of these MRSA cases that I mentioned and the fact that the how and the why have not been determined. Frankly, I am mystified and concerned."

"They are obviously therapeutic complications," Bingham said. "The how I have no idea, although I know several epidemiologists are working on it. And the number: Well, I knew there were quite a few, but I was not aware it had reached the twenties."

"How did you hear about them?"

"From two sources, first from Dr. Dawson, several months ago. She wanted me to know that she'd contacted the Department of Health and had the city epidemiologist on the case. Then from a surgeon friend of mine. He's one of the investors in the company as well as on the Angels Orthopedic staff. In fact, he had been doing most of his affluent-patient cases there before this MRSA problem started. He's been keeping me abreast of the situation because a year or so ago he'd talked me and Calvin into picking up some of the founders' stock."

"What?" Laurie demanded. "You are an investor in Angels Healthcare?"

"Certainly not a heavy investor," Bingham said. "When my friend Jason recommended it because he had learned it was going to go public, I had my broker check it out. He thought it looked promising. He actually took a larger stake than I."

Laurie's jaw slowly dropped open. She stared at Bingham with astonishment.

"What's got into you?" Bingham questioned. "Why are you acting so surprised? Specialty hospitals are serving a need."

"I'm shocked," Laurie admitted. "Do you know this Dr. Angela Dawson?"

"I can't say I know her. I'd spoken with her, as I just mentioned, and even met her at a mayoral function. She's very impressive. Why do you ask?"

"Is she an M.D. or Ph.D.?"

"She's an M.D. She has her boards in internal medicine."

Laurie was even more taken aback.

"You have a strange expression, Laurie. What are you thinking?"

"I'm thinking it is a little weird for you to be essentially ordering me to stay away from Angels Healthcare hospitals when you are an investor and there is a problem going on."

The web of capillaries on Bingham's nose dilated. "I resent the implication," he boomed out.

"I don't mean to sound insubordinate," Laurie added quickly. "I'm actually thinking of your best interests. It might be best for you to recuse yourself."

"You better be careful, young lady," Bingham snapped patronizingly while pointing one of his thick fingers at Laurie. "Let's get this straight. I'm not in any form or fashion restricting your investigation of your case, especially not for my investment. I'm just telling you not to go to those hospitals yourself, angering politically connected people, and putting me in a difficult situation. All I'm saying is to use the forensic investigators to do your legwork, as I've been telling you for years. Are we clear on this?"

"Quite clear," Laurie said. "But I'd like you to know that my intuition is telling me there is something decidedly odd going on."

"Maybe so," Bingham reluctantly agreed. He was clearly more irritated now than when Laurie had first arrived. "Now get out of here and get back to work so that I can get back to mine."

Laurie did as she was told, but before she could open the door, Bingham called out, "Actually, it's my recollection your intuition has always been right, so keep me informed and, for God's sake, stay away from the press."

"I'll do that," Laurie promised. There had been a few times in the past when she had unknowingly leaked confidential information to the media.

In the elevator on the way up to the fifth floor, Laurie couldn't decide if she was pleased with herself for holding back her tears or disgusted with herself for provoking Bingham. She was leaning in the direction of the latter. It had served no purpose whatsoever to accuse him of impropriety; she didn't believe it herself. Her response had been from shock that her own chief was supporting an organization whose ethics seemed questionable at best.

With both her emotional and her rational brain in turmoil, Laurie bypassed her office for Jack's. She needed a little reassurance from having been abused by Bingham and the powerful and politically connected Angela Dawson. But Jack's desk chair was disappointingly empty.

"Where's Jack?" Laurie asked Chet, whose eyes were glued to his microscope. He hadn't heard her come in.

"He's out on one of his field trips," Chet said, looking up from his work.

"Meaning?"

"You know Jack: The more controversy, the better! He posted a case where the three involved stakeholders are at each other's throats over the manner of death. It was a construction worker at a high-rise site who fell ten stories onto concrete."

"I know the case," Laurie said. "What's he up to?" As irritated as Laurie had made Bingham, she hoped Jack would be discreet, a virtue he often ignored.

"How should I know. He said something about reenacting the crime, but short of his jumping off the building himself, I have no idea what he meant."

"When he comes back, tell him I was looking for him."

"Will do," Chet said agreeably

Laurie was about to leave when she remembered to ask Chet about his MRSA case.

"Right," Chet responded. "Jack had mentioned you were interested in it, so I got it out." He pulled himself along his desk with his chair's casters squeaking shrilly enough to make Laurie wince. He grabbed a case file from the top of his file cabinet and handed it to her. "The name was Julia Francova."

"Terrific," Laurie exclaimed. "I'm glad you still had it." She slid out the contents to make certain it was another Angels Healthcare case.

"What's the big interest?"

"I had a similar case this morning," Laurie explained. "There have been quite a few over the last three months or so: twenty-four, to be exact. It hadn't appeared on anyone's radar screen, since the cases have been widely distributed among the staff, including cases in Queens and Brooklyn."

"I didn't know about any others," Chet admitted.

"Nor did anyone else. I'm looking into it, and I'm psyched. There is something weird about these cases, and I'm going to figure it out if it kills me. I've already managed to provoke our fearless leader."

"Let me know if I can help. The reason I still have the case is that I've been waiting for the CDC to get back to me before signing it out."

"Don't tell me you sent an isolate for subtyping," Laurie questioned while trying to keep her excitement in check.

"I did. I sent a sample to a Dr. Ralph Percy. I got him through the CDC's central switchboard."

"That's more than terrific. I'll call Dr. Percy for you, and I'll put the results in the case file. It will save you a step."

Eager to add yet another name to her matrix, Laurie again tried to leave. This time, Chet called her back.

"I took your advice you gave me this morning and called my new lady friend this afternoon," Chet said.

"And? What happened?"

"I was shot out of the sky, and I was as direct as you suggested I be. I put my ego out there on the table, but she blew me off. I had even sent some flowers to soften her up, but no luck."

"Was she rude?"

"No. Actually, I'm exaggerating. She was

pretty nice about it, even though I stuck my foot in my mouth with my opening ploy. She had confided to me the evening before that she was desperately trying to raise a couple of hundred thousand dollars for the company she works for. I started the conversation by saying I'd found the money in my bedside table, and I wanted to invest."

"Bad strategy."

"Obviously. She said she felt I was mocking her."

"I think I would have felt the same," Laurie agreed. "How did you leave things?"

"Open-ended. I gave her my cell phone number."

"She's not going to call," Laurie said with a wry chuckle. "That's asking too much. You'd be making her feel like the aggressor. You have to call her back and apologize for your supposed joke."

"You mean I should call her back after she shot me down twice."

"If you want to go out with her, you have to call. If she didn't want you to call she would have said so."

"When do you think I should do it?"

"Whenever you'd like to see her. It's up to you."

"Do you think I should call her back again today? I mean, isn't that a little too pushy?"

"I wasn't a party to your conversation," Laurie said. "But you said you left things open-ended. There's a slight risk she might be perturbed, but I think the chances are better than even she'll be flattered. Call her! Take a chance," Laurie said as she backed out into the hall. "Obviously, you want to see her. What do you have to lose?"

"The rest of my self-esteem."

"Oh, baloney!" Laurie said, heading toward her office.

Chet put his hands behind his head and leaned back, staring up at the ceiling. He felt indecisive, yet he trusted Laurie's counsel. She was smart, intuitive, and, above all, female. With sudden resolve, he tipped forward, got out the Post-it note on which he'd written the number of Angels Healthcare, and placed the call. He wanted to do it quickly, before he lost his nerve.

As on the previous call, he had to go through the operator to get Angela's secretary. Then, after identifying himself appropriately, he was put on hold. While he waited, he debated whether to be humorous or serious, but ultimately decided to be merely straightforward. When Angela finally came on the line, he simply told her that he'd been thinking of her and had just had another conversation with his colleague, who'd again urged him to call.

When Angela didn't immediately respond, Chet quickly added, "I hope I'm not annoying you. I was reassured that wouldn't be the case. She said there was always a small risk but that in all likelihood you'd be flattered. When I told her I had given you my cell number, she laughed and said you wouldn't call."

"It sounds to me that your colleague is socially astute."

"I'm counting on it," Chet said. "Anyway, I'm calling for two reasons: The first is to apologize for my earlier insensitive attempt at humor."

"Thank you, but an apology is not necessary. Actually, I overreacted because I am a bit desperate and preoccupied. Your apology is accepted. What's the second reason for your call?"

"I thought I'd ask you out to dinner again. I promise it will be the last time, but you have to eat, and perhaps a break from your routine will give you some fresh insight to where you can find the capital you need."

"Your persistence is indeed flattering," Angela said with a chuckle. "But I really am wickedly busy. But I appreciate the call, especially since I imagine as a doctor you still have a waiting room full of patients."

"That might be true," Chet said, slipping into his defensive humor, "but they are all dead."

"Really?" Angela questioned. She assumed there was humor involved but didn't get it. "I don't understand."

"I'm a medical examiner," Chet answered. "It was supposed to be funny. Actually, I'm free anytime this evening, starting now. What I have left to do, I could always come back later to finish."

"Do you work here in Manhattan?"

"I do. I've been here for twelve years. I know it's not as sexy as being a brain surgeon, but in my book it's intellectually more challenging. Every day we learn something and see something we've never seen before. Neurosurgeons pretty much do the same thing every day. Truthfully, doing craniotomies day in and day out would drive me batty. I suppose the company you work for employs clinical pathologists. . . ." Chet trailed off, unsure how Angela was responding to his line of work. In his experience, women were either fascinated or turned off. There was little middle ground. Unfortunately, Angela didn't respond to his last sentence, which was purposefully a half question. For a moment there was a pause, which progressively made Chet uncomfortable. He worried he'd made a faux pas by bringing up his medical specialty.

"Are you there, Angela?" Chet questioned.

"Yes, I'm here," Angela responded. "So you work at the OCME under Dr. Harold Bingham?"

"That's correct. Do you know him?"

"To a degree. Do you also work with a Dr. Laurie Montgomery?"

"I do. In fact, she just left my office. It's funny you should ask. She happens also to be my social adviser."

"You know, I just remembered something," Angela said to change the subject. "Just a few minutes before you called, I'd had a call from my daughter. She called from her best friend's house. She'd been invited to stay for dinner and was asking if she could. I said yes."

"Does that mean that you might be rethinking your evening plans?" Chet questioned, trying not to get his hopes up.

"It does," Angela said. "Maybe you are right about a change in routine, and you are certainly right about the need to eat. Today I only managed a sandwich on the run."

"Does that mean you'll join me for dinner?"

"Why not," Angela said, as a declarative statement, not as a question.

For the next few minutes, they discussed a time and place. At Angela's suggestion, they decided on the San Pietro on 54th Street between Madison and Fifth. Chet had never heard of it, but Angela told him it was one of those best-kept New York secrets. She said she'd make a reservation for seven-fifteen, and Chet agreed with alacrity.

8
APRIL 3, 2007
4:05 P.M.

It had not been a good day for Ramona Torres, age thirty-seven, mother of three children ranging in age from five to eleven. Her husband had awakened her at the first blush of dawn in order to drive her to the Angels Cosmetic Surgery and Eye Hospital for her surgery. It was so early that she had to wake the children to say good-bye. Once at the hospital, he had had to drop her off at the posh entrance, where the doorman had relieved her of her overnight bag. She had waved as he pulled away to return home to the Bronx and see that the children had their breakfast before school. She really would have preferred that he'd come in with her to lend moral support.

Ramona had always had a general fear of hospitals, but her fears had been significantly magnified during her last hospitalization by the difficult delivery of her youngest child. The rocky, postpartum course during which she had almost died had required emergency surgery. Although it had been carefully explained to her after the fact that the venous embolism she'd suffered had not been anyone's fault and that everything had been done to avoid such a complication, Ramona had still blamed the hospital. Even Ramona's husband, an attorney, had been unable to change her opinion, such that when Ramona had entered the hospital that morning, her heart had been beating faster than usual and the perspiration dotting her forehead had not been from being too warm.

As Ramona had changed out of her clothes and donned the traditional hospital garb in the same-day-surgery area, she had been tense and had tried to hide her trembling from the nurses and nurse's aides. If someone had asked her what she was afraid of, she wouldn't have been able to tell them, although suffering another venous embolism would have been high on the list. Also on the list was undergoing anesthesia. The idea of another person, no matter how well trained, being in control of whether she lived or died was enormously unsettling. Mistakes happened, and Ramona did not want to be another mistake. As a medical secretary, she had had more than enough knowledge of all that could go wrong.

With such a mind-set, Ramona had almost changed her mind about having the surgery while she had waited on the gurney in the admitting area. But then her vanity had intervened. With her last child, she'd experienced a significant weight gain, which had never melted away as it was supposed to; in fact, it had substantially worsened to the point that Ramona herself admitted she was obese. Although Ricardo, her husband, had never said anything about being disenchanted, she knew he didn't like it. She didn't like it herself, especially when her oldest, Javier, said it embarrassed him. Since Ramona had struggled to restrict her caloric intake, she had reluctantly decided on liposuction, which a friend had had with great success. Hoping for a similar result, Ramona had visited her friend's plastic surgeon, and she'd been scheduled.

After a three-and-a-half-hour operation, Ramona had awakened vomiting, and as unpleasant as that had been, things got progressively worse. The only high point had been a quick visit with Ricardo, who'd taken time off from the office to visit when Ramona had been moved from the post-anesthesia unit to her luxurious room. He'd not been able to stay long, which Ramona did not regret because she'd been remarkably uncomfortable. She'd not been able to find a position that didn't aggravate her pain, and her painkillers, which she could self-administer, seemed to have no discernable effect whatsoever.

Then, a half-hour after Ricardo left, she'd suffered a shaking chill, the likes of which she'd never experienced. It started in the core of her body and then spread out to the very tips of her fingers. Alarmed at such a development and with her teeth chattering, she'd immediately called the nurse, who had responded quickly with a blanket. The nurse also had taken Ramona's temperature and recorded it as 101.8 degrees, a respectable fever.

"It's not uncommon," the nurse had said. "With an extensive liposuction like yours, it's as if you have a very large wound, even when all you can see are the small incisions on your skin."

Ramona had been content with that explanation until the moment when more disturbing symptoms emerged. All at once, she was aware of a vague feeling of pressure in her chest, an urge to cough, and a sense that she couldn't quite get a full breath of air. If Ramona had not had the experience with venous embolism after her last delivery, she might not have panicked as she did. She reached for her call button and pressed it repeatedly.

"Mrs. Torres, you only have to ring once," the nurse admonished, as she quickly came into the room and arrived at Ramona's bedside.

Ramona explained her symptoms and her fear of having a pulmonary embolism. The nurse rapidly retook her temperature, which had climbed only a tenth of a degree, and retook her blood pressure, which was mildly lower.

"Am I having an embolism?" Ramona anxiously asked.

"I don't think so," the nurse said. "But I'm going to call your surgeon just the same."

At that moment Ramona coughed, which she had been trying to avoid, because any movement aggravated the postoperative pain. When she coughed and expectorated into a tissue, she saw something that alarmed her even more. It alarmed the nurse as well. The considerable mucus was bloody through and through, and not merely streaked.

9
APRIL 3, 2007
4:15 P.M.

It had been one of those frustrating days for Detective Lieutenant Lou Soldano. The only positive thing that had happened was learning from Jack that his detective sergeant friend's daughter was apparently off the hook as far as being charged for murder, and likewise for the boyfriend in the other case. But in the case Lou was really into, he'd gotten nowhere. He still had no idea who the Asian floater was, even after a lot of effort. He didn't even know for sure whether the guy was American.

After his powwow with Freddie Capuso, where he learned that the victim was whacked because he was about to rat about something, Lou had driven back to headquarters, where he sought out Sergeant Detective Ronnie Madden in Organized Crime. Ronnie had not heard about the hit, so he couldn't add anything. Instead, he'd given Lou some background on Louie Barbera, including the fact that as a cover he ran a restaurant in Elmhurst called the Venetian. Ronnie confirmed Freddie's opinion that relations between the Lucia and Vaccarro organizations were hardly copacetic, but a turf war was not imminent.

Lou then went to Missing Persons to see if they had made any headway identifying the victim. They hadn't, and Lou got the impression they were waiting for a missing-person report to come in and do their work for them. Lou tried to suggest that it might be important to be a bit more proactive, but it got him nowhere.

Lou had even forced himself to go over to the FBI, which he was generally loath to do. He hated the way they acted superior, as if they thought of themselves as the aristocrats and the PD as a bunch of ignorant commoners. In contrast to Missing Persons, they had yet to be alerted about the case. Lou tried his best to do that, but they said they'd prefer to hear about it through official channels, meaning "Leave us alone because we're too busy to look into your particular lowbrow pet project."

At this point Lou got the idea of going back out to Queens to visit Louie Barbera. As he drove over the Queensboro Bridge, he admitted to himself that he'd become fixated on a single case to the detriment of all the others he had pending, but it was his personality to do so. Whenever he got involved in a task which he thought would be easy but wasn't, he took it personally. Such was the case in the current situation, and as he got off the bridge and into Queens, he was doggedly committed to finding out the who, the why, and the wherefore of the Asian floater, come what may.

Lou found the Venetian on Elmhurst Avenue without difficulty. It was part of a relatively new strip mall sandwiched between Fred's DVDs and Gene's liquor store. Lou parked in the small lot in front of the strip. Two cars down was the traditional black Cadillac, which made Lou smile. The midlevel wiseguys made an attempt to be nondescript so as not to stand out, and then they all drove the same vehicle. It didn't make sense, although in this particular instance, it gave Lou the encouragement that Louie Barbera was available.

The first thing Lou noticed when he walked in were all the black velvet paintings of Venice. He'd recalled such paintings in Italian restaurants when he was growing up but hadn't seen any for some time. He also noticed that all the tables had red-and-white checked tablecloths, which was also a throwback. The only things the Venetian lacked were the old Chianti bottles with candles and several years' worth of drippings clinging to the sides.

"We're closed," a voice said out of the gloom. There was very low-level illumination and, coming in from the sunshine, Lou's eyes had to adjust. When they did, he could make out five men playing cards at a round table. Espresso cups dotted its surface. Ashtrays were overflowing.

"I assumed so," Lou said. "I'm looking for Louie Barbera. I was told I could find him here."

For a moment, all five people sat like statues. Finally, one of them who was directly facing Lou said, "Who are you?"

"Detective Lieutenant Lou Soldano of the NYPD. I'm an old friend of Paulie Cerino." Lou thought he saw the group stiffen at his announcement, but it could have been his imagination.

"I never heard of him," the same man said.

"Well, no matter," Lou said. "Are you Louie Barbera?"

"I might be."

"I'd appreciate a moment of your time."

With merely a nod from Louie, the four men seated with him stood up. Two went to the deserted bar. The other two moved over to the wall opposite the bar. Everyone had taken their playing cards with them. Louie gestured toward the seat directly opposite him, and Lou sat down.

"I'm sorry to interrupt your game," Lou said, eyeing the man's ordinary clothes and overweight body. He obviously wasn't at the same level as Vinnie Dominick.

"No matter. Why are you looking for Louie Barbera?"

"I want to ask him a question."

"Like what?"

"Like whether there's any more than the usual animosity between the Lucia people and the Vaccarro people."

"And why do you want to know?"

"There's a rumor on the street that there'd been a professional hit last night. Now, when something like that goes down, and the victim happens to be associated with one of the two families, hostile feelings can boil over, resulting in a major blowup. We at the NYPD don't mind if you professionals bump each other off, but we get aggravated when innocent people get hurt. Then we'd have to come out here and clean things up. Am I making sense?"

"You're making sense," Louie conceded. "But I don't know anything about any hit."

"Are you sure? I mean, I have your best interests in mind. It's always better to keep the peace for your real line of work and for mine, too."

"I'm a restaurateur. What do you mean my 'real line of work'?"

Lou thought for a minute. He was tempted to tell the bozo sitting in front of him that an identity game was a pitiful waste of time, but he thought better of it. He coughed into his closed fist and then said, "Then let me put it this way: Are you sure all your waiters, busboys, and kitchen help are going to show up today, particularly those of Asian extraction?"

Louie leaned back and called over to the men lounging on the bar stools, "Hey, Carlo, has the whole staff checked in today?"

"Everybody's accounted for," Carlo said.

"There you go, Lieutenant," Louie said.

Lou stood up and took out one of his business cards. He placed it on the table. "In case you suddenly hear something about the hit, give me a call." He then headed for the door. A few paces away, he turned back into the room. "I'd also heard a rumor that Paulie Cerino is getting out on parole. Give him my best; we go way back."

"I'll do that," Louie said.

As soon as the door closed, the four hoodlums returned to the table, taking the same seats they had vacated earlier. Carlo Paparo was seated directly to Louie's right. He was a muscular man with large ears and a pug nose. He wore a black turtleneck under a gray silk sports jacket and black slacks.

"Did you know that clown?" Carlo asked.

"I'd heard of him from Cerino, but I'd never met him. Paulie hated him so much he loved him. Apparently, they'd butted heads for so long they'd come to respect each other."

"He's got balls just showing up like this. None of the cops in Jersey would do such a thing without a partner and backup SWAT team waiting outside."

Louie had been recruited from Bayonne, New Jersey, to fill in as boss for the Vaccarro Queens operation. In Bayonne, he'd run a similar but smaller enterprise. When he'd made the transition, he'd brought over his most trusted underlings, including Carlo Paparo, who had been with him the longest, Brennan Monaghan, Arthur MacEwan, and Ted Polowski. Tuesday and Thursday afternoons they played penny ante, unless there was something big going down.

"Have any of you guys heard anything about Vinnie Dominick and his pack of assholes knocking anybody off?"

Everybody shook his head.

"I think we ought to check it out," Louie said. "The detective is right. We don't want any trouble with the police nosing around just when we're about to jack up operations, especially cops from downtown. Most of the local guys we can handle, but even that might change if the big boys come causing trouble."

"How do you propose to check it out?"

"We could contact that skinny Freddie Capuso," Brennan suggested. "It would cost a few bucks, but he might know who got bumped off."

"He'll know shit," Carlo said. "Half the time we used him, it turned out he gave us crap. He's just a damn gofer."

"I think we should tail Franco Ponti for a few days," Louie said. "If Vinnie needs somebody whacked, he always uses Franco, and if there's to be more killing, I'd like to know sooner rather than later who's getting bumped off. The Lucias are causing enough trouble in general. I don't want them ruining our expansion plans."

"It'll be easy to follow Franco with that ancient hog he drives around," Arthur MacEwan said, giving everybody a good laugh. Franco's car was famous in the neighborhood, with its black-and-white foam dice and a picture of him and his then girlfriend,

Maria Provolone, at the senior prom hanging from his rearview mirror.

"It's the tail fins that crack me up," Ted Polowski said. "What's it from, the nineteen fifties?"

"You know, I'm liking this idea of tailing Ponti better and better," Louie said, while thinking over his own suggestion. "Remember last year when we were wracking our brains about how they get their drugs into the city and never figured it out."

"We never thought of tailing Ponti!" Carlo said, knocking his forehead with the heel of his hand. "How come we were so stupid? I mean, we tried everything else."

"Maybe this little episode will have an unexpected payoff," Louie said, not knowing how prophetic his comment would turn out to be.

"When should we start?" Carlo asked.

"My mother, God rest her soul, always said, 'Don't put off until tomorrow what you can do today' . . ."

"Yeah, yeah," Carlo said. "Because today is yesterday's tomorrow."

Brennan, Arthur, and Ted smiled wanly. Like a lot of Louie's pet sayings, they'd heard both of the proverbs one too many times.

"Time is money," Louie said, raising his eyebrows teasingly. He knew his minions found his adages sappy.

"All right!" Carlo said. "We'll have to do this in shifts. I'll start. Who wants to come along?"

"I'll come," Brennan said.

"Keep me posted," Louie said.

10
APRIL 3, 2007
4:45 P.M.

Armed with yet another MRSA case from Chet, Laurie retreated to her office, still marveling that a series of infections were occurring despite the fact that it was impossible for them to be doing so, and it made her wish she'd studied more epidemiology during her training. Silently, she reiterated to herself the primary reason it couldn't be occurring. First off, the patients were all seemingly healthy, and healthy people usually could deal with a small number of staph being introduced into their nose or mouth. Ergo, for primary pneumonia to occur, there would have had to have been a large enough dose of staph introduced in a relatively short time to overcome the patients' natural defenses. But as Laurie had learned that very day, the HVAC systems of the Angels Healthcare hospitals were designed so that such a scenario could not happen. Above and beyond the fact that staph cannot be aerosolized, it was impossible for there to be a sudden surge of airborne bacteria in a room whose air intake was through a HEPA filter, whose air was changed every six minutes, and whose occupants were tested clean for MRSA, and who were all wearing surgical masks.

From an epidemiological and scientific perspective, Laurie became progressively concerned that the MRSA problem in the Angels hospitals could not be caused naturally, and that understanding led her to the more unsettling notion that the outbreak had to be deliberate. Then suddenly Laurie had an idea. There was one person in the OR who could conceivably manage to cause the pneumonias, and that was the person giving the anesthesia. With control of the airway and often ignored, the anesthetist or the anesthesiologist could conceivably manage in some devilish fashion to introduce secretly enough viable staph deep into the respiratory tree to cause the fatal pneumonia.

With a sense of urgency, Laurie snapped up her matrix and was immediately relieved. The matrix was at an early stage, but even with the small number of entries she had, she saw that there were different anesthetists and different anesthesiologists. But then she had another thought. What if it wasn't a single person but rather a cabal of anesthetists or anesthesiologists who were involved in some sort of vicious contract dispute with Angels Healthcare? But the second she'd conceived the conspiracy theory, she dismissed it as the product of how desperate she was to find an explanation. She even mocked herself for entertaining such a ridiculous, paranoid hypothesis, and she immediately vowed not to confess to anyone, especially Jack, that she had thought of such a thing. And after she'd returned to rationality, she realized the hypothetical bad guys couldn't be anesthetists or anesthesiologists because a number of the cases were not primary necrotizing pneumonia but rather fulminant surgical-site infections resulting in toxic shock syndrome.

Having run out of ideas, Laurie went back to expanding her matrix and filling in the blanks. When she'd first walked into her office, there was a note from Cheryl stuck on her monitor screen that indicated that most of the records Laurie had requested from the various Angels hospitals were in her e-mail inbox and that the rest should arrive the following day. Laurie had also found the packages sent from the ME offices in Brooklyn and Queens containing the files of their six cases and, in a separate envelope, the case files of the two missing cases of Besserman and Southgate, which had not been in their office when Laurie had gotten the four others.

Laurie went into her e-mail and scrolled through all the hospital records Cheryl had amassed for her. One by one, she queued them up and sent them to the printer down in administration. For ease of reading, she wanted hard copies. Next, she organized the cases by hospital. Considering case files and hospital records, she had a lot of information, which made her wonder if she should computerize her matrix. Although the idea had merit, she decided to stick with the simple legal-pad variety for the time being.

When she thought she'd allowed enough time to pass she made a rapid trip down to the computer room and retrieved the stack of printed hospital records.

On the way back up in the elevator, she noticed it was nearing five, and wondered if and when Jack would be returning. As she got out on the fourth floor to stop in and see Agnes in the microbiology lab, she pulled out her cell phone to make sure it was turned on in case Jack called. It was conceivable he might be closer to home than to the OCME on his field trip, as Chet had called it, and head home afterward rather than return to the office.

"We're making headway," Agnes said. Laurie had caught her in the process of putting on her coat to go home. It had been another of her normal ten-hour days. Agnes went over everything she had done, which included reaffirming that all the cases in Laurie's series were definitely methicillin-resistant staphylococcus aureus. She then ticked off where she had sent David Jeffries's samples for more definitive subtyping: the state reference lab, the CDC, and Ted Lynch in the OCME DNA lab. She advised Laurie that the CDC would be more efficient than the state reference lab and that Laurie could expect to hear from them in two to three days — four, tops.

Agnes's comment about the CDC reminded Laurie that she had meant to call Dr. Ralph Percy about Chet's case, but a glance at her watch suggested she might be too late. After quickly thanking Agnes for everything she was doing, Laurie dashed up a flight to save time. Since she'd not gotten the number from Chet, she had to call directory assistance for the main CDC switchboard. When the CDC operator connected her to the doctor's line, Laurie got voice mail.

"Damn!" she murmured before Dr.

Percy's outgoing message had terminated. The doctor had already left for the day, and Laurie was irritated at herself for not having called the moment she'd returned from Chet's. After the beep, Laurie gave her name, her direct-dial number, the patient's name, and the fact that she was interested in the MRSA typing he'd done for Dr. Chet McGovern. Then, as an afterthought, she mentioned she was a medical examiner and a colleague of Dr. McGovern.

"What's going on?" Riva asked. She'd returned to the office while Laurie had retrieved her printed documents and had overheard Laurie's voice-mail message.

"It's been one busy day," Laurie complained. "I wanted to talk to someone at the CDC, but he's left for the day."

"There's always tomorrow," Riva said.

"I hope you are not trying to aggravate me," Laurie said. Such a patronizing comment reminded Laurie of her mother.

"Oh, no. If anything, I was trying to calm you down. You look frazzled. I know you've been preoccupied most of the day."

"That's an understatement," Laurie said. She then told Riva what she'd been up to all day and why she wanted to talk with the doctor from the CDC.

"What about the woman at the CDC I

dealt with?" Riva suggested. "Did you call her?"

"I did. She was helpful and said she'd get back to me."

"Why not try her? I'm certain she'd have access to Chet's case."

"Good idea," Laurie said. She had Silvia Salerno's number on a Post-it stuck to the edge of her monitor. As the direct-dial connection went through, she glanced at her watch. It was now significantly after five. Once again, she got voice mail. On this occasion, she didn't leave a message since the woman had already agreed to call her back. Laurie hung up the phone and shook her head.

"Two for two!" Riva said lightly. "They must have a curfew at the CDC!"

Laurie laughed. Riva's comment about the world-renowned CDC amused her, as unlikely as it was, and laughing for possibly the first time all day made her realize how tense she was.

Riva stood up and took her coat from behind the door. "I think I will follow the CDC's example and head home. Working with Bingham this morning on the police custody case exhausted me."

"Oh, yeah!" Laurie said. "As preoccupied as I've been, I forgot to ask you what the

317

outcome was."

"Not good for the police or the city," Riva said, "although it could turn out to be a windfall for the family. The hyoid bone was fractured in several places, so there was obviously excessive force."

"The only good part is that Bingham will take over the inevitable political and legal fallout."

"That's true," Riva said. "We pathologists can only say it was a homicide. Whether justified will be up to a jury."

With her coat on, Riva said good-bye, but before she left Laurie asked, "If there are any more MRSA cases over the next week while you're assigning cases, would you give them to me?"

"I certainly will," Riva said before leaving.

Laurie turned back to her desk with the three stacks of case files from the three Angels Healthcare hospitals and the stack of printed hospital records. Over the next three minutes, she combined the case files with their hospital records. There were still a few hospital records missing, as Cheryl had indicated.

Putting her matrix in front of her, Laurie picked up David Jeffries's hospital record and began reading. As she read, she filled in the boxes that she'd not been able to do without the hospital record. Since she still felt the operating room had to be where he was infected, she read through the anesthesia record, paying attention to the detail. When she did so she came up with some additional categories that she had not thought of earlier, namely the OR room number, how long the operation took, duration of time spent in the PACU, and which drugs were given in the PACU. Reading through the nurses' notes, she found the names of the scrub nurse and the circulating nurse. With a ruler, she made more vertical lines to create boxes for this additional information.

When she finished with David Jeffries's hospital record, she reached for another. It happened to be one of Paul Plodget's patients: a forty-eight-year-old man named Gordon Stanek. Like Jeffries, he was a patient of Angels Orthopedic Hospital. And as she'd done with Jeffries, she used the hospital record to fill in the boxes of her matrix. As she'd noticed earlier with Riva's two cases, the anesthesiologists were different. Unsurprisingly, she recorded that the other people involved with the patient, including the surgeon and the nurses, were also different, as was the operating room itself. Even the anesthesia was different. Although both patients had general anesthesia, the agents employed were different. There was also a difference in the way the anesthesia was administered. Jeffries had had an endotracheal tube, while Stanek had had a laryngeal mask airway.

Laurie sat back and glanced first at her matrix, then at all the case files and hospital records. It was going to be a long process. In the end, what she hoped to find was some kind of commonality they all shared.

Laurie was about to pick up another hospital record when a rhythmic thumping coming from the hallway caught her attention. It was low in pitch and distant, and had the building not been as quiet as it was, since it was after five, Laurie might not have heard it. Straightening up in her chair, Laurie cocked her head to try to hear better. Although the beat stayed the same, it was becoming progressively louder. It was as if someone was beating on the floor with a rubber mallet and coming closer and closer.

Irrational fear spread through Laurie like a jolt of electricity. The thought of jumping up and slamming and locking her door flashed through her mind, yet she was frozen in place.

"Hey, sweetie," Jack said as he appeared in the doorway and proceeded into Laurie's office on his crutches. Leaning over, he gave her forehead a kiss. "You'll never guess what

I've been up to." He leaned his crutches up against Riva's file cabinet and sat down in her chair. "I've been having a ball," he added and started to explain but then stopped in mid-sentence when he looked closer at Laurie's expression. He leaned forward and waved his hand in front of her face. "Hey! Hello! Anybody home?"

Laurie batted his hand away. "As quiet as it is around here, you and your crutches scared me," she said, not sure for the moment if she was more relieved or miffed.

"How did I do that?" Jack asked with confusion.

"Because . . ." Laurie started to say, but then realized with some embarrassment how ridiculous it was for her to have been frightened by the sound of Jack's crutches on the corridor's vinyl floor. She guessed it was a symptom of how overwrought she was.

"I'm sorry," Jack said.

Laurie reached out and gave his knee a pat. "You don't have to apologize. If anybody is to blame, I am. I've had one hell of a day."

"No matter," Jack said, regaining the excitement with which he had arrived. "I wanted to tell you what I've been doing for the last couple of hours."

"I'd like to hear," Laurie said. "But you see all these case files and these printouts of hospital records on my desk?"

"Of course I see them," Jack interrupted. "It's hard to see your desk underneath them. But first let me tell you about the case you passed up."

"I think we should talk about these cases on my desk," Laurie said.

"In a minute!" Jack snapped. Then, in a more normal tone, he said, "God, you've got such a one-track mind."

You're the one to talk about a one-track mind, Laurie thought but did not say. Sometimes Jack could be a lesson in patience control.

"I'm the visitor. I'm the one who came to you, so my story goes first. Okay?"

"Fine," Laurie intoned in frustration.

"Anyway, thanks for passing up the Rodriguez case."

"You're welcome," Laurie said insincerely.

"The cause of death was straightforward, as I'm sure you assumed it would be. I mean, the victim, a construction worker, fell ten stories onto concrete from a building under construction."

"Can you get to the point!" Laurie complained.

Jack stared at Laurie for a beat. "You're in a crummy mood."

"No, I'm just a little impatient to talk

about something which, with due respect, I think is more important."

"Okay, okay," Jack said. "So as not to hear about this for a week, tell your story!"

"No, I agreed for you to talk first, so finish! Just pick up the pace."

Jack smiled wryly before continuing. "The internal exam showed all sorts of blunt-trauma injury, including detached heart, ruptured liver, and bilateral compound fractures of the femurs. But I knew that wasn't going to help with the manner of death, so I visited the scene."

"I hope you didn't cause your own *scene,*" Laurie quipped. "Because I did a site visit myself and inadvertently caused a *scene,* which has Bingham spitting bullets."

"Not diplomatic me!" Jack said. "Actually, everyone had a ball. What I did was fill a plastic body bag with sand courtesy of the contractor so that it was the same weight as the victim. Then, up on the tenth floor . . ."

"I hope you didn't climb ten stories on your injured knee," Laurie interjected.

"No!" Jack said as it if was totally out of the question. "They took me up in the construction elevator. Up there, I checked where the guy was working when he fell. Ironically enough, he was putting up temporary guardrails. With a guy down on the ground with a stopwatch, we first rolled the bag off the ledge like what would happen if Mr. Rodriguez had accidentally fallen. And do you know how far away from the building the bag ended up?"

"I can't imagine."

"Six feet, and it took two and a half seconds. When we heaved the body bag off as if he were pushed or leaped on his own accord, guess where it landed in two-point-six seconds?"

"Please, just tell me your story?"

"Twenty-one feet on the nose. Pretty cool, huh? It proves it wasn't an accident."

"What if he stood at the edge of the building, closed his eyes, and took a baby step?"

"Wouldn't happen. He wouldn't want to hurt himself by hitting the building on the way down."

"You're sure of that?"

"I am. I thought about it myself once, a few months after the plane crash."

"Oh," Laurie merely said. It was an area she didn't want to revisit at the moment. Jack still struggled with depression on occasion.

"I'm going to sign the case out as suicide. Do you know why?"

"I can't guess," Laurie said. "Why?" Despite her initial pique, she was interested.

"Why not homicide? He could have been pushed or thrown."

"Because on external exam, he had healed scars across both wrists. He'd attempted suicide before. This time, he used a more efficacious and guaranteed method."

"Very interesting," Laurie said with questionable sincerity. "Now, can I speak?"

"Of course," Jack responded. "But I think I know what you are going to say."

"Do you?" Laurie questioned, with a touch of superciliousness.

"You are going to tell me by the looks of all these case files that there has been a surge at Angels Orthopedic of MRSA postoperative infections, and that I have to cancel my surgery or at least reschedule it for some indeterminate later date. Am I close?"

"You are right on the nose," Laurie said, "but, smarty pants, I think you should hear the details."

"Can't we do it over a bite to eat somewhere along Columbus Avenue?"

"I want to tell you now," Laurie insisted. "These MRSA cases are truly a mystery. In my opinion, what is happening actually cannot be happening, either naturally or intentionally."

Jack's eyebrows raised when Laurie mentioned the idea that the MRSA was being spread intentionally. He asked her if she truly thought it was possible. When she said yes, he didn't dismiss the idea out of hand. Laurie had a track record of ferreting out several equally bizarre situations some years earlier that everyone else had dismissed.

"Okay. Let's hear the unexpurgated version, and I promise not to interrupt."

First, Laurie handed over her unfinished matrix and then went on to tell Jack everything she did that day, and everything she'd learned and everything that was pending. She finished up with: "There shouldn't even be a discussion whether or not you should proceed with your operation. You shouldn't, plain and simple."

"Well, I'm sorry that Blowhard Bingham gave you a hard time. I think your visit to the Angels Orthopedic Hospital should be a source of commendation, certainly not the opposite. I'm intrigued myself by all you have told me, except for your final conclusion. Now, don't argue with me!"

Laurie had tried to complain.

"I let you speak without interruption, so let me have the same courtesy. I have been proactive today anticipating your attempting to change my mind, so I've learned some things as well. First off, these MRSA infections in your series are not technically nosocomial, since they are not within the time period of forty-eight hours."

"That's true," Laurie agreed, "but that definition is more for statistical purposes."

"The forty-eight-hour limit is because infections within that time very often are from organisms carried in by the patient. And that will undoubtedly turn out to be the case with your series, and my reason for believing that is twofold: One is because of what you have learned in your investigation — namely, that the contamination cannot be occurring naturally or by intention, ergo, it is being brought in by the patients; secondly, the cases all seem to be community-acquired MRSA, which by definition comes from the community, or in other words from outside the hospital."

"Can I say something now?" Laurie questioned.

"If you must."

"The CA-MRSA, or community-acquired, has definitely shown up as a problem in hospitals, and that's been over a number of years at an ever-increasing rate."

"That may be so, but I believe the fact that the bug is the CA-MRSA exclusively lends more credence to my theory. But be that as it may, I also called Dr. Wendell Anderson's office and spoke to his scheduling nurse.

Thinking of you, I asked her whether it would be possible, if I put off the surgery, to again be scheduled at the seven-thirty slot. She said it would be up to the doctor, because he always starts at eight-thirty or nine and that he was doing me a favor by coming in early on Thursday."

"Well then let's delay it," Laurie said.

"I don't want to delay it. That's the point. Yet I wanted to ask in case I changed my mind, but I didn't."

"Why not?" Laurie demanded with obvious irritation at Jack's intransigence.

"Because the sooner it gets done," Jack growled, "the sooner I'll be on the bike and on the b-ball court."

"Jesus Christ!" Laurie exclaimed, throwing up her hands in frustration. "How can you be so foolishly stubborn?"

"I'll tell you how," Jack snapped back. "Before I hung up with Anderson's secretary, I asked her to have Anderson call me back, which he did within the hour. I put the questions to him very directly. First, I asked him if he knew about the MRSA in the Angels hospitals. He said he did, and he admitted there was a significant mystery to it, because he told me all the infection-control mechanisms that the hospital had instituted at great expense. He said infections had de-

328

creased but were still occurring at a much-reduced rate. He also told me that he had himself instituted some control measures above and beyond what the hospital was doing."

"What were they?"

"On his own cases he insists the anesthesiologist give supplemental oxygen, maintain the patient's body temperature, and even monitor and maintain glucose levels."

"Has he had any recent postoperative infection?" Laurie asked incisively.

"I'm glad you asked that question," Jack said smugly. "Although I know it's an egotistical sore point with surgeons, I asked him directly if he had. Surprisingly enough, he said he's only had three postoperative infections in all his career, and all three had been open compound fracture repairs, meaning the cases were dirty to begin with. Also, all three were at University Hospital, not Angels Orthopedic."

"So he's not had an MRSA case."

"Well, I don't know what the bacteria was involving his cases at University, but the point is, he's had no infection problem at Angels."

Laurie stared off. She could sense she was losing the argument.

"I even went a step further," Jack said. "I

asked him from one doctor to another if he would go ahead and have the surgery as scheduled given the timing in relation to my injury and the fact that Angels is struggling with an MRSA problem." Jack paused for maximum impact.

"And?" Laurie was forced to say. She wanted to know.

"He said in a heartbeat he would do it. And furthermore, he said he wouldn't operate at Angels if he didn't feel that confident. He said the only thing he would personally do was use an antibiotic soap for several days before the procedure. When I admitted to already doing that, he said I'd be fine. He also said that when I go in for my pre-op blood-work tomorrow, that he would arrange that I be screened for MRSA, and that if I turned out to be a carrier, he would insist I be treated and that the operation would be delayed. The last thing he said was that he'd see me Thursday morning at seven-thirty a.m., and I'd be back on my bike in three months and playing b-ball in six."

Laurie looked over at her pile of cases and hospital records. She felt a mixture of frustration, anger, and despondency. Jack had certainly made some cogent points, especially talking directly to his surgeon, who was highly regarded and rather famous for operating on celebrity athletes. Yet still, Laurie could not help but feel it was a wrong decision to proceed with the surgery under the circumstances. It would be okay if it were an emergency, but as elective surgery, it still seemed crazy to her.

"Come on!" Jack said, standing up and touching her shoulder in the process.

As if she were in molasses, Laurie got to her feet.

Jack handed her matrix back to her. "I still think you should proceed with investigating this series. There has to be an explanation, and I for one would certainly like to hear it."

Laurie nodded, took the matrix, and tossed it casually onto the rest of the debris on her desk.

Jack wrapped his arms about her and hugged her. "Thanks for caring," he said.

Laurie hugged back.

"I love you," Jack said.

"I love you, too." Laurie said.

11
APRIL 3, 2007
5:25 P.M.

"So, how are we going to work this?" Angelo asked Franco.

He and Franco were in Franco's car, having pulled over to the left side of Fifth Avenue between 56th and 57th streets. There was a row of massive concrete urns sitting on the sidewalk, presumably for protection of the Trump Tower from wayward vehicles. The commercial entrance to the building was behind them, forcing one of them at any given time to be looking back over his shoulder to keep the area under observation.

"That's a good question," Franco answered. "This isn't the easiest assignment I've ever had. Where's that description again?"

Angelo handed over the sheet of paper.

"Your turn to watch the entrance," Franco said. Facing forward, he quickly reread the description. "I guess we will have to rely on the hair. I can't even imagine what blond with lime-green highlights will look like. It sounds almost scary."

"I think the size issue will tip us off, at least initially," Angelo said. It was easier for him to look back while sitting in the front passenger seat. "It's hard to see the hair color with the angle of the sun, and there's a lot more people coming out. I guess it's quitting time."

"If we don't see her soon, I'm going to start worrying we've missed her."

"That won't bother me," Angelo said. "I have a nagging feeling about this hit."

"Oh, come on, you pessimist," Franco said. "Enjoy the challenge of it. By the way, where are the date-rape pills and the gas you got from old Doc Trevino?"

"The pills are in my pocket, and the ethylene is on the floor of the backseat along with the plastic bags. That stuff is unbelievable how fast it works. Two seconds, the person is out."

"Well, we sure can't use the gas here in broad daylight. Well, maybe it isn't so broad anymore."

"Of course not, but it might come in handy if she kicks up a fuss once we get her in the car. I don't want to be forced to shoot her in the car."

"Hell, no," Franco said. "Not on my upholstery. Let me see the pills."

Angelo reached into his jacket pocket and pulled out a letter-sized envelope, which he handed to Franco. Franco squeezed the ends of the envelope together and looked in at the contents. There were ten small white pills nestled in the bottom crease.

"How many of these things do you have to use?" Franco asked.

"Doc said just one. All you have to do is plop it into a cocktail, and twenty minutes later you can pop it to her."

"How come he gave us so many?"

"Beats me. Maybe he thought we could have fun with the others."

Franco tipped the envelope and poured half of the pills into his hand. Then he dropped them into his jacket pocket and handed the envelope back to Angelo. "If we use one tonight and it works, maybe I'll give it a try."

"Sounds like it would be a great evening," Angelo said teasingly. "Viagra for you and Rohypnol for your honey."

Refusing to be baited, Franco said, "I think one of us should walk down there to the entrance and get a better look at each and every one coming out. There would be less chance of missing her."

"That's not a bad idea," Angelo agreed.

"But what are we going to do when we see her? We can't strong-arm her with all these people around."

"What about your Ozone Park police badge? You've always said it works wonders."

"It does, but not always in a crowd. People are emboldened when other people are around. She could yell and scream, and there's lots of cops in the neighborhood."

"I've noticed. I'm amazed they haven't approached us to leave."

"You've spoken a bit too soon. Here comes one now."

Franco glanced back over his shoulder. A burly policeman with a strikingly large gut was heading toward them, carrying a pad of traffic tickets in his hand.

Franco looked at Angelo and back at the policeman. In ten seconds, the cop would be at the door.

"I'll jump out," Franco said. "You drive around the block!"

"Why don't I jump out?"

"Because I'm in charge," Franco said. "Make sure your cell phone is on. And most importantly, don't wreck my car."

Franco climbed out onto the sidewalk. "Good evening, officer," he said. The policeman arrived just as Franco reached full height.

"There's no parking or standing," the cop said, as he eyed Franco and then bent down to look in at Angelo.

"He's just dropping me off, officer," Franco said as he also bent down to wave good-bye to Angelo. Angelo had slid across the bench seat to be behind the wheel. Franco closed the door lovingly.

"Hey!" the officer called out suddenly as Angelo started to pull away. Angelo stopped with his heart racing. "Your seat belt!" the policeman yelled.

"Thank you, officer," Angelo said in a tense voice after putting down the window halfway.

Franco's heart had raced as well. With definite relief, he smiled at the policeman, then walked north toward the Trump Tower commercial entrance.

Amy Lucas looked over at the clock high on the wall across from her desk. With utter relief, she saw that it was finally five-thirty, her normal quitting time. The day had been a mixture of anxiety and tedium. The anxiety had been getting called into the CEO's office and being questioned about Paul. She'd never even met the CEO before, much less been called into her office. Although she suspected it would be about Paul, she wasn't entirely sure. There was always the concern about being fired, not that she'd done anything to deserve it but more because she couldn't afford to be fired. Financial need evoked a kind of paranoia, and her finances were being strained by her contribution toward keeping her mother in an assisted-living facility. Each month was a struggle to stay in the black.

Paul's absence had also been the source of anxiety. She'd been working for the man for about ten years and had moved with him from their previous job to Angels Healthcare about five years ago. When he'd not shown up by ten that morning, Amy feared something was wrong, because Paul Yang was generally very precise and methodical, like most accountants, unless he had been drinking. That was the worry. As the day wore on and he didn't appear or call, she came to believe he was on one of his binges, like he'd had before the move to Angels Healthcare, and it saddened her. Back then it had been difficult, because she'd had to make excuses for his absence on a regular basis, and even on one occasion rescue him from a fleabag motel.

After the motel incident, he'd seen the light, and overnight he became thankfully motivated to stay away from alcohol. Only

Amy knew he'd gone to AA meetings and had kept it up for years now. She'd hoped he'd stay away from alcohol for good, but now, five-thirty in the afternoon, she was certain he'd relapsed.

If it was true, as she expected it was, that he'd gone back to alcohol, she blamed the stress he'd been under regarding the stupid 8-K form and the ballyhoo about whether or not to file it. She knew he was upset about it because he had specifically told her so, but he didn't tell her why he was so agitated. Amy wasn't an accountant, and had never even gone to secretarial school. She was pretty much self-taught, although she did take appropriate courses in high school and was exceptionally good with the computer.

Sometime after she had typed the 8-K on Paul's laptop, he had called her into his office, and then, as if there was a great conspiracy afoot, gave her a USB drive, which contained the 8-K file.

"I want you to keep this," he'd whispered. "Just put it someplace safe. On a separate file is the Securities and Exchange Commission's website."

"But why?" she'd asked.

"Don't ask! Just keep it unless something happens to me."

Amy could remember looking into his

eyes. He was being so melodramatic that she'd thought he was joking with her, because he did have a sense of humor. But he apparently wasn't joking, because he dismissed her and never mentioned the USB drive again.

Now, as she was ready to leave for home, she opened her bag and took out the USB storage device and looked at it as if she expected it to communicate with her. She couldn't help but wonder if Paul's absence fulfilled his request for her to file the 8-K. When he'd given her the charge, he'd never described what he meant by "unless something happens to me." Certainly, going on a binge qualified as something happening to him, but Amy wasn't confident. She slipped the drive back into its side pocket and closed her purse. Her last thought before leaving was whether she should call his home. She'd considered doing it off and on all day but wasn't sure if she should. She'd even considered calling one of his old girlfriends, whose number she still had, but she decided not to do it since he'd had no contact with her for five years, as far as she knew. With a sigh, her indecision was such that she thought it better to do nothing than to do something that might make the situation worse. With that thought she turned off her desk lamp and left the office.

"What the hell is going on?" Carlo said with a shake of his head. He was mystified.

"I haven't the slightest idea," Brennan said.

Carlo and Brennan were in Carlo's black GMC Denali, pulled over to the right side of Fifth Avenue at Grand Army Plaza. Just to their right was the Pulitzer fountain with the statue of a naked Abundance in all her glory.

Carlo and Brennan had picked up Franco and Angelo the moment they'd emerged from the Neapolitan Restaurant. At a safe distance in Johnny's parking lot, they had joked about the two Lucia enforcers, trying to decide which one was the weirdest-looking. To them, Franco looked like a hawk with his narrow, hatchetlike nose and beady eyes, while Angelo looked like someone from a horror movie with his extensive facial scarring.

"What a pair," Carlo had commented as he'd put his sub sandwich down on the center console and put his car in gear.

Tailing the two had been easy, since Franco's car stood out from the crowd with its erect tail fins and whiter-than-white sidewall tires. The only problem spot had been getting on the Queensboro Bridge, since they had missed a traffic light, and Franco's

340

car had driven out of sight. After a short period of anxiety, they had been able to catch up to their quarry, thanks to the traffic light on the Manhattan side of the bridge. From there, they had proceeded to Fifth Avenue without a problem until Franco had suddenly pulled to the side a bit beyond the commercial entrance to the Trump Tower.

Franco's parking had been so precipitous that Carlo had had to drive by and make a right at 55th Street, and go around the block. That maneuver had also caused a bit of concern about losing them until they'd returned to Fifth Avenue and saw Franco's car still standing where it had been.

For the next thirty-five minutes, Carlo and Brennan had stayed where they were next to naked Abundance, alternately watching Franco's car with a pair of binoculars Brennan had thoughtfully brought along. They couldn't see much, just two silhouettes having an active conversation from the looks of their intermittent hand gestures. While they waited, they finished the sandwiches they'd gotten at Johnny's. Without knowing where they were going or how long it would take, they'd jumped at the chance to have some food.

The stakeout had gradually become boring until both men sat up a little straighter when the NYPD officer had appeared and closed in on the car.

"What's going down?" Carlo had questioned. Brennan had the binoculars at the time.

"I don't know. They're just talking."

"Let me see!" Carlo said. He took the binoculars from his colleague, who was lower in the organizational hierarchy. Carlo and Brennan had known each other for years from living in the same neighborhood and attending the same high school.

"Franco's walking toward us," Carlo said as he continued watching through the binoculars.

"Uh-oh," Brennan said urgently. "Angelo is driving away! What should we do?"

"Let's stick with Franco," Carlo said. "He's stopped at the Trump Tower entrance. My guess is he's waiting for someone to come out of the building."

"What about Angelo? I could get out and stick with Franco while you tail Angelo."

Carlo shook his head. "My bet is Angelo's just going around the block. Let's stick where we are. I'm starting to think they're planning on snatching someone."

"That's crazy with all these people around, not to mention the cops."

"I can't argue with you there," Carlo said,

and then quickly added, "I think he sees who he is after. He just tossed his cigarette into the gutter."

"Who is it, a man or a woman?" Brennan questioned. He eyed the binoculars and had to resist an urge to grab them away from Carlo. After all, he'd had the sense to bring them along.

"I think it must be that girl with the green coat. She's taking a cab, and he is, too. I bet he's pissed because Angelo's not in sight."

Carlo tossed the binoculars into Brennan's lap and put the Denali in gear.

"What are we going to do?" Brennan asked while searching for Franco and the girl. "God, the girl looks like she's twelve. What could Franco and Angelo be after her for?"

"It doesn't make much sense."

"Uh-oh! The girl's got a cab and is about to leave Franco high and dry. Should we try to follow her or stick with Franco?"

"We'll stick with Franco, you dope."

Brennan pulled his eyes from the binoculars and cast an angry look at Carlo. He didn't like being called a dope.

"Well, lucky for Franco. He's caught himself a cab as well. Hang on! We're off to the races."

"You must be joking," the taxi driver said,

twisting around to look at Franco sitting in the backseat. " 'Follow that cab!' That's the first time I've actually heard that outside of the movies. Are you for real, man, or is this a joke?"

"It's no joke," Franco said. "Keep that cab in sight and you got yourself a twenty-dollar tip."

The driver shrugged and turned back to drive. A twenty-dollar tip was well worth a little extra effort.

Franco bounced around in the backseat and had trouble handling his cell phone. Giving up for the moment, he struggled with the seat belt instead. Once he got that secured, he wasn't being thrown about quite as much, especially since the car had steadied to a degree once it had gotten up to speed. It was still relatively hard to dial the number, because the driver was weaving in and out of the lanes.

"Where are you?" Franco demanded the moment Angelo answered.

"I'm stuck in traffic on Sixth Avenue going north. Where are you?"

"In a cab heading south on Fifth. The bird has flown."

"Okay. As soon as I can, I'll head south."

Franco flipped his phone closed. He was irritated at himself for two reasons: He should have had some sort of a plan when the girl or woman, whichever she was, appeared. More important, he should have insisted they take Angelo's humdrum Lincoln Town Car for their evening activities instead of his babied Cadillac. The idea of Angelo wrecking his car or even denting it in New York City's rush-hour traffic made him sick.

"We're coming up on the cab in question," the driver said proudly. "Want me to pull up alongside?"

"No!" Franco said quickly. "Just stay behind."

The two taxis made good progress down Fifth Avenue, catching the lights. Franco began to wonder if Paul Yang gave them the wrong information about her living in New Jersey, of if she did, whether she was going out on the town for the evening, which would complicate things.

Franco's fears were dispelled near the New York Public Library, when Amy's taxi suddenly braked and turned right. Franco relaxed a degree, sensing they were headed toward the Port Authority Bus Terminal.

Flipping open his phone, Franco called Angelo. "Where are you?" he demanded, as he'd done previously.

"I'm just turning south on Seventh Avenue," Angelo said. "Where are you?"

"We're heading west. I'm pretty sure we're going to the bus terminal, but I'll know better once we hit Eighth Avenue."

"What are you going to do?"

"I don't know, especially not knowing if you are going to be in the area. I suppose I have to follow her into the terminal and get on the bus with her."

"Yeah, well, lucky you."

"Screw you," Franco said. He regretted not thinking faster when the cop came up to the car. He should have had Angelo get out instead.

"If I don't hear from you sooner, I'll call you when I'm at the bus station."

"Okay."

"I hope this is worth it."

"It's worth it," Franco said. "There's millions at stake."

Franco flipped his phone closed as they came to the traffic light at Eighth Avenue. As he expected, they turned right. A minute or so later, he tossed the fare plus some change and an extra twenty dollars through the opening in the Plexiglas divider and jumped out before the taxi had come to a complete stop. Amy was already entering the terminal.

As usual during rush hour, the terminal was a sea of people. Tailing Amy was easy in one respect and hard in another. The easy part was her strange hair color, which was like a neon light. The hard part was her height. If Franco didn't stay directly on her, she disappeared out of sight within seconds.

Suddenly, a problem reared its ugly head, one that Franco had failed to anticipate. Amy got into a line to purchase a ticket, but Franco had no idea where she was going. As the ticket line quickly moved forward, Franco panicked. He thought about pushing ahead and just standing to the side when she ordered her ticket so he could overhear where she was going. But he dismissed it out of hand. He didn't want to call attention to himself, because he didn't want her to recognize him later. Just another face in the crowd was not a problem, but doing something out of the ordinary right next to her was quite another story.

Franco was the fourth person behind Amy, and when it was her turn at the ticket window, he strained forward in an attempt to hear, but it was futile. As she retreated from the ticket window, she had her ticket in her hand, and she passed within several feet.

That was when Franco realized there was yet another problem. Amy was walking away, and there were three people in front of him. Panicking again, trying to keep Amy in sight, he pushed ahead, saying, "Excuse me, I'm going to miss my bus, do you mind?" Several of the people grudgingly let him pass. The third, however, stood his ground.

"I don't want to miss my bus neither, pal," the man said. His face was coated in a fine white dust, suggesting he was a plasterer or a painter.

Unaccustomed to being opposed and worried about losing Amy, Franco felt a surge of anger well up inside him. Controlling himself with some difficulty, he said, "I can't miss my bus. My wife's having a baby."

Without a word and with obvious irritation, the painter reluctantly stepped aside and motioned for Franco to go before him.

"Where you going, Dad?" the agent said, having overheard Franco's statement.

For a second, Franco froze. With everything going on, he hadn't thought about his needing a destination. Frantically, his mind tried to remember some place in New Jersey, any place, and luckily, Hackensack popped into his consciousness. He didn't know why Hackensack but was thankful nonetheless. He told the agent the name of the town, and while getting out a twenty-dollar bill, he glanced back over his shoulder. Amy was a distance away, being engulfed by a crowd at the base of an escalator. She disappeared quickly.

Franco paid, then ran for the escalator.

When he got there, he pushed ahead using the same line that had worked so well at the ticket window. Once he got to the top, he frantically searched the area and was immediately relieved to see Amy waiting in line alongside a number 166 bus with her petite face buried in a *New York Daily News.*

With a sense of relief on one hand and a new worry on the other, Franco went to the end of the line. The new problem was that his ticket wasn't for the number 166 bus.

Despite being out of breath, Franco called Angelo and found out that Angelo was just outside the bus terminal.

"I'll be on a one sixty-six bus," Franco said, trying to cover the phone with his hand. "Find out the bus's route once it gets out of the Lincoln Tunnel, because I have no idea. Then drive over to Jersey yourself. I'll keep you posted where Amy and I are, and obviously when we get off. Try to get as close as possible so when we do get off, we can end this circus."

"I'll give it my best shot. Meanwhile, you got any more pictures of Maria Provolone in this hog of yours to keep me company?"

"Up yours," Franco said and flipped his phone closed. He didn't like Angelo razzing him about Maria, his one true love, who'd been shot and killed their senior year in high school by a rival gang.

At last, the line began to move. Franco wasn't as concerned about the ticket discrepancy as he'd been about having no ticket at all, and he was proved to be right. The bored driver making his umpteenth run just took the ticket without checking it, as he did with all the passengers. Franco moved down the center aisle. He saw Amy almost immediately. She'd taken a window seat in the middle of the bus and was back into her newspaper. By coincidence, the seat next to her was vacant. For a second, he thought about sitting next to her and engaging her in conversation, but he quickly nixed the idea. On this kind of job, surprise was critical. Instead, he took an aisle seat several rows behind her.

The bus didn't leave for another fifteen minutes, making Franco wish he'd had an opportunity to grab a paper himself. Instead, he had to just sit there. At least he had the opportunity to plan the rest of the evening. It wasn't easy, because what was to happen depended on what Amy Lucas did at the other end of her bus ride. He knew worst case would be if a companion picked her up. Ultimately, that could mean he and Angelo might have to ice two people, which doubled the opportunity for trouble.

When the bus finally closed its door and pulled away from the loading platform, it had to wend its way within the terminal until exiting onto a multistory-high ramp that dove down directly into the Lincoln Tunnel. The good part was that ramp avoided the clogged city streets; the bad part was that he was going to be significantly ahead of Angelo.

Thanks to the gentle rocking, the soothing drone of the engine, and the overheated bus interior, Franco was practically asleep by the time the bus burst forth into the glory of the New Jersey twilight. Rousing himself, he asked his seatmate where the bus went. The man gave Franco a confused questioning glare before asking, "You mean the end of the line?"

"Yeah, I guess," Franco answered.

"I know it goes to Tenafly because my sister lives there. Ultimately, where it goes from there, I don't know."

"How long does it take to get to Tenafly?"

"I'd guess a little over an hour."

Franco thanked the man. He was hoping Amy wasn't going to Tenafly or beyond. The idea of spending that kind of time on the bus with fifty or so apparently depressed people smelling of wet wool was daunting. To keep himself occupied, he went back to musing about what would happen when Amy got off the bus. Somehow, he'd have to approach her and get her involved in a conversation, probably by talking to her about her boss. Since there had been nothing in the newspapers, his disappearance had gone essentially unnoticed and apparently unreported, except, of course, by the fish. Although he didn't have Angelo's police badge, he could pose as an authority, perhaps even someone from the SEC. He didn't know if the SEC had investigators like the police, but he assumed they'd have to. At least it was a plan. Giving credence to such a plan was that he and Angelo were dressed to the nines. Both appreciated elegant clothing almost to a competitive level. Both leaned toward Brioni and were that evening, as usual, decked out in their Brioni splendor. Franco couldn't help but believe that such attention to their appearance gave them an aura of credibility.

Mulling over confronting Amy made him think about calling Angelo, but he decided to wait. He didn't have anything to report, and Angelo was undoubtedly about to get into or was already inside the tunnel.

Going back to Amy again, he thought that the best thing he could do was talk her into entering a public place so they could talk more easily and wait for Angelo, and a bar

fitted that description, with the added benefit of them being able to have a drink. Reflexively Franco slipped his hand into his
pocket and reassured himself that the date-
rape pills were where he put them. The question then arose if he should try to get one in
Amy's drink before Angelo got there or after.
There was no doubt in his mind that timing
was paramount.

Glancing out the window, Franco noticed
they had left the main highway leading from
the Lincoln Tunnel and were now heading
north on city streets. Franco reached for his
cell phone.

"Where are you?"

"At the Twenty-one Club, having a nice
dinner," Angelo said sarcastically. "I'm stuck
in traffic. I'm not even into the tunnel yet."

"Good work!" Franco said, with equal sarcasm. "Did you find out where the number
one sixty-six bus goes?"

"Not exactly. Someplace in Bergen
County. That's up around the George Washington Bridge and beyond."

"Call me when you are out of the tunnel!"

Franco replaced the phone in his inner
jacket pocket and then tried again to
settle back. The second he did, the bus
made its first stop. Several people got off,
but not Amy.

Franco sat up straighter, worried that if he did happen to fall asleep, he might miss Amy getting off, and all their effort would be for naught. If that were to happen, Franco could just hear Vinnie's reaction.

Twenty minutes later, Franco's phone shocked him into full wakefulness since it was on buzz mode and was against his chest in his jacket's inner pocket. It was Angelo, who'd finally made it into the tunnel and out the other side.

"Should I take the first exit?" Angelo asked frantically, suggesting he was rapidly approaching it.

"Have you looked at the goddamn map?"

"Of course."

"Then take the first exit and come north, for chrissake. And hold on!" Franco leaned over toward his seatmate once again and asked if he knew what town they currently were in. Then Franco put his cell back to his ear. "The gentleman I'm sitting next to believes we've just entered Cliffside Park, so get your ass up in this neck of the woods."

Franco's seatmate smiled cordially when Franco stole a glance in his direction, which made Franco nervous. He always wanted to keep his interaction with people to a minimum when on a job. When the man tried to start a friendly conversation, Franco was vague and ended it gracefully as soon as he could.

Ten minutes later, Franco's seatmate disturbed Franco by tapping him on the shoulder. "My stop is next," he said, and motioned to stand up.

Franco got up to let the man pass. As the man reached the aisle, Franco asked what town it was.

"Ridgefield," the man said indifferently.

Franco sat down and called Angelo to give him a quick update on his progress.

"That means I'm about fifteen to twenty minutes behind."

As if answering a prayer, ten minutes later Amy stood up and the bus began to slow. Quickly, Franco pulled out his cell and leaned across the aisle and asked the woman passenger if she knew what town they were stopping in. She said she didn't know, but the man next to her said it was Palisades Park.

Franco hurriedly gave a call to Angelo. "It's Palisades Park." Bending down as the bus came to a stop, he saw a street sign. "Broad Avenue, Palisades Park."

"Got it," Angelo said.

Franco moved forward. Other people got up as well, blocking Franco from Amy. By the time he got out onto the street, he panicked because he didn't see Amy in either direction. Momentarily confused, he ran to the end of the bus. Thankfully, he saw her on the other side of the street walking south. It was a commercial area with a medley of lighted shops and a number of people bustling in various directions. Franco hustled across the street and rapidly bore down on the unsuspecting Amy. After the sodden warmth of the bus, it seemed excessively cold, causing him to turn up his jacket lapels.

"Ms. Amy Lucas," Franco called out a few steps behind the young woman. In Franco's estimate, there was just the right amount of passersby to keep Amy at relative ease.

Amy stopped and looked up into Franco's face. She took a wary step back as Franco approached to arm's length away from her.

"I'm sorry to bother you, ma'am," Franco said, imitating a very old TV show he'd enjoyed. "But I need to ask you a few questions."

"What about?" Amy asked. She looked from side to side nervously.

"Your boss, Paul Yang?"

Amy's demeanor changed from guarded to solicitous in a blink of an eye. "Is he all right? Where is he?"

"He's in federal custody, ma'am. He wanted us to contact you."

Amy's expression now changed from solicitous to concerned. "Why is he in custody, and why did he want you to contact me? I don't know anything."

"Excuse me, ma'am," Franco said, low and authoritative. "I believe you do. There is the very serious issue of the eight-K, which I have been led to believe a copy of which is in your possession, either at your home, on your person, or in your desk at work."

Amy's expression changed to something akin to a scared rabbit, but to her detriment, she didn't flee.

"I'm an SEC investigator, so I believe you can understand why we need to talk."

"I guess so," she said without enthusiasm.

"It is rather cold. Perhaps there is a public place where we can talk, and you will feel comfortable talking to a stranger."

Amy glanced around the immediate area.

"How about a bar. It's a place people can talk more privately than most other places. It is our hope you are not pulled into this unfortunate serious legal problem."

"There's Pete's across the street," Amy said, pointing.

"Do you go there often?" Franco asked. From where they were standing, it looked like a local dive, just what he wanted, but not if she were a known customer.

"I never go there. It's considered to be kinda a rough hangout."

"I think it will work fine. Let me call my partner, Investigator Facciolo."

Franco pulled out his cell phone and connected to Angelo. "Agent Facciolo," he said, trying to hold back a smile. "I have the witness in front of me. She's being cooperative. We are going into a bar to talk. The bar's name is Pete's on Broad Avenue, Palisades Park. The nearest cross street is . . ." Franco took the phone from his ear and asked Amy what the nearest cross street was.

Amy pointed a block ahead. "See those concrete balustrades on the sides of the road? That's route forty-six."

Franco repeated the information to Angelo and then rang off. He pointed toward the bar, and he and Amy ran across the street.

From Franco's point of view the bar was perfect, despite its miasma of stale beer. The lighting was low and the music rather high as it pounded out mostly rap. The joint was not crowded, with only five people sitting at the bar nursing drinks and a dozen or so in the rear playing pool. To the right were a series of empty wooden booths. Franco guided Amy over to one booth, being careful not to touch her. He was pleased and amazed that she was being so cooperative. He couldn't help but think that basing the interview on her missing boss had been a stroke of genius.

Once they were seated across from each other, Franco put down his lapels. He rubbed his hands together rapidly. "It seems cold for this time of year."

Amy merely nodded. She was terrified that she was about to be arrested, and angry at Paul for putting her in such a situation.

"I'm sure they aren't going to let us sit here without drinking something. What would you like? And I'll tell you what, I won't tell anybody if you won't. I'm not supposed to drink while on duty, but I'd love to have a cocktail."

Amy was not a big drinker, but she did like vodka on occasion. It calmed her down, and if there was any time she needed to be calmed down, it was at that moment. "I guess I'll have a dirty vodka martini," she said shyly.

"That sounds terrific," Franco said, still rubbing his palms together to generate heat. "I think we have to order them from the bar. I don't think there's a waitress, so I'll be right back."

At the bar, Franco ordered the martini, then a neat bourbon for himself. The burly, whiskered, and tattooed bartender gave Franco a good stare. "Nice duds," he said, before mixing Amy's drink and then reaching for the bourbon to pour Franco's. While the bartender was so occupied, Franco surreptitiously dropped one of the date-rape pills into Amy's drink. He did it by palming the small white pill and then releasing it as he picked up the glass by its rim.

After the bartender filled Franco's glass, he asked if Franco wanted to run a tab. Franco responded by placing a twenty on the bar, which he had had in his other hand. "Keep the change," he said.

Back at the table, he slid Amy's drink toward her and checked his watch. He wanted to see how long it was before the pill took effect. Despite the music, they could talk reasonably well, since the sides of the booth were shoulder height and shielded out some of the higher notes, although certainly not the jarring bass. The problem that Franco now had to face was thinking up enough things to talk about while, at the same time, bolstering his story that Paul Yang had been arrested and was being held incommunicado.

After about ten minutes, Franco was running out of innocuous questions. On the positive side, he began to sense that Amy's speech was becoming slurred, and her movements, when she picked up her drink, were becoming wobbly. Next, it appeared her eyelids were becoming heavy, requiring her to make an extra effort to keep them open.

"What about the eight-K?" Franco asked. In truth, he didn't have the slightest idea what an 8-K was despite having overheard Vinnie's talk with Paul the previous evening.

"What ablout it?" Amy questioned, inserting an inappropriate L into *about.* She took another sip from her cocktail, which she was certainly doing rapid justice to. After she put her drink down, Franco noticed her torso was now starting to wobble slightly, even when she was not moving her extremities. For all practical purposes, she was beginning to act as if she'd already had two or three drinks.

"Where is it?" Franco persisted.

"Right here in my trusty old purse," Amy said, tapping her bag repeatedly.

"Why don't you give it to me!"

"Sure, why not," Amy said. Her hand wandered in the air before she was able to seize the bag. With some difficulty, she got the inner zipped compartment open and then handed the USB storage device to Franco.

Franco turned the device over in his hand, then pulled it open. He'd never seen one.

Out of the corner of his eye, he saw Angelo come into the room. A few of the people at the bar turned and gaped at him. Angelo stared back with what Franco guessed was rising fury. Angelo had learned to deal with his facial deformity and the reaction it evoked but not with people he deemed to be the dregs of society, such as a handful of winos in a dumpy tavern.

Franco stood up, slipping the USB drive into his jacket pocket in the process. "Agent Facciolo, we're over here." For a second, Franco feared he would have to step over and drag him back to the table, but Angelo finally broke off and approached the table on his own.

"Fucking scumbags," Angelo voiced, looking back over his shoulder.

"Yeah, well, they're jealous of your Brioni jacket."

"Yeah, sure!" Angelo growled.

"This is Amy Lucas," Franco said, as he motioned toward Amy. Then he put his arms on Angelo's shoulders. "And this is Agent Facciolo, who I told you about."

"Oh, dear!" Amy said with a wince while looking up at Angelo. "I'm so sorry you've burned your face."

"Has she had one of Dr. Trevino's specials?"

"Just one, and only a little more than ten minutes ago."

"Terrific," Angelo said. "Let's give her another one. It looks like she's finished her drink."

"If we give her another one, she might pass out."

"Hey! Don't you remember, that was the idea. What is she drinking? I'll get it and we can blow this shithole. I want to finish this job. It's aggravating me."

"Wait!" Franco said, restraining Angelo. "Let me get it. I don't want you shooting up this joint because of those drunks at the bar."

"Fair enough," Angelo said. "I'll stay here with this beautiful young lady."

Franco pulled Angelo a step away from the table and, cupping his hand over his mouth, whispered, "We're SEC agents, so act according."

"Yeah, sure," Angelo said. He sat down next to Amy, and she moved in to accommodate him.

It was only fifteen minutes later when it was evident to Franco that Amy had had quite enough and was enjoying herself, perhaps even a little too much. Franco had seen the bartender look over on several occasions when she laughed. It was a high-pitched squeal.

Franco looked across at Angelo and motioned toward the door with his head, and Angelo nodded his.

"Where's the Black Beauty?" Franco asked.

"Just around the corner," Angelo said. Then, to Amy, he said, "I'll be back in a moment, hon."

Franco watched Amy sip her drink. "Why do you do that with your hair?"

Amy shrugged and then laughed. "It's fun. Before I did it, nobody noticed me."

Franco stared across the table. Amy was now evincing slight intermittent jerky motions just to keep herself sitting upright.

A few minutes later, Angelo came back. "The car's right outside."

"Come on, Amy," Franco said, giving her arm a tug.

"I haven't finished my drink," Amy said, with an exaggerated expression of sadness. She laughed.

"I think you've had enough," Franco responded. He motioned to Angelo, and together they got her onto her wobbly feet. With both men supporting her, she walked out of the bar. With a little difficulty, they got her into the backseat.

"Sit with her," Franco said. "If it looks like she's going to throw up, get her head out the window."

As they positioned Amy in the backseat with her head in the far corner and with the window down, they didn't notice the man who came out of the bar. He was dressed in casual hip-hop gear with a long, ill-fitting sweatshirt and a Yankees baseball hat on backward. Without stopping to watch Franco and Angelo's antics, he walked north up Broad Avenue.

"Are you ready?" Franco asked, looking in the rearview mirror.

"All set," Angelo said. Amy now had her seat belt on and her face practically out the window. Angelo was supporting her head with his outstretched hand. Amy herself was passed out cold.

After checking the map for the fastest route back toward Hoboken, Franco made a U-turn in the middle of Broad Avenue and accelerated south.

For a time, they drove in silence. It was Angelo who spoke up first. "I certainly hope Vinnie appreciates all this effort. Driving in the city during rush hour was bad enough, but it was nothing compared to getting into the tunnel and then out here in New Jersey. I mean, it was a bitch."

"I would have traded places in a heartbeat," Franco said. "Commuting day in and day out on a bus like the one I was on is a nightmare."

They didn't talk again until they pulled into the marina. Franco drove to the same place he had the night before and parked at the base of the main pier. He turned out the headlights. As it was the previous night, it was completely dark. Both men got out of the car and converged at the driver's-side rear door. As they opened it, Amy's head sagged to the left.

"Okay, baby!" Angelo said. "Time to rise and shine." He poked his head into the vehicle and released the seat belt. With that accomplished, they got Amy out of the car.

"She doesn't weigh much, does she?" Franco commented.

"When her boss last night said she was small, he wasn't joking."

With relative ease, they walked Amy out the pier. The cold air off the river revived her to a degree, and she actually helped them so they didn't have to support her entire weight. The only relatively difficult part was getting her across the narrow gangplank and into the stern of the boat.

"What should we do with her while we get under way?" Angelo asked.

"Well, she hasn't gotten sick, so let's put her into one of the forward cabins. I don't want her getting up and just falling overboard. Wait here and hang on to her while I turn the light on in the main saloon and below."

It was a little more difficult moving Amy on the boat than it had been on the open pier, but they managed to get her into a cabin and draped her over a bed with her feet still on the floor. Just in case she did get sick, they spread towels under her head. When they were finished, they stood up and looked down at the woman.

Suddenly, Franco bent over, grasped the lapels of Amy's coat, and rudely ripped it open. The buttons flew off in various directions and clattered to the floor.

"You know something?" he said. "If you don't look at the hair and you ignore the zits, she's not bad. What do you say?"

"We did give her a date-rape drug," Angelo said, as his scarred lips twisted into a half-smile. "We shouldn't waste things."

"Yeah, it would be like the stem cell and frozen embryo hassle. I mean, if you're going to flush them down the toilet, why not use them?"

Franco and Angelo regarded each other. Their respective smiles broadened until they laughed.

"Okay," Franco said. "Once we're under way, we'll flip for who goes first."

"You got a deal, man!"

With more alacrity than they'd shown all evening, Franco and Angelo went back up on deck. Franco continued up to the bridge deck while Angelo disembarked to handle the mooring lines. By the time Angelo had the bowline free and tossed onto the bow, Franco had the diesel engine purring like a contented cat. Angelo ran back and loosened the stern line from its massive dockside cleat. Just as he was about to toss it into the stern, his eye caught a glint of light back along the pier in the area of the fuel pump. For a second, Angelo stared into the darkness. When it didn't recur, he assumed it was a brief reflection of the light issuing from the *Full Speed Ahead* on the fuel pump's glass gauge cover.

Angelo tossed the mooring line onto the boat, scampered across the gangplank, and pulled the gangplank aboard. "All clear," he shouted up to the bridge deck. As the yacht began to move out of its slip, Angelo went around and pulled in the thick, white bumpers. As he did so, he was caught in the reddish glow of the running lights that Franco had just turned on.

Brennan hovered behind the fuel pump for longer than he thought necessary. He didn't want to take any additional chances. He was worried that while he was trying to make out the name of the yacht, he'd caught Angelo's attention. The problem had been that in the corner of his field of vision, Brennan had seen Angelo suddenly stand bolt upright and stare directly toward him for a beat. Brennan realized after the fact that it was possible for light from the yacht to reflect off the front of his rather large binoculars.

When the sound of the yacht's engines had receded enough that he was reasonably sure he'd not be seen, Brennan hazarded a glance around the pump and saw the *Full Speed Ahead*'s running lights close to two hundred yards beyond the end of the pier. Believing there was no way he could be seen at such a distance, he jogged back down the pier, past Franco's car, and then all the way up to the rear of the marina's parking lot. He didn't see Carlo's black Denali until he was almost upon it. He quickly climbed into the front passenger seat. He was out of breath.

"Well?" Carlo demanded.

Brennan held up his hand to give himself a few deep breaths.

"They took her onto a yacht," Brennan managed.

"Since we've come to a marina, that's not all that enlightening, especially since you thought they drugged her in the bar."

"I'm sure they drugged her!" Brennan shot back. He didn't like being ordered around by Carlo. "They had to practically carry her out of the bar."

"Okay, okay! Don't take offense."

"You should do some of the running around if you don't trust me."

"I said okay, they drugged her," Carlo said. "Do you think this ridiculous shenanigan was just to pork her? I mean, this has been a lot of effort. There's certainly enough broads out in Queens so that they didn't need to come all the way out here in the sticks."

"It can't be just to get laid," Brennan said disparagingly. "What's the matter with you; are you stupid?"

For a moment, the two men stayed quiet. The strain of the evening's activities had gotten to them. Finally, Carlo spoke: "We shouldn't be busting each other's balls. This has not been a picnic like I thought it would be. With that said, we have to come up with something to tell the boss."

"They made the effort to take the yacht out. I can't imagine they'd bother if they just planned on getting laid, nor would they make such an effort with a chick that certainly wasn't special. We are missing some major piece of information."

"You really didn't hear anything they said back at the bar?"

Brennan glared at Carlo.

"Okay, okay, you already said you didn't. It's too bad, though. It was the perfect opportunity."

"The music was too loud. It was boom, boom, boom," Brennan said while repeatedly slapping his fist into his open palm. "I couldn't hear myself think, much less someone else's conversation."

"Maybe they took the boat out so after they finish with her, they'll just dump her into the drink."

"That seems like a weak explanation to me," Brennan said, suppressing the urge to make a stronger value judgment. He knew that one of the benefits of a date-rape pill, if that was what they probably gave her, was that the woman remembered zilch.

"Well, we can't follow them anymore tonight unless they come back."

Give me a break, Brennan thought but did not say. Instead, he said, "Thanks to my binoculars, which I brought along, I think I know the name of the boat. I mean, I couldn't see it too well, and it was bouncing up and down, but it looked like *Full Speed Ahead.*"

Carlo turned to Brennan. "Hey, that might

be something Barbera would like to know."

Oh, really? Brennan questioned silently and sarcastically. Sometimes he truly wondered how Carlo had gotten to where he was in the organization.

Carlo got out his cell phone and called Louie Barbera.

When Barbera was on the line, Carlo gave a quick description of their evening so far. Louie was instantly taken aback. His first question was the name of the business where the girl worked, but unfortunately, Carlo and Brennan had no idea. Louie then asked them if by any slim chance they knew the name of the boat.

"We think it is *Full Speed Ahead.* It was dark and hard to see, but Brennan brought along some binoculars, and that was what it looked like."

Brennan nodded to acknowledge Carlo's giving him the credit.

"You guys are doing a good job," Louie said. "That could be very interesting information. As far as I know, no one is aware Vinnie Dominick is hiding a yacht in New Jersey. It could be the answer to how he's getting his drugs these days."

"What do you want us to do?"

"Hang out and see when they come back and whether the girl's with them or not. If it's early enough, go back to the Trump Tower. I want a list of the businesses with office space. Something's going on with one of those businesses, and I'd like to know what it is."

Carlo disconnected with Louie and turned to Brennan. "Did you hear? We've got to sit tight."

"Thanks for giving me credit about the boat's name."

"Hey, you deserved it. What do you say we go find some coffee? Who knows how long these dorks will be out for their romantic cruise."

"That's the best idea you've had today," Brennan said.

"Well?" Franco asked when Angelo came back up onto the bridge deck. Franco had the big boat up to a reasonable speed so that it was just planing. He could have gone considerably faster, but there was no need, and the diesels made a tremendous, earsplitting roar when they were pushed much faster.

"She said she liked me better because your dick is so small."

Franco took a playful swing at Angelo, which Angelo easily evaded. Earlier, Franco had won the coin toss, and while Angelo piloted the boat, he'd gone down to have his way with the unconscious Amy. After that, it had been Angelo's turn.

"How far are we going to go?" Angelo asked. He looked out at the New York City skyline to the left and the Jersey shoreline to the right. In the middle distance ahead was the illuminated Statue of Liberty.

"About the same as last night. Did you get the chain out?"

"Not yet."

They rode in silence for a short while until Angelo said, "What are we going to do?"

"Why are you asking? We're going to do just what we did last night. Shoot her and throw her overboard."

"Why bother to shoot her?"

Franco took his eyes off the water in front and regarded Angelo in the half-light of the bridge. "She'd be still alive when we tossed her into the drink."

"So what?"

Franco shrugged. "It doesn't seem right throwing her into the water alive. It's not human."

"So you think you are human. Is that it, Franco?"

Franco redirected his attention to the water in front. He saw some running lights of a boat off the starboard side on a course across their bow. He backed down the engines and the boat slowed quickly.

"What the hell are you driving at?" Franco questioned angrily. "Are you trying to play with my mind somehow?"

"Hell, no!" Angelo exclaimed. "Jeez, calm down! I'm just asking because actually, I feel the same way. It's just not right throwing her in without icing her first. But that makes me wonder if we're two old softies."

"Hey, speak for yourself."

"Franco, this is a discussion, not an argument. In comparison with the wiseguys of old, particularly the enforcers like us, we're pussycats."

"What the hell are you talking about?"

"I saw a movie once about what it was like when the real bosses were in control. When one of the musclemen of the day took someone out to knock 'em off like we're doing, they tied the person to a chair and put their feet in cement, and while the cement dried, the person being knocked off could think about what was soon to happen. Now, those guys were the real baddies, not like us."

"You're out of your freakin' mind."

"Maybe, but someday I'd like to have a chance to do it. Besides, it would be easier and faster today, with stuff like quick-set and the like on the market."

"Well, I can tell you one thing for sure.

We're not going back to Home Depot tonight so you can have some fun and games."

12
April 3, 2007
7:17 P.M.

Angela hurried out onto Fifth Avenue from the commercial entrance to the Trump Tower, and merged into the heavy pedestrian traffic heading south. She had to wait for the light at 56th Street, and glanced at her watch. She was already late for her scheduled seven-fifteen dinner with Chet McGovern. It seemed that lately she was always running and always late. The pressure was unrelenting. She knew she shouldn't be taking the time to dine formally, but the coincidence of having had a confrontation of sorts with Dr. Laurie Montgomery and being persistently asked to dinner by one of the medical examiner's colleagues on the same day was too much not to take advantage of. Angela was concerned that Laurie Montgomery could be the biggest current threat to the secrecy Angels Healthcare had managed vis-à-vis the MRSA problem and its cash-flow consequence. Angela needed to know how big a threat.

When the light changed, Angela's mind went back to her other problems. Paul Yang still had not returned, and just before leaving the office, Angela had checked with Bob. She thought he would have called if the accountant had contacted him, but Angela wanted to be sure. It would have been nice to be able to cross off one of her concerns. At the same time Angela was checking with Bob about Paul Yang, she had asked him if all had been arranged with Michael about the extra fifty thousand. Bob had said everything had been taken care of except the money itself, which he hoped would be wired in the morning.

The last thing Angela had had to take care of before she left the office was a blowup between Cynthia Sarpoulus and Herman Straus, the president of Angels Orthopedic Hospital. Cynthia demanded to keep David Jeffries's OR closed for another twenty-four hours, while Herman wanted it available. It was his contention that there had been four operations after Jeffries, which had had no infections, and the OR had been fastidiously cleaned. Cynthia, on the other hand, wanted to wait a day to check it again before giving it a green light. Under normal circumstances the chief operating officer, Carl Palanco, would have handled the problem, but mercurial Cynthia had threatened to quit, meaning Angela had to step in to mediate. Angela did not want to lose their infection-control professional with MRSA still a potential threat.

At 54th Street, Angela turned left and hurried her step. Despite all the current problems and pressures, she resigned herself to at least enjoy the meal even if it was, like everything else she was doing, in the line of work. After all, on the positive side, it was one of her favorite restaurants.

Coming through the front door and then the inner door, she peeled off her coat and gave it to the coat check person. Approaching the hostess desk, she expected to see one of the owners, of which there were two. Although she didn't know for certain, she suspected they were brothers. The one whom she expected to see, since he acted as the maître d', was the elegant Italian male with the omnipresent and superbly fitted Italian suit, crisp white shirt, bold Italian silk tie with matching pocket square, and luxuriously dark, rather long and flowing hair. The other was the tough, no-nonsense Italian male exuding testosterone, who could have played the part of a mobster. He dressed considerably more casually yet commanded significant respect tinged with a touch of fear. He usually hung out behind the small bar, and when Angela stepped farther into the room, she caught sight of him in his usual location. When he caught sight of her, he waved and greeted her by name. Prior to the disastrous MRSA problem, Angela had patronized the restaurant nearly on a weekly basis, but it had been for lunch, not dinner. She quickly surmised the brothers probably rotated evenings, since the power lunch was the establishment's forte.

One of the waiters recognized her as well. He was a youthful-appearing Italian with a pervasive smile, who also greeted her by name. With a grand gesture he pointed her toward the front corner table and said, "Your guest has already arrived."

Standing behind the table, Chet waved and smiled a greeting.

As Angela approached, she sized him up. She'd forgotten his engaging, nonchalant smile as well as his boyish appeal. She never would have suspected he was a physician, and certainly not a medical examiner. During her medical training, pathology had not been her favorite course. She couldn't help but wonder why anyone would choose to make a career of it.

When she reached the table, Chet surprised her by stepping out and giving her a hug. She limply hugged back. After all, this was business, even if he didn't know it.

"Thanks for coming out, knowing how busy you are."

"Thanks for having me. I'm not sure I would have gotten much dinner had you not been so persistent."

"As I said, you have to eat."

They sat down.

"First things first," Chet said. "This is my treat."

"I think I'm going to get the best of this exchange," Angela said. She knew that in keeping with its quality, San Pietro was not inexpensive.

They engaged in superficial banter for a time, after which Angela signaled for the waiter. She was committed to having a short evening.

The youthful, smiling waiter came over and rattled off an impressive description of more than a dozen appetizer specials and more than a dozen entrée specials. Then he handed out the menus.

"That was incredible," Chet whispered to Angela. "How does he remember all that?"

After they had made their selections, including a bottle of 1995 Brunello, they went back to their conversation. As had been the case the night before, Angela found Chet an extremely facile conversationalist, and she couldn't help but enjoy his humor and refreshing candor. He was, as he openly admitted, an irrepressible lothario. Yet by admitting it so freely, it seemed to erase its usual tawdry shallowness. Once again, as was the case the previous evening and in spite of all the pressure she was under, she began to enjoy herself. Of course, the wine significantly helped, as it was truly delicious to the point of making her feel a bit guilty: She imagined the bottle was pricey.

As the conversation proceeded, and not wanting to be rude by essentially delving into her true interest for coming out to dinner, namely, to find out about Laurie Montgomery, she took advantage of Chet's openness by asking him why he chose medicine and why forensics.

"You want the expurgated version or the truth?" Chet said, flashing one of his playful smiles.

"The truth!" Angela said with exaggerated forcefulness. She took another sip of the heavenly wine.

"Most people, like ninety-eight percent, go into medicine because they are truly motivated to help people. Not me. I had no idea what I wanted to be until about the eighth grade."

"What happened?"

"One of my friends, whom I thought of as somewhat of a nerd — I mean, he was the chairman of the chess club — suddenly decided he truly wanted to be a doctor, and for the standard reason. And do you know what happened?"

"I cannot wait to hear."

"Overnight, he became really popular with the girls. I couldn't believe it. It was like a metamorphosis. Even the girl I was trying to date, Stacey Cockburn, suddenly wanted to date Herbie Dick. Really, those were the names. I'm not joking."

Angela suppressed a laugh.

"So, suddenly I wanted to be a doctor," Chet continued. "And it worked. Two weeks later, I took Stacey to the Saturday-night dance."

"But was the motivation enough to make you actually study medicine?"

"It was for me. I'd always liked biology, so medicine wasn't generally contrary to my interests. And having a real sense of direction at that age was somehow reassuring. And my parents and sisters were wild about me being a doctor, because in a small midwestern town, the doctor is still considered a rather respectable individual."

"Okay," Angela said. "But why forensics?"

"I suppose because I like puzzles and I like to learn new things. For me, that's what forensics is all about. Also, in medical school I sensed I wasn't all that good with patients, especially when they were alive."

Angela smiled and nodded. She could understand to a degree philosophically what he was saying, but not the part about having to do the autopsy itself.

"Okay, it's your turn," Chet said. "Why did you choose business?"

Angela hesitated for a moment, thinking how she cared to answer. Her first inclination was to brush the question off by offering some pat answer, but a combination of Chet's forthrightness, her recent misgivings about her motivations, and even perhaps the wine made her want to be frank. "I guess I should ask you the same question you asked me," she said. "Do you want the stereotypical version or the honest one?"

"The honest one for sure."

"Actually, I never wanted to be a businesswoman, at least not until about five years ago."

"What did you want to be?"

"I wanted to be a doctor."

"No shit?" Chet questioned, as a wry, uncertain smile appeared on his face.

"No shit," Angela echoed. "And I was part of the herd. I was part of the ninety-eight percent you mentioned. I truly wanted to take care of and hopefully cure people. It might sound overly sappy, but I even had it in mind to bring medicine into the inner city like a kind of modern-day Dr. Livingstone."

"How come you didn't do it?"

"I did do it," Angela said. "I went the whole nine yards. I did a residency in internal medicine, got my boards, and opened a practice in Harlem."

Chet sat back and put his fork down. He was momentarily at a loss for words. He'd sensed from the moment he'd begun talking with Angela at the health club that there was something special about her, but he never would have guessed she was a doctor. The shocking news challenged his self-esteem, since being an M.D. and a high-level businesswoman certainly trumped his being only a doctor. But at the same time, the news fanned his interest in Angela.

"Are you surprised?" Angela asked. Chet looked as if a cannon had gone off next to him.

"I'm flabbergasted."

"Why?"

"I don't really know," Chet stammered.

"I'm surprised myself," Angela admitted.

"But perhaps my motivations for medicine weren't quite as altruistic as I've always believed."

"Oh?" Chet voiced. He leaned forward. "Why not?"

"Part of the reason I wanted to go to medical school, and I suppose to take care of people, because that's generally what you do after you graduate, was to get back at my father."

"Really?"

"Really!" Angela repeated. In truth of fact, she was as surprised by her statement about her father as Chet was. It wasn't that the idea hadn't vaguely occurred to her in rare moments over the years, but rather because she'd never truly visited the issue.

"Forgive me if I'm being too personal," Chet said, readjusting himself in his seat. "Why would you want to get back at your father? For some reason, I guess I just assumed you experienced an idyllic childhood."

"In all outward appearances, it was," Angela said. She was again surprised at herself. As a private person, she was admitting things she'd admitted only to a few close girlfriends while in college. "And it was important for my father that it appeared that way. But our perfect little family had its secrets." Angela paused, unsure if she wanted to go on. "I hope I'm not boring you. Are you sure you want to hear this?"

"Oh, come on!" Chet complained. "I'm fascinated. And if it is a concern for you, I give you my word that whatever you feel comfortable telling me will go no further."

"I appreciate that," Angela said. She took a sip of wine, thought for a moment, and then said, "Regrettably, my father abused me, not in any sexual sense but rather in an emotional sense. Of course, I had no idea of this as a child. It was only after I'd matured to whatever degree I have. When I was very young, I was the apple of my father's eye. I remember it very well, and I was crazy about him. But with my father's guarded emotions and reliance on appearances, the cost for me, and for my mother, for that matter, was absolute, petlike allegiance. As long as I was his little automaton darling doll, everything was picture-perfect. The problem was that I was slowly growing up, and the moment I expressed any autonomy by being my own person, he turned away from me and dropped small comments about me abandoning him, which made me feel horribly guilty. For a time, I tried desperately to please him, but invariably I'd disappoint him as my interests turned progressively away from home and more toward my friends and school. My poor mom, who had remained entirely allegiant, perhaps suffered the most, because he seemed to become bored with her and had the stereotypic midlife crisis, complete with affairs and alcohol. Of course, he never took responsibility. He blamed both my mother and myself for his need to act out, claiming no one cared about him. For some reason, which I'll never understand, my poor mom stayed with him until he divorced her for a younger woman."

"I'm sorry for you," Chet said. "It's tragic that people like your father can be their own worst enemies. Obviously, your father should have been proud of your accomplishments, not feel threatened by them. But how did this influence your wanting to go to medical school?"

"My father was a dentist, quite a successful and good one, actually, but he had in one of his rare flashes of honesty admitted he'd wanted to be a doctor but had been unable to get into medical school. To please him, back when I was only ten or eleven I told him I would go to medical school, which wasn't entirely a surprise, since one of my favorite child games was being a nurse or a doctor, which at the time I thought was the same thing."

"You were just being clairvoyant. Year by year, the two fields are coming closer and closer. The major difference now is nurses work harder and doctors are paid more."

Angela smiled but was preoccupied by her own story. She had never before expressed it even to herself quite so succinctly.

"So part of your motivation to go to medical school was to spite your father?" Chet asked.

"I think it was a part. It was like a personally rewarding way to get a kind of revenge. My getting an M.D. challenged him to the extent he skipped my graduation."

"I don't know if I can quite buy this theory in its entirety," Chet remarked.

"Why?"

"The fact that you subsequently did an internal-medicine residency, one of the most demanding, took a lot of commitment."

"I'm still not practicing."

"And why is that?"

"Actually, because my practice literally went bankrupt. I ran up a considerable debt because the Medicaid reimbursement was either slow or nonexistent, and the Medicare too low to cover the shortfall."

"Wow," Chet said. "My life in comparison with yours has been a walk in the park. As a child growing up, my most emotionally draining moment was when some older kids kicked in the face of my Halloween pumpkin. My folks are still together, my father came to every athletic event and graduation I ever had from kindergarten on up."

"With that kind of stable background, how come you're such a Casanova? I hope you don't mind me asking, especially since I don't know it's true. You seemed so at ease when you approached me last night, and your repartee seems so polished."

Chet laughed. "It's all an act. I'm always nervous on the inside and worried about being rejected. Calling me Casanova gives me more credit than I deserve. Casanova was successful; I'm usually not, although once I do go out with a woman a half a dozen times or so, I find myself yearning for the chase. Whether it represents a problem or not, I don't know. It started in medical school, when I had to work as well as go to school. I didn't have time for a real relationship, because a real relationship takes time." Chet shrugged. "So the seeds were planted back then."

"Well, that sounds honest."

"Honest, yes; admirable, probably not. I'd like to say I just haven't met the right woman, but I can't because I usually don't hang around long enough to find out."

"Have you ever had a long-term relationship?"

"Oh, yeah! Practically all the way through college. My girlfriend and I had plans for her to follow me to Chicago where I went to medical school, but at the last minute she ditched me for somebody here in New York."

"I'm sorry."

"All's fair in love and war."

"Maybe that episode affected you more than you give it credit for."

"Maybe," Chet said. Then, to change the subject back to her, he said, "You mentioned you were divorced. Do you want to talk about that?"

Angela hesitated. Normally, she avoided talking about her divorce, not only because she was by nature a private person but because the whole sad affair could still infuriate her even after six years. Yet, since Chet had been so open and she herself had already related even more private matters, she suppressed her usual reticence and said, "At the very end of medical school I was, like a teenage girl, swept off my feet by a man who I thought was the antithesis of my father. Sadly, that was not the case. He too was ultimately threatened by my medical degree. He also had affairs and, worst of all, developed a penchant for hitting me."

"Ouch," Chet said with a wince. "Domestic violence is intolerable and inexcusable. Unfortunately, we see more of it in the morgue than people realize."

The waiter suddenly appeared and whisked away their plates, then asked if they cared for dessert. Chet looked across at Angela.

"I'm not a big dessert person," she confessed.

"Nor I," said Chet. "But a cappuccino would hit the spot."

"I'll finish the wine," Angela said, pointing to the bottle. The waiter happily poured it and took the empty bottle away.

"Okay," Chet said, sitting back in his chair. "Your inner-city practice went bankrupt. When was that?"

"Two thousand one," Angela said. "Hopefully, that year will be my nadir. I mean, it couldn't get much worse. My medical practice went bankrupt and I got divorced, two ugly experiences that I don't recommend for anyone. It's the one year I would not like to live over again."

"I can well imagine. So, how did you make the transition from private medical practice to a company executive? By the way, what is your position, some sort of medical adviser?"

"I'm the founder and the CEO."

Chet's wry smile reappeared, and he shook his head in disbelief. "You are a trip! Founder and CEO! I'm awestruck. How did that happen?"

"The bankruptcy was a humiliating disaster, but it did have one saving grace. It impressed upon me the detrimental power that economics plays in medicine. I mean, I was somewhat aware before my bankruptcy, but not the extent I was after. Anyway, I had an idea to try to do something about it, but medical school taught me nothing about medical economics. In fact, I knew nothing about economics or business, which medical care has unfortunately become a slave to, so I went back to school and got an MBA at Columbia."

Chet put his head back and slapped a hand to his forehead. "That's enough," he pleaded. "I can't take any more. You're making me feel too blasted inadequate."

"You're kidding, of course?"

"I suppose," he admitted. "But, lady, you have one hell of a CV."

The waiter came and served Chet's cappuccino.

"I have a question for you," Angela said, suddenly realizing she'd been so engrossed in their conversation that she'd not yet touched on the issue that had brought her out to dine.

"Shoot," Chet responded.

"I wanted to ask you about Dr. Laurie Montgomery."

"What would you like to know?"

"Would you characterize her as a persistent, get-the-job-done person, or would you think of her as laid-back?"

"The former for sure. In fact, I'd characterize her as one of the most persistent people I know, both she and her husband. A few of the other MEs think of them as such compulsive workers that they make the rest of us look like slackers."

Angela felt the muscles in her gut tighten. She had hoped and expected Chet would say something to mitigate her worries, not fan them. "I actually met her today. It wasn't under the best of circumstances. We have had an outbreak of postoperative methicillin-resistant staph that has bedeviled us for a month or so and which has required us to go to extraordinary effort to control, even to the point of hiring a full-time epidemiologist and infection-control specialist."

"Laurie mentioned the problem," Chet said. "She also reminded me that I had posted one of your cases."

"Oh, she did?"

"Yes. She came by my office to pick up the

case, which I'd done a number of weeks ago, and was still waiting for some lab results. She had just done a similar one this morning. I guess both cases came from one of your hospitals."

"Did she say what she was going to do about it, if anything? I mean, we are already doing everything in our power. I personally have authorized our infection-control person free rein."

"Well, you can relax, because Laurie specifically said she was going to solve your problem if it kills her."

Angela's throat went dry. She took a sip of wine. "Did she use those exact words?"

"Absolutely."

Suddenly, Angela wanted the evening to be over. Although she had enjoyed herself more than she would have imagined prior to talking about Laurie Montgomery, she now had a problem that could not wait. Without concern of its precipitousness, she put down her glass, folded her napkin, and placed it on the table. She then made a show of looking at her watch.

"How is it I sense our most delightful evening is over?" Chet said, with a touch of melancholy. "I was hoping you'd be willing to walk one block north for a drink at the elegant Saint Regis King Cole Bar."

"Not tonight. Duty calls," Angela said. "Let's get the check, and how about we split it?"

"Oh, no!" Chet said. "This is my treat. I made that clear at the beginning."

"Okay, if you insist, and if you'll pardon me, I have to get back to the office. There's a call I must make." Angela pushed back her chair and stood. Chet did the same. The unexpectedly precipitous end to such an enjoyable evening flummoxed him.

"We'll talk soon," Angela said, extending her hand, which Chet shook.

"I hope so," Chet said.

With a final smile, Angela threaded her way across the room, got her coat from the coat check, and after casting a final glance and wave toward Chet, hurried out of the restaurant.

Chet slowly sat down. His eyes caught those of the waiter, who shrugged in sympathy.

13
APRIL 3, 2007
9:05 P.M.

Michael flipped his cell phone closed and gritted his teeth. He was in the lavatory on the mezzanine floor of Downtown Cipriani in SoHo. Before he'd fled to the restroom from the intimate private club on the second floor to escape the pounding disco music, he'd been with two of his buddies, entertaining three chicks from New Jersey. His phone had buzzed, and since it was Angela, he'd taken the call but, unable to hear, he'd fled to the john. Now he wished he hadn't.

With great restraint, Michael resisted the temptation to pound the graffiti-covered wall, which was smart, since the wall was lath and plaster, not plasterboard.

"Fuck!" Michael shouted as loud as he could. Within the confines of the small room, the expletive careened around the walls in an explosion of acoustical energy, making Michael's ears ring in protest. He gripped the sides of the only sink and tensed his muscles as if he were about to rip it off the wall. Slowly, he let his eyes rise up and stare at himself in the mirror. He looked terrible. His product-coated hair was standing on end as if ten thousand volts of electricity had gripped his body, and his eyes looked like those of Dracula.

He then breathed out. He was furious but under control. His bitch of an ex had just thrown another problem at him, as if he were some pissant lackey. If he weren't already in up to his eyeballs, he would have simply told her with glee to go screw herself, but that was not possible. He had to handle it, and the only way was to go out to Queens and again grovel at Vinnie's highly polished, wingtipped feet.

Suddenly giving in to his urges, he pounded the wall, but he was smart enough to use his palm, not his fist, so that the force of the blow was delivered over a wider area. Still, his hand tingled when he pulled it away.

Even calmer after the blow, he opened his phone. With trembling fingers, he punched in Vinnie's private cell phone number. It was the phone Vinnie carried with him night and day.

"Tell me you are calling me with some good news for a change," Vinnie said, in the overly calm voice Michael feared. Michael remembered a time that Vinnie had used that very same voice when he dismissed a guy. Then, as soon as the fellow was out of sight, Vinnie merely nodded to Franco, who also left. And that was the end of the guy, who was never seen again.

"I got to talk to you," Michael said, with as much equanimity as he could muster.

"Tonight?" Vinnie questioned serenely. In the background, Michael could hear festive chatter and the sound of Frank Sinatra crooning, a sure indication that Vinnie was still at the Neapolitan.

"The sooner, the better," Michael said. "Sorry to bother you, and I wouldn't have done so it if wasn't important."

"Well, suit yourself, Mikey, but don't dilly-dally. The later it gets, the less tolerant I am for screwups, if that's what you are coming to tell me."

Michael put himself in high gear. He dashed back to the club, which was all but empty, save for his two friends and the three Jersey girls, since it didn't start to rock until after eleven. He told them he had an important meeting but that he'd be back. He then dashed down the fire-escape stairs that were used as the entrance to the club, jumped in his Mercedes parked across the street, and motored off. Since he was so far downtown, he took the Williamsburg Bridge and then the expressway all the way to 108th Street in Corona. In just slightly more than twenty minutes, he had the Neapolitan in sight.

Michael had calmed down significantly during the short drive. He'd even pondered what plan B might be if Vinnie simply refused to help, as he'd done that morning. Michael couldn't come up with any likely alternatives, meaning he had to convince Vinnie that he had to help. Such reasoning may have been well and good while Michael had been in the car, but now that he was crossing the street and about to confront Vinnie, his fears came back with a vengeance.

Just outside the door, he stopped, trying to think up an appropriate intro. Vaguely, he thought he'd try to appeal to Vinnie's vanity, which was at least a big target. With that thought in mind, Michael went through the door and slipped through the curtain.

The restaurant was filled with birthday party revelers. The ceiling was clogged with balloons, and streamers were everywhere. The tiny dance floor was littered with confetti, and a large banner hung behind the bar with the words *Happy Birthday Victorio*. Vinnie was at the same table as he was in the afternoon, with Carol at his side. Michael did not recognize his other friends. Frank Sinatra was still droning away.

When Michael looked at Vinnie, he did a minor double take. He couldn't help but be buoyed. Vinnie was laughing so hard his eyes were apparently tearing. Michael stayed rooted where he was in hopes of catching Vinnie's eye, but after five minutes it was apparent it wasn't going to happen. With reluctance, Michael started off in Vinnie's direction. He recognized a few people, but most everybody else was a stranger. Michael couldn't help but notice that neither Franco nor Angelo seemed to be present, although he did see Freddie and Richie at the bar.

As he neared the table, he finally caught Vinnie's eye, and he was pleased that Vinnie's smile did not falter. Vinnie introduced everyone, and Michael dutifully shook hands around the table. Then Vinnie excused himself, waved for Michael to follow, and walked deeper into the restaurant, waving at some of the guests and shaking hands with others. They then walked quickly through the kitchen, which was in a mild panic to get out the entrées. In the far back of the kitchen was a door to an office. Vinnie went through without hesitation. Paolo Salvato, the owner, looked up from his desk in surprise.

"Paolo, my friend," Vinnie intoned.

"Would it be an imposition if we used your office for a few moments?"

Paolo stood up. "Not at all." He hustled out from behind the desk and disappeared into the kitchen, pulling the office door closed in the process.

"Okay, Mikey," Vinnie said, turning to Michael. "What's this new problem that couldn't wait until morning?"

Michael started by saying it was the kind of problem that only Vinnie could deal with. That was the attempt at appeasing Vinnie's ego. Then Michael hurriedly outlined what Angela had told him, namely that there was a woman doctor — a medical examiner, to be precise — who had suddenly taken it upon herself to solve the problem of the bacteria that had been causing the problems at the Angels hospitals. Michael added that this was a very unfortunate development, in that this doctor could go to the media and the IPO would be dead. He finished by saying that someone uniquely persuasive had to talk with her and convince her it was in her interest to cease and desist.

To Michael's relief, Vinnie didn't respond negatively, nor did his expression change while Michael had run through his quick summary. But when Michael was through, in the most unexpected manner, Vinnie cocked his head to the side and with an impenetrably wry smile asked, "By any chance, is the doctor's name Laurie Montgomery?"

"It is," Michael replied with amazement and not a little confusion.

"Oh, what a tragedy," Vinnie said, clapping his hands in delight.

"Do you know this individual?"

"Oh, yes," Vinnie said calmly. "Miss Montgomery and I have a history. She caused me one hell of a blowup with my wife over her brother's funeral home and also got me indicted and thrown in prison for two years. I'd say that means we know each other. But do you know who has had even more trouble than I have had with this bitch?"

"I can't guess," Michael said. He was astounded and thankful at this unexpected but fortuitous situation.

"Angelo! Fifteen years ago, she was responsible for his face getting so badly burned he almost died."

Vinnie fumbled in the side pocket of his jacket and tried to pull out his cell phone. In his haste, the phone seemed to resist. When he finally got it free, he quickly made a call. Franco answered. Vinnie put the phone on speaker.

"How are you two guys doing? Enjoying the cruise?"

"We're having a ball," Franco said. "The first part of the evening was a pain in the balls, but the second part has made up for it. The fish have been fed."

"Terrific," Vinnie said. "Is Angelo there?"

"He's right here."

"Put him on."

Angelo's unique voice came through the phone's speaker. Since he could barely oppose his lips, his b's, d's, m's, and p's had a distinctive muted quality.

"Angelo," Vinnie said. "What if I were to tell you that Dr. Laurie Montgomery . . . You remember her, don't you?"

Instead of answering, Angelo merely laughed in a decisively mordant fashion.

"What if I were to tell you she is endangering an important deal of ours and that you and Franco need to talk some sense into her like you boys did yesterday with Mr. Yang."

Angelo laughed again, but this time with obvious glee. "I'd tell you that you wouldn't even have to pay me. I'd do it for free, provided I could do it my way."

"Guess what? Frankie boy just sang that song a few minutes ago here at the Neapolitan. It appears that you're going to get your wish."

Vinnie disconnected. He put his arm around Michael's shoulder and guided him back through the kitchen. "Seems that this is your lucky day, too. The eight-K problem has been put to bed, and you can stop worrying about Laurie Montgomery. Not bad for a night's work."

Michael merely nodded that he'd heard. He was speechless. Twenty minutes later, after having a glass of wine at Vinnie's table, he sat in his car, still marveling at the unpredictability of life.

14
APRIL 3, 2007
9:45 P.M.

Adam Williamson was nestled into his Range Rover like a hand in a perfect-fitting, cashmere-lined leather glove. Ludwig van Beethoven's remarkable Ninth Symphony had been playing for the last hundred or so miles, and the astonishing final choir was about to begin. Adam had the volume almost full blast so the sound was as if he were seated in the center of the Berlin Philharmonic Orchestra. As the choir suddenly commenced, Adam sang along in German, his voice drowning out the professional singers. It was so moving that Adam could feel goose pimples spread over his back and down his extremities. It was nearly orgasmic.

With almost precise timing the last few notes of the symphony died away as Adam completed a wide three-hundred-sixty-degree right-hand turn that culminated in a row of toll booths blocking the entrance to the Lincoln Tunnel leading from New Jersey to New York. After paying the toll he entered the tunnel.

A Bach CD was the next selection, and the sounds of the fragile strings and harpsichord were the perfect foil for the brooding drama of Beethoven, and Adam's fingers began to play lightly on the steering wheel in time to the music.

It had been a pleasant drive from Washington, D.C., up to New York City, but Adam was now eager to arrive and eager to carry out his mission. He knew very little about his target, and that was the way he preferred it, a fact that his handlers appreciated. In his current line of work, too much knowledge served only to complicate the issue. All he needed was a name, an address of either work or home, and a few photos. If no photo was available, then a description would suffice. On those missions where there was no photo and only a description, he always allowed himself more time. Adam was not the kind of person who brooked mistakes, so the setup invariably took longer. And this current mission happened to be one of the no-photo types, so he had reserved three full days on the outside chance he might have difficulty with the ID.

The Range Rover emerged from the tunnel into the very heart of midtown Manhattan.

Adam had not been back to New York since he'd come home from Iraq. As he headed north up Eighth Avenue, he observed the city dispassionately, which was hardly strange, since in his current persona he viewed everything dispassionately. When he was young, even while in college, he'd come to the big city on numerous occasions with great excitement, at first with his family and then alone, and even on occasion with his fiancée, but now as he drove north along Eighth Avenue with its tawdry shops, it seemed as though it had been in a previous life, and in some respects, it had been. Adam had been a totally different person back then. In fact, he labeled his life as BI and AI, meaning before Iraq and after Iraq.

BI Adam Williamson had been a rather reserved, gentlemanly, quietly intelligent young man with clean-cut good looks who'd fit into his upper-class New England life in an exemplary fashion. He'd gone to a respected boarding school, had learned and respected good manners, and had gone to Harvard, as did his father and his grandfather and back ad infinitum, back to when the *Mayflower*'s long boat had scraped ashore in Plymouth, Massachusetts.

The beginning of the interim between BI and AI hadn't been a nativity but rather the horrific event of 9/11, which had jolted Adam's comfortable and predictable world, akin to one of the planets being knocked out of its orbit. At the instant the first plane crashed into the north tower of the World Trade Center, Adam had been brushing his teeth in the Harvard Business School dorm, where he was dutifully learning the ins and outs of business as preparation ultimately to assume control of the family owned financial company.

Against his parents' wishes as well as his law-student fiancée's, Adam insisted on volunteering for the military in a sudden burst of messianic zeal to do his part for America and democracy. As a natural athlete who'd been an all-American lacrosse player as well as a polo devotee, combined with a personality that motivated him to approach everything he did with one hundred percent effort, once in the military, which he'd previously known nothing about, he became fixated on becoming a member of the Special Forces. And in keeping with his personality, even that wasn't enough, and he wasn't satisfied until he became a member of the Delta Force.

Adam had enjoyed the training and reveled in its difficulty, as if the training in and of itself was helping the cause of democracy. But the real thing, meaning actual combat, came as an utter shock, because Adam was far more cerebral than physical. On his second night mission in Iraq, he was forced to kill with a knife another living, breathing human being, and his reaction shocked and shamed him. The experience had triggered a transcendental guilt and sadness, which he hid from his squadmates. To overcome what he construed as a weakness and a failing, he went out of his way on subsequent missions to kill. Over time and with equal horror and relief, he came to accept what he was doing as well as accept that he'd been metamorphosed into a true killing machine with little or no emotional response. It wasn't something he was happy about or proud of. It was just what he thought was expected of him.

Adam turned right at Columbus Circle, and the Bach Brandenburg Concertos seemed so apropos with the sudden appearance of Central Park, with its lacy, budding trees providing a welcome relief from the hard, angular, and mostly concrete city. Adam's route was to take him along Central Park South all the way to Madison Avenue where he'd turn north. At that point, it was a matter of going around the block to arrive at his destination, the Hotel Pierre, a New York City landmark from the Gilded Age.

The Pierre had been the hotel Adam had stayed in ever since he'd visited the city as a small child, all the way up to and including when he was in business school. On this trip, he'd insisted on staying there, to his handler's chagrin. His primary handler, in particular, had tried to get him to stay in some less vigilant surroundings and where he'd have his Range Rover instantly at his disposal. But Adam had insisted. He was curious if he'd feel any nostalgia. He didn't think he would. It was as if his experiences in Iraq, particularly the covert missions, has sucked all the emotion out of him from both witnessing and participating in the kind of atrocities that before Iraq, BI, he couldn't have ever imagined. And most disturbing of all, he'd come to enjoy what he was doing, even the killing.

His Iraq experience came to a disastrous conclusion. It happened during an ill-fated covert action that went horribly wrong. He and the rest of his team had ended up being decimated by misdirected friendly fire, which he and his colleagues had called in. Although he'd not been killed, as were his squadmates, Adam had had a leg broken and had been rendered unconscious. In such a vulnerable state, he'd been taken hostage by the very people he and his team had been sent to kill or capture.

Despite supposed preparatory training as a POW, Adam was unprepared for his ordeal as a captive. He leg was never appropriately attended to and was a source of constant pain. But worse, he was tortured by repeated episodes during which he was certain he was about to be shot or beheaded.

Although it had been explained to him as a common psychological response called the Stockholm syndrome, he was shocked when it happened to him. After several months, he began to identify with his captors and their twisted ideology. He'd even made a tape that was shown on Al Jazeera satellite TV in which he lauded the insurgents' cause and cast aspersions on the United States' motives for the Iraq intervention. His mind had been so twisted that when his release was eventually brokered by an FBI negotiator for the secret exchange of a number of insurgent detainees, he didn't know whether to rejoice or bewail his release and ultimate repatriation. Intuitively, he'd known he could never return to his former life; it was simply out of the question.

Adam turned left on 61st Street, and halfway down the block pulled over to the Pierre's entrance marquee. The doorman tipped his hat and opened the Range Rover's door. "Checking in, sir?"

Adam merely nodded as he climbed out of the car. Following the doorman to the car's rear, Adam insisted on taking the tennis bag, which contained the tools of his trade, the moment the doorman opened the hatchback. The small overnight bag he allowed to be carried for him.

"Will you be needing your vehicle this evening?" the doorman asked as he held open the hotel's door.

Adam nodded again.

"Fine, I'll keep it right here at the door," the doorman said as he gestured toward the registration desk.

Directions weren't necessary for Adam, as the lobby had barely changed over the twenty or so years he had intermittently stayed at the hotel. Pausing at the flower-bedecked center table in the middle of the carpet, Adam let his eyes take in the familiar surroundings, including the raised sitting area to the right and mostly nineteenth-century English furniture. As he'd expected, he didn't feel anything. The scene evoked no emotion whatsoever. It was like his memories were of someone else's life.

The check-in was dispatched with commendable speed, after which the receptionist called for a porter, saying, "Hector, this is

Mr. Bramford from Connecticut. Would you show him to his room? By the way, Mr. Bramford, we've given you a very nice park view."

Bramford was one of the several identities Adam carried on this particular mission, along with all the associated documentation. His handlers in Washington ran a discreet risk-management/security firm with branches in major cities around the world, and Adam worked for them for special operations as an independent contractor. The clients for the current mission, all former lawyers and politicians, had contacts in the highest levels of government, so obtaining the identities had been relatively simple.

"This way, Mr. Bramford," Hector said, pointing toward the elevators.

The interior of the elevator was unique in regard to its French style, and Adam remembered it the moment he stepped in. Its frivolousness as well as its cleanliness stood in such sharp juxtaposition to his war experience that he marveled it could exist on the same planet as Iraq. And as he rose up in the fussy décor, the sheer contrast of the total situation made him think back to his release from captivity. At that time, he'd been picked up in the scrubby, battle-scarred desert dressed only in a soiled pair of boxer shorts and limping on a deformed leg.

Within hours, he'd been airlifted to Germany where his leg was rebroken and reset, and he began treatment for what was called a post-traumatic stress disorder variant. Under the psychiatrist's guidance, Adam made considerable strides in dealing with his anxiety, his inability to concentrate, his joylessness, and his difficulty sleeping. He had had less success with generating any interest whatsoever in returning to any semblance of his former life, which included resurrecting his relationships with his family, his family's business, his fiancée, or Harvard Business School. He also had had no success in adjusting to the loss of the camaraderie of his Delta Force colleagues and the unique and addictive risk of making a kill.

Adam's psychiatrist had become frustrated by what she considered Adam's lack of progress, until she suggested a new strategy: namely, for Adam to embrace what he'd been morphed into from his military experience rather than attempting to suppress or ignore it. It was even she, as an Alexandria, Virginia, resident, who had introduced Adam to the founder and CEO of Risk Control and Security Solutions, which was extremely receptive to the combination of his Special Forces training and his experience of having been a POW. To protect his identity, they worked out an employment relationship, which didn't show up on their books. In return, they paid him extremely well.

The Pierre elevator reached the correct floor. Hector allowed Adam to disembark first, then pushed ahead to open the door to Adam's room. He gave Adam a rapid tour of the room, including how to navigate the hotel's simple entertainment systems and the location of the minibar. Then he backed out of the room, obsequiously clutching Adam's tip.

For a few minutes, Adam stood in front of the window that gave out onto Central Park. The most apparent object was the skating rink, brightly illuminated in the center of the park's mostly dark expanse. He then turned back into the room. He took his tennis bag from his shoulder and unzipped it. Inside was a selection of favorite firearms, carefully wrapped in towels and tape. He took each out, unwrapped them, and checked to make sure they were all in the same working order as they had been when he had packed them. When he was satisfied that his arsenal was unscathed by the drive, he pulled out a single sheet of paper from an inner zipped pocket. On it was the target's name, a brief and probably useless description, and the rather odd address of the Office of the Chief Medical Examiner of the City of New York.

15
APRIL 3, 2007
10:15 P.M.

"It doesn't look good," Dr. Tom Flanagan said. "It doesn't look good at all."

Dr. Tom Flanagan was one of eight intensivists employed by University Hospital at great cost to supervise care in the intensive-care unit, or ICU. He was either there at the unit or on call 24/7. He was speaking to Dr. Marlene Ravelo, who was board-certified in internal medicine and infectious disease and who ran the University Hospital department of infectious disease.

"Unfortunately, I agree," Dr. Ravelo said.

They were standing at the foot of Ramona Torres's bed in a special isolation cubicle off the main ICU room.

On the right side of the bed was Dr. Raymond Grady, a pulmonologist. He was busy adjusting her positive-pressure ventilating machine in an attempt to give adequate volume. It was becoming difficult. He glanced at the readout for the central venous pressure and the other one for the pulmonary wedge pressure. "We're not ventilating her very well," he called across the bed to Dr. Phyllis Bohrman, the cardiologist consult they'd called. She was watching the ECG on another monitor. Next to her was the chief resident in medicine, Marvin Poole.

"It's pretty clear why," Dr. Bohrman said. "Look at that last chest X-ray. The lungs are full of fluid."

"Let's look on the bright side," Dr. Flanagan said. "We're getting a lot more practice handling sepsis with septic shock than usual with these Angels Healthcare patients."

"That's true," Dr. Ravelo agreed. "But it would be nice to save one of them now and then."

"We can't be faulted. Having had a liposuction, this individual's surgical site infection covered a significant percentage of her body's surface area."

"Let's not forget what I believe is necrotizing pneumonia," Dr. Ravelo said.

"Do you think the pneumonia is a result of seeding by her surgical-site infection, or do you think it is primary — I mean, isn't primary staph pneumonia rather rare?"

"It is, but the time interval seems strange. Weren't we told the pulmonary symptoms preceded the symptoms of cellulitis?"

"That was what was on the record."

"It's very strange, especially considering last night's case was so similar, although the surgical-site infection was so much smaller."

"Okay, guys and girls," Dr. Flanagan called out. "Pulmonary function is heading south to Antarctica, cardiac function is going in the same direction so that the blood pressure is in the basement. There's no longer any urinary output, so that tells us what's happening in the kidneys, and the liver is not doing what it should be doing. Thank you all for your hard work, but we've clearly lost the battle."

Dr. Flanagan and Dr. Ravelo turned and walked back to the central desk, where they got Ramona Torres's chart to write their final notes.

"Do you think we should have done anything differently?" Dr. Ravelo asked as they took seats side by side.

Dr. Flanagan shook his head. "We followed the newer protocol to a T, so I don't think so. Hell, we gave her everything we've got, including the activated protein C and corticosteroids. Equally as important, you changed the antibiotics the instant we knew we were again dealing with MRSA, so we can be confident we had the right cocktail. And remember her APACHE II score was off the charts when she arrived, so we didn't have much to work with."

"Why can't we get Angels hospitals to send these patients sooner?"

"That's a damn good question. What I'm guessing is these patients' infections develop just too damn quickly postsurgery. I mean, this woman was operated on just this morning at seven-thirty a.m. In her chart, it says the first nonspecific symptoms started a little after four p.m. That's one hell of a rapid course."

"With all the nasty toxins potentially at staphylococcus's disposal, it's understandable. I'd be willing to put some money on this patient's bug to have the Panton-Valentine leukocidin, or PVL, gene."

"Does it surprise you that the Angels hospitals are having so many MRSA cases?" Dr. Flanagan asked.

"Yes and no. Staph is the most common surgical site pathogen, and whereas MRSA comprised only two percent back in the nineteen seventies, today it is sixty percent and rising all the time."

"Actually, what bothers me most about these cases is the whole specialty hospital dilemma. They don't have the resources for this kind of case, and they have to outsource it. In fact, in one specialty hospital, I think it was also an orthopedic hospital, a patient had a heart attack. And you know how they dealt with it?"

"No."

"They called nine-one-one."

"You are kidding!" Dr. Ravelo blurted in total disbelief.

"They didn't have any doctors on duty. Can you believe it?"

"Did the patient survive?"

"I don't think so."

"That's a travesty."

"I agree, but what can you do? Are you aware of the specialty hospital debate in general?"

"I know a little about it, I suppose. It's one of the advantages of being in academic medicine. We don't have to get so involved in various private-sector squabbles."

"I would not be so sure. It might eventually influence our salaries. The biggest problem most people see in these private specialty hospitals is that they are only interested in the cream of the patients: i.e., the healthy, well-insured who come in to have a quick procedure and then are out. It's really a moneymaking machine, because they get paid the same as the university gets paid, but because they don't have ICUs like ours or an ER like ours, which are not moneymakers, their costs are significantly less."

"I heard the government had a moratorium against them for a while. Was that the reason?"

"No," Dr. Flanagan said. "The government was against them for a time, actually from late 2003 to late 2006, because the specialty hospitals involve some level of physician ownership to guarantee a continual flow of patients. There is an existing ban in Medicare law for physicians to refer patients to medical service organizations in which they have ownership interest, like imaging centers or clinical laboratories or the like. But there is a loophole as far as a whole hospital is concerned. Ownership in that situation was not banned because it was thought that in a whole hospital, there would be little risk of a conflict of interest."

"But a specialty hospital is not a whole hospital!" Dr. Ravelo said indignantly. "They only do a very limited number of services."

"Exactly! Yet it is by claiming they are a whole hospital that they are taking advantage of the loophole."

"Why was the moratorium lifted then?"

"I haven't the foggiest idea. There were a number of hearings on the issue in which all these points were clearly raised. Most people familiar with the debate, who'd either attended the hearings or read about them, thought for sure the moratorium should be sustained and actually strengthened because the existing moratorium was only against new specialty hospitals getting Medicare provider numbers, which are necessary for reimbursement."

"What happened?"

"Suddenly, the moratorium was lifted with little explanation. My guess is that it was a behind-the-scenes lobby competition, with the lobbyists from the AMA pitted against the lobbyists for the AHA, or American Hospital Association, and the FAH, or Federation of American Hospitals. I guess the doctors spent more money than the hospital admin groups."

"That's awful. Everything comes down to money. I'm embarrassed for our profession."

"Well, it's not all bad. Patients generally like specialty hospitals, and for routine procedures, they are certainly more comfortable."

"Maybe we should ask Ramona Torres," Dr. Ravelo said. "Maybe she'd have an opinion about which is best: a specialty hospital and its comforts or a truly full-service hospital. If she'd been here from the start, from our statistics, she would have had a significantly higher chance of surviving her infection."

"Good point," Dr. Flanagan said. "A very good point."

16
APRIL 3, 2007
11:05 P.M.

"Hey, asshole!" Carlo called while giving Brennan's shoulder a sudden forceful shake.

Brennan, who'd fallen asleep and had slowly slipped down in his seat until his knees were pressing against the dash, overreacted to being awakened so roughly by sitting bolt upright. Frantically, he searched the immediate area outside the windshield for a beast or foe. As soon as he heard Carlo begin to chuckle in the darkness of the car's interior, he became oriented to time, place, and person. And just when he was about to say he'd had quite enough of Carlo for one night, Carlo pointed out something beyond the windshield.

"I think our charges are returning to port," Carlo said. "Front and center!" He'd spent a year and a half in the armed forces before earning a dishonorable discharge. He'd hated the regimented experience, but he still indulged in the phraseology on occasion.

Brennan had to squint into the distance beyond the pier. A sliver of a moon had arisen over the New York City skyline, throwing a limpid line of reflections toward them across the Hudson River. Brennan and Carlo were still in Carlo's Denali parked high on the hill at the very back of the marina's parking lot, waiting for Franco and Angelo's return.

"I don't see them," Brennan said. Hardly had the words escaped his mouth before a sizable yacht silently slipped through the moon's reflection. "Okay. I see a boat. How do you know it's them?"

"How many boats have we seen go in and out tonight?"

"You still don't know it's them," Brennan said, as he raised his binoculars. With the magnification, the boat looked ghostly as it slipped through the mist suspended over the water's surface. "Aren't they supposed to have some lights on?"

"How do I know?"

"What are we going to do?"

"We're going to sit here and watch them leave and see if they are still accompanied by the young lady. Then we are going to take a look at their boat."

It seemed to take forever as the boat backed into its slip and Franco and Angelo made it secure. When it was finally done, the two men walked along the pier toward dry land.

Carlo put down his window. Even from the distance, Carlo and Brennan could hear that Franco and Angelo were carrying on as if they'd been to a party. They were laughing as they climbed into Franco's finned Cadillac, slammed the doors, and drove away.

"It must have been quite a boat ride."

"At the girl's expense," Carlo commented as he started the car. "What a couple of pigs."

"It doesn't make much sense. I wonder who she was. Why all the effort? She certainly didn't look like anything special."

"It doesn't make sense to us, but maybe Louie can make sense out of it," Carlo said. Then, turning to Brennan, he asked, "Did you bring your locksmith's tools?"

"I always do."

"Let's take a quick look around the inside of the *Full Speed Ahead,* if you can manage the door and the alarm system."

"I'll manage them," Brennan said confidently. Two of Brennan's skills were lock picking and understanding electronic equipment, including alarms and computers. He'd gone to a technical school for electronics after he'd been kicked out of regular high school.

Carlo reparked in approximately the same place Franco's car had been. He took a flashlight from the dash before he and Brennan walked out the pier. They proceeded in silence, listening to the waves softly lapping against the pilings. When they got to the gangplank of *Full Speed Ahead,* Carlo hesitated. He looked back at his vehicle. "I hope they didn't forget something and come back."

"Want me to run back and move the car?"

Carlo shook his head. "Let's just keep a sharp eye out for headlights. We'd have a lot of warning. It's not like this is the only boat on the pier."

They boarded the yacht quickly. "Start on the door," Carlo said. "I'll keep an eye out."

"Posh boat," Brennan said. Then he stopped. "What do you think this stack of cinder blocks is for?"

"Three guesses and the first two don't count, lunkhead."

Brennan looked back at the cinder blocks and suppressed a shiver at the thought. Proceeding on to the glazed double doors leading into the yacht's interior, he got out his set of tiny locksmith's tools. He didn't have much light, but he didn't need much. Lock picking was a skill done mostly by feel.

"What do you think?" Carlo asked. He was sitting on the gunwale at the very stern where he had a good view of the approach into the marina, as well as the entire parking lot.

"A piece of cake," Brennan said. Two minutes later he had the lock open but had to deal with the primitive alarm system. With that taken care of, he called to Carlo.

Carlo used his handheld light to quickly scan the interior of the main saloon. He pointed to the glasses on the bar. "So they were drinking. Explains their mood."

"What if we find the girl? What are we going to do?"

"We'll have to improvise." His light found the steps and the gangway forward. After taking another look up at the entranceway into the marina, which he could barely see, thanks to the neighboring boat, which was almost as large as the one they were on, Carlo led the way down the stairs and into the galley and dining area. Moving quickly to avoid being out of sight of land, they crossed the galley into the gangway leading forward. Carlo briefly tried each door, but the staterooms were all empty and undisturbed until they came to the last one. In it, the queen-sized bed cover was in disarray, as was a towel on its surface.

"I'd say this was the scene of the crime," Carlo said. He shone the light around the room, which was otherwise totally ship-shape. "The girl's gone. That's what we came here to find out, so now let's blow."

They rapidly backtracked. Carlo didn't feel comfortable until he had a reasonable view of the marina and the parking area at the boat's stern. All was serene. He turned back to Brennan. "I just had an idea. How easy would it be to hide a tracking device on this yacht?"

"Easy," Brennan said. "What kind of tracking device are you interested in: one that records exactly where the boat's been or one that tracks in real time and you can watch where the boat goes."

"The second one," Carlo said, warming to the idea.

"No sweat. We can put a thing about the size of a deck of cards someplace here on the boat and then set up a situation where we can follow it on the Internet."

"Good. Let's run it by Louie first."

"Ah, come on," Angelo pleaded. "It's not that much out of the way."

"But it's going to midnight, and I'm exhausted," Franco said.

They were in the Lincoln Tunnel heading

back to New York City, where Franco was intending to drive directly across Manhattan to connect with the Queens Midtown Tunnel.

"I want to stop at the Neapolitan," Franco continued. "The party will be breaking up soon, and I'd like a chance to make sure Vinnie understands the secretary is history."

"It's only twenty blocks out the way. I just want to see if she still lives in the same place, because if she does, the job will be a piece of cake. You can't believe how much I'm looking forward to getting some revenge. I've done two stints in the slammer for that bitch, got coldcocked by her damn boyfriend, and she's the one responsible for my face looking the way it does."

Franco glanced over at Angelo in the half-light of the car. He'd become accustomed to Angelo's horrific facial scarring. He wondered if it were his own face, would he ever get used to it?

"What would it take?" Angelo said. "Ten minutes, fifteen at most."

"Okay, okay," Franco said reluctantly.

Twenty minutes later, Franco's big black car was creeping along 19th Street with Angelo bent down to see the building's façades. The last time he'd been there had been ten years earlier, but the experience had been burned into his memory. He'd been certain he'd remember the building, but it wasn't happening.

"Which one, for chrissake?" Franco demanded. He'd made the decision to sacrifice the time because he'd momentarily felt sorry for Angelo, but the rationale was wearing thin with Angelo taking so freaking long merely to pick out the right building. Earlier, Angelo had assured him there wouldn't be a problem.

"There it is!" Angelo exclaimed suddenly. He pointed.

"Are you sure?" Franco questioned. He looked at the building Angelo was pointing at. It was brick, in a mild state of disrepair, exactly like the buildings on either side. "How can you tell?"

"Trust me! I can tell."

As Angelo climbed out of the car, Franco called after him to remind him that their visit was only a quick reconnoiter. Angelo waved over his shoulder to indicate he'd heard.

Angelo glanced up at the top of the building. Lights were on in the fifth-floor apartment. Dr. Laurie Montgomery's had been the apartment in the back: 5B. Angelo pulled open the outer door and stepped into the foyer. As soon as he did, he remembered his crazy partner, Tony Ruggerio, blasting away in that particular foyer at a woman who both of them thought was Laurie Montgomery but who turned out to be someone else. Partnering with Tony had been a frustrating handicap for Angelo, but he'd had no choice in the matter until the guy's recklessness got him killed.

Hoping for pay dirt, Angelo checked the names alongside the buzzers and mailboxes. To his great disappointment, the name for 5B was Martin Soloway.

Having keyed himself up to such an extent, Angelo felt a momentarily paralyzing letdown. But then he remembered that he knew where she worked, and his mind-set took a rapid about-face, only to be halted by the very real possibility that after twelve years she might have switched jobs, as well as apartments. In a mood hovering between unbridled anticipation and abject despondency, Angelo returned to the car and climbed in.

Although the retracted scarring of Angelo's face restricted his range of facial expression, Franco had learned to interpret subtle small changes. He knew instantly that Angelo was dejected.

"She's no longer there?" Franco questioned.

"No longer there," Angelo confirmed. He

then told Franco his concerns that she might have left town.

"Hey, buck up! She's got to be here. She wouldn't be causing trouble if she wasn't."

Although there wasn't a lot of facial movement, Franco could tell that Angelo's mood had changed for the better.

17
APRIL 4, 2007
4:15 A.M.

Angela had had difficulty falling asleep. She'd tried reading, but after several hours she'd given up. Instead she tried the TV, which usually put her to sleep within ten minutes, but on this occasion was no better than the book. While struggling to pay attention to the late-night talk show, her mind kept reverting to her major worries: the capital shortfall, Paul Yang's apparent binge with a prepared 8-K sitting in his laptop a mere click away from submission to the SEC, and Dr. Laurie Montgomery's potential of turning the MRSA problem into a public-relations disaster, either by discouraging doctors and patients to use the Angels hospitals or by alerting the SEC to a major problem, which had major financial consequences.

Angela finally gave in and took an Ambien. She knew she'd been reverting to the crutch of using a hypnotic drug too frequently over the previous few months, but she felt it was warranted. Of all the people at Angels Healthcare, she was the only one who could be trusted to keep the IPO on track in the current crisis. To do that she needed her wits, which certainly required sleep.

As had been the case in the recent past, the tiny, white, racetrack-shaped tablet worked its wonders, and Angela fell into a deep, albeit drugged, sleep with disturbing dreams. The worst dream was about being forced to move along a narrow ledge on a horrendously high and otherwise perfectly perpendicular cliff. Although not knowing exactly why, she had to get to the other side of the cliff or there would be a catastrophe. The ledge became progressively more and more narrow, and within sight of her goal, her foot slipped off the edge. Although she was able to grasp the edge with her hands, she was unable to haul herself back up onto the narrow ledge. Gradually, her fingers and arms tired, and she slipped off and fell into the abyss.

Angela awoke with her heart racing, relieved to be alive. Although she could understand the origin of the theme of the dream, she wondered where the idea of being on a cliff had come from.

Although not looking forward to the cold marble floor of the bathroom, she had no choice, so she eased out from under the covers to keep her spot as warm as possible. She tried to be quick, just as she tried to keep her mind a blank. What she was worried about was not falling back asleep. She guesstimated she'd only slept for about five hours.

Unfortunately, Angela's fears became a reality. Although she still felt exhausted and even drugged, to a degree she could not quiet her mind, which ignored her orders and quickly went into high gear. It was going to be a busy day. First, she wanted to reassure herself that Michael's fifty thousand had been wired into the company's account. Next, she wanted to hear from Bob if Paul had resurfaced and, more important, if he had filed or not.

By four-thirty, Angela acknowledged that more sleep, no matter how necessary, was out of the question. Reluctantly, she got up, and on her way to the kitchen, she stopped at her daughter's door. After briefly wondering if it was worth waking her, Angela pushed open the child's door. With enough illumination spilling in from the nightlight in the hall, she could see Michelle's familiar form, with her dark, luxurious hair pulled back from her angelic face. In the dim lighting, her flawless skin seemed to radiate supernaturally from within.

For a moment, Angela stood there looking down at her daughter as only a parent can do. She felt a surge of love that eclipsed by a millionfold all the heartache and venom associated with Michael, the ignominy of the bankruptcy, and the anxiety of all the current problems with Angels Healthcare. It was a way for Angela to reorganize her priorities as she considered what was really important. And as she did so, she thought about the previous evening. After the fact far more than during her dinner with Chet McGovern, she'd realized she enjoyed herself in a way she'd not anticipated. Although she'd agreed to go for utilitarian purposes — namely, to find out whether Laurie Montgomery was a real threat — she'd relearned that honest conversation and general interaction with an apparently healthy man could be self-revealing. She'd never had such a frank discussion about her motivations with anyone, including herself.

As quietly as she'd entered Michelle's room, she left, pulling the door shut but not closed, exactly as she had found it. Michelle had always needed a bit of light as a connection to the real world cutting through the darkness of her room.

Advancing into the kitchen, Angela quietly readied the espresso machine. Haydee's bedroom and bath were off the kitchen, and Angela didn't want to disturb her.

As she waited for the light to indicate that the machine temperature and pressure were up to the proper level, Angela went back to her musing about the dinner experience with Chet McGovern. What she had admitted to him about going to medical school partly to get revenge against her father was not particularly flattering. What she failed to tell him was how much she had enjoyed medical school, particularly the clinical years, and, even more so, how much she had loved medical residency. Although most of her contemporaries had found residency training a grind, she truly thought of it as the crowning experience of her life: a perfect combination of service and learning.

The coffeemaker light indicated that it was ready. Angela loaded one of the sealed capsules, tightened the handle into the unit, and turned it on. She grimaced at the noise in the stillness of the apartment.

As the coffee ran into the cup, Angela reminisced about individual episodes she'd had with patients and families during her residency and during the year she'd had her private practice. They ranged from the sublimely joyous to the sublimely sad, but always uniquely human. Then she found herself comparing how she'd felt after a day of practicing medicine to how she felt after a day working at Angels Healthcare and acknowledged how fundamentally different the rewards were. With medicine, it was deeply personal; at the end of the day, she could almost always revel in the fact that she had helped at least a few people in the most direct way possible. With business, it was more vague and had to do with accomplishing something, even if it was difficult to define exactly what it was, although it invariably had something to do with money.

Angela took her coffee back to her study. It was her favorite room in the apartment, with one entire wall of floor-to-ceiling bookshelves, complete with a ladder that was attached to a track across the bookshelves' face. Angela had loved books as a child and was proud that she'd never thrown one away.

At the desk, Angela got out a legal pad and began writing down the problems she was currently facing and what she would try to do about them that day. When she wrote Paul's name down, she thought about the man having an alcohol problem, which she hadn't known about. From the standpoint of a CEO, it made her angry that the information had been kept from her, and she was surprised Bob had done so. But then, thanks to her recent reflections about her medical training, she thought about the problem from a physician's point of view and remembered how difficult all addictions could be. Angela then wondered if the company should pay for inpatient rehab, which might be important if he was truly relapsed. She wrote the idea down. It was an issue that should be considered after the IPO.

When Angela wrote Dr. Laurie Montgomery's name down, she paused. There was little she could do about that problem. It was in Michael's hands, for whatever that was worth. The previous evening, when she'd called him to tell him the disturbing news about Laurie's apparent personality and the fact that she had voiced that she was going to solve the Angels Healthcare problem with MRSA if it killed her, he'd said that he'd do something about it immediately. Knowing him as well as she did, she had no idea whether he was telling her the truth or just placating her for the moment. With her intuition telling her loud and clear that Laurie Montgomery was the biggest threat to keeping their infection problem out of the media since the problem began, there was no time to delay. With all the trouble and effort they were going through with the cash-flow problem, it would be tragic if the IPO stumbled from the work of an overenthusiastic medical examiner.

Angela's eyes strayed over to her telephone and then on to the Tiffany desk clock. It was four-thirty-five in the morning, hardly the time for a personal call. Yet she was so certain of Laurie's threat potential that she seriously debated calling. From sore experience, she knew Michael sometimes partied to such an hour, even five a.m., on numerous occasions when they were married.

Talking herself into making the call, Angela justified it because of the importance of starting some sort of offense against Laurie and because Michael deserved it. All those times he'd stayed out to such an hour he'd return and wake her with his drunkenness, and sometimes even Michelle.

With a certain vengeful glee Angela dialed the number. As the number rang, she fully expected his voice mail, especially since he had caller ID and she had a private line.

To her surprise, he answered, sounding mildly intoxicated.

"This better be important," he said, slurring his words.

"Michael, it's Angela."

There was a pause. In the background, Angela could hear a woman's voice with a heavy New Jersey accent complaining and demanding to know who was calling in the middle of the night.

"Did you hear me?" Angela demanded. Now that she'd awakened him, she felt a tad guilty, but she was determined not to show it.

"For chrissake. It's four-thirty in the fucking morning."

"It's four-thirty-five, to be exact. I'm concerned about the Dr. Laurie Montgomery issue I called you about last night."

"I said I'd take care of it."

"Have you?"

"I told you I'd take care of it, and I did. It's over, it's done, so go back to sleep!"

"How are you so sure? As I was told, she has a reputation of being very persistent."

"It's not going to matter how persistent she is. My client actually knows her personally. He said he'd be happy to talk with her, and he's confident she'll be amenable to his position. What I gathered was that the doctor owes my client big-time."

Michael's explanation didn't make too much sense, but his assuredness did. Angela thanked him and told him to go back to sleep.

18
APRIL 4, 2007
4:45 A.M.

Laurie had been awake for a while; she didn't know exactly how long when she finally looked at the clock. By then it was quarter to five, an hour before Jack would be getting up to shower and an hour and fifteen minutes before he would come back and drag her out of bed. That was the normal routine, and the fact that she was already awake spoke volumes about her mental state. Laurie was a night person. Along about ten o'clock, when Jack was finding it hard to hold up his eyelids, Laurie would usually get a second wind. She loved to read at night and would stay up after midnight engrossed in a novel more often than she liked to admit, always to deride herself the following morning and vow never to do it again.

Now, as she lay there, fully awake and staring up at the dark ceiling, she knew exactly what the problem was; she was depressed. It wasn't a major, incapacitating depression, which she'd never had but could imagine was like, but rather a nagging melancholy that she was inexorably being set up for a major disappointment. She'd always wanted a child from as early as she could remember, and she always thought of herself as a mother-in-waiting through her long medical training, which she'd blamed for not having had the time to find a spouse. Then she'd fallen in love with Jack and had to deal with his guilt over the loss of his family and whether or not he could commit to another. But that was now behind them and they were trying to have a family, but over the last year, it hadn't happened despite temperature charts and careful monitoring of her cycles. The problem, as she saw it, was her age now that she was in her forties. Every month that went by, she was terrified that her chances of naturally conceiving had sunk, and now Jack was insisting on having an operation, which would take him out of commission for God knew how long, and not only that, he was choosing to have it at a time when he was putting himself at significant risk.

Laurie rolled over on her side facing Jack and propped herself up on an elbow. She gazed at his profile, the picture of tranquility lying on his back with one arm casually thrown onto the pillow behind his head. She did indeed love him, but his obstinacy could drive her to distraction, as was the case with the surgery issue. For the life of her, she could not understand how he could dismiss the data and believe it was prudent to have the procedure.

Recognizing that more sleep was not in the cards, Laurie got out of bed. With her bathrobe and slippers on, she padded into the study they had made facing out onto 106th Street. It was just becoming light. She looked down from the window onto Jack's beloved basketball court, wishing it would suddenly disappear. Then she turned back to the partner's desk. Her side was piled high with the MRSA case files and hospital records of the twenty-four cases, along with her uncompleted matrix. She'd hauled all the material home with the intention of working on it the previous evening, but she hadn't done it. And now that she was awake early, she thought she would take advantage of the time, but before even sitting down, she recognized she felt the same as she had the night before. Her despondency kept telling her that her efforts were in vain. Jack was just going to do what Jack wanted.

In the kitchen, Laurie made herself some coffee. Sitting down at the breakfast table, she began thinking about the process of in vitro fertilization and how Jack would respond to the idea. Although it would be a natural progression, they'd not discussed it. In truth, Laurie had been afraid. She knew that Jack's agreement to have children was more to please her than something he intrinsically wanted to do.

To Laurie's surprise and despite being unable to fall back asleep in bed, she fell asleep at the kitchen table as evidence of how tired she was. What woke her was Jack standing in the doorway completely naked with his hands on his hips and an exaggerated expression of confusion on his face.

"What the hell are you doing snoozing in the kitchen?" he asked.

"I couldn't sleep," Laurie said, conscious of the irony.

Jack advanced into the room and put a hand on her shoulder. "If you are still fretting about this surgery, I'll promise you I'll be fine."

"Oh, yeah, sure," Laurie said sarcastically. "As if you have control. Why do you have to be so headstrong?"

"Look who's talking!"

"Well, if the situation was reversed, I sure as hell wouldn't be taking the kind of gamble you're planning on taking."

"Hey!" Jack said. "We've been through

this, remember? Let's agree to disagree. I have to go over to the hospital this morning on the way to work for a quick pre-op blood and urine test, get the MRSA swab I told you about, and have a quick chat with the anesthesiologist. That's why I'm up early. Why don't you come along? Witnessing all such preparation, maybe you'll feel better."

Laurie thought for a moment about the suggestion. At first she thought she didn't want any further association with Jack's surgical plans as a way of protest, but rethinking the issue, she didn't want to cut off her nose to spite her face. On this visit, she'd be invited as a spouse of a patient, so she wouldn't be blamed for making an official ME visit. Laurie couldn't help but feel that if the MRSA cases weren't intentional, then it had to be some sort of systems error involving all three hospitals, and if there was any chance of her guessing what such an error could be, she'd have to have opportunities to visit, which Jack was obviously affording.

"Okay, I'll come," Laurie said with such sudden decisiveness that Jack was mildly taken aback.

"Wonderful," he said. "Let's hit the shower and be on our way."

Franco awoke but opened only one eye. His

cell phone was ringing, but before he answered it, he looked at his radio alarm to see the time. It was five-forty-five. Accompanied by an extended string of blasphemy and expletives, he snaked a hand out from beneath the covers and put the phone to his ear.

"Yeah?" he said with a tone that would let the caller know he was not happy about being disturbed at such an hour. The only reason he answered was because it might be Vinnie.

"Let's get a move on," Angelo said. "But let's not take your boat. Let's take a van."

With a few more carefully chosen expletives, Franco reminded Angelo what time it was.

"I know it's early," Angelo admitted. "But when I got back to my apartment last night, I called the ME office. I asked about Dr. Laurie Montgomery and was told she still works there. I also asked what time she comes into work, in case we can snatch her. I know these people work long hours."

"You're too damn eager," Franco complained.

"Vinnie wanted it done yesterday, don't you remember?"

"Yeah, I remember," Franco said reluctantly.

"Okay, let's meet up at the Neapolitan. I'll

get the van."

"The Neapolitan's not going to be open."

"Oh, you're right."

"Angelo, you're too into this. Slow down! It's when you're all keyed up that mistakes are made, like forgetting that nobody's at the damn restaurant until after ten."

"You're right. I am keyed up, but you would be, too, if you was me. I tell you what! I'll pick you up at your apartment at six-thirty. Okay?"

"You can still pick me up at the restaurant," Franco said. He didn't want to be without his car later on in the day. "There's always a place to park right in front as early as it is." He disconnected and threw his feet out from under the blankets. He sensed it was going to be a long day trying to tamp down Angelo's zeal, especially since knocking off a public servant who worked in a reasonably secure environment was not going to be a walk in the park.

Adam Williamson answered the phone on the first ring. Especially on a mission, he slept like a nervous cat, always prepared to leap up at the slightest provocation.

"Mr. Bramford, it is six o'clock, as you requested. The weather is expected to be cloudy with a possible shower and with a high temperature of sixty-two degrees."

Adam thanked the operator and immediately called room service for a full breakfast of juice, eggs, bacon, fried potatoes, and coffee. On missions like this one, he never knew when he'd have a chance to eat again on a stakeout of the target's home or place of work. To help him, his handlers always provided commercial plates in the particular state the operation was to take place, along with lettering on the Range Rover's doors. On this occasion, it was an interior design and antiques store on 10th Street called Biedermeier Heaven.

With a contented feeling that all was in order, Adam stepped into the shower. Ever since returning from Iraq, it was only at times like this that he felt whole: He was on a mission, and all was going according to plan. The only way it could have been better was if he were doing it with several of his fellow Delta Force buddies who'd been with him on his last, fateful military mission. Of course, the apogee was yet to come. That was when he made the kill.

Laurie stayed a few steps behind Jack as they entered Angels Orthopedic Hospital. It was significantly busier at six-fifteen in the morning than it had been at two-thirty the previous afternoon. As Jack went to the information booth, Laurie stayed close. Although she had a legitimate reason for being there, she was not interested in causing any sort of confrontation, such as what might happen if she had the misfortune of running into either Angela Dawson or Cynthia Sarpoulus. Loraine Newman probably would have been a different story, but even she might feel obligated to call the others if she saw Laurie. After all, they were her bosses.

Jack was given directions to the second floor. As they waited for an elevator, Jack noticed Laurie's vigilant behavior.

"What the devil's gotten into you?" he questioned. "You're like a squirrel expecting there's a dog in the neighborhood."

"I told you I wasn't treated with much hospitality yesterday. I'd just as soon avoid meeting the organization's CEO or their infection-control specialist."

"Don't be so paranoid. You have full right to be here."

"Maybe so, but I prefer not to get in any row about it."

On the second floor, they found their way with ease to the pre-op waiting area. The space was decorated more like a living room in a private mansion than part of a hospital. Even the name was a misnomer, as there was little waiting involved. Although there were a number of other patients for surgery the next day, there was adequate staff available. Jack and Laurie didn't even have to sit down before Jack was about to be taken back to an examination room where his blood was to be drawn.

"Do you have your cell phone?" Laurie asked Jack.

"Of course. Why?"

"I have mine as well. I'm going to run up to the fourth floor and visit the clinical pathology lab. Call me if I'm not back here when you're ready to go."

Jack winked. "So, you are going to make constructive use of your time?"

"Something like that," Laurie admitted.

Although Laurie initially didn't want to be recognized while visiting the hospital, she now changed her mind. She thought she'd use the opportunity to see if Walter Osgood was there. Remembering that she would be calling the CDC sometime during the day, she wanted to know if Walter Osgood would like to know if the MRSA infecting the hospitals, at least in three patients, was the self-same subtype, meaning they'd have to all three come from the same source. It had irked her the previous afternoon when he'd tried to justify not subtyping the bacteria on all the cases. From an epidemiological point of view, it was mandatory, especially in a situation where the source and the method of spread were unknown.

On the fourth floor, Laurie walked into the laboratory and asked the first technician she encountered if Dr. Osgood was there.

"I have no idea," the technician admitted. "You'd have to ask Dr. Friedlander, the supervisor of the clinical lab. His office is against the back wall. You can't miss it." She pointed across the room.

"I've heard that before," Laurie mumbled to herself as she walked in the direction she was shown. Despite her misgivings, she did stumble directly onto the office as the technician had suggested. Advancing to the open door, Laurie looked in at a thin, bearded man in a spotless, crisply ironed long white coat, engaged in paperwork at his desk.

"Excuse me," Laurie called out.

"Can I help you?"

"I'm looking for Dr. Osgood. Can you tell me if he is here this morning?"

"No, not today. Today he is . . ." Simon spun around in his chair to gaze at the bulletin board behind him. "He is at Angels Heart Hospital. He's here only Monday and Thursday."

"Thanks," Laurie said.

"Is there something I can help you with? I'm the supervisor of the clinical pathology lab."

"I think I need to talk directly with Dr. Osgood," Laurie said, although she briefly thought about asking Dr. Friedlander to convey the message.

"Is it urgent? We could always call. He's usually available on his cell."

"It involves the MRSA outbreak."

"I'd say that was important enough. And who exactly are you?"

After Laurie had identified herself, Dr. Friedlander made the call. As soon as he got Osgood on the line, he told him that a Dr. Laurie Montgomery was standing in his office and wanted to speak with him. Laurie reached out for the phone, but Dr. Friedlander put up his hand to have her wait. Laurie could not hear what Dr. Osgood was saying, but Dr. Friedlander locked eyes with her as he intermittently said "yes" into the phone with a final "I understand." He then dropped the receiver into its cradle before returning his attention to Laurie and said, "Sorry, I'm afraid Dr. Osgood is fully engaged. He asked that you call him back sometime today at the home office. I can give you the number." Taking one of his own business cards, he circled the Angels Healthcare number and, leaning across his desk, handed it over to Laurie.

Mildly chagrined at being so impersonally rejected when she thought she was about to do the man a favor, Laurie turned on her heels and walked out of the windowless office.

Now it was definitely an emergency, Walter Osgood reasoned. The first time it had been vague intuition, based mostly on Dr. Laurie Montgomery's resistance to accepting his rationale for failing to have the MRSA completely characterized. But now it was different. She was back in the Angels Orthopedic Hospital, despite the company's CEO all but telling her directly not to return, and on this occasion requesting to speak with him of all people.

Getting out the emergency number again, Walter called Washington. This time the phone rang even more times than it had the previous day, yet it was eventually answered. The deep, wary voice on this occasion sounded sleep-addled. "What is it this time?"

"The same problem."

"Are you on a landline?"

"Yes."

"Call me back at this number." The man

gave Walter another number, then disconnected.

Walter waited for several minutes before dialing. The same man answered, although the slight hoarseness was gone. "Are you talking about the medical examiner?"

"Yes, she came back this morning, apparently investigating even though she was all but told not to. She worries me. I'm not sure I want to continue if something is not done about her."

"Something is surely being done. You have to be patient."

"Like what is being done?" Walter demanded. He hated all the secrecy, especially since he was the one out in the cold.

"We have an individual in the city at this moment whose specialty is to take care of this kind of problem."

"You are going to have to be more specific."

"I think the less you know, the better."

"Are you saying someone is here in New York right now?"

"That's exactly what I am saying."

"How about his or her name and a number."

"Sorry, I can't do that."

"I'm not sure I want to continue with all this."

"I'm afraid you don't have any choice at this point. It was your option to begin, but it is not your option to stop. The pressure must be maintained at least for a few more days."

Walter felt a mixture of anger and fear, but the fear won out. He didn't respond.

"I hope your silence means you understand the reality of your situation."

"If she shows up again in the next few days, can I call you to let you know whomever you sent here hasn't convinced her to stop her meddling?"

"Yes, you do that, but rest assured, we have sent our best negotiator."

"One other question. I don't know your name."

"There's no need for you to know my name."

Similar to the call the day before, the line was cut off precipitously and Walter found himself listening to a dead line. Slowly, he hung up the receiver. Despite the reassurances the man had given, Walter panicked and wondered how bad a decision to become involved it would turn out to be when all was said and done. His only consolation was that his son had seemingly stabilized, and the doctors who were administering the supposed experimental treatment were moderately optimistic.

By the time Laurie had had the time to read only a few of the day's op-ed pieces in the *Times,* Jack had appeared accompanied by a youthful doctor dressed in scrubs but covered by a long, white coat as crisp and clean as Dr. Friedlander's. Apparently, such smartness was hospital policy. Laurie had to admit that it appeared far superior to some of the residents at the University Hospital who seemed to revel in having the most soiled white coats, as if it were testament to how hard they were working.

Jack introduced the man as Dr. Jeff Albright. To Laurie, he had the bluest eyes she'd ever seen.

"I'm lucky," Jack continued. "Dr. Albright has agreed to pass gas for me in the morning. I told him you were concerned about MRSA and me having surgery, so he graciously offered to come out and have a word with you and hopefully put your mind at ease."

Laurie shook hands with the anesthesiologist, and noting how young he appeared made her feel old by comparison. She also felt abashed from Jack's introduction, as if she were an oversolicitous mother. Jeff gave the usual stereotypical assurance and said that Jack was as healthy as an ox, making Laurie wonder just how healthy oxen were, since she thought the expression was "strong as an ox." When Jeff finished his prepared speech, Laurie asked him how many cases he'd done after which the patient came down with an MRSA infection.

Somewhat nervously, his eyes flicked back and forth between Laurie and Jack. Apparently, Jack had not asked such a specific question. "One," he finally admitted. "It was several months ago, after a shoulder rotator cuff repair. Like the others, it was totally unexpected and unfortunately fatal."

"What was the name?" Laurie asked.

"I'm not sure I'm at liberty to divulge that," Jeff said.

Laurie knew she had the right to ask, as it was undoubtedly a medical examiner case, but she didn't push the issue. The name didn't matter, other than to reassure herself she'd not missed a case. She was more interested in Jack's upcoming surgery.

"Was there anything you can remember about the case that was unusual?"

Jeff shook his head. "It went entirely smoothly. Well, there was one thing. We staff have been regularly tested for MRSA ourselves on a weekly basis. During the week that the death occurred, I did turn positive.

Whether it happened from that patient, I don't know. But I can safely say I'm free now. I was screened just yesterday."

"I'm happy to report I'm also free of those buggers," Jack said.

"Were you the anesthesiologist for David Jeffries on Monday?" Laurie asked.

"No, I wasn't. That was Dolores Suarez."

"Thank you for talking with me," Laurie said. She smiled weakly. Jeff's efforts didn't make her any more confident.

"We'll take good care of your husband," Jeff promised. He said good-bye and disappeared back into the examining area.

"So," Jack said. "You have to admit this is a nice operation, so to speak. Just the fact there's no waiting makes it unique."

"It's neat, it's clean, it's pleasant," Laurie admitted. "But there is obviously a problem here, despite its apparent cleanliness."

"Don't tell me you are not reassured."

"MRSA is surely not respecting the luxurious venue."

"You are impossible," Jack said with a sigh. "Every hospital is seeing MRSA."

"But every hospital is not seeing multiple cases of MRSA necrotizing pneumonia that's killing people as if it were a raging hemorrhagic fever like Ebola."

"Come on!" Jack said with some frustra-

462

tion. "Let's get to work."

"This is a fucking mess," Franco complained. "This is what you got me out of bed for?" He gestured ahead through the van's windshield. In front of the medical examiner's office was an unruly crowd of fifty or sixty people staging an unauthorized protest over the medical examiner's initial report regarding Concepcion Lopez, whom Bingham had posted the day before. Most of the protestors were Hispanic. And most were carrying amateurish placards taped or stapled to broom handles attesting to a supposed cover-up and complaining of police brutality to the Hispanic community.

"What I can't figure is what they're doing here so goddamn early," Angelo said.

"I'd guess to get on the morning news," Franco said. "Besides, they get more bang for the buck if they block rush-hour traffic, which they are obviously doing."

Many of the protestors were wandering out into First Avenue. Police in riot gear were waiting to be called out of their bus parked on 30th Street. For the time being, the regular police were trying to keep the crowd out of the streets and confined to an area directly in front of the OCME but with minimal success.

Franco and Angelo were sitting in the Lucia organization's van, which was mostly used for hijacking and other forms of thieving at Kennedy Airport. They were parked at the curb between 29th and 30th streets in a no parking/no standing area in front of one of the original Bellevue Hospital buildings. They had a good view of the entrance to the OCME, except for a Range Rover parked in front of them.

"What's with this SUV?" Angelo complained. "This is a no-parking zone for chrissake. It's amazing how people just ignore the law."

"Calm down!" Franco responded.

Angelo hit the steering wheel several times in frustrated anger. "Of all days, why do they have to have their protest today?"

"You're getting yourself all worked up," Franco warned. "Why don't we just leave. With all these cops around, much less all these bellyaching nuts, there's no way we're going to be able to make a grab."

"I want to at least see her," Angelo groused. "Then I want to go to Home Depot."

With a dumbfounded expression, Franco looked over at Angelo. "Home Depot? What the hell are you going to get at Home Depot?"

Angelo returned the stare, and in the process raised his eyebrows as much as he was able.

"Wait a second!" Franco said, suddenly remembering. "Tell me you're not going to get a bucket and quick-set!"

"Vinnie specifically said I could do it my way, and that is exactly what I plan to do. Ever since I saw it in that movie, I've wanted to do it to someone who deserved it, and no one deserves it more than Laurie Montgomery, as I'm sure Vinnie would agree."

"Oh, for the love of God." Franco groaned, raising his eyes heavenward.

"There she is!" Angelo shouted excitedly, pointing out his side window. He reached for the door handle and had the door open before Franco was able to get ahold of his arm.

"What the hell do you think you're doing?" Franco shouted as Angelo struggled to free his arm. "The place is crawling with cops. It's suicide to go out there."

Angelo stopped struggling, pulled his foot in, and closed the door. He knew Franco was right. There was no way he could approach Laurie under the circumstances. As tense with anticipation as he'd been all morning, he'd reacted by reflex when he'd caught sight of her getting out of a taxi on the opposite side of the street, obviously avoiding the crowd of protesters in front of the OCME. Suffering from acute and frustrating impotence, he was forced to watch Laurie a mere fifty or so feet away as she leaned back into the taxi and extracted a pair of crutches. Next to emerge was Jack.

"That's her boyfriend," Angelo growled. "I wouldn't mind icing him at the same time."

"Calm down!" Franco said again. "I feel like I'm sitting with a mad dog."

For almost a minute, Laurie and Jack stood in plain sight, severely testing Angelo's restraint, waiting for the light to change. Then, like a cat forced to watch a tempting mouse walk directly in front of its nose, Angelo had to find the self-control to witness their slow progress across First Avenue. When they turned to cross 30th Street, they were only the length of the Range Rover in front.

"This would have been perfect, if it hadn't been for the protest."

"Maybe so, maybe not," Franco said philosophically. "So now you've seen her, let's get the hell out of here."

Angelo started the van. "I'm thinking," he said. "She's going to recognize me just as easily as I recognized her."

"Maybe easier," Franco agreed.

"That means we should have more people." Angelo put the van in gear, looked behind him down First Avenue, and pulled away from the curb. "When we come back later this afternoon, I think we should have Freddie and Richie with us."

"I think that's a good idea," Franco agreed.

Adam had scouted the area around the OCME the night before and had come up with a plan to make a definitive ID on the target. He'd arrived that morning just before seven and had parked his Range Rover in an appropriate no-parking zone where he was reasonably confident the commercial plates would work their usual magic. He hadn't been happy about the protest, which was just beginning to form, not because of the people and the confusion they would cause but because of the TV vans and crews he assumed would be sent to cover the event. Adam wanted to avoid at all costs being caught on film.

As he'd expected, the outer door to the OCME had been open, although it had been locked the night before. Why he'd been so sure it would be open in the morning was that by peering in the previous night, he had been able to see a reception desk inside and another set of glass doors beyond.

Once inside, Adam had retreated to a vinyl

couch with a copy of *The New York Times*. The receptionist asked Adam if she could be of assistance. He had told her that he was told to wait for one of the medical examiners.

For fifteen minutes, Adam had sat in the reception area. Several people had come in, including one medical examiner whom the receptionist had greeted as Dr. Mehta. The other people had been addressed by their first names. The receptionist's name he learned was Marlene Wilson.

At exactly seven-fifteen, the outer door opened. The first person to come in did so on crutches. Adam lowered the paper so he could see over the top. The second person looked encouraging. She was of medium height with sculptured features, brunette hair with auburn highlights, and a surprisingly pale, almost blond complexion. In Adam's mind she matched the description, as meager as it was, but he had to be certain.

"Good morning, you two," the receptionist said to Adam's chagrin, meaning he was forced to go to plan B. He'd quickly learned the modus operandi for entry was for the receptionist to make verbal contact before buzzing the employees in. The regular employees went through the double doors directly opposite doors to the street. The one medical doctor who'd come in went to a door beyond the receptionist's desk to be buzzed in, requiring her to walk across the room in front of Adam. The person Adam believed to be the target proceeded to follow the route of the previous doctor, as did the man on the crutches.

"Excuse me," Adam called out. "Are you Dr. Laurie Montgomery?"

Laurie stopped a step beyond Adam, as did Jack, who was almost even with the man's location.

Adam got to his feet and regarded Laurie for a beat. In keeping with her light complexion, her eyes were a pale blue-green. Adam asked again if she were Laurie Montgomery.

"Why do you ask?" Laurie questioned.

"I'm from ABC Collection," Adam said. "Could you tell me if you have ever lived in the SoHo section of Greenwich Village?"

Laurie exchanged a questioning glance with Jack. "No, I haven't," Laurie said.

"But your name is Laurie Montgomery."

"Yes, but I've never lived in SoHo."

"Sorry to bother you, then," Adam said and started for the door.

"Why are you looking for a Laurie Montgomery in SoHo, if I may ask?"

"For a phone bill which was unpaid when

she moved."

"Sorry," Laurie said as she turned toward the ID room door.

Adam continued outside. The protest was in full swing, with the protesters marching in a circle in front of the building, chanting over and over in unison, "Police brutality must be stopped! Cover-up! Cover-up!"

Being careful to avoid any chance of being caught by any of the cameras, Adam returned to his vehicle, climbed in, and then skirted the commotion. Heading north on First Avenue, he thought he'd return to the hotel, do a little planning over a second cup of coffee, and then head up to the Metropolitan Museum. It had been a favorite destination in his youth. He was quite certain he'd not see Laurie Montgomery until late that afternoon. Since he had yet to have her home address, he was going to have to rely on the OCME to provide access.

19
April 4, 2007
7:20 a.m.

"Well, it's about time, you guys," Detective Lieutenant Lou Soldano said. He tossed his newspaper aside and made a production out of examining his watch. "You've always bragged how early you get here. This ain't that early."

"What is this?" Jack questioned. "Is this today, or is it yesterday? We don't see you for months, and here you are two days in a row. What gives?"

"I imagine my appearance gives away the fact that once again I've been up all night."

"How come you don't let anyone else in your department do any work?"

Lou thought for a minute. It was a question he'd never asked himself. "I guess because I don't have anything else to do. I suppose that sounds rather pathetic."

"You said it, I didn't," Jack said, as he settled into one of the brown vinyl chairs and elevated his bad knee.

"We would have been earlier," Laurie said, "but we had to stop at the hospital for Jack's pre-op workup."

Lou looked from Laurie to Jack. "Are you still going through with the surgery tomorrow?"

"Let's not get into that," Jack said. "Rather, let's hear why you were up all night!"

"It was a bit of déjà vu," Lou said.

Laurie called over to Jack to ask if he wanted coffee, and he gave the usual thumbs-up sign. He then motioned for Lou to continue.

"I was out with the harbor guys once again. Just like the previous night, they'd come across a floater who'd been shot in the exact same fashion as the one the previous night. I'd left word to call me if it happened, and they did. It's just what I didn't want to see. Most of the other wars the competing organized-crime syndicates have waged have started out the same way. First a hit, then another, and then a goddamn avalanche."

Laurie brought over Jack's coffee in one hand and hers in another. She sat on the arm of Jack's chair, listening to Lou.

"The only hopeful sign is that this hit was a little different."

"How so?" Jack asked.

472

"The victim's a girl," Lou said, but then quickly added, "I mean, a woman." He glanced up guiltily at Laurie. He knew she was sensitive to feminist issues, such as calling women *girls*. "That's rather novel," he continued. "We haven't seen too many women bumped off gangland-style, so I suppose there's hope this episode is unrelated to yesterday's, meaning it's not necessarily an escalation of whatever was the cause of yesterday's hit."

"The floater is not the only bit of déjà vu," Dr. Riva Mehta called out from the desk where she was going over all the cases that had come in overnight and deciding which ones needed to be autopsied and who in the ME staff would do them. "Laurie, you asked about MRSA cases. There's another one here. I assume you want it."

"Absolutely," Laurie said, slipping off the arm of Jack's chair and scooting over toward Riva. "Is it from an Angels Healthcare hospital?"

"Nope. It's from University Hospital."

Laurie took the case folder and walked over to the chair next to Vinnie's, who was engrossed as per usual in the sports section of the *Daily News*.

"Damn!" Jack whispered, returning his attention to Lou. "She's probably going to use

473

this new case as more grist for her mill about canceling my surgery tomorrow. So please, don't bring it up."

"I'll try, but when it comes to common sense, you are not even in Laurie's league. Are you sure you shouldn't follow her advice?"

"Don't start," Jack said, holding up his hand as if to ward off a literal attack. "Let's get back to your case. Was the floater clothed or naked?"

"Interesting you should ask. She was half and half."

"What the hell does that mean? Bottom but no top or vice versa?"

"Sort of. She had outerwear but no underwear. She had on one of those shirtdresses. I think that's what you call them, and she was wearing a coat but no bra and no panties. I don't know if it's significant or not. I mean, isn't it kind of a fad these days for some girls, I mean women, to go out without underwear?"

"You got me," Jack said. "I haven't the faintest idea. Regardless, we're obligated to use a rape kit to cover all bases."

"I think I was born too early," Lou said with a laugh.

"Has this floater been IDed?"

"No, in that way, it's similar to yesterday's."

"How about yesterday's? Have you identified the victim?"

"No. And I put some serious time in on it yesterday. I can't figure it out. The guy was wearing a wedding ring and was well dressed. I don't understand why the family hasn't called in. In such a case, Missing Persons ordinarily solves the mystery in twenty-four hours or less. My only thought is that maybe he's a foreigner. Now, with today's case, who I suspect is single, I will be less surprised if it takes a few days, unless the woman has a roommate or the kind of employment where a supervisor or a coworker will call the police."

"How old approximately?"

"Young, late teens, early twenties."

"Does she look like a hooker?"

"How can you tell these days the way the kids dress? The only thing unique is some lime-green highlights in her hair."

"Lime green?" Jack questioned with disbelief.

"As I said, it's unique."

"Does she have the same depressions in her legs like she was chained, possibly to a weight, like yesterday's?"

"She does, which is why I've tried to keep that fact quiet. If there is to be more of these gangland executions, I want them to keep bobbing up. I want the perps to continue making the same mistake."

"What do you expect out of the autopsy?"

"Hey, I don't know," Lou said, throwing his hands into the air. "You're the magician."

"I wish that were the case."

"I do want the slug. If it's again a Remington high-velocity hollow point like I believe yesterday's was, we'll at least have to consider the same gun was used for both cases."

"Was the body found where the other one was?"

"Not really, but not that far away, either. The way the current and tides move around out there, it's anybody's guess where flotsam will end up."

"All right, let's do it," Jack said. He got to his feet and collected his crutches, then hobbled over to Riva. "Is the new floater file handy?" he asked her. "And can I do the case?" Riva was happy to hand over the case file, and Jack used it to swat Vinnie's newspaper. "Let's go, big guy," Jack said, as he dropped the case file into Vinnie's lap. "Let's lend a hand to the halls of justice."

Vinnie groused, as was his habit, but to his credit, he put away the paper and got to his feet.

"We'll need a rape kit," Jack added.

Vinnie nodded and headed toward communications on his way down to the autopsy room.

Jack looked over Riva's shoulder at the stack of cases she was reviewing. "Looks like a busy day."

"Even busier than yesterday," Riva said.

"Hey, I'll meet you downstairs," Lou called over to Jack. Jack waved for him to go ahead.

"Have any corkers?" Jack asked. He tried to rifle through several of Riva's carefully organized case files, but she smacked the back of his hand with the ruler she kept handy for that very purpose. "Ouch," Jack said as he grabbed his hand and rubbed it, pretending he'd been truly hurt.

"There's a couple in here which I think will be a challenge," Riva said.

"That sounds good," Jack said. "How many can I expect?"

"At least three," Riva said. "I've got two people who've requested paper days, so the rest of us will have to pick up the slack." Paper days were days that medical examiners did not do autopsies but rather concentrated on getting all the information needed to finish their pending cases and finalize the death certificates.

"Jack, I'm afraid you have to look at this," Laurie said. She'd gone through the MRSA case that Riva had given her.

Jack rolled his eyes. It wasn't difficult for him to guess that Laurie was about to mount one more effort to get him to change his mind.

"This case is a repeat of David Jeffries's," Laurie began. "She also had been operated on at an Angels Healthcare hospital, only to suffer a fulminant MRSA infection, for which she was shipped off to the University Hospital in hope of saving her."

"Thank the good Lord it wasn't at the orthopedic hospital," Jack said.

"Jack, be serious!" Laurie complained. "This is the second astoundingly fulminant staph infection in as many days. You must rethink your decision. The vast majority of MRSA infections don't kill their victims, and surely not within hours of the initial symptoms. These are very unusual in all regards. Why can't you see this?"

"I do see it. It is a mystery, and I'm supportive of your efforts to figure it out. As for me, I've put myself in Dr. Wendell Anderson's very capable hands. If he's confident, I'm confident. If you can come up with something specific why I am specifically at risk, I'll consider it more seriously, but otherwise my mind is made up. I've even been tested for MRSA, and I don't have it. Dr.

Anderson has not had a case. In short, I'm going to have my surgery tomorrow, and that's it." Jack stopped and took several breaths. He'd worked himself up during his monologue. He and Laurie locked eyes for a beat, then he said, "Now I'm going down and do my first case. Okay?"

Laurie nodded. The melancholy she'd experienced on awakening drifted back. She felt tears bubble up from somewhere behind her eyes, but she fought them off. "Okay," she said, with a slightly hesitant voice. "I'll see you in the pit."

"I'll see you in the pit," Jack echoed, and walked from the room.

Riva and Laurie stared at each other, with Laurie wanting support and Riva wanting to give it.

"The trouble with men," Riva pontificated, "is that they are men, and they don't think like we do. The irony is that they accuse us of emotionalism, whereas they are equally capable. He'd made an emotional decision to have the surgery and, at this point, he's incapable of rationality."

Laurie smiled in spite of herself. "Thank you," she said. "I needed that."

"Interesting that he did offer you an out," Riva said. "And I can be the witness. He said if you could come up with something that could specifically put him at risk, he'd be amenable to hear it. Of course, he didn't offer to change his mind, but he might. What you need to do is find out the how and the why of these infections. I know it is a tall order in less than twenty-four hours, but from your past record, if anybody could do it, you can."

Laurie nodded agreement, not the part about her being the most capable of the challenge but rather the idea of her possibly changing Jack's mind by her solving the apparent mystery. Suddenly, Laurie stood up and headed out of the room. Her melancholy had been overwhelmed by a surge of adrenaline. She was committed to the puzzle, no matter how unlikely the success, and undaunted by the seemingly impossible time constraint.

"I'm afraid I will have to assign you a few other cases," Riva called after her.

Laurie waved to indicate she'd heard.

"Do you want the case files now or later?" Riva yelled.

Laurie stopped and hurried back to Riva.

"They should be both interesting and quick," Riva said, while handing over the two envelopes. "Both are young, seemingly healthy people in their early thirties, so the posts will be quick and you can get back to your MRSA mystery."

"What's the presumed cause of death?"

"There isn't any. One died at the dentist's office after getting injected with a local anesthetic. I know it sounds like a drug reaction, but there were no symptoms of anaphylaxis. The other collapsed at a health club while riding a stationary bike."

"I'm here!" a voice called out. "The day can now officially begin."

Both Laurie and Riva looked up as Chet bounded into the room. He swirled his jacket over his head like a lariat and let it fly into one of the vinyl club chairs.

"Where is everyone?" he asked, looking confused. He'd expected to see Jack.

"Jack and Vinnie are already downstairs," Laurie said. "You're even more chipper than yesterday, and almost on time two days in a row. What gives? Don't tell me you scored a dinner date with your new woman friend."

Chet stood up straight, flashed a Boy Scout signal with his raised right hand, and clicked his heels. "Scouts never lie. I did indeed, and I'm happy to report she was more intriguing and beautiful than I had remembered. I actually enjoyed talking with her."

"Listen to this, Riva! We are witnessing the

possible stirring of maturity in this heretofore juvenile. He was content merely to learn about another human, female being."

"Now, I wouldn't go that far," Chet said. "I was still plotting to get her back to my apartment or me over to hers, but she cut me off with just dinner."

"Darn," Laurie said, snapping her fingers in sham disappointment.

"I have to thank you for your advice, Laurie. I'm sure the date wouldn't have happened had it not been for your encouragement and advice."

"You're very welcome," Laurie said. She turned to Riva. "Thanks for these cases. They're perfect." Laurie started once again to leave.

"She took me completely by surprise," Chet continued, forcing Laurie to hold up. "She's a doctor; she's boarded in internal medicine. On top of that, she's CEO of what has to be a multimillion-dollar company that builds and runs specialty hospitals. I mean she is one impressive lady."

Laurie experienced an unpleasant visceral contraction accompanied by a sensation akin to dizziness which resolved as quickly as it had appeared. She cleared her throat before asking, "Is her name by any chance Angela Dawson?"

"It is!" Chet exclaimed. "Do you know her?"

"Vaguely," Laurie said with surprise. "I have met her, and unfortunately I have to say I wasn't as impressed as you are."

"Why not?"

"I'm afraid I don't have time to explain now, but let me just say that I sensed her priorities as a businesswoman were trumping those of a physician."

Laurie knew Chet would undoubtedly have more questions, but she had to move on. Despite his protests, she excused herself. Walking quickly through communications, where notification of all the deaths of the city were received, she began to plan her day. With as little time as she had before Jack went under the knife, she would need to be efficient. The first stop was the forensic investigator's office. Janice Jaeger had done the site visit on the new MRSA case, and Laurie wanted to question her. More than once, Laurie had learned something important from Janice's wealth of experience that had not gotten into the report. Forensic investigators were tasked to include only facts, not impressions.

Laurie found Janice finishing up after a long night. She was the sole PA officially working from eleven to seven but rarely left before eight. She was aided, if need be, by forensic pathology residents who rotated night call. If even more backup was needed or the case was particularly challenging, one of the medical examiners was also available.

"Did I miss something?" Janice asked, as Laurie came up to her desk. Laurie got along famously with all the PA's but particularly with Janice, who appreciated Laurie's recognition of her work. More than any of the MEs, Laurie was constantly coming to her and asking questions and valuing her opinion.

"I'm about to do Ramona Torres," Laurie said. "I gathered from your note you made a site visit to the University Hospital."

"I did indeed."

"Did you sense anything about the case that you thought was interesting or unique but not appropriate for your report?"

Janice smiled. Laurie was always asking her probing questions. "I did, actually," Janice said. "I got the feeling the doctors were upset that they weren't getting the Angels Healthcare septic patients soon enough to make a difference concerning survival."

"Did you make a visit to the Angels Healthcare Cosmetic Surgery and Eye Hospital?"

"No, I did not," Janice said. "Not in this

case. Do you think I should have?"

"I can't say," Laurie admitted. "But you have visited Angels Healthcare hospitals in conjunction with other MRSA cases."

"Absolutely," Janice said. "On a number of occasions."

"I've read several of your reports. What's your general feeling about the hospitals and these recurrent MRSA cases?"

Janice smiled again. "Do you want the truth?"

"Of course! I wouldn't be asking if I didn't."

"I don't know how to explain it, but I feel like something strange is going on. I mean, it's nothing I can write in my report, but they keep having these infections and yet keep doing the surgery. Whenever I ask any type of question in this regard, they say that they are doing everything they possibly can. Meanwhile, people are dying."

"I've had the same response," Laurie admitted. "Thanks for your opinion. Is Cheryl around?"

"She's out on a call. Bart Arnold is around. Do you want to speak with him?" Bart Arnold was the chief of forensic investigation and ran the department.

"No. Just leave a message that I need the hospital record for Ramona Torres. They can e-mail it to me like they did with the others."

"Not a problem."

Laurie rushed all the way to the front elevators to save time: Not only were they faster, there were more of them. She bounded into her office, laid the three case files on her desk, and hung up her coat. Snatching up the phone, she called down to the mortuary office and asked for Marvin. When she got him on the line, she asked him if he would work with her again that day. She said she wanted to be expeditious. He agreed with his usual cheerful readiness. Laurie gave him Ramona Torres's accession number, said she wanted to do her first, and then rang off.

She looked at the clock. One of the first things she wanted to do that day was call the CDC, but fearing they might not be functioning as early as it was, she turned her attention to reviewing the day's autopsy cases. That required rereading the case file of Ramona Torres. After doing so, she felt confident the post would be similar to David Jeffries's. Putting that one aside, she picked up the first of the two sudden-death cases and pulled out the PA's report.

The patient's name was Alexandra Zuben, age twenty-nine. She had visited the dentist for a root canal and had received the local anesthesia as Riva had described. At the very outset of the procedure, the patient suddenly had fallen unconscious. After she had been placed in a head-down position, she'd revived and insisted the procedure continue. A few minutes later, the same situation had developed, although on this occasion she did not revive, 911 had been called, and the patient had been rushed to the hospital, where she was found to have an arrhythmia, a markedly elevated blood pressure, and little or no respiratory efforts. She'd been put on a ventilator, but despite aggressive therapy, she had progressed to a cardiac arrest that could not be reversed. The emergency-room diagnosis had been recorded as respiratory failure compounded with cardiac failure secondary to severe allergic reaction and anaphylaxis to Novocain. The PAs concluded with the fact that a family member had said that the patient was remarkably healthy but had had, on occasion, several syncopal attacks involving palpitations, flushing, and heavy perspiration.

Laurie slipped the PA's report back into its folder. Her initial impression was that the emergency-room diagnosis was in error, and she had a reasonable idea of what she would find on the autopsy. Of particular note, she was reasonably certain she would not need any special equipment for the post.

Next, Laurie took out the PA's report on her third case. It was very short. It merely said that Ronald Carpentu had been on a semirecumbent stationary bike, which he used most every day, and had suddenly collapsed. Immediate CPR had been given by the health club's personnel but without success, 911 had been called, and the CPR was continued en route to the emergency room. On arrival, the patient was declared dead with the diagnosis of a severe heart attack.

Laurie replaced the PA's report. On this third case, she was quite certain the emergency-room diagnosis would prove to be correct, but there was still the question of why. Laurie guessed atheromatous heart disease. Again, she would not need any specialized equipment.

Picking up the phone, she called down to the autopsy room. It rang six times, causing Laurie to drum her fingers on her desk. While she waited, she thought about the weird coincidence of her giving Chet advice about dating Angela Dawson, of all people.

"Hello," a voice said, sounding more like "Yellow."

Laurie asked for Marvin, and after only a few seconds, he came on the line. "Are we ready?" Laurie asked.

"We've been ready for hours," Marvin joked.

Less than five minutes later, Laurie was suited up and staring down at Ramona's corpse. As with David Jeffries, an endotracheal tube and a number of intravenous lines were still in place. But the most striking thing was the extensive bruising over much of her body from the liposuction.

"You are motivated today," Marvin said, in a reference to how quickly Laurie had gotten down to the basement level, changed into her barrier protective gear, and come into the autopsy room. Besides her case, there was only one other under way, and that was the floater. Laurie hadn't even stopped to see how it was going.

"I want to be as efficient as I can," Laurie admitted. "I promise I won't leave you high and dry like I did yesterday. I apologize again. I got sidetracked and lost all idea of the time."

"No sweat," Marvin said, seemingly embarrassed that Laurie felt she needed to apologize.

Laurie palpated Ramona's skin and looked at it closely. It had a spongy feel, and there were multiple tiny abscesses such that Laurie felt that had she lived, she would probably have sloughed off a large part of her epidermis.

After taking a number of photographs, Laurie began the case. She worked quickly and silently. When Marvin asked questions, she answered as if preoccupied, and he soon stopped. Since they worked together so often, there was little need to talk.

As with David Jeffries, the most notable pathological finding, besides the extensive cellulitis, was in the lungs. Both were fluid-filled and contained innumerable small abscesses that would have coalesced into larger and larger ones had the patient lived. As with Jeffries, the necrosis was substantial.

When the final suture had been placed, closing the autopsy incision, Laurie stepped back from the table. She glanced around the room. Now, all eight tables were being utilized. Looking over near the door, she could see that Jack, Lou, and Vinnie were still involved with the floater.

"That was one of the fastest autopsies I've seen," Marvin commented, as he began to clean up.

"How soon can you have the next case?" Laurie asked.

"Fifteen minutes or so," Marvin said. "Do you have a preference as to which one of the two should be next?"

"It doesn't matter," Laurie said. "I wouldn't

fault you if you don't believe me, but I'm going upstairs to make one phone call, and then I'll be back."

Marvin smiled.

Laurie stopped briefly at Jack's table and jokingly asked why he was taking so long. Jack was known to be one of the fastest prosectors.

"Because these two windbags talk like a couple of old ladies," Vinnie said disgustingly.

"We're being thorough," Jack said. "Even before the micro and the lab contribute, we know this young woman was raped rather brutally."

"Which raises the question," Lou said, "was it a rape followed by a homicide, or was it a homicide and an incidental rape?"

"Unfortunately, the autopsy is not going to provide us with an answer to that question," Jack said.

Laurie excused herself and exited via the washroom to ditch her gloves and Tyvek disposable suit. Her face mask she wiped clean with alcohol and left it in her locker. Intent on not keeping Marvin waiting, she dashed upstairs.

Back in her office, Laurie dialed Dr. Silvia Salerno at the CDC. As the call went through, she wedged the phone between her head and shoulder to free her hands. Shuffling through the case files on her desk, she located Chet's case, Julia Francova. She opened it up with the hopes of being able to add the subtyping of the patient's MRSA.

When the phone wasn't answered immediately, Laurie looked at the time. It was now going on nine, and she was certain the CDC had to be open for business. "Come on, come on!" Laurie urged. "Answer the damn phone."

Just when she thought about checking to see if the CDC had a paging system, the line was picked up. It was Silvia, and she was mildly out of breath. She immediately apologized, saying she had been in a neighboring office.

"I hope I'm not bothering you," Laurie said. "I know you said you'd be calling me, but the sooner I have some information, the better."

"Don't be silly," Silvia said. "You certainly aren't bothering me, and I was planning on calling this morning. I did check on those two MRSA cases of Dr. Mehta's. They are the same organism, and I can say that with definite certainty. Because we are adding these strains to the national library of MRSA, we go out of our way to characterize them, and we do this with multiple genetic methods, such as high-throughput amplified fragment-length polymorphism analysis. I could send you a list of the other methods we use."

"Thank you, but I don't believe that will be necessary," Laurie said. She had no idea what Silvia was talking about. "But I do have another case, which had been sent to you people a number of weeks ago for typing. Specifically, it was sent to a Dr. Percy."

"Dr. Percy is a colleague. What was the referring doctor's name?"

"Dr. Chet McGovern. He's a colleague of mine here at the OCME."

"What was the patient's name?"

Laurie spelled out the name to avoid any confusion.

"Hang on for a minute."

Laurie could hear the familiar sound of Silvia's keyboard, making her wonder how anything got done before digital computers.

"Yes, here it is," Silvia said. "Interesting! It's also CA-MRSA, USA four hundred, MWtwo, SCCmecIV, PVL, exactly like the two previous cases. Is it from the same institution?"

"It's from one of the same institutions," Laurie said. "Remember, the first two were from two separate hospitals."

"Yes, I remember. Concerning the two

cases at the same institution, are they close to each other in time, maybe even the same date?"

Laurie turned to her unfinished matrix, but she did have the data from Mehta's case from the Angels Cosmetic Surgery and Eye Hospital. The patient's name was Diane Lucente, and like Ramona, she'd had liposuction. Laurie checked the date of Diane's death and Chet's case. "No," Laurie said. "They occurred almost three weeks apart."

"How odd," Silvia said. "I guess you know how genetically versatile staphylococcus is."

"I'm on a rather steep learning curve," Laurie admitted. "But I was informed of that yesterday."

"I find that the exact subtype being separated by institution and time quite amazing. All three must have been in contact with the same carrier."

"Did you have this specific subtype in your collection before Dr. Mehta sent you the isolate?"

"Yes, we did. As I told you last time, it is one of the most virulent subtypes we've seen for all sorts of test animals as well as humans."

"Do you send out cultures of these organisms?"

"We do. We support any number of researchers willing to work with these organisms."

"Have you ever sent this particular organism to New York City?"

"I don't know offhand, but I can find out."

"I'd appreciate it," Laurie said. The nagging concern of the bacteria being spread purposefully resurfaced in Laurie's brain, yet the old arguments against such an idea resurfaced as well, each essentially canceling the other.

"I have asked around the center if anyone was aware of the cluster of MRSA cases you are investigating, but no had heard about it."

"Is that odd or not?" Laurie asked.

"No. It's up to the individual institutions if they want to contact us for assistance. There's no mandatory reporting to us, but there probably is to the state or city authorities."

"Did you get the other isolates I had our microbiology department overnight to you?"

"Yes, I did. They are in the works. I shall have some results in two to three days — four, tops."

Laurie thanked the woman for her help and rang off. For a moment, she sat at her desk and went over the conversation. She had to admit that the call had deepened the mystery, not solved it.

Suddenly remembering the time, she leaped up from her desk and dashed for the elevator. She was afraid she had once again kept Marvin waiting despite her promise not to do so.

Carlo followed Brennan out of the electronics store on Lexington Avenue in Manhattan. Brennan had purchased a GPS tracking device from a company that specialized in marine as well as terrestrial applications. Once outside, they found that it had started to sprinkle, so they ran for the black GMC Denali.

"I'm glad to see it started to rain," Carlo said, as he revved the engine before pulling out into the traffic.

"How come?" Brennan asked, absorbed in slitting the cellophane wrapping of the box containing the tracking device. He loved electronic contrivances and had had a ball picking out the item. He'd spent such a long time discussing with the salesman the pluses and minuses of the array of tracking devices the store carried that Carlo had become totally bored.

"Because there'll be less chance of people hanging around the marina. I don't want anyone seeing us hiding the thing on the boat. You know what I'm saying?"

Brennan didn't answer. Instead, he was easing the tracking device out of the box's foam interior.

"Hey!" Carlo demanded. He didn't like to be ignored. "Are you listening to me?"

"Sort of," Brennan admitted. He looked into the depths of the molded foam packing material.

"I'm talking about the rain and the marina. I asked you if you agreed it was to our advantage it was raining."

Brennan at last found what he was looking for. It was a packet containing an operating directions booklet but, more important, an online registration code.

"Well?" Carlo questioned with irritation.

Brennan next used his penknife on the packaging for the device itself, but before he could free it from its cellophane mummification, his head snapped forward from an openhanded blow from Carlo.

"What the hell!" Brennan yelled. He turned and glared at Carlo. "What did you hit me for?" he growled.

"I was talking to you," Carlo yelled back. "You were ignoring me. I don't like to be ignored. It pisses me off."

Brennan stared at Carlo. He was in a momentary rage. Luckily, he controlled himself, since Carlo was behind the wheel and they were hurtling down Lexington Avenue in a clot of traffic. Carlo might have been bigger and older, but he sure as hell wasn't wiser. In fact, he was somewhat of a lunkhead, and it was that realization that enabled Brennan to calm down a degree.

"Don't hit me ever again," Brennan voiced slowly, emphasizing each syllable.

"Then don't ignore me when I'm talking to you," Carlo snapped back.

Brennan rolled his eyes, shook his head, and went back to the operating instructions. He was pretty sure how the tracking device worked, but he wanted to read up on registering it for the real-time online services.

"I'm sorry I hit you," Carlo said after a few blocks. "Being ignored is a pet peeve of mine."

"Sorry to hear that," Brennan said.

They drove in silence for a while, to Brennan's relief. He finished reading how to register the device and then skimmed over the operating directions. Armed with all that information, he got his laptop from the rear seat and his cell phone from his jacket pocket. Once the laptop was booted up, he called the company. Not only did he want to register, he wanted to make sure that if the device was lost, it could not be traced back to him. Apparently, it was not an unusual request, because the service individual was able to oblige with ease.

"How long will it take to be online?" Brennan asked.

"Since I just got an okay on your credit card, I'm doing it as we speak."

Brennan thanked the man. Next, he opened the back of the device and inserted the four triple-A Copper Tops he'd bought as well. Going back to the company's website, he clicked on the position icon, then added the password and user name he'd just gotten. With another click, he got an hourglass, and a few seconds later, a query appeared asking him to select the size of the area he wanted to display. Brennan clicked 5 miles by 2.8 miles. A second later, there was a small blinking dot moving slowly along Lexington Avenue.

Turning the laptop screen in Carlo's direction, he said, "It works. It shows us heading south."

"Impressive," Carlo said. "How does it work?"

"It would take too long to explain," Brennan said. "But in essence, it's simple triangulation using satellite signals."

"That's enough," Carlo said. His lack of knowledge of current electronic devices made him feel inadequate.

As usual, the traffic was bad going across town, and the rain, as light as it was, made it worse. The driving was stop-and-go the whole way.

Carlo's cell phone startled both of them. With a bit of a struggle, Carlo got it out and checked the caller ID. Satisfied, he accepted the call, put it on speakerphone, and nestled the phone into a cubby on the center console.

"What's up?" Carlo questioned

"Nothing," Arthur MacEwan said in his high-pitched, shrill voice that drove everybody nuts. "Absolutely nothing. We've been here for over two hours, and Franco Ponti's hog of a car hasn't moved an inch."

Arthur MacEwan and Ted Polowski were parked in the back of Johnny's parking lot and had been there staking out Franco's car since before eight that morning.

"Have you seen the Hawk?"

"Nope. No sign of Franco. We did see Vinnie Dominick when he arrived with Freddie Capuso and Richie Herns. They've been inside the Neapolitan and have yet to reappear."

"How about scarface?"

"Haven't seen Angelo, either. We're getting tired of sitting here, and I'm wondering if it's a good idea. What if they spot us?"

"You've got a point, but you heard Louie this morning. He went nuts about them knocking off that girl last night after the hit the night before. Franco and Angelo are probably sleeping off their shenanigans. He wants them followed because he's trying to figure out what's going on, and if they do it again, he's going to let that detective know it's a Lucia problem and has nothing to do with the Vaccarros."

"Holy shit," Arthur said suddenly. Then he lowered his voice. "A blue van pulled up a second ago that says Sonny's Plumbing Supply, and Angelo just got out. And there's Franco, too. They're going into the Neapolitan."

"At least you found them," Carlo said. "Now keep track of them. And concerning your worry about being spotted: Make sure you eat a sandwich or something to justify sitting there."

"Okay," Arthur said, without much enthusiasm.

Once Carlo and Brennan got into the tunnel, the traffic lightened up considerably. They made good time to the marina in Hoboken. Although there were a number of cars in the parking lot, thanks to the rain that had continued, there was no one on the pier.

Carlo parked close to the water's edge and

a good distance from the marina's sole building, where all the other cars were. Wasting no time, they stepped from the car and hustled out the pier. They stopped at the stern of *Full Speed Ahead*.

"I'll watch while you find a place to hide the device," Carlo said. He looked back toward the building. Not a soul had appeared.

Brennan crossed the gangplank and immediately began to search for an appropriate cranny. He found one at the very stern under some attached bait containers. With his hand, he inserted the tracking device as far back into the nook as he could. There was even a hidden lip that would keep the device from sliding out. A few moments later, he was back on the pier, and the two men started back to the car.

"Did you see anyone?" Brennan asked.

"Not a soul. How'd you make out?"

"I found a perfect spot."

Back in the car, Brennan brought his laptop out of sleep mode and went through the process of logging on again. When it was appropriate, he clicked the position icon as he'd done earlier and then the scale. Within seconds, there was a stylized representation of the area, even including the pier where *Full Speed Ahead* was moored. A blinking red dot was exactly where it was supposed to be.

Brennan moved the laptop into Carlo's lap.

"Pretty nifty, wouldn't you say?" Brennan offered.

Carlo nodded. He was impressed but also intimidated by Brennan's expertise.

"I'm not surprised we didn't get her this morning," Franco said. "Snatching this medical examiner lady is not going to be easy. The area around the medical examiner's office is a busy place, with Bellevue on one side and NYU Medical Center on the other side."

"The problem was the damn protest," Angelo butted in. "If it hadn't been for all those Hispanics carrying on, we would have had an opportunity. Hell, she and her boyfriend, who was on crutches, walked in front of our van."

"You're making it sound too easy," Franco said. "First of all, there was an SUV in front of us. Second of all, there were two of them and only two of us. What are you thinking? There's no way we could muscle the two of them into the van without causing a major scene. I say we should just shoot her from a distance and walk away."

"No!" Angelo blurted. "I want to snatch her. That's the only way to be sure the job gets done, and I want to make sure."

"Paul Yang and Amy Lucas were both a piece of cake," Franco said. "They were unsuspecting and easy to lure. But this Montgomery chick is in a totally different ballpark. There's no way we are going to be able to talk her into getting into the van peacefully, and that assumes we can even get her by herself. With her boyfriend on crutches, she'll be helping him. I say we shoot her and be done with it. As a medical examiner, I'm sure there's a dozen people who wouldn't mind seeing her put away."

"What's the plan?" Vinnie asked Angelo in his most serene tone. For those who knew him, it was a sign that he was major-league perturbed.

Franco, Angelo, Freddie, and Richie were all sitting in one of the Neapolitan booths, talking with Vinnie Dominick. Espresso cups, overflowing ashtrays, and a platter of cannoli cluttered the tabletop.

"I agree with Franco, it's a challenge," Angelo said. "Unfortunately, she moved out of her digs on Nineteenth Street, which would have otherwise made it a breeze. We may be forced to find out where she lives, but for now I think we should continue to try at the medical examiner's office. Franco's also right about needing more bodies, especially if we have to deal with the boyfriend, something I wouldn't mind doing. And we need another van."

"Why another van?" Vinnie questioned.

"For backup. If the snatch goes bad, we have an alternate getaway vehicle."

Vinnie nodded while staring at Angelo. Everyone stayed quiet while Vinnie ruminated.

"I want to be sure about this, too," Vinnie said finally. "In the past, it seems as if she has had nine lives, and with two hospitals right in the same area, a shot would have to be damn good. It would be just our luck if we got her good and they saved her. Snatch her and get rid of her once and for all! As far as another van goes, we've got more than we need. Are you going back to the OCME at lunchtime? We can't wait around for a week for this to go down, you know what I'm saying."

"We are aware," Angelo said. He was relieved Vinnie didn't jump at the easy way out. The more Angelo thought about it, the more intent he was on a slow demise for Dr. Laurie Montgomery.

"Are you okay with this?" Vinnie asked Franco.

"It has its merits," Franco said grudgingly. "But I'm worried about one thing."

"What's that?"

"In all due respect, Angelo is a bit too juiced up over this job. This morning, after we left the stakeout, we had to stop at Home Depot for a big bucket and a couple of bags of quick-set. I get nervous when there's this degree of emotion. I mean, he's thinking about this purely as payback, not a job. When emotions are involved like this, mistakes happen. People don't think right."

A wry smile appeared on Vinnie's face as he turned to Angelo. Clearly, he did not disapprove of Angelo's vengeful plans. At the same time, Vinnie knew Franco was right.

"So you want Laurie Montgomery to stew for a while before you drop her in the drink?"

"Something like that," Angelo admitted.

"What about Franco's point about mistakes can be made if emotions are involved and you're too eager?"

"I'll keep it in mind, and tone myself down."

Vinnie switched his attention to Franco. "Satisfied?" he questioned.

Franco nodded. "If he listens to me."

Vinnie nodded as well and looked back at Angelo. "You two are a team. Talk to each other! Don't take chances! Be cool!"

Angelo nodded.

"Okay," Vinnie said. "It's decided. Freddie and Richie, get another van. Keep in touch with each other and keep me informed."

"Right!" the men said in unison as they slipped out of the booth.

After the men had left, Vinnie had Paolo Salvato make him yet another espresso. As Vinnie sat in the silent, empty restaurant, he thought of Angelo's plans for Laurie Montgomery. It was perfect, and he fantasized about being there himself. After all the troubles she'd caused him, he'd wanted to whack her when he'd been released from prison, but he hadn't because Lou Soldano had specifically warned him that if something were to happen to Laurie, he'd personally come after Vinnie, suspecting the worst. But now, ten years later, Vinnie was confident that enough time had elapsed.

20
APRIL 4, 2007
11:44 A.M.

Laurie hurried out of the autopsy room after completing her final postmortem for the day. She was anxious about the time, since the final two cases had taken longer than she'd expected, and she was desperate to get back to the MRSA mystery. She was also anxious about not knowing what else to do. She'd put a lot of stock in what she thought she might learn from the CDC, and although she sensed it was important to have learned that the three cases that had been extensively subtyped were all the exact same bacterium, she didn't quite know what to make of it. She'd also hoped that Silvia, a recognized MRSA expert, would have come up with some ideas and suggestions, but she hadn't.

As Laurie removed her Tyvek coverall, she stopped for a minute and looked at her hands. They were shaking, as if she'd had twenty cups of coffee. Preoccupied as to what she should do next, Laurie ducked into the locker room to change back into her clothes.

"Are you just finishing now?" Riva asked as Laurie appeared.

"I'm afraid so," Laurie said, spinning the combination lock on her locker.

"I thought I'd assigned you cases that would have been quick. Sorry."

"Maybe I should have been able to do them quicker, but I felt the medical condition should be carefully documented. Both can be teaching cases."

"Really! Why?"

"The first one, the death at the dentist's office, turned out to be preventable, which is why it would be a good teaching case, particularly for primary-care and emergency-care physicians. The patient was reported by a family member to have had syncopal attacks involving palpitations, flushing, and diaphoresis, but it was never investigated."

"Hyperthyroidism," Riva said.

"You are exactly right," Laurie said. "It was not an allergic reaction as was suspected. The thyroid gland and the thymus gland were both diffusely enlarged, as were the heart and the spleen. That was why her blood pressure was so high in the emergency room."

"What about the second case?" Riva asked.

"The stationary bike rider."

"That was also interesting. I thought I was going to find atheromatous coronary heart disease, but I didn't."

"That was what I suspected as well. I'm glad I put it in the pile to be autopsied."

"Everything was normal with the heart and the coronary arteries."

"Really?" Riva questioned with surprise.

"Except for one thing," Laurie said. "The right coronary artery had an exceptionally acute angle takeoff. Suddenly, something the patient had unfortunately done while riding the bike cut off flow to the artery."

"I've heard of that but have never seen it," Riva said.

"Which is why I thought it too would be a good teaching case. I carefully dissected the area free and will have it preserved."

In contrast to Riva, who was taking a break between cases, Laurie had continued changing from scrubs to her clothes during the conversation. When she was finished, she slammed her locker closed, spun the combination lock, and waved to her office mate.

"I'll see you upstairs," Riva called after her.

Not willing to take the time for lunch, Laurie went to the front elevator and rode directly up to the fifth floor. Before retreating to her office, she went into the histology lab to see if her pulmonary slides were available on David Jeffries. She had little hope they would add anything significant at this point. She felt obliged to get the slides, since she'd specifically asked Maureen O'Connor to put a rush on them.

"You are eager," Maureen said in her colorful Irish accent when she caught sight of Laurie. "When I said I'd have them today, I didn't say I'd have them this morning."

"I hate to be a pest," Laurie said. "I'll be in my office."

"I'll have someone run them down when they're ready."

Laurie hastened down the hall. After sitting at her desk, she surveyed the jumble of case files and hospital records, with the matrix front and center. She picked up the matrix. It was far from complete. Glancing back to the pile of cases, she felt a drain on her enthusiasm and optimism. Transferring the information took longer than she expected, yet it seemed as if the matrix was the only hope she had of understanding what was going on with the Angels Healthcare hospitals.

As Laurie was about to start, she remembered she did not have Ramona's hospital record, as well as a few others. Picking up her phone, she called down to the PA's office. When Bart Arnold, the chief PA, answered, she asked to speak with Cheryl.

"What can I do for you?" Cheryl asked when she came on the line.

"I left word with Janice earlier this morning I needed a hospital chart on Ramona Torres."

"I got the message and put in the call. They promised me they'd send it with the others. I'd be surprised if it wasn't already in your e-mail."

"Hang on," Laurie said. Quickly, she opened her e-mail. As Cheryl suggested, the missing hospital records were there waiting for her.

"Sorry," Laurie said. "You're right. They are all here."

After hanging up with Cheryl, Laurie put the large file in the printing queue and then headed down to the first floor to pick up her printouts.

Adam had had a pleasant morning. After his second cup of coffee that morning back at the hotel, he'd made his way to the Metropolitan Museum. As one of the first people through its imposing front entrance, he'd felt as though he had the place to himself. He didn't try to cover too much, but viewed objects he'd appreciated in his youth, including Athenian red figure vases, several classical

Greek statues, and the old masters exhibits.

When noon approached, Adam had decided to return to the OCME for a short stay and had parked in the same location he'd parked that morning. As he'd told himself earlier that morning, he thought the chances of seeing the target over the lunch hour were slim, but he now came prepared. On the seat beside him, he had a rolled-up towel from the Hotel Pierre in the form of a cone and held in place with clear tape. Inside the cone was one of his favorite weapons: a nine-millimeter Beretta fitted with a three-inch-long suppressor. The suppressor's tip could just be seen at the pointed end of the cone. In the open end, he could insert his hand and seize the automatic pistol's handgrip. In this fashion, he could use the weapon in public without causing a panic, which it invariably did when it wasn't so camouflaged. Of course, even with the towel, the amount of time the weapon was out from under his coat was kept to an absolute minimum of only a few seconds.

With his seat tilted back, his elbows on the armrests, and his hands on his stomach and fingers intertwined, Adam had made himself snugly comfortable, especially with Arthur Rubinstein playing Chopin at a moderate volume on the vehicle's CD player. The light rain outside added to his tense contentment.

In contrast to that morning, relative calm prevailed at the corner of First Avenue and 30th Street, except for the traffic, with its incessant thundering medley of city buses, dump trucks, paneled vans, taxis, and private cars heading north. The protesters were gone, as were the police, and there was minimal pedestrian traffic, particularly in and out of the oddly designed OCME.

Shielded from the hum of the traffic by his vehicle's impressive soundproofing as well as the CD player, Adam calmly went through a number of possible scenarios in case Laurie Montgomery fooled him and suddenly appeared, preferably alone. Of course, he would immediately step from the car with his borrowed Hotel Pierre towel and close the gap between himself and Miss Montgomery. At that point, he could not predict what would happen, as it would depend on what had transpired between the time he'd left the car and the time he got within striking distance of approximately arm's length. The variables included passersby, particularly if anyone showed any interest in his activities whatsoever. If all was copacetic, the towel would come out and he'd fire from three feet into the back of the head. He would then calmly return to the Range

Rover and motor away, driving directly to the Lincoln Tunnel. He had his belongings in the car, and his handlers would take care of Mr. Bramford's hotel charges. At least that's how it had happened on most of Adam's previous operations.

In the middle of his musings, Adam, who was continually aware of what was transpiring in his surroundings, noticed in his rearview mirror that the occupants of the blue van that had pulled up behind him were arguing to beat the band. What had caught his attention, besides their mouths going a mile a minute, was that each was rudely stabbing a finger at the other, interspersed with angry waves of dismissal. Since violent arguments were not common in public and because of his line of work, Adam was always sensitive to unexpected behavior. As he watched, the driver made what looked like the final wave of dismissal before opening his door. As the driver tried to climb out, the companion attempted to stop him by grabbing his arm. But it was to no avail. The driver easily shook himself free and alighted from the vehicle. The passenger responded by following suit and leaping out of the van as well.

Adam had watched this simulated silent movie in his rearview mirror, but suddenly he was aware that the driver had come alongside the Range Rover. Adam turned and stared at him. Adam did not like to be approached while on a mission. It made the possibility of recognition after the fact much more possible.

Adam noticed two things about the man. First, his extensive scarring from burns and his careful attention to his clothes, which seemed out of place in relation to the condition of the van. Adam's first thought was that the man was an Iraq veteran like himself. Adam had seen many people with similar burns during his long rehab. The driver then shocked Adam by rapping noisily against the Range Rover's window.

There were two choices: Either open the window or just drive away. Just driving away was the most rational, since the hit was now off even if Laurie were to come out, but as curious as Adam was, especially if the man was an Iraq veteran, he opened the window.

"There's no parking here, mister," Angelo snapped vehemently.

The van's passenger had joined the driver. He seemed equally angry, not at Adam but at the driver. He even ordered the driver back to the van, but the driver would have none of it.

"Did you hear me!" Angelo demanded,

talking to Adam. Franco threw up his hands in disgust and returned to the van.

"Are you an Iraq vet?" Adam asked. After the totality of the experience in that nightmarish country and the long process of rehabilitation because of his leg, Adam felt a unique and immediate bonding with anyone who'd suffered similarly.

"What kind of question is that, you asshole?" Angelo hissed.

"I thought because of your burns you might have served," Adam said, controlling himself against taking offense from the man's rudeness.

"Are you making fun of me?" Angelo snarled.

"Quite the contrary. I thought you and I had something in common."

Angelo gave a short, derisive laugh. "Listen, fruitcake, I love your music, but I want you to move this trash heap of yours out of here. It's a no-parking area."

"I'm not parking at the moment, I'm standing."

"Okay, wise guy," Angelo growled. "Out of the vehicle."

Adam stared at the grotesque man ordering him out of the car. In such a confrontation, Adam had several advantages. First, he truly didn't care what happened to himself and in many ways wished he'd died with his buddies, and second, his martial arts training had been so intense, he reacted by pure reflex.

Once again Adam debated. The wise thing for everyone, including the nattily dressed apparent hoodlum and his companion, was for him to drive away, but the problem was that Adam had allowed himself to get angry, and it fused with all the anger he was actively suppressing.

Adam opened the door and slowly got out. Every muscle in his body was tensed, ready to uncoil.

Angelo stepped back. Although the blond stranger was more heavily built, Angelo felt he had the trump card. He was, as usual, packing his Walther, and he slipped his hand under the lapel of his jacket and grasped the gun. He wasn't going to shoot the man. He was just going to pistol-whip him once to get him the hell away from the area.

The nanosecond that Adam saw the direction of Angelo's hand movement, he sprang forward with lightning speed, sending a flurry of karate chops that took Angelo by complete and total surprise. The first hit his right forearm, producing an electriclike numbness to Angelo's hand, causing him to drop his weapon onto the pavement. The second and third landed on Angelo's head and the side of his neck, causing him to stumble backward but remain on his feet. The final blow was a kick to the chest that hurled him down to the wet pavement.

With equal speed, Adam snatched up Angelo's gun and quickly glanced through the van's windshield at the companion. Luckily, Franco didn't move, and for a beat he and Adam locked eyes. Adam was concerned he, too, might be armed.

Adam broke off, backed up, and quickly climbed back into the Range Rover. He started the engine, and then tossed Angelo's gun out into First Avenue where it was repeatedly run over. He then pulled from the curb and accelerated down First Avenue.

"Holy shit," Arthur MacEwan cried. "Did you see that?"

"I never saw anybody move so quickly," Ted Polowski said. "It was unbelievable. And look at Angelo. He's having trouble getting up."

"There goes Franco. He's got the gun."

Arthur and Ted had followed Angelo and Franco into Manhattan, and when the two had pulled up behind the silver Range Rover and parked, Arthur and Ted had gone around the block and pulled over to the curb at a hydrant on 30th Street. From there, they had a good view of the blue van, and they settled in for what they thought might be a long wait. But it turned out not to be the case. Almost immediately, a white van pulled up behind the blue one, and Ted, who knew most of the Lucia people, recognized Richie Herns as the driver. And then it was only a few minutes later that Angelo had bounded out of his vehicle to confront the guy in the Range Rover.

Still shaking his head over what he had just witnessed, Arthur called Carlo, who, along with Brennan, was having lunch with the boss, Louie. "You'll never believe what we just saw," he said excitedly. He then went on to describe the shellacking Angelo had just suffered from a guy in a Range Rover who Angelo had tried to pick a fight with. "You would not believe how fast this guy was," Arthur continued excitedly. "Angelo didn't stand a chance. Angelo even pulled a gun, but the guy knocked it out of his hand, then threw it out into the street. I'm telling you, it was unbelievable."

"Where are you?"

"We're across the street from the city morgue in Manhattan."

"City morgue?" Carlo questioned "Why the hell the city morgue?

"We don't have the foggiest idea."

"Why did Angelo pick a fight?"

"No clue about that, either."

"Is Angelo okay?"

"I think so. He's walking a little strange, but he's getting into the blue van just now."

"Hang on," Carlo said. "Let me tell Louie about this."

Arthur could hear Carlo relate the story, and Louie's bewildered reaction.

Carlo came back on the line. "Louie wants to know if you recognized the guy."

"No," Arthur said. "But his Range Rover had the name of a business called Bieder-something Heaven."

"Any phone number or address?"

"We couldn't see from where we were. The lettering was too small, but there was several more lines of print."

"Do you know if Franco is there as well?"

"Oh, yeah! He's here. He tried to stop Angelo from bothering the guy, and after the scuffle, he went out and got Angelo's gun from the middle of the street. Oh, one other thing. There's a second van, too, parked just behind Angelo and Franco's. Whoa, Angelo's started the blue van. I'm going to have to sign off here. Nope! False alarm! Angelo just pulled up a car length to be on the corner, and Richie's pulling up behind him. There's someone else in Richie's van, but we don't know who it is. Should one of us walk over there and check it out?"

"No! Absolutely not. They don't expect anyone to be watching, and we don't want them to have any reason to believe so. Hold on again. Let me tell Louie the rest of this weird story."

Once again, Arthur could hear Carlo relate the details, but he couldn't hear Louie's responses. Carlo came back on the line. "Louie said you're doing a good job. He wants you to stay with them. Later this afternoon, Brennan and I will come over and relieve you."

"Sounds good," Arthur said.

Carlo put his phone back in his jacket pocket and looked across at Louie. Louie stared back. His fleshy face was scrunched together, his brow deeply knitted. It was obvious he was deep in thought. Carlo and Brennan knew enough to stay silent and eat their pasta.

Finally, Louie broke the silence and took the napkin away from his neck where he'd poked it under his collar. "I don't understand any of this, but what I do understand is that it's got to stop. They are acting weird to say the least, knocking people off and brawling in broad daylight on a Manhattan street. And what's this about the city morgue?"

Carlo and Brennan knew Louie well enough not to respond until Louie directly asked them a question. Louie had always had a propensity to think out loud. As Louie heaved his considerable bulk out of the chair and began to pace, Carlo and Brennan exchanged a glance, wondering what was coming.

Louie wandered over to the bar, continuing his dialogue. After mindlessly playing with a shot glass full of toothpicks for several minutes, he came back to the table. "You guys are sure there was no company at the Trump Tower that you recognized when you stopped there this morning?"

Carlo and Brennan both shook their heads.

"Get a phone book!" Louie ordered Brennan. Dutifully, Brennan left his seat to bring a phone book to the table. "Try to look up Bieder-something Heaven!" Louie ordered when Brennan returned.

Louie looked at Carlo. "If they keep up this irresponsible behavior, we're going to have the entire NYPD out here on our backs sooner or later. What do you think?"

Carlo nodded. Since he was asked a specific question, he said, "They are taking big chances, so it must be important business."

"That's exactly what I was thinking. I mean, that detective came all the way out here to warn us."

"Nothing in the phone book," Brennan reported.

"I didn't think there would be," Louie said. "Not with a guy who could handle Angelo Facciolo so easily. The name's undoubtedly a cover."

"Do you think they could have been waiting at the city morgue for the same thing?" Brennan asked, risking putting in his own two cents. "I mean, why would Angelo pick a fight with someone in broad daylight unless there was competition or some sort of existing bad feelings?"

"Good thought, " Louie said. "I'm glad we're watching them. I'd like to know what's going on, but if they knock off someone else, I'm going to let that detective know we're not involved."

After the adrenaline rush evoked by Angelo, it took Adam a while to calm down, but by the time he arrived at the hotel, he was composed enough to think clearly about the unfortunate and totally unexpected incident. Although nothing untoward had happened, it still could if someone had observed the altercation and had called the police with a description of Adam's Range Rover. Consequently, Adam was disappointed in himself for not having driven off immediately. He certainly did not get any secondary gain from the useless confrontation — in fact, quite the contrary.

"Will you be needing your car soon, Mr. Bramford?" the doorman said, opening Adam's driver's-side door.

"No, thank you," Adam said as he alighted. He specifically wanted the car put into the garage.

Adam went up to his room. He needed to make a call and did not want to use his cell. He wanted a landline. One of the fallouts of his one-sided fight was a reluctance to return to the OCME area for fear of again running into the smartly dressed thug.

Seated at a desk in the changing room of his junior suite, Adam placed his call. The protocol was for him to ask for a fictitious individual by the name of Charles Palmer and then be given another number to call. Once he had the second number, he'd leave his direct-dial number. At that point, he had to wait. The return call usually came within a minute.

There was no small talk when Adam spoke

to one of his handlers. "I'm in need of a home address," he said, without reference even to a name. Adam didn't have to question if the information could or could not be obtained. With his handlers' access to the highest levels of government, it was always available.

"We will have it in a few minutes. You'll have it on your BlackBerry."

That was it. Adam pressed the disconnect button on the phone and then called room service. He thought he'd have lunch before heading over to his second-favorite attraction in New York City: the natural history museum.

"How was I to know he'd be a karate expert," Angelo snapped back.

"That's not the point," Franco said. "The point is you didn't think, and when you don't think, you make mistakes. Luckily nothing drastic happened."

"That's easy for you to say. I feel like I got run over by a truck; my chest hurts, and so does the side of my neck."

"Consider your bruises as a warning to keep your cool. I've never seen you like this, Angelo. You're just too damn eager. As I said to Vinnie, you're juiced up something awful."

"You'd be juiced up if the broad had burned your face such that you look like a freak."

"You said that, I didn't."

"What did you do with my gun?"

"It's here under my seat," Franco said. He took out the scratched handgun and handed it to Angelo. Angelo looked it over carefully. He removed the clip, made sure there was no bullet in the chamber, then pulled the trigger several times. The mechanism worked smoothly. "It seems okay."

"It might be a good idea to fire it a couple of times to be sure."

Angelo nodded as he pushed the clip back into the base of the butt.

"You haven't answered the question I asked you earlier," Franco said. "Are you going to be able to control yourself? Otherwise, I'm going to send you home for a few days. Mark my word! I'll take care of Montgomery myself."

"Yeah," Angelo said irritably. "I'll control myself! Maybe I shouldn't have gotten out of the van, but at least I got rid of the SUV, which was blocking our view."

"At too great a risk, I might add. I mean, you understand that, don't you?"

"I do now. I suppose."

"From now on, I want everything done my

way until we get her on the boat. Then I don't care what you do. Apparently, Vinnie likes your cement shoes idea. That's fine. I couldn't care less if you and Vinnie want some payback beyond just whacking her. But I don't want any more reckless behavior. Are we on the same page here or what?"

"Yeah, we're on the same page," Angelo said.

"Look at me!"

Angelo reluctantly glanced over at Franco.

"Say it again."

"We're on the same fucking page," Angelo repeated irritably.

"Good," Franco said. "We got that cleared up. Now let's go get some lunch. Montgomery's not being cooperative. We'll have to come back and try to get her when she leaves tonight."

21
April 4, 2007
3:05 P.M.

"Hello, excuse me!" a voice called.

Laurie looked up from her work. One of the histology technicians was standing in the doorway, clutching a cardboard tray for microscope slides.

"Maureen asked me to run these down," the woman said. "She also asked me to apologize for not getting them to you sooner. Two people called in sick today."

"No problem," Laurie said. She reached over and took the tray. "Thanks for bringing them, and thank Maureen for getting them to me so quickly."

"Will do," the woman said amiably.

Clutching the tray, Laurie looked back at her cluttered desk. Working nonstop, she had filled in only approximately two-thirds of her matrix, although the process, as painstaking as it was, was speeding up, since she had become accustomed to where in the hospital records she'd find the specific information she wanted. She'd also added more categories as she'd gone on, which forced her to go back to cases she thought she'd finished. One thing was certain: With as many categories as she now had, constructing the matrix was significantly more work than she'd originally imagined.

Although Laurie enjoyed a certain compulsive contentment about her progress, it had to contend with a growing disappointment that her efforts were probably not going to provide any insight into the mystery. As she worked, she'd hoped that she'd see some unexpected commonality, but it wasn't happening. If a few cases were in the same OR, the next one would be in a different OR; if several patients were on the same floor, the next one would be on a different floor; and so on and so forth. Yet she had persisted and would continue to do so, since it was all she had.

Relishing a break from what was essentially tedious data entry, Laurie cleared a space on her desk for her microscope. Turning on the lamp, she slipped the first slide of David Jeffries's lung section into the stage clip, rotated the revolving nosepiece to the lowest objective, and lowered the objective close to but not touching the slide. Putting her eyes to the eyepiece, she used the coarse adjustment knobs to pull the objective back up from the slide until she got an image. Reflexively, her hand went to the fine-adjustment knob and brought the image into sharp focus.

Laurie was again awed by the degree of damage wrought by the bacteria, many of which she could see as disclike clusters in the microscope's two-dimensional field. The normal alveolar structure of the lung was being dissolved by the bacteria's flesh-eating toxins such that abscesses of varying sizes were being formed. As she moved around with the help of the mechanical stage, she could see capillary walls in various stages of sepsis, causing hemorrhages into the septic soup that filled the lungs. The amount of destruction of the lungs' normal architecture reminded her of images of a city following a carpet bombing or a trailer park directly ravaged by a category five hurricane.

For more than an hour Laurie went through the tray of slides one by one. Using a higher-power lens, Laurie was even more impressed with the bacteria's pathogenicity. Focusing in on fibrous tissue responsible for maintaining the lung's normal structural architecture, she could see that the tissue was coming apart like the skin of an onion. Covalent bonds were being broken and collagen itself was dissolving into its constituent molecules.

"Hey, sweetie," Jack said as he quietly breezed in. He was becoming progressively adept on his crutches. "How's your day going?"

Laurie looked up, her face paler than usual.

"What's up?" Jack questioned. His smile waned. "You look terrible."

Laurie took in a deep breath and let it out. The tissue destruction she had been viewing had had a visceral effect on her. The fact that it had occurred within hours in a previously healthy person couldn't help but underline how fragile human beings ultimately were. The idea of enjoying any sort of health seemed a miracle.

Jack put his hand on her shoulder. "Really, are you okay?"

Laurie nodded and took another breath. She tapped the barrel of her microscope. "I think you ought to take a look at this. Keep in mind it was a normal, healthy person just a few hours earlier."

Laurie pushed herself back from the desk to give Jack room.

Jack put his crutches aside and leaned down toward the eyepiece, but about halfway he hesitated, then regained full height.

"Wait a second," he said suspiciously. "Is this a setup? Am I being slyly seduced into looking at a slide of your MRSA case from yesterday?"

"Remind me never to try to slip something by you," Laurie said with a wan smile. Her blood pressure had quickly risen back to normal, returning color to her face and clearing the accompanying queasiness. She admitted it was a section of lung from David Jeffries.

Jack looked into the microscope, and, moving the mechanical stage, he took a quick tour of the section. "Wow," he said. "It's totally destroyed. I see hardly any normal architecture."

"Does it change your mind about elective surgery where you might find yourself dealing with such a pathogen?"

"Laurie!" Jack scolded.

"Okay," Laurie said, pretending to be nonchalant. "I just thought I'd ask."

"How were your cases today? You seemed to have been engrossed more than usual."

"They were fine, particularly from a teaching perspective, such that they took longer than I hoped. I wanted to get up here ASAP and work on my matrix." She patted the legal pad. "It's the only thing left that I have that has a snowball's chance in hell to convince you that you are specifically at risk for being exposed to MRSA during your scheduled surgery."

"And?" Jack asked, looking at Laurie askance.

"I haven't found anything yet," she admitted before looking at her watch. "But I still have about fifteen hours."

"Ye gods. And you call me bullheaded."

"You are bullheaded. I'm merely persistent, and, of course, I have the added benefit of being right."

Jack waved Laurie away and gathered his crutches. "I'm heading to my office to clean things up since I'll be gone for a few days." He emphasized the *few days.*

"How were your cases today?"

"Don't ask. Riva promised some good ones; instead she gave me two natural deaths and an accidental one, none of which were at all challenging. Lou's case was more interesting. The slug's caliber and the indentations from an apparent chain to keep her sunk suggested the same killer. The difference was she was raped."

"Tragic."

"Another testament to the inherent wickedness of man."

"I'm glad you said man. Now get out of here. I only have fifteen hours."

"What time do you want to leave this evening?"

"Actually, we should take separate cabs, unless you want to stay late. I want to finish this matrix."

"I'll come back here when I'm done in case you change your mind. I don't want to hang around, because I want to watch my buddies play basketball to remind me why I'm willing to go under the knife."

On that issue, Laurie had to hold her tongue. Instead, she said, "Is Chet still in your office, or has he left for the day?"

"I wouldn't know. I stopped in here first."

"Well, if he is, you should try to dampen his enthusiasm for his new lady friend."

"Oh? How come?"

"By coincidence, she's the CEO of the company that has built the three Angels specialty hospitals."

"Really?" Jack said, raising his eyebrows. "That is a coincidence. Why dampen his enthusiasm?"

"She's the one who all but ordered me out of the orthopedic hospital yesterday. I don't know about long-term, but right now I question her motivation."

"Not to worry," Jack said. "I'm sure Chet will have eyes for someone else tonight. A week from now, he won't even remember her name."

"I hope so, for his sake."

With Jack out of her office, Laurie went back to the microscope. Although she had made an effort to appear upbeat with Jack, she was again feeling despondent. She'd joked about the fifteen hours, but in reality, it was far too little time to solve a mystery that had been confounding people with Ph.D.s in epidemiology.

Suddenly, Laurie's hand stopped twirling the horizontal mechanical stage control. She'd seen something unusual zip past the microscope's field. Since she was viewing at high-power, objects moved very quickly in and out of the field with very little rotation of the control. She slowly reversed direction with the control, and the strange object came into view.

Laurie was entranced. It appeared to be in the middle of what had been a bronchiole, probably close to what had been an alveolus, or the terminal sac in the bronchial tree where oxygen entered the blood and carbon dioxide came out. Laurie immediately questioned whether it had been there originally or was an artifact, inadvertently introduced or formed during the slide's preparation. It was about the size of the white cells Laurie had seen, which were the body's defensive cells, but there was no nucleus. It had absorbed almost none of the standard stain used by histology.

Most remarkable, it was a nearly round disk, symmetrical with a scalloped border, giving it a stellate appearance. Why she thought the symmetry was important was that most artifacts she'd seen didn't have such symmetry. Laurie looked at the object itself. The scalloped border comprised about one-fifth the diameter. The center of the object was opaque, with the mere hint of either nodularity or being mottled. One minute she'd see it, the next minute she wouldn't. She wished the object had taken the stain, because if it had, she would have known if what she was seeing was real or something she was conjuring up. Trying to keep her excitement in check, Laurie took out a grease pencil to mark the glass slide so that if the scope's mechanical stage were to accidentally move, she could find the object again. She did this by placing four dots in the cardinal directions. Satisfied, Laurie then shifted to low power. When she looked in again, the object was significantly smaller, and because it lacked staining, it tended to blend in to the chaotic surroundings.

Switching back to high power, she made sure the object, whatever it was, was still in the field. With that ascertained, she quickly went down to get Jack.

When Jack looked at the object, he said, "My gosh, how did one of my grandmother's butter cookies get into David Jeffries's lung?"

"Be serious," Laurie said. "What do you think it is?"

"I'm not fooling. It looks just like it came from one of my grandmother's cookie cutters. We called it a star, but obviously it has far too many rounded points."

"Do you think it is an artifact?"

"That would be my first guess, but it is surprisingly symmetrical. I suppose that's due to the dynamic tension between the hydrophilic and hydrophobic forces at the interface of the menisci."

"What the hell is that?"

"How should I know?" Jack said, still looking at the microscopic object. "I'm just running off at the mouth, speaking pseudo-scientific gibberish."

Laurie swatted Jack's shoulder playfully. "Here I thought you knew what you were talking about."

Jack looked up. "Sorry, I have no idea what it is. I don't even know if it is real or artifact."

"Nor do I," Laurie admitted.

"Have you found any others, or is this it?"

"So far that's it. Now that I found it, though, I'm eager to see if there are more."

"Do you have any idea what it could be?"

"I know what I think it looks like, but it can't be."

"Come on! Run it by me!"

"It looks like a diatom. Do you remember those from biology?"

"I can't say that I do."

"You must. They're a type of algae or phytoplankton with silicate cell walls."

"Give me a break," Jack said. "Now, how do you remember that?"

"They're so beautiful, kinda like snowflakes. I did sketches of them in high-school biology."

"Well, congratulations on your discovery. But if you're interested in my vote, I'd say I'd lean toward artifact rather than a pelagic diatom unless the university gave him a glass of Antarctic sea water as part of his terminal treatment."

"Very funny," Laurie said sarcastically. "Artifact or not, I'm going to look for more."

"Good luck! Say, I'm about to head out. Do you want to change your mind and come along?"

"Thank you but no thank you. I'm going to look at these slides for a while, then finish my matrix. Don't wait up for me. I know you're going to bed early."

"Good grief, Laurie. You're beating a dead horse."

"Maybe so, but I'm not sure I'm going to sleep that much tonight, one way or the other."

Jack bent down to give Laurie a hug, but she stood up and gave him a real one.

"See you later," Jack said, affectionately touching the end of Laurie's nose with his index finger.

"What's that for?" Laurie asked, reflexively backing away.

Jack shrugged. "Beats me. I just wanted to touch you because, I guess . . ." Jack paused, acting suddenly self-conscious. "I guess I think you are terrific."

"Get out of here, you oaf," Laurie said, nudging him. Jack's clumsy sentiment threatened to break down Laurie's carefully constructed defenses. In truth, her own emotions were barely under the surface. On the one hand, she wanted to support him through his surgery, as she assumed he could use, as everyone could, but on the other hand, she didn't want to lose him and was furious that he was putting her in such a conflicted state.

Gathering up his crutches and giving Laurie a final smile, Jack left. Laurie stood for a moment, looking at the stacks representing her twenty-five MRSA cases. Quickly leaning out into the hall, she called down to Jack, "Remember to use that antibiotic soap tonight!"

"It's on my list," Jack yelled back without turning around.

Laurie ducked back into her office. She stood for a moment, recognizing that one of the struggles with having a real relationship with another was to allow the person to be themselves and make some decisions independently, with hopefully enlightened self-interest. What it boiled down to from Laurie's perspective, and the question of whether to have the surgery or not was a good example, was that a real lover had to recognize that there were two centers of the universe.

Pushing what she feared was sophomoric philosophizing out of her mind, Laurie sat back down at her desk. Her eyes flicked back and forth between her microscope and her matrix. Both beckoned. Although she thought the matrix the most promising in the long haul, the diatomlike apparent artifact was the most seductive.

Leaning forward, Laurie put her face to the eyepiece. What she wanted to do was scan the entire slide methodically to see if there were any more of the diatomlike objects.

Angelo pulled to a stop at the same location he and Franco had been when they'd left their stakeout earlier. They were at the curb on First Avenue where it crossed 30th Street. The OCME was just off to the right. Traffic was rush-hour heavy.

Angelo put the van in park and used the emergency brake. "No Range Rover," he said, making a stab at justifying his behavior at noontime.

"Don't even go there," Franco said, making himself comfortable. He'd gotten a coffee and a hero at Johnny's, as had Angelo.

"Here come Richie and Freddie," Angelo said, looking in the rearview mirror and watching the white van pull up within a foot behind them.

Franco didn't answer. He was intent on surveying the area to make sure there were no apparent problems, such as parked police cars or loitering flatfoot patrolmen.

Angelo took a swig from his coffee, then unwrapped his sub. When he was finished, he glanced out the windshield and started.

"The boyfriend!" Angelo called out loud enough to make Franco slosh a dollop of coffee into his crotch. Angelo blindly reached for the small cast-iron bottle of eth-ylene and a plastic bag.

"Shit!" Franco yelled, straightening his back to lift his butt off the seat.

Angelo ditched the ethylene onto the floor and reached behind his seat for a roll of paper towels without taking his eyes off the OCME's front door.

Franco used a few towels to blot up the coffee from his seat, and a few more to wipe his pants. Only then did he look out the windshield. "Where's Montgomery?"

"I don't know," Angelo said dejectedly. "Jesus. This woman is such a pain in the ass. Where the hell is she?"

They watched as Jack stood with his arm raised and crutches tucked into his armpits. He had advanced out into the street as far as he dared with the traffic zooming past him.

"This is probably better," Franco said. "Without the boyfriend interfering, the snatch will be far easier."

"You're probably right," Angelo said. "I just hope she didn't leave early."

"Relax!" Franco countered. "Don't be such a pessimist."

"Would you like some more tea?" the waiter asked.

Adam shook his head. He was sitting in the

Pierre's oval high-tea room jutting off the main corridor leading to the hotel's Fifth Avenue entrance. When he'd been a preteen, it had been his favorite room in the hotel, with its whimsical murals and, more important, with its afternoon selection of cookies and crumpets. As he turned the page of the Arts section of the *Times*, he felt his BlackBerry vibrate. Taking the mobile device out, he saw that he had an e-mail. Using the appropriate buttons, he opened it. It was short and simple: 63 West 106th.

After signing the check to his room, Adam went up to gather his things. He was encouraged. The timing seemed to be impeccable. Ten minutes later, he was climbing back into the Range Rover. Sensing that the mission would soon be over, he changed the selection on the CD changer from Bach back to Beethoven.

Laurie leaned way back in her chair, and it squeaked in protest. With the tips of her fingers, she rubbed her eyes. She'd been so intent on staring into the microscope's eyepiece that she'd seemingly failed to blink as often as she should have. Her eyes had a gritty feeling, but the massage was rapidly therapeutic, and after only five seconds of rubbing followed by a series of rapid blinks, she was fine.

Although Laurie still had no idea whatsoever what the scalloped, disc-shaped object was, she'd found two more on the slide. And since all three were mirror images of each other, she felt they could not be artifacts introduced when the slides had been prepared. They were definite objects that had been in David Jeffries's lung at the time of his death.

Laurie's excitement soared. She even allowed herself to fantasize that she'd discovered a new infectious agent that in conjunction with staph made for an exceptionally lethal combination. At that point, she dashed down to histology and confronted Maureen, who was about to lock up for the night. After pleading her cause, Laurie convinced the woman to locate filed pulmonary slides on a handful of the former MRSA cases. After thanking her effusively, Laurie dashed back to her office.

To her delight, she found more of the diatomlike objects, and she noticed that the amounts differed from case to case, with some cases having none. They were extremely rare and consistently unstained, which excused her colleagues from having not seen them. It was at that point that the matrix had provided its first payoff. Although the matrix had not been completed, it had provided a seeming corroboration of the pathogenicity of the discs. The shorter the period between the onset of the individual patient's symptoms and the time of death, the more diatomlike objects Laurie found. Although this discovery hadn't been akin to fulfilling Koch's postulate confirming a microorganism as the source of a particular disease, Laurie felt encouraged. Very encouraged.

With her eyes feeling as though they were back to normal, Laurie grabbed her Rolodex. Obviously, she had to try to identify the scalloped, microscopic objects. A few years earlier, Jack had had a similar situation about a liver cyst, and he'd taken the slide over to the NYU Medical Center and had it looked at by a giant in the field of pathology, Dr. Peter Malovar. Despite being in his nineties and a professor emeritus, he still maintained an office and a reputation of maintaining his encyclopedic mind. The man's life was his work, especially since his wife had died twenty years earlier.

With a shaking hand, Laurie punched the numbers of Malovar's extension into her phone, hoping that the rumors of the long hours the aged pathologist maintained were correct. She kept her fingers crossed as the phone rang once, then twice, and to her delight was picked up at the commencement of the third ring.

Dr. Malovar's voice had a slight but pleasing English accent, a grandfatherlike calmness, and a surprising clarity for a nonagenarian. Laurie told her story in a rapid monologue, tripping over her words at times in her haste. When she finished, there was a pause. For a second, she'd feared that she'd been cut off.

"Well, this is an unexpected treat," Dr. Malovar said happily. "Offhand, I have no idea what this diatomlike object is but I would love to see it. It sounds perfectly intriguing."

"Would there be any chance of my bringing it over now?" Laurie questioned.

"I would be delighted," Dr. Malovar insisted.

"It's not too late? I mean, I don't want to keep you."

"Nonsense, Dr. Montgomery. I'm here until ten or eleven every evening. I'm at your disposal."

"Thank you. I'll be over shortly. Is it difficult to find your office?"

Laurie was given explicit instructions before she hung up. She got her coat and hurried out to the elevator. As she boarded, her stomach growled as a visceral reminder that she'd skipped lunch. With Dr. Malovar having assured her he was not about to leave, she pressed the second-floor button. There wasn't much choice in the lunchroom's vending machines, but she trusted she could find something of caloric value, if nothing else.

The lunchroom was a favorite hangout for the support staff, especially during meal hours, and that evening was no exception. It was just after seven, and half of the three-to-eleven shift were present. With its stark concrete walls, the sound level in the room was almost painful for Laurie in contrast to her office's silence. As she stood in front of one of the vending machines, anxiously trying to decide which selection was the least bad for her, she heard her name over the din. Turning, she saw the smiling faces of Jeff Cooper and Pete Molimo. They were the evening shift Health and Hospital Corporation van drivers who went out to fetch the bodies. As with most of the rest of the staff, Laurie had become friendly with them over the years. Laurie and Jack, in contrast to their colleagues, were more apt to visit scenes during the evening and night hours, because they both felt such visits were exceedingly helpful.

The men were enjoying a break in their routine. They had finished their meals, as evidenced by the debris on their table. Except for rush-hour auto accidents, calls of deaths during mealtime were relatively rare and didn't pick up again until after nine. Both had their feet up on the opposing empty chairs at their four-top table.

"Haven't seen you much, Dr. Montgomery," Jeff said.

"Yeah, where've you been hiding?" Pete added.

Laurie smiled. "Either in my office or in the pit."

"You're a little late for going home, aren't you?" Pete asked. "Most of the other MEs are out of here before five."

"I've been working on a special project," Laurie said. "In fact, I'm not even going home now. I'm heading over to NYU Medical Center."

"How are you getting over there? I don't know what it's doing now, but it was sprinkling an hour or so ago."

"I'm walking," Laurie said. "It's too short for a cab ride."

"Why don't I run you over?" Pete offered. "We're just sitting here, and I'm tired of talking to this die-hard Boston fan."

"What if you get a call?" Laurie asked.

"What's the difference. I got a radio."

It took Laurie two seconds to make up her

mind. "Are you ready to go now?"

"You bet," Pete said, gathering up his trash.

In a lot of ways, it was ludicrous to ride, because the medical center entrance was on the same block as the OCME, and when they backed out of the morgue's receiving dock onto 30th Street, it was not raining. In fact, there was a patch of pale blue-green sky off to the west and moving closer.

"This is rather silly," Laurie said, as Pete almost immediately turned into the curved driveway at the medical center's entrance several hundred feet down First Avenue. He managed to get up to only about twenty miles per hour. "I'm sorry to trouble you."

"No trouble at all," Pete assured her. "I was glad to get away from Jeff, the bum. He's so sure the Sox are going to beat the Yankees that he won't shut up about it."

Laurie hopped out of the van, thanked Pete, and used the microscope slide box she was carrying to wave as she hurried through the revolving door. The center was crowded with visitors, but Laurie quickly left them behind on her way to the academic portion of the institution. Using the elevator, she rose to the sixth floor. As she exited, she noticed that the corridor was as silent as the one outside her own office. Most all doors were closed, and she didn't pass a single person.

She found the renowned doctor in a small, windowless interior space that could have been a storeroom but which the aged man had decorated with all his diplomas, rewards, and honors, all protected in simple, glazed black frames. A very large freestanding bookcase filled with all his favorite pathology tomes, some with tooled leather bindings, dominated one wall. Most of the rest of the room was filled by a large mahogany desk piled high with reprints and legal pads covered with erratic cursive.

He stood up and extended a hand as Laurie entered. She was surprised how much he looked like Einstein, with a cumulus of white hair. His back was kyphotic, as if he were anatomically built to look into a microscope.

"I see you have brought the slides," he said, eagerly eyeing Laurie's slide box.

In anticipation of her arrival, he'd positioned his impressive microscope on a customized shelf that pulled out of the end of the desk. It was a teaching scope with double-binocular eyepieces. An impressive digital camera was mounted on top and shared the same view as the eyepieces.

"Should we?" he continued, motioning for Laurie to take the seat positioned on her side of the scope.

Laurie sat. She could see out of the corner of her eye how zealously he watched as she opened her tray and carefully extracted one of the slides marked with grease pencil. Respecting that the microscope was his, she handed him the slide. Eagerly, he placed it onto the mechanical stage and lined up the grease-pencil markings. After he'd lowered the low-power objective, he told her to use the mechanical stage control to find the object of interest.

Having become quite proficient at locating the objects despite their lack of staining, Laurie quickly located one. "I don't know if you can quite see it, but it's under the pointer now."

"I think I see it," Dr. Malovar said. He backed up the objective, changed to higher power, then refocused. "Ah, yes!" he said, as if experiencing visceral pleasure. "Most interesting! Are they all similar?"

"They are," Laurie said. "Strikingly so."

"Such symmetry, such an elegant border. Have you observed them on end?"

"No, I haven't," Laurie admitted, "so I don't know if it is disc-shaped or spherical."

"I'd say disc-shaped. Have you noted the slight nodularity?"

"I have, but I didn't know if it was real."

"It's real, all right. Fascinating, as is the degree of necrosis of the lung tissue."

Laurie was dying for him to tell her what it was and questioned why he was teasing her by withholding the information.

"It is quite apparent they are in the bronchioles and not within the alveolar walls."

"I felt the same way," Laurie admitted.

"I can see why you said they looked like diatoms, but I wouldn't have thought of it myself."

Laurie was becoming impatient. Finally, she just asked, "What is it?"

"I have no idea," Dr. Malovar said.

Laurie was stunned. Particularly from the appreciative way he was describing the object, she thought for sure he knew what it was the very instant he'd seen it. Shock turned into dismay when she realized she could not charge home to Jack with new, decisive information. It also made her consider that maybe some of her colleagues had seen them, but dismissed them as being unimportant.

"Do you think that they had anything to do with the fulminant MRSA infections these people had?"

"I have no idea."

"Do you have any idea of how we might identify them?"

"For that, I do have an idea. I'd like to look at them under the scanning electron microscope, especially after slicing one open."

"Is that a lengthy procedure? Can we do it tonight?"

Dr. Malovar leaned back and laughed. "Your eagerness is commendable. No, we cannot do it tonight. There's some skill involved. We do have a talented person, but of course he is gone for the night. I can see if he can at least start tomorrow."

"How about a microbiologist?" Laurie suggested. "Should I show it to a microbiologist?"

"You could, but I'm not optimistic. I've had a bit of microbiology myself." He pointed to a Ph.D. diploma in microbiology.

Laurie was crestfallen.

"But I believe I do know who will be able to identify it at a glance."

Laurie's eyes brightened. Her emotional roller coaster was taking her up once again. "Who?" she asked eagerly.

"Our own Dr. Collin Wiley. My sense is that what we are seeing is a parasite, and Dr. Wiley is department head of parasitology."

"Can we get him to look at it tonight? Do you think he is still here?"

"He is not here. In fact, Dr. Wiley is in New Zealand for a parasitology meeting."

"Good Lord," Laurie murmured. The roller coaster was on its way down again. She visibly sagged in her seat.

"Don't look so forlorn, my dear," Dr. Malovar said, leaning to the side to gaze directly at Laurie with his glacial blue eyes. "We live in the information age. I will simply take a few high-definition digital photos tonight and e-mail them to Dr. Wiley, along with a description of the case. I know for a fact he has his laptop with him, since it has his lectures' PowerPoints. Could you give me your e-mail address?"

Laurie rummaged in her bag for one of her ME business cards. She handed it over.

"Perfect," Dr. Malovar said, putting it on the corner of his desk.

"When do you suppose I might get an answer?"

"That's totally up to Dr. Wiley. And remember, he's halfway around the world."

After discussing with Dr. Malovar the process of getting a sample of David Jeffries's lung to him, perhaps even the paraffin block used by histology, Laurie left the pathologist's office. As she rode down in the empty elevator, she made a decision. Although she was eager to finish her matrix, she decided to forgo it for the time being and go home. She thought there was a significant chance, maybe not huge but at least possible, that the discovery of the unknown objects might be enough in and of itself to make Jack see the risk issue her way.

Down at the hospital entrance, she was able to catch a taxi with relative ease.

As soon as Adam had turned onto 106th Street, he had sensed his thoughts about the imminent end to the mission were probably unduly optimistic. Instead of being a quiet side street, it had been alive with all sorts of people and children enjoying the improving weather. Driving by Laurie Montgomery's house had added to his feeling, because directly across the street was a sizable and popular playground with an impressive array of mercury vapor lights capable of turning the entire area into day. But what had totally convinced him was when he'd stopped for a few moments to survey the area, he'd spotted Montgomery's injured spouse or boyfriend on the sidelines of an active neighborhood basketball game with more than fifty people either playing or watching. Seeing the man standing there leaning on his crutches strongly suggested to Adam that Laurie was probably already home as well.

But Adam had not been discouraged.

Quite the contrary. He still thought the area a far better location than in front of the OCME for the hit. It just meant he'd have to wait for morning, when she would appear at her door on her way to work and either walk east to catch a cab on Central Park West or walk west and snag one on Columbus Avenue. Either way, he'd have his opportunity to take her out. And considering Laurie had arrived at work that morning at seven-fifteen, he estimated that she'd left the house around six-forty-five. With that decided, Adam had vowed to be parked in front of Montgomery's house by six-fifteen at the latest the following day.

"Good evening, Mr. Bramford," the doorman said when Adam climbed from the Range Rover back at the Pierre. "Will you be needing your vehicle again this evening?"

"No, but I'd like it to be available at six a.m. sharp. Will that be a problem?"

"No problem whatsoever, Mr. Bramford. It will be waiting for you."

After collecting his things, particularly his tennis case, Adam hurried into the Pierre. He wanted to see if it wasn't too late for the concierge to get him a symphony ticket or a ticket for whatever else was happening that evening at Lincoln Center.

■ ■ ■ ■

To get Angelo's attention about the hour, Franco made a production of looking at his watch by sticking out his left arm full length, pulling back his jacket sleeve, rebending his elbow, and rotating his wrist. Next to him, Angelo was staring straight ahead out through the windshield at the darkened scene. Had his eyes not been open with an occasional blink, Franco would have thought he was asleep. The vehicular traffic racing past them on First Avenue had slowed to a mere trickle. Had it not been for the street-lights, it would have been pitch dark. The sun had long since set, and no moon had arisen to take its place.

"It's not going to happen," Franco said at length. "At least not tonight. We can't sit here all night."

"The bitch!" Angelo murmured.

"I know it's frustrating. It's as if she were taunting us. I guess she went home early, just before we got here, or maybe she's working late. Either way, I think we should go. The troops behind us are getting antsy."

"I want to stay another fifteen minutes."

"Angelo! That's what you said a half-hour ago. It's time to move on. We'll come back tomorrow morning. You'll get your revenge soon enough."

"Ten minutes."

"No! We're going now! I wanted to leave a half-hour ago. I've already extended our sitting here longer than I feel comfortable with. I don't want someone noticing us and getting suspicious. Start the van and signal the guys in back!"

Angelo got the engine going and then turned the headlights on and off a few times.

"All right, we're out of here."

Reluctantly, Angelo pulled away from the curb. He drove slowly so that when they came abreast of the OCME, he could look through the front door into the building's interior.

"The place looks dead," Franco said. "How appropriate."

As they drove up First Avenue, Angelo broke the silence. "Maybe we'll have to check out the boyfriend's apartment if we can't get her here at the OCME."

"That's on the bottom of the list," Franco blurted with a shake of his head. He and Angelo had visited Jack's apartment ten years earlier, with disastrous results. "Those neighborhood gang friends of his are a menace to society, and they are always on alert for other gangs. We're going to stick with what we got. I mean, it's not like we've been sitting here for a week, you know what I'm saying."

Angelo nodded, but he wasn't happy. He felt like a kid promised a present but being forced to wait.

As Laurie climbed out of the taxi in front of her house, she looked over at the lighted basketball court. It seemed like a particularly crowded evening, which always made the competition that much more fierce. As evidence, Laurie could hear that the cries of accomplishment and derision were more strident than usual. Standing on her tiptoes, Laurie scanned the spectators for Jack. As much as he enjoyed the game, she wouldn't have been surprised if she saw him, but she didn't.

A few minutes later, she found him soaking in the bathtub.

"You're early," he said. "With as much work as you looked like you had with your matrix, I didn't expect to see you until after ten at the earliest. Did you finish already?"

"No, I did not finish," Laurie admitted, as she stripped off her coat and tossed it out into the hallway. She shut the bathroom door to keep in the steamy heat. After putting down the toilet seat cover she sat and locked eyes with Jack.

"I'm soaking in antibiotic soap," Jack said, averting his gaze. Laurie's serious expression and the fact that she was willing to sit in the steamy bathroom gave him the uncomfortable feeling that she was in one of her talking moods and, considering the timing, there was only one subject. "I thought you'd like to know how responsible I'm being," he added.

"I didn't finish my matrix because I found more of those diatomlike objects."

"Really?" Jack said without a lot of enthusiasm.

"Really," Laurie repeated. She then went on to describe how she'd first found more in David Jeffries's slides, and then found them in most of the cases whose slides she was able to get.

"Were they in all cases whose slides you had?" Jack asked. Despite knowing where the discussion was going, Jack found himself interested. He'd convinced himself that the object he'd seen was an artifact of some sort.

"Not all but most. And most interesting is that I discovered with the help of my unseen matrix that the shorter the interval from the onset of symptoms until death, the greater the number of these particles were."

"So you just randomly counted the number on each slide."

"Exactly."

"Well, that's hardly scientific."

"I know," Laurie admitted. "It's just suggestive, but it was consistent, and therefore very supportive."

Jack ran a soapy hand through his hair. "This is all very interesting, but I'm not sure how to interpret it. I mean, neither one of us knows what it is."

"I didn't leave it at that. I called up Dr. Malovar, whom you had praised so highly about your liver cyst."

"How is he? He's a trip, isn't he? I admire the guy. I hope I'm still around at his age, much less still contributing."

"He's fine, but don't you want to know what he said?"

"Of course. What was his diagnosis?"

"He said he didn't know."

Jack gave a short laugh of amazement. "He didn't know at all? I'm shocked."

"He said he thought it was a parasite."

"That's more like it. Then did you get Dr. Wiley to look at it?"

"Dr. Wiley, unfortunately, is in New Zealand at a parasitology conference."

"Well, then I guess we'll have to wait, because Wiley in his field is like Malovar in his."

"Dr. Malovar sent a digital photo, so I'm

562

certain we'll hear when Dr. Wiley gets it."

"Of course, there's no accounting of when that may be."

"I'm afraid not."

"Okay, Laurie," Jack said, sitting up. "What's your real point here? Is this another attempt at getting me to cancel my surgery? If it is, out with it!"

"Of course it is," Laurie said with some heat. "How could it not be, I've found an unknown parasite associated with a rapidly fatal postoperative course. What seems to be happening is a synergism with MRSA, which I have agreed is in every hospital. But this unknown parasite is apparently in only three hospitals, one of which you are scheduled to enter and allow yourself to become a potential victim."

"Laurie, let me remind you that I'm going to have my operation with a surgeon who has not had one case of whatever this is, and he's been operating nonstop at the Angels Ortho Hospital. Well, that's not entirely true. He had to stop when they closed the ORs to fumigate them. But since then, he's been back with a full schedule day in, day out, with no problems whatsoever. Secondly, I do not have a parasitic disease. Maybe that's the basis of this outbreak: These people have visited the backwaters of the Amazon and picked up this parasite unbeknownst to anyone. Hey! I commend your work, and certainly keep at it. If it turns out that this unknown parasite is infectious and you've discovered some new illness, all the power to you. Hell, you might even win a Nobel Prize."

Laurie stood up abruptly. "Don't patronize me!"

"I'm not patronizing you," Jack contended. "I'm just trying to fend off your negativity and prepare myself for this operation tomorrow. You know how I feel about it. What I'd really like is some support on your side, not fearmongering."

Laurie felt a rush of emotion dominated, for the moment, by frustrated anger. Yanking open the bathroom door and slamming it behind her, she stalked down the hall to the darkened living room, where she threw herself onto the couch to brood. Jack had touched the sore spot of her ambivalence.

Carlo nosed his Denali into one of the few parking places along the front of the strip mall. What that meant at nine-thirty on a Wednesday night was that the Venetian was doing a brisk business. Both Carlo and Brennan alighted. The weather had completely cleared up. Despite the garish light coming from a neon gondola on the roof, two stars could be faintly seen in the sky.

Brennan stretched with a few noisy grunts and groans as they walked down the sidewalk toward the restaurant's entrance and passed the open DVD rental store in the process. Brennan's whole body was stiff after sitting in the SUV since five o'clock.

Inside, they had to search the crowd for Louie. Carlo finally found him at a four-top table near the bar. "Wait here!" he said to Brennan and struck off, weaving in and out among the tables. Carlo thought it ironic that the restaurant was doing as well as it was, considering it was in reality a cover for the Vaccarro family's real work. Carlo attributed it to Louie's influence. Louie loved good food and red wine, as was suggested by his body's profile.

When Louie caught sight of Carlo, he excused himself from his buddies, heaved himself to his feet, and took Carlo off to the side. Despite the crowd, it was easy to talk, thanks to the assemblage of black-velvet paintings that crowded every wall and the acoustic ceiling tiles.

"What's up?" Louie asked. "You're early."

"They closed up shop," Carlo explained. "All four of them went back to the Neapolitan, parked the vans, and went inside. We waited a good hour and a half, and when none of them reappeared, we came here to let you know what was up."

"I'm listening."

"Well, nothing, actually. From the moment Arthur and Ted hooked up with Angelo and Franco mid-morning, they've been staking out the medical examiner's office. Except for the one-sided scuffle between Angelo and some unknown guy nothing's happened. They've just sat in their vans, and us in my Denali."

"Any idea why they sat in two vans?"

"No idea whatsoever."

"None of this makes sense," Louie complained. "It's one hell of an effort on their part, but why?"

Carlo shrugged. He had no idea, either, despite the fact that he and Brennan spent part of the afternoon batting around ideas.

"Yet because it doesn't make sense, my intuition tells me it's important," Louie said, and then paused for a minute. "I want you guys to keep up the surveillance, that's for certain. I want to know where Angelo and Franco are and what they are doing. And have Arthur and Ted start early, like at six. I think the reason they didn't hook up with them until the middle of the morning was they went out too late."

"I'll tell them. Anything else?"

"What about the tracking device."

"We got it, and we've got it on the boat. How it works, you'll have to ask Brennan."

"I don't care how it works. I just want to know when the boat goes out and where it goes, so tell Brennan to stay on top of it."

22
APRIL 5, 2007
3:15 A.M.

Trying not to wake Jack, Laurie rolled over and looked at the clock. She'd been awake for almost an hour, and she was now convinced that more sleep was not an option. She didn't know if it was depression, frustration, or dread, or a mixture of all three, but she couldn't stay in bed a moment longer. Her mind was constantly going over the same issues, with the same results.

Being as quiet as she could, she slipped from under the covers, gathered up the clothes she had set out for the day by feel, since the only light came from the clock face, and slowly inched toward the open bathroom door. Once she was in the bathroom, she leaned back into the bedroom to listen to the sound of Jack's breathing. It hadn't changed, which pleased her.

Waking up as early as she had and wanting something to occupy her overly busy mind, Laurie had suddenly thought of heading into work early. She thought she could at least finish her matrix, and whether it would have any effect on Jack's thinking was not the point. As the discussion the previous evening had proved, he was not about to be deterred, and besides, it was clearly too late. His surgery was only four hours and fifteen minutes away.

Laurie showered quickly and put on her usual small amount of makeup. As she did so, she thought about the evening before. It had gone badly at first, with both of them irritated at the other. But that had soon changed, and once again they'd agreed to disagree. Although Laurie said she didn't want to have anything to do with the operation itself, such as going with him to the hospital in the morning, she promised she'd be there in the afternoon to support him one hundred percent in his rehabilitation. He had been warned by Dr. Anderson that his mobility postsurgery would be restricted because he would be waking up with a device that would be constantly flexing and extending his knee, and that he would be attached to it for at least twenty-four hours.

Laurie dressed quickly. While she had a quick bite to eat in the kitchen, she wrote a note for Jack, telling him she'd gone to work early and why, and asked him to have Dr.

Anderson call her at the OCME when the procedure was done. She signed the note by telling him she loved him and that she'd see him around noon.

Unsure of where to put the note to be certain he saw it, Laurie took some tape from the kitchen and returned to the bathroom, using the door from the hall. They had designed the bathroom with two doors, one from the bedroom and one from the hall, for exactly this kind of situation when one of them was up before the other. With a piece of tape, she adhered the note to the center of the mirror such that there was no way he could argue he'd not seen it.

Getting her coat, key, the tray of slides, and her bag, Laurie opened the hallway door and was about to close it behind her when she remembered her cell phone was charging at her bedside table. For a moment, she debated whether she wanted to risk waking Jack. Believing Jack should get as much sleep as possible and that she would not need her cell, since she would be spending the first half of the day at her OCME desk and the second half in Jack's hospital room, she decided to forgo its convenience.

Outside, it was still dark with only a hint of dawn in the eastern sky, and the street was completely deserted in both directions.

Thinking it would have been wiser to have called a radio cab, Laurie hesitated on the front stoop. But not wanting to take the time now that she was already down, she ran toward Columbus Avenue. In her experience, it was a lot easier getting a taxi there than on Central Park West, and she was proved to be correct as one pulled to the curb the moment she extended her hand.

As the cab zipped downtown in the nearly empty streets, Laurie admitted to herself that April 5, 2007, was not going to be a day she would ever want to relive. The level of general anxiety she was experiencing was as high as she'd ever felt, evidenced by the abdominal distress she'd suffered after eating her skimpy breakfast, which was now being made worse by the jolting and rocking of the taxi. At one point she sensed she was about to vomit, but it passed. It was with definite relief that the taxi finally reached the OCME. Laurie directed the driver to the side of the building and down the ramp to the receiving dock. Still queasy, Laurie quickly paid the fare and climbed out.

She waited a half-minute or so to let a mild wave of dizziness dissipate, then mounted the stairs to the receiving dock. As she passed down the hall, she said hello to the night security man in his cubbyhole office.

Surprised to see her, Mr. Novak jumped up from his desk, poked his head out, and called down to Laurie, who'd already reached the back elevator. "Good morning, Dr. Montgomery," he called. "What brings you in so early?"

"Just a little extra work," she lied. She waved as she boarded.

Laurie stopped again on the second floor, as she had the evening before. She bought herself a cup of vendor coffee. Strangely, coffee tended to calm her stomach. At least it had in the past.

Laurie turned on her office light, and after hanging up her coat, she surveyed her cluttered desk. Her microscope still occupied center stage. The piles of case files and hospital records looked daunting. Her matrix was balanced on the top of one of them.

After putting her scope to the side along with the trays of slides, Laurie sat down. She moved the matrix in front of her. Before beginning, she opened the lid of the coffee and took a tentative sip. A grimace followed by reflex. It wasn't because it was too hot, which was what she feared, but because it tasted horrid. If she hadn't known, she wouldn't have even suspected it was coffee. With the lid replaced, she put it aside, intending to go down to the ID room when she thought Vinnie would have the communal coffee made.

Laurie then took the next case file and hospital record and set to work. Not quite an hour later, the phone rang. As much as she'd been concentrating combined with the near-absolute silence of the deserted fifth floor, the phone's old-style raucous jangle totally startled her. She answered it in a panic before she'd even had a chance to guess who it might be. It was Jack.

"What time did you leave?" he asked.

"I'm not sure. It was three-fifteen when I got up."

"Why didn't you wake me? I missed you when I awoke a few minutes ago."

"I wanted you to get as much sleep as you could."

"Are you exhausted?"

"I've been exhausted for days. Luckily, I didn't have any trouble getting to sleep."

"I'm glad we talked again last night," Jack said, "even if I wasn't when we began."

"I'm glad, too."

"Well, I had better jump into the shower with my antibiotic soap. I'm supposed to be over there at six-fifteen, and it's already twenty after five."

"I forgot to ask: How long does this patella tendon graft take?"

"Dr. Anderson told me a little more than an hour."

"I'm impressed. That's fast."

"He does them so often, he's got it down to a science."

"I'll see you around noon," Laurie said.

"I love you."

"I love you, too," Laurie closed. She heard the click. It sounded so final. Slowly, she replaced the receiver. *What was the day going to bring?* she asked herself uneasily. She wished she'd hung up first, because she kept hearing the metaphoric disturbing finality of the click over and over in the depths of her brain.

Shaking off any morbid thoughts engendered by the phone, Laurie went back to her matrix, taking yet another case file and its accompanying hospital record from the slowly dwindling stack. To keep from thinking about anything other than the busywork of data entry, Laurie kept at her task compulsively, as if it were a life-or-death necessity. Close to seven, she had only two more to go when Riva arrived.

"What on earth are you doing here so early?"

"I couldn't sleep," Laurie said. "I thought I might as well work."

Riva looked over her shoulder at Laurie's

nearly complete matrix. "Very impressive! Have you learned anything earth-shattering?"

"Hardly," Laurie said. She thought for a moment about telling Riva about the unknown and possibly infectious agent she'd found microscopically, but then changed her mind. Riva would undoubtedly want to see it, and Laurie was intent on finishing her matrix.

"Are you still planning on a paper day today?" Riva questioned.

"Absolutely," Laurie said. "I want to finish what I'm doing and then go over to see Jack. He's having his surgery today."

"Oh, that's right," Riva said. "I'd forgotten. I don't have Jack to schedule, either. I'd better get down there and see what's come in overnight."

By seven-twenty-five, Laurie had finally made the last entry. She held the matrix up. It was quite extensive, with every known variable she had been able to conjure up to compare the cases.

Quickly she scanned the document, looking for gross, unexpected commonalities among the twenty-five cases that might suggest the how and the why the patients had gotten infected. But nothing seemed to jump out until she looked back at the column for date of surgery. Having always had a facility with mathematics and numbers in general, there seemed to be a pattern. Believing it was only some sort of coincidence, Laurie got out her daily calendar and translated the dates of her series into days of the week. To her surprise, there was a pattern in that all the eye or cosmetic cases were on Tuesday, the heart cases were on Wednesday or Friday, and the orthopedic cases were on Monday or Thursday. With her knowledge of statistics, Laurie immediately knew that twenty-five cases were not nearly enough to give any credence whatsoever to her finding, yet she found it curious.

Returning to the matrix and slowing down, she let her eyes pause at each entry in each of the categories, such as age, duration of the procedure, type of anesthesia, et cetera, but still nothing significant caught her attention. Coming to the end of the matrix, Laurie switched her gaze to the wall clock. It was seven-thirty exactly, and Jack's surgery was starting. Laurie could visualize the scalpel cut through the skin, and she winced at the thought. Looking back at her matrix, she felt sorry she had finished filling it in. The process itself had been effective in keeping her mind from thinking about what she preferred not to think about.

Suddenly, Laurie thought of something

else she could do to avoid obsessing over what was happening to Jack. She thought of Dr. Collin Wylie in New Zealand and the possibility that he'd gotten the photomicrograph, and the possibility he'd had an opportunity to look at it, and if he had, whether he'd been able to recognize it and respond. There were a lot of ifs, but, undeterred, Laurie went to her e-mail. The main reason she'd not thought about doing so earlier was because the outgoing e-mail had been sent during the night, and she'd forgotten to factor in that New Zealand was on the opposite side of the world, meaning in Auckland it had been morning.

The moment after she'd clicked the appropriate icon and her e-mail opened, she saw it: C_Wylie@NYU.EDU. Eagerly, Laurie opened it.

Dr. Montgomery: Greetings from Down Under
I received the photomicrographs from Peter, and I have already duly chastised him for not recognizing an acanthamoeba polyphaga cyst, although I gave him some slack because of the location. I have never seen one in the lung. If you want to see it better, use an iodine stain. As for the evanescent nodularity Peter mentioned, I

can only assume that it represents encasement of more of the same MRSA as is seen free in the microscopic field. It has been recently demonstrated in Bath, England, that MRSA can invade and multiply within acanthamoeba, similar to legionella, the cause of Legionnaire's disease. Since acanthamoeba normally eat bacteria, it is interesting to wonder how the MRSA and legionella have developed antiamoebic resistance, if you will, and how molecularly similar the process is to their antibiotic resistance. I will be back in the city on Monday. If I can be of any additional assistance please do not hesitate to contact me.
ALL THE BEST,
COLLIN WYLIE

As astonished as she was about what she was reading, Laurie had read the e-mail without blinking, and she had to make up for it by squeezing her eyes shut and then blinking several times in a row. She knew next to nothing about amoebas in general or acanthamoeba in particular. Leaning over, she pulled her Harrison's *Principles of Internal Medicine* from the shelf and rapidly looked up acanthamoeba. The reference was short, and merely part of a general article about infection with free-living amoeba. It talked about acanthamoeba causing an encephalitis, but nothing about pneumonia. It also mentioned that the CDC had a fluorescein-labeled antiserum available for definitive diagnosis, which Laurie thought might be helpful to confirm Dr. Wylie's impression.

Laurie replaced the textbook and scanned her shelf for a possible second source. Not seeing one, she repositioned herself at her monitor screen and Googled acanthamoeba. A large number of hits appeared in seconds. She chose a general one.

With a growing sense of urgency, Laurie scanned the first part of the article, which described the protozoa as one of the most common in soil and fresh water. It described some of its characteristics, including the fact that it was a free-living bacterivore but could on rare occasions cause infections in humans. The next paragraph elaborated this issue at length, and Laurie quickly skimmed it.

It was at that point that Laurie's eyes encountered the caption of the next paragraph: *Acanthamoeba and MRSA!* With a surge of adrenaline coursing through her body, Laurie read an elaboration of what Dr. Wylie had mentioned, namely, that MRSA had recently been shown to be able to infect acanthamoeba. But in addition to what he'd cited, the article stated that the MRSA that emerged from the amoeba was frequently more virulent. And then, experiencing a reaction akin to a bolt of electricity passing through her, Laurie read that acanthamoeba cysts infected with MRSA can act as a mode of airborne dispersal for MRSA!

Laurie rocked back in her chair and stared blankly at her monitor screen. She was stunned. She'd been confident that MRSA could not be aerosolized, but now she was aware it could be, so all potential scenarios concerning how the MRSA was spread were back on the table, particularly the idea that the Angels hospitals HVAC systems could be involved.

With some difficulty, Laurie tried to calm herself. She had to think, and with her pulse racing and ideas flying around inside her brain, it was difficult. She took a few deep breaths, and after doing so, she remembered another reason she'd dismissed airborne spread as a serious possibility: The patients never breathed room air after being inducted. It was always bottled air or cleaned and piped-in air.

Laurie thought about this stumbling point. It seemed so definitive, or was it? With a mounting fear that her concerns were legitimate, she snapped her phone off the hook.

Even though a quarter to eight might have been the worst time to call an anesthesiologist, as all the seven-thirty cases were being inducted, Laurie called over to the Manhattan General Hospital. She'd worked on a case with the MGH's chief of anesthesia, Dr. Ronald Havermeyer, and he'd been extraordinarily helpful. Laurie was sure he, of all people, could reassure her about patients never breathing OR air and would be happy to do so. Additionally, his being chief meant that he was in a supervisory role and might be available.

Nervously tapping her fingers on her desktop, Laurie willed the connection to go through as quickly as possible.

"Dr. Havermeyer," a voice finally said.

Laurie quickly explained who she was and without explaining why, asked her question.

"It's true," Dr. Havermeyer said. "The patient never breathes room air after induction until they get to the PACU, and even there they are often maintained on piped-in sources."

"Thank you," Laurie said.

"Not at all. I'm glad I could help."

Laurie was about to hang up when Dr. Havermeyer asked why she wanted to know.

Quickly, Laurie sketched out her concern

— namely, whether bacteria in the HVAC system could be responsible for postoperative nosocomial pneumonia.

"Are you talking about an extended period of breathing ambient air, or just three or four breaths over fifteen or twenty seconds?"

Laurie felt her throat go dry as she intuitively sensed she was about to hear something she did not want to hear.

"Because if it's the latter, there usually is a time," Dr. Havermeyer said. "When the surgeon gives the word and it's time to wake the patient up, or at least terminate the anesthesia, the anesthetist frequently flushes the system with pure oxygen in order to get a faster turnover time for the OR. During the flush, the patient might take two, three, or even four breaths. So it's possible."

Laurie thanked the doctor and hung up.

Suddenly, her fears coalesced. MRSA could spread airborne if encysted with acanthamoeba, and patients having general anesthesia did, even if for only a few seconds, breathe ambient OR air. Laurie snapped up the paper on which she'd written the days of the week her cases had occurred. Her memory told her that orthopedic cases were on Monday and Thursday, and it was unfortunately true. It was also unfortunately true that it was Thursday that very day, the day

Jack had to have his surgery.

With growing desperation, Laurie grabbed one of her cases' hospital charts. Frantically, she searched for the anesthesia record to check the time anesthesia commenced. Anesthesia time was one variable she'd not included in her matrix. To her horror, it was seven-thirty-five a.m. Literally tossing the record to the side, Laurie grabbed another: seven-thirty-one a.m. Swearing under her breath, Laurie grabbed yet another: seven-thirty-four a.m.

"Damn!" Laurie shouted. She got another: seven-thirty a.m.

With four cases out of twenty-five enough for Laurie to fear for the worst in relation to Jack, she ran from her office and beat the elevator down button in hopes of hurrying its arrival. She checked her watch as she waited. It was just after eight. Jack's procedure was supposed to take a little more than an hour, so she might make it if she got a taxi immediately. Luckily, First Avenue was a good place to get a cab in the morning because of the hospitals and other services in the area. What Laurie had decided was that she wanted to be in the Angels Orthopedic Hospital's engineering spaces above the OR as soon as possible to make absolutely certain no one else did.

■ ■ ■ ■

As much as Angelo thought he was depressed the previous evening, he now felt worse. They'd been waiting for almost two hours after arriving at six-fifteen, and still no Laurie Montgomery. Since she and her boyfriend had arrived the previous morning from 30th Street, he'd positioned the van so as to be able to see as far up the street as possible. Every time he'd see a taxi approach, his heart would speed up in anticipation, only to be disappointed again and again.

"I don't think she's coming to work today," Angelo growled.

"Kinda looks that way," Franco said while licking his finger to turn the page of his newspaper.

"As if you give a shit!"

Franco lowered his paper and glared over at Angelo, who'd turned to look back up 30th Street. He felt like lashing out at his partner in crime but didn't. It wasn't worth the effort. Instead, he started to go back to the paper when he caught sight of a figure bursting out from the OCME and descending the front steps as if being chased.

"It's her!" Franco yelled.

Angelo's head spun around. He started to

demand where when he caught sight of Laurie. She was standing at the curb, holding open a taxi door so a passenger could disembark.

"Holy shit!" Angelo yelled. He reached behind his seat for the ethylene, but Franco grabbed his arm.

"There's no time," Franco asserted. "We've got to follow her. Start the damn car!"

They watched while Laurie's hand anxiously waved for the obese woman passenger to hurry. Laurie even resorted to giving the woman one of her hands and attempting to help by pulling, as if the woman were stuck. As soon as the woman was barely out of the way, Laurie threw herself into the cab and pulled the door shut. A moment later, the cab was off with a screech of rubber.

"My God!" Angelo said. "The guy must be a NASCAR nut."

"Don't lose them," Franco cried, as he blindly reached for parts of the vehicle that could keep him from being thrown from his seat.

Angelo didn't need to be reminded about not losing Laurie, and he had the accelerator to the floor. The aged van responded admirably, and it shot forward with its own screech of complaint from its tires.

Briefly, Angelo glanced in the rearview mirror to see if Richie was on the ball. He was, and was not too far behind.

"Do you think she stayed the night in the morgue?" Angelo questioned, as he wove in and out of the traffic.

Franco didn't answer. He was too busy holding on and looking out for police cruisers. Luckily, he saw none. Soon Laurie's taxi and Angelo's van had to stop for a traffic light, and Franco had an opportunity to put on his seat belt.

When Laurie had finally managed to get into the taxi, she had hurriedly told the driver the name of the hospital, the address, and that she was a doctor. As a plea for speed, she'd said she was on a life-and-death emergency. The cab driver, who was a young individual, had taken the request to heart, and Laurie was pleased how quickly he took them up First Avenue. Although he'd not run any red lights as far as Laurie could tell, some of them had been debatably close and had required him to accelerate through the amber.

Unfortunately, going across town was different, and Laurie's feet began a nervous tap as they were forced to wait for a taxi to unload ahead of them at the corner of Park Avenue. Not only did the stop increase her anxiety of being too late, it also gave her a chance to add to her fears. If it were true that all the cases involved the seven-thirty OR time slot, then it was understandable why Wendell Anderson had never had an MRSA case; he didn't start his surgery until significantly later by choice, at least not before doing so, as a favor to Jack.

Laurie gritted her teeth. If she hadn't been so anxious, she could have gotten angry at Jack all over again about his headstrong insistence on having his surgery that day.

As they neared the destination, having just turned down Fifth Avenue, Laurie got out more than enough money and poked it through the Plexiglas divider. She had the door open before the cab came to a complete stop, and she was out on the pavement in a flash, slamming the taxi door behind her. She ran toward the entrance but then slowed as she neared the liveried doorman for fear of making him suspicious and delaying her. Seemingly unperturbed by Laurie's dash from the taxi, the man touched the brim of his hat as a kind of welcoming salute before giving the revolving door a push for her benefit.

Once inside, Laurie continued to force herself to walk at a nearly normal gait. She was conscious of her reception on Tuesday and did not want to call attention to herself, especially since there was a uniformed security man standing off to the side of the lobby. Laurie reached the elevators and pushed the call button. Looking up to the floor indicator, she could see that one car was nearing the lobby.

Out of the corner of her eye, to her chagrin, Laurie glimpsed the security man push off the wall and walk in her direction. Self-consciously, she looked the other way. She could sense his presence at her side but slightly behind.

The elevator arrived. With relief Laurie boarded and in the process pushed the fourth-floor button. For a beat she faced into the car, fearing the man was about to accost her, but he didn't. Yet when she turned to face the elevator doors, he boarded and their eyes briefly met. They were the only two people in the elevator as the doors closed.

Laurie quickly shifted her gaze up to the cab's floor indicator above the doors and held her breath. Expecting to be questioned at any moment, the doors closed, the elevator rose but then immediately stopped.

To her surprise and relief, the security man exited on the second floor, apparently having pressed the button when Laurie had been purposefully keeping her eyes on the floor indicator. When the doors re-closed, Laurie breathed a sigh of relief.

The elevator then rose up to the fourth floor. As the doors opened, Laurie dashed out and ran headlong down the aseptically white corridor. Coming up to the engine room door, she hesitated, praying she was wrong and that her suspicions and fears were a product of an overly active imagination. Looking at her watch, she saw it was eight-forty; the timing would be correct.

Grasping the doorknob and with a bit of effort, Laurie pushed into the engineering room and was immediately enveloped in the throaty, deep hum of the machinery in the heavily insulated, high-ceilinged room.

The heavy door made a loud mechanical click that caught the attention of a surgically masked, hooded, and gowned figure who straightened up from where he had been otherwise hidden among the ducting. In one hand he held a wrench, hardly a surgical instrument, in the other a stoppered Erlenmeyer flask.

In took only a second for Laurie to believe her worst fears were confirmed. Shouting "No!" at the top of her lungs, she raced toward the man, who took a few steps back as if he were going to flee but then changed his mind and stood his ground. Laurie ran into him at full speed with her hands clawing at his mask and ripping it away. Instantly, she recognized who it was. It was Walter Osgood.

The unexpected contact forced Walter to stagger back. As he desperately tried to grasp something to keep him on his feet, he dropped both the wrench and the flask. The wrench clattered safely to the floor but the flask smashed into a dozen shards. The contained white powder was ignominiously dumped onto the floor.

Laurie screamed like a banshee and pounded Walter, who tried to protect himself by raising his crossed arms and briefly allowing Laurie to hit against them. She even got an arm through to his face, striking it as hard as she could, which jolted him out of his inaction. With a surge of defensive anger, he balled his hand into a fist and swung it wide in a roundhouse blow, catching Laurie above the ear. Laurie went down hard. Still, she shook herself and then tried to get up but felt her head yanked painfully to the side. Walter had roughly grabbed a handful of her hair and was dragging her. With Walter twice her size and weight, it was difficult for Laurie to resist, but she reached up and hit and then scratched his forearms. Walter's reaction was to strike her again, almost as hard, with his left hand.

She tried to break the hold he had on her hair as he pulled her over to a door. Opening it with his left hand, he dragged her inside. She tried to kick his legs, but he released the grip he had on her hair and hit her again on the side of her head with his fist. As she flopped back supine, he dashed back out through the door. Although dizzy, Laurie regained her feet and lunged for the doorknob only to feel and hear it make a loud mechanical click. She was locked in.

Walter gingerly touched the side of his face. Pulling his fingers away, he saw a small amount of blood. Quickly, he retrieved his N95 mask and secured it to his face, despite the fact that one of its ties had been snapped apart when Laurie had torn it off. Next, he ran to a large, deep sink, where he found a towel. Wetting it, he rushed back to the smashed flask and, being careful not to cause even the slightest air disturbance, laid the wet towel over the white powder.

Ignoring Laurie's muffled yells as she pounded on the storeroom's door, Walter pulled out his cell phone. He was pleased there was a signal. Quickly, he dialed the emergency number in Washington. Once again, it had to ring a number of times. As he waited, he winced at the new crashing sounds coming from the storeroom. Laurie was apparently throwing large metal containers against the door, which was more worrisome than her previous yelling or pounding against the door with her fists. Walter was concerned someone might hear the commotion, despite the extensive sound insulation with which the room had been equipped. There was no doubt in Walter's mind that Dr. Montgomery had to be removed, and she had to be removed quickly.

Finally, the phone was answered. Walter had no patience with the heretofore cloak-and-dagger routine. When the man started to ask whether Walter was on a cell phone, Walter yelled that he didn't have time for such intrigue. "I've got Dr. Laurie Montgomery locked in a storeroom in the OR HVAC room," he yelled. "Should I let you listen to her yelling and screaming and pounding on the walls? This whole mess is over if she's not dealt with. Do you understand what I'm saying? Whoever your best negotiator, as you called him, is, he's doing a hell of a lousy job. She burst in here and ruined my sample, so today's attempt isn't going to happen. I warned you about this two days ago."

"You say Miss Montgomery is locked in a closet?"

"I said a storeroom," Walter yelled.

"What floor?"

"Fourth floor. It's left down the corridor from the elevator. The door plaque says *Engineering*."

"Don't let anyone in!"

Walter laughed sarcastically. "You don't understand. If one of the engineers needs to come up here for any reason, I couldn't stop them. How often they do come, I have no idea."

"I'll have someone there momentarily."

This time it was Walter who hung up first. For a moment he just stood there, furious at what he had been dragged into and everything that was happening, all because the company's health insurance wouldn't pay for his boy's lymphoma treatment.

Another crash brought Walter abruptly back to the present. He walked over to the storeroom door, pounded it himself, and told Laurie to shut up and that he'd let her out when she'd calmed down.

"Let me out now," Laurie yelled back.

"I've called security. They are on their way," Walter yelled, but his comment only resulted in another horrendous crash from within the storeroom. Giving up, he set his mind to clean up the airborne infection powder.

Adam was parked on the playground side of the street just opposite Laurie Montgomery's house. He'd gotten there slightly earlier than he'd planned to give himself an extra cushion of time, but something had obviously gone awry. Although a few people had exited the building, neither Laurie nor her boyfriend had shown their faces.

Just when Adam was about to admit he'd have to return in the morning, his phone buzzed against his leg. It was one of his handlers in Washington.

"Where are you?" the man demanded.

"One hundred sixth Street on the Upper West Side."

"Get over to the Angels Orthopedic Hospital. The target is locked in a closet in a fourth-floor engineering space. An operative of ours is there. His name is Walter Osgood. Miss Montgomery must be extracted ASAP and then dealt with accordingly. It should be a challenge, but we trust you are up to it."

Adam quickly hung up and started his vehicle. He then switched on the Beethoven and turned up the volume.

In the darkness, Laurie was becoming desperate. She'd always been somewhat claustrophobic, and being locked in the way she was had awakened her childhood fears. The only sliver of light was found beneath the stout door, and she'd been unable to locate a light switch. After the first few minutes of pounding on the door and yelling in hopes of being heard by someone other than Walter Osgood, she'd groped about in the utter blackness. The storeroom was about ten by twenty feet, with shelving on both sides. It was in the very back that she'd found the sizable metal containers whose tops were secured like paint cans. She had no idea what they contained and thought they may well have been paint. By rolling one forward, she'd used it to heave repeatedly against the door. It had had no perceivable effect despite its weight, and she had to be careful in the darkness that it didn't bounce off the door and injure her.

For a moment, she did nothing except try to listen. It had been some time since she'd heard Walter moving about in the outer room. Unable to hear anything and finding that standing in the darkness was more harrowing than trying to avoid hitting herself with the multi-gallon container, she went back to heaving it at the door. On her second try, she heard a deeper sound as the can struck the door and a softer one when it hit the floor. Laurie guessed that the top had come off and the contents spilled.

Bending down, Laurie gingerly patted the floor as she moved her hand forward. There was no smell of paint, so Laurie assumed it had to be something else. All at once, she encountered a fine powder with her fingers. Slowly, she moved her fingers toward her face, warily sniffing the closer she came. It wasn't until her fingers were close to her face that she smelled anything, and even then she wasn't sure what it was. She guessed it was a type of cleaning product.

Laurie righted the container. It still contained about half of its contents. She pushed it to the side so as not to stumble on it. Then she was about to get another one when she heard sounds coming from out in the other room. It sounded as if it were a door closing.

Hoping it was someone other than Walter, Laurie began rattling the doorknob with one hand and pounding on the door with the other, all the while yelling "Help" over and over. Within the confines of the storeroom, her yells were almost painfully loud, but she imagined they weren't so in the other room. Everything was so insulated.

Laurie stopped her clamor. No one had come to her rescue. She heard muttering voices. Obviously, someone had joined Walter and hadn't rushed to her aid. It wasn't hard for her to imagine that whoever it was was in league with Walter, probably coming to get her out of the hospital. Panicking, Laurie tried to think of what she could do. She'd not even been able to defend herself from one man, much less two. Suddenly, she thought of the fine powder. It certainly wouldn't hold them off for long, but may be enough to get a step on them. Maybe she could get out into the corridor, where yelling and screaming could bring someone . . . anyone.

Moving up to the door, Laurie felt around for the open container. Reaching in with her two hands, she scooped up as much of the powder as she could. Then, stepping forward, she pressed herself against the wall on the side of the door that opened. It was none too soon, as the door was suddenly unlocked and thrown completely ajar. For a second nothing happened, and then a head cautiously came in along with what could have been a gun. Laurie threw the powder into the face, then rolled around into the doorway and pushed the man backward.

Without waiting for an instant, Laurie took off running. She saw Walter grab the man who had his free hand slapped over his eyes.

The ruse had caught both unawares and had been more effective than Laurie had even hoped. The problem was that she'd not been able to run toward the door to the corridor but rather toward the far door that Laurie had been told led to a second HVAC room. More important for her at the moment was that she'd also been told it too had an exit leading to a back stairway.

Although the powder had provided Laurie with the opportunity to run, it was not caustic enough to hold Adam down for long. Laurie had just managed to get through the adjoining door when Adam got his sight more or less back to normal, and he was able to pursue, although he was still coughing to a degree.

When Adam dashed into the second HVAC room, he had to come to a full stop. For a second, he did not see Laurie. Rapidly, his eyes scanned the high-ceilinged room with its tangle of ducting. He didn't see Laurie, but he did see the room's second door settling into its jamb.

There were large service elevators, but Laurie ignored them. Going through yet another door that Laurie sensed was locked in the other direction, she plunged down the stairs, which had two runs per floor. Originally, she was going to run back into the hospital on the OR floor below and make a large ruckus, but she had to ditch that idea with the fear of the door being locked from the stairwell side. Instead, Laurie continued down. Behind her, she heard Adam burst out through the door on the fourth floor.

Reaching the ground floor, Laurie exited out to the deserted receiving dock. To her right was the parking garage, to the left the ramp leading up to Fifth Avenue. Without a second's hesitation, Laurie ran to the left. At least she was confident the avenue would be filled with moving traffic.

Halfway up the ramp and despite her heavy breathing, she heard behind her the exit door bang open against the side of the building. At this point of full-fledged, head-long sprinting, her muscles were complaining in agony and each breath gave her a searing sensation in her chest.

Laurie got to the street. To her left almost a half a block away was the liveried door-man. At the moment, the sidewalk was devoid of activity. The street was a different story. As she'd expected, it was all but clotted with traffic moving at a slow pace. For lack of any other alternative, Laurie ran directly out into the middle of the one-way multilaned avenue, causing several cars to brake precipitously before drivers angrily drove on. With both hands waving, Laurie tried to get a car, a taxi, a bus, anything to stop. When she saw Adam sprinting in the middle of the street, she started to run north against the traffic while still waving her hands and pleading for someone to stop.

"It's her, for chrissake!" Angelo yelled the moment he'd seen Laurie appear, dashing from the hospital's parking ramp. He was out of the van in an instant. He and Richie had parked their respective vans just south of the ramp entrance at the north end of the hospital. Since the traffic went north to south, they'd decided it was the best place to be when Laurie came out the front entrance, which was what they had expected.

Franco leaped out of his side of the blue van while Richie and Freddie jumped from the white one. All four men were running up the sidewalk on the park side of Fifth Avenue, with Angelo slightly in the lead. Suddenly, Angelo stopped, as did the others. All saw Adam race out into the street in pursuit of Laurie, at whom he was yelling to stop. They all saw that he was carrying something wrapped in a towel.

Because Laurie was not moving ahead exclusively but rather trying to get cars to stop by slapping their hoods, Adam rapidly closed the narrow gap between them.

Laurie turned to look at him. Although she'd thought upstairs in the HVAC room that he was a stranger, now she thought she recognized him as the bill collector at the OCME. But before she could say anything and before he said anything, he slowly raised the cone-shaped towel he was carrying such that Laurie could see a black cylinder just concealed in its tip.

The sound of the gun was muffled, and Laurie reflexively winced and closed her eyes. Strangely, nothing happened. She re-opened her eyes. At her feet lay Adam, still clutching his pistol, which had partially come out from behind its towel. Laurie was shocked into momentary immobility, staring down at her attacker, who was on his stomach, slightly twitching. But Laurie's trance didn't last long. A moment later, she was set on by four men, one of whom was yelling "Police" and showing several motorists who'd finally stopped his police badge. Two other cars had actually pulled to the side of the road, and the drivers were climbing out.

Laurie was relieved as she allowed herself to be rapidly escorted to the park-side sidewalk. It was there that her relief dissolved in a totally new whirl of fear. One of the men was Angelo Facciolo, an old nemesis of hers going back fifteen years. She tried to slow the rapid progress being made as the four men hustled her toward the vans. "Excuse me," she called out, still wanting to believe the men had saved her. "Let's stop! I'm fine."

She was ignored. No one spoke. Suddenly, she tried desperately to break from their collective grasp but to no avail. She found herself being hoisted up into the air with her feet only lightly touching the pavement. It was at that point that Laurie belatedly tried to verbally protest, but even that was of limited value as a hand snaked from behind and was clasped over her mouth.

Reaching the vans, the sliding door of the white one was thrown open, and Laurie was pulled inside as if devoured. She tried to struggle, but the four men crushed her under them, making it hard for her to breathe. She felt her legs being bound with duct tape, then her arms. She still tried to struggle, and she screamed when the hand over her mouth had been removed. But her shouting didn't persist for long, as she was gagged with an oily rag held in by several turns of the duct tape.

23
APRIL 5, 2007
2:15 P.M.

Jack cringed from a new stab of pain from his freshly traumatized knee, as he'd forgotten where he was while reaching for the glass of water on his bedside table. Although the general, background pain hadn't gone away, the blissful narcotic had changed the pain's character such that Jack could easily ignore it. Jack had an intravenous setup with which he could control how much pain medicine he got. In that way, he was certain to get less, which was his goal. He knew that all the strong pain meds had a price to pay down the road, even if it was something seemingly simple like constipation.

From about noon on, Jack had been multitasking, meaning watching TV and flipping through magazines simultaneously. He'd brought some more serious reading, but he had a sneaking suspicion he might not get around to it until the following day, or the day after that, or maybe never. He liked just relaxing now that the big stress was over. The operation was history, and Dr. Anderson had popped in around eleven and reported that it had gone exceedingly smoothly. There was only one problem: Laurie had said she'd be by around noontime, and so far there had been no Laurie and no call.

By one, Jack had called the OCME, as he assumed she'd gotten held up, perhaps by there being so many autopsies such that she had to pitch in. But he learned the day had not been overwhelming. Speaking with Riva, Jack was told Laurie was in her office around seven that morning but that no one had seen her since. Thinking that she might have gone home, Jack had tried her there. When he didn't catch her, he left a message for her to call. With no other ideas of where she might be, Jack could only wait. Now that it was after two, he began to get seriously concerned.

After drinking his water, Jack was about to go back to his magazine and the TV when Lou Soldano walked in. He was doubly solicitous when he saw the contraption Jack's operated leg was Velcroed into. It was constantly flexing and extending the knee, which Lou envisioned as being constantly painful. After assuring the detective that it wasn't bothering him, Jack asked if he'd seen or heard from Laurie.

"That's why I'm here," Lou said in a very serious tone. He pulled over an upholstered chair.

"I think you'd better tell me what's going on."

"There was a very bizarre shooting this morning while you were under the knife," Lou said. "It was right below your window, in fact. The victim was a man we knew little about since he was carrying false identification."

Jack nodded. He had no idea how Laurie possibly could be in any way involved.

"As you know, New Yorkers are rather high on the hard-hearted scale, and when this shooting went down, not too many stopped, although we are hearing from more people as the day progresses. Of those who stopped, we haven't gotten consistent reports. Be that as it may, the individual had been chasing a woman out from behind the hospital."

"So the woman shot this guy?"

"No, not the woman but some passerby who had leaped from a van with three other people. This guy shot the man who was about to shoot the woman, at least according to a couple of witnesses, but to corroborate the story, the shooting victim was carrying a silenced automatic nine-millimeter pistol rolled up in a towel."

"Is the victim dead?"

"No! He's critical but not dead."

"Have you been able to talk to him?"

"Nope. He had to undergo emergency surgery down the street at Beth Israel."

"What about the woman? Have you talked to her?"

"Nope again. The woman was whisked off in a white van by the four men who had, of all things, pretended to be plainclothes police. I'm telling you, this is one weird case."

"So how does this relate to Laurie?" Jack asked, although he was unsure if he wanted to hear.

"The descriptions of the woman, although they're not terribly consistent, could be describing Laurie, with some more so than others."

Jack stared at Lou. His anesthesia-addled mind was struggling to process the information Lou was providing. Jack didn't like what he was hearing but wanted to remain hopeful. "Let me get this straight," he said. "You don't have any specific association of this apparently abducted woman with Laurie?"

Lou nodded. "Nothing specific, just the suggestive descriptions. That and the fact that no one knows where Laurie is at the moment. I mean, no one at the OCME, and certainly not you."

"Good God!" Jack murmured. "And me a total invalid with a totally bum knee."

Lou stood up and replaced the chair. He came back to the bed, where the flexing and extending machine was making a constant, low-pitched grinding noise. He reached out and gave Jack's arm a squeeze. "I just want you to know that I've got a thousand people, including myself, working on this and will be twenty-four-seven. We've been stopping white vans all over the city."

Jack nodded. Although his knee felt reasonably well, he was now sick with fear.

24
APRIL 5, 2007
8:05 P.M.

By a little after eight, it was finally dark enough to suit Angelo for the quick ride over to the marina. That morning after they made the snatch, they'd driven south to a parking garage where Franco was known. With ease, they'd transferred a terrified Laurie from the white van to the blue one. At that point, Richie and Freddie had driven the white one back to Queens, where it disappeared into the motor pool.

Meanwhile, Angelo and Franco had driven the blue van with Laurie in it out to New Jersey, where they'd found a run-down motel of questionable morals with rooms rentable by the hour. What was most significant to Angelo was that the entrance to the units was up and around the back of the grubby office. Angelo had wanted privacy for escorting Laurie inside, and he had had it in spades. At that time of the morning, the motel had all but been deserted.

Richie and Freddie had returned just before noon, bringing with them takeout from Johnny's and a couple six-packs. The four men then had spent the early afternoon playing cards, eating subs, and generally enjoying themselves.

It had been after the card game that Angelo had finally attended to Laurie. After getting her to promise not to make a scene, he'd removed the duct tape from across her mouth and allowed her to spit out the gag. He'd then asked if she were thirsty, and when she'd admitted she was, he held a glass he'd prepared for her. Laurie had taken it despite its taste, and from then on, she'd been easy to take care of. Angelo had spiked the drink with one of his small, white date-rape pills. Later in the afternoon, they'd added another to make the switch from the van to the boat a piece of cake.

"Okay, come on, baby doll," Angelo said, as he shook Laurie's shoulder. "We're going for a nice little boat ride."

Without any trouble, they got Laurie from the motel room into the van. With two of the Rohypnol tablets on board, they didn't even need to rely on the duct tape, yet they elected to leave it on. With Angelo driving and Franco sitting shotgun in the van, and Richie and Freddie in Richie's car, the group made their way to the waterfront. Once there, they headed directly to the marina. All was going well until the pier itself came into view. At that point, they noted something they'd not seen the previous nights: another car.

Angelo braked and stopped the van. Richie pulled directly behind Angelo.

"Can you make out the make of the car?" Angelo asked.

Franco leaned forward so that his nose was practically touching the windshield. "It's hard to say, but if I had to, I'd say it was a Cadillac. A black Cadillac."

Sitting back, Franco looked at Angelo. "Did Vinnie say he was coming?"

"Not to me he didn't. You think it's Vinnie's?"

Franco shrugged. "It could be."

Angelo put the van back in gear and slowly drove forward. He didn't like surprises, and he knew Franco didn't, either. When they were fifty to sixty feet away, Angelo stopped again. This time, both men strained to see forward. "I think it is Vinnie's," Angelo said.

Franco got out. And as he closed on the car, he could see it was Vinnie's. Franco walked around to the driver's-side window and knocked. Because of the tinting, he couldn't see in. But then, looking out the pier, he could see why. A light from one of the lower gallery's portholes was casting a dim, flickering beam across the water.

Walking back to the van, Franco approached on the driver's side. Angelo lowered the window. "It's okay," Franco said. "It's the boss. He's already out on the boat."

"I wonder how come," Angelo said. He wasn't sure he wanted to share the upcoming experience with the whole city.

"Beats me."

They parked, got Laurie out of the van, took the duct tape off her ankles, and walked her out the pier. Reminiscent of the snatch that morning, they had to hoist her practically off her feet, but not because she was resisting.

"I think you might have overdone the date-rape drug," Franco said. Being nearly comatose, Laurie seemed to weigh a surprising amount considering her trim figure.

"Hello, men!" Vinnie called to them when they drew near. He had been standing in the shadows of the afterdeck, but now he walked out more into the open. Ice could be heard clinking in his old-fashioned glass. "I hope you don't mind me dropping by. I realized I didn't want to miss the fun. And I see you men have already got the quick-set and the other gear."

"We got it yesterday," Angelo said, "and got it on board today."

"Good work," Vinnie said calmly. "I also brought someone else with me." He gestured back into the shadows. Reluctantly, Michael Calabrese stepped forward with a weak smile. "I got to thinking," Vinnie explained, putting an arm around Michael's shoulders. "Mikey here seems to come up with all this work for you guys and for me but never gets his hands dirty. You know what I'm saying? It's just prudent business practice to have him participate. If push ever came to shove, he couldn't throw up his hands and say he didn't know what was going down when these nice people disappear.

"Angelo, I know this is mostly your show, but I didn't think you would mind sharing. Is that too much to ask?"

Angelo held his tongue as he and Franco maneuvered Laurie across the gangplank onto the yacht.

"I didn't hear your response," Vinnie said.

"It's okay," Angelo murmured, as he and Franco helped Laurie across the open afterdeck.

"There you go, Mikey!" Vinnie said, thumping Michael on the back. "Your fears are over. Angelo's glad to have you on board, so let's party."

While Franco and Angelo were below, putting the deeply sleeping Laurie in one of the staterooms, Richie and Freddie manned the mooring lines. Vinnie happily climbed to the bridge, and with his scotch at his side, he started the twin diesels and eased the boat from its slip. As they motored out into the middle of the river, Vinnie called down for someone to put on one of his Frank Sinatra CDs. A few minutes later, Hoboken's favorite son was crooning away and massaging everyone's mental state.

It was a pleasant night. There was little wind and the water was calm. A scimitar moon was just peeking over the jagged, twinkling skyline of the city. To the north was the lighted George Washington Bridge with the Martha Washington level demurely beneath. To the south in the middle distance was their approximate destination: the illuminated Statue of Liberty. Within ten minutes, all worries, concerns, or irritation were blown away by the soft breeze and the loud but lulling sound of the engines. Everyone was either on the bridge or sitting on the gunwales in the stern, except for Laurie, who was sleeping off her unexpected medication, and Angelo, who was apparently beginning the preparation for the real reason they were all there.

Ten minutes later, Angelo appeared and asked Franco to help him move Laurie up to the afterdeck. "You are right. We overdid the date-rape pill. She won't wake up."

Franco followed Angelo below, and Richie went as well, in case they needed more help. A few minutes later, the group appeared, carrying both Laurie and the five-gallon bucket into which her feet were sticking. Freddie jumped out of a folding chair so they could sit her down.

The group gathered around. Even Vinnie came down after putting the boat on autopilot. While Freddie ducked below for some rope to keep Laurie upright, Vinnie stuck his hand into the bucket to feel the consistency of the cement.

"Impressive," Vinnie said, looking down into the bucket. Laurie's feet were buried up to mid-calf. "It's almost dry."

"It only takes a half-hour," Angelo said. "It's actually called hydrophilic cement. The guy at the Home Depot recommended it."

Vinnie looked at Angelo and joked, "You didn't tell him what you were going to do with it, did you?"

Everyone had a good laugh.

"The problem is, she's passed out," Angelo said, changing the subject. "I wanted her to suffer. Instead, she looks like she's enjoying herself."

"Try to wake her," Vinnie offered. "Maybe the fresh air will help."

Angelo patted Laurie's cheek with the flat of his hand, but there was no response. He tried it harder. Still no response.

Vinnie looked across at Richie. "Head up to the bridge and drive this brute of a boat. We shouldn't leave it on autopilot. We don't want to take a chance of hitting anything."

Richie reluctantly climbed the ship's ladder. He didn't want to miss the fun.

"You and me are just going to have to take what we get," Vinnie said to Angelo. Then, to the group, he added, "Let's all have another drink and toast to Angelo's vengeance!"

As the boat bore down on the Statue of Liberty, the festivities hit high gear. A second Frank Sinatra CD had been put into the player, and when "My Way" came on, everyone sang. A few minutes later, when they got to the world-famous landmark, Vinnie yelled up to Richie to head out toward the Verrazano Bridge.

"Hey, it's my turn to join the fun," Richie said. "How about someone else run this hulk!"

Vinnie looked at Freddie and hooked a finger in the direction of the ladder to the bridge. "Your turn," he said with a slightly inebriated smile.

Twenty minutes later, Vinnie poked his finger into Laurie's bucket. The hydrophilic cement felt like it was supposed to feel. It was even cool. "I think she's ready," he yelled at Angelo. Angelo came over and felt as well and nodded.

Vinnie went over and yelled up to Freddie to ease back on the throttle. Vinnie looked at Angelo. "This looks like as good a place as any." They were in the mouth of the narrows with the Verrazano-Narrows Bridge dead ahead.

"Fine with me," Angelo said, slurring his words.

"Freddie!" Vinnie yelled up the ladder. "Put it in neutral and come on down if you want."

"Hey, everybody," Angelo said. "It looks like the evening air has done her a world of good: She seems to be waking up!"

"Yes, she does," Vinnie agreed.

"Let's give her a little time," Angelo suggested. "I'd like her to know what's going on when we balance her on the stern with her cement boot on."

"Perfect," Vinnie said. "Time for another round." Everyone cheered, even Richie, until Vinnie added, "Except you, Richie. Tonight, you're the designated driver."

A half-hour slipped comfortably by as the men sat around Laurie and watched her slowly revive. There had been a lot of jerky movements over a fifteen-minute period, and finally her eyes had opened halfway.

Although it was obvious to everyone except Angelo that Laurie's lights were on but no one was home as of yet, Angelo insisted on talking with her in an attempt to get her to comprehend exactly what was about to transpire. Finally, he realized his efforts were in vain.

Standing up, Angelo steadied himself with his hand on the stern's gunwale. "Let's do it," he said. He undid the rope around Laurie's torso, which had been holding her upright in the chair.

"I want you to help!" Vinnie said to Michael, giving him yet another slap on the back.

"That's quite okay," Michael said. "I don't want to horn in on the fun."

"Nonsense," Vinnie countered. "It's a community activity. I insist."

Michael studied Vinnie's face. He could tell the man was dead serious. Reluctantly, he moved to one side of Laurie's rag doll figure.

"All right, everyone!" Angelo said. "First,

we stand her up!"

Although the boat was in neutral, the engines still made considerable noise, especially when the exhaust pipes went under the water's surface, a situation that produced loud popping noises reminiscent of gunfire.

Moving Laurie from the chair to the very back of the boat was more difficult than they had expected. She was so flaccid, several people had to keep her upright while the others had to lift the five-gallon bucket of concrete. At that point, they faced the daunting task of lifting Laurie and the concrete up onto the stern gunwale.

"All right on three," Angelo said. Everyone was either grasping the weighty bucket or Laurie's floppy body.

Not everyone was immediately aware of a giant presence that had silently loomed out of the darkness, but certainly became so within seconds of each other. On the other hand, everyone was instantly frozen by the powerful and blinding searchlight beam, and everyone heard the word "freeze" as it was suddenly and loudly projected from a sizable directional speaker mounted on one of the larger vessels of the Harbor Police fleet. A second later, a grappling hook dropped over the yacht's gunwale and the two boats were quickly made fast. A moment later, uniformed police swarmed out of the blinding light and relieved the revelers of the burden of Laurie and her concrete boot.

EPILOGUE
APRIL 10, 2007
2:30 P.M.

Detective Lieutenant Lou Soldano quickly stubbed his cigarette out in his car's ashtray when he turned onto 106th Street. Whenever he even got close to Laurie, and even to Jack, for that matter, he always felt guilty about his smoking on account of having promised both of them he was stopping about nine million times. Slowing down, Lou parked in a no-parking access to the neighborhood playground across from Jack and Laurie's. He tossed his NYPD auto identification onto the dashboard and got out of the vehicle.

Although spring often would take a long time to appear in the city, it was doing fine as Lou looked around the neighborhood. A few crocuses had poked their delicate heads out of the ground in a small plot in the playground and even in a few window boxes on Jack and Laurie's side of the street. In the small wedge of Central Park that Lou could see at the end of the street was a patch of lacy yellow forsythia.

Starting across the street, Lou couldn't help but notice how Jack and Laurie's building stood out. They had just renovated it the year before when they had gotten married. Now several other buildings were in the process. The neighborhood was definitely on the upswing.

Before the renovation, Lou could just push in through the outer door, since its lock had been broken some time before the war and never fixed. Jack used to joke that it was the Civil War. Now Lou had to ring the bell, which he did. Jack and Laurie lived on the top two floors. The rest of the building had been divided into rental apartments, but Lou had the suspicion that Jack and Laurie let them for little or no money to deserving families, particularly single-parent families.

Presently, Laurie answered, which made sense, since Jack was still hobbled from his recent operation. Her voice sounded disgruntled. Knowing what they both had been through, he asked if he should come back at another time after identifying himself. Having come directly from court, he'd not phoned ahead.

"Are you joking?" she questioned with exasperation, as if Lou were adding to her woe.

"I was just asking. Maybe I should have called?"

"Lou, for chrissake, get your ass up here!"

Behind him, Lou could hear the door release activated. Quickly, he pushed it open, then held it with an extended foot. "I'm on my way."

"You'd better be."

Lou had no real idea what Laurie's mind-set was. At first she'd sounded purely vexed, but then it had seemingly turned to pique. As he climbed the final flight, suffering from all the cigarettes he'd smoked in his life, he vowed once again to quit tomorrow or maybe the next day.

Before he could knock and with his arm raised to do so, the door opened. Laurie was standing just inside the threshold, with one fist jammed in the crook of her hip. "Am I glad to see you," she said, motioning over her shoulder with her head. "Would you mind talking to King Louis Quatorze over there?"

Lou leaned in and looked into the living room. Jack was sprawled out on the couch, surrounded by all manner of treats, including juices, fruit, and cookies. Lou looked back at Laurie. He had to admit she looked good considering her horrid experience less than a week previously at the hands of vengeful two-bit mafioso types. Her face had her normal color, and her eyes were bright and fully open.

"He thinks he can order in a semirecumbent exercise bike today and just hop on. Can you imagine?"

"That might be rushing it," Lou agreed.

"Now, don't you gang up on me," Jack warned, but with a smile.

"I'm not getting involved," Lou said, raising his hands. "I'm just calling it as I see it. But let me ask the two of you a question: Are you getting a little stir-crazy locked up in here together?" Lou knew that Laurie had been essentially ordered to take sick leave after her abduction and torture.

Laurie and Jack glanced irritably at each other, then simultaneously laughed.

"All right!" Lou ordered. "What's so funny now? Am I the butt of a joke?"

Jacked waved Lou away. "Not at all. I think we both realized at the same instant that you were correct. Is that right, Laurie?"

"I'm afraid so. I think we've been getting on each other's nerves because neither one of us can do what we want to do. We both want to get out."

Clearly happier than they had been five minutes earlier, Jack and Laurie welcomed a visit with Lou, for whom Laurie had quickly made fresh coffee. Laurie was sitting on the couch next to Jack, and Lou in a side chair on the opposite side of the coffee table.

"So, how are both you guys?" Lou asked, balancing his coffee on his knee.

Laurie looked at Jack and motioned for him to go first.

"I'm as good as can be expected," Jack said. "The surgery went fine, and, thanks to Laurie, I didn't get anything I hadn't signed up for, meaning a fulminant MRSA infection. I'm chagrined, to say the least, that I didn't give the threat more credence. But I have to say, if a doctor tells you you're going to have a little discomfort after a surgery, don't believe him or her. Surgeons lie like crazy. But with that proviso, in general I guess I'm doing okay. It's just hard looking out my living-room window at night seeing the guys having a run. I feel like a kid quarantined."

"What about you, Laur?" Louis asked, switching his line of vision. *Laur* had been the name given to Laurie by Lou's kids back when Lou had first met her fifteen years previously.

Laurie flashed a questioning expression. "I feel a heck of a lot better than people think I should. I'm sure it's a function of the Rohypnol I was given. I mean, I'd heard date-rape pills frequently caused considerable amnesia, but I had no idea how total it would be or that it could involve retrograde events. I remember only sketchily confronting Osgood and then being locked in the storeroom. I'm not sure how I got out, although I do remember being chased by what's his name."

"Adam Williamson," Lou put in. "A tragic figure, I might add. At least in some regards. He's an Iraq veteran who went through hell and has a lot of resultant mental problems."

"Did he pull through?" Jack asked. He noticed that Lou used the present tense.

"He did. He's going to make it. What we're not sure about is whether he's going to be willing to plea bargain with us. Obviously, we have him on attempted murder and conspiracy. You do know he was about to shoot you at point-blank range, don't you, Laurie?"

"That's what I was told. Isn't there a witness to the fact?"

"We have two good witnesses," Lou said. "And the king of all ironies is that Angelo is the one who saved you by shooting Adam before Adam shot you."

"That part I don't remember," Laurie admitted. "In fact, I don't remember anything else until gradually waking up in the hospital."

"It's a good thing," Lou said. "When we got there in the middle of Upper New York Bay, they had you rigged up with what they used to call cement boots."

"So I heard," Laurie said with a shudder.

"That reminds me," Jack said. "First, how did you know she was out there, and once you did, how in tarnation did you find them out there in the middle of New York Bay in the dark?"

"That's the best part," Lou said. "And truthfully, I don't mind taking a little credit. The floater we picked up Monday night scared the bejesus out of us, making me worry about a Mob war breaking out, like I told you. When I found out that the word on the street was that Vinnie Dominick was behind it, I went over to Paul Cerino's old organization to tip them off, thinking the floater might have been in cahoots with them. As it turned out, he wasn't, but the Vaccarros were concerned enough to follow Vinnie's principle enforcers, Angelo and Franco, and discovered Vinnie had squirreled away a sizable yacht, which they were using for nasty purposes. The next part is the cleverest. What they did was to figure out a way to get the city, meaning me, to get rid of the competition Vinnie represented. And how they did it was secretly to put a GPS tracking device on the yacht and then wait until a good opportunity arose. Louie Barbera, Paul Cerino's replacement, called me up Thursday evening right at the point I was despairing and offered me the website and the password and user name for the GPS device. He also told me what he thought was about to happen so we wouldn't waste time, and we didn't. It was just lucky we got there when we did for your benefit. At the same time, the opportunity couldn't have been any better from a law-enforcement angle. We reeled in Vinnie Dominick and all his top guys in one fell swoop, plus another guy by the name of Michael Calabrese. And best of all, we got them all for attempted first-degree murder, hardly a minor charge. Furthermore, while the crime guys have been poring over the boat, trace blood was discovered that belonged to the two floaters, whom we have identified as Paul Yang and Amy Lucas, both from New Jersey, and both worked for Angels Healthcare."

Laurie stiffened. "Angels Healthcare that runs the Angels hospitals?"

"None other. It's a relatively complicated story and the investigation is ongoing, involving the FBI and the SEC. Sadly, it is just another one involving huge amounts of potential money, the kind of corruption we've all heard a bit too much of these days, although in this case there was a generous amount of old-fashioned crime involved, like murder, as well as the newer white-collar variety. As you correctly sensed, Laurie, the MRSA was being purposefully spread, and not just for terrorist purposes. There was a method to the madness. What a group of people was trying to do was sabotage the IPO and, in a sense, the specialty-hospital concept."

"Who was responsible?" Laurie asked.

"Ultimately, the people behind it are lobbyists, mostly former lawyer-politicians who had morphed into becoming lobbyists after either retiring or being voted out of office. Of the particular organization we are speaking of, they had landed the perfect clients: the AHA and the FAH. What they had been hired to do was to make absolutely sure that the Senate moratorium on building specialty hospitals and registering them with CMS, or Centers for Medicaid and Medicare Services, be changed into law. But they didn't do it. Somehow, they dropped the ball. Wanting to keep the AHA and the FAH as clients, they shouldered the responsibility to make absolutely certain the first IPO after the moratorium was lifted would not be successful. Hence, they conjured up the MRSA initiative, as I've been calling it. Their thinking was that it would be viewed as a natural phenomenon, and that investors would be driven away by the cash crunch the post-op infections would cause."

"So it was they who recruited Walter Osgood. Was he just a pawn in this affair?"

"I'm afraid so. We know that he wasn't extorted but did it on his own free will. He had both the background to pull it off and some very specific needs that motivated him. As I think you know, he trained in microbiology, so it wasn't difficult for him to requisition the MRSA from the CDC and the amoeba from National Culture. He had a little private lab where he cooked up what turns out to be a pretty good bioterrorism agent, at least that's what our consults have been telling us. He got the MRSA to invade the amoeba, proliferate, and then he got the amoeba to encyst. Once he got the amoeba to form cysts, which is apparently easy, he could dry the cysts to form an airborne infectious agent. Perhaps the cleverest part, he could use the cysts to flood an OR at the moment when patients with anesthesia with endotracheal tubes are about to be awakened. Timing was critical, and it didn't work a hundred percent of the time, but as Osgood became more and more familiar with particular surgeons and the lengths of particular procedures, he got better and better."

"Sounds like you have all these terms and concepts down pat," Laurie said.

"On a case like this, I needed to be prepared for the sake of the prosecutors. All the arraignments were this morning."

"What were Walter Osgood's needs you mentioned?"

"He had a son who came down with a very severe form of some sort of cancer. The only treatment was deemed experimental, and the Angels Healthcare employees' health insurance company would not pay. Walter had been paying on his own. The involved pharmaceutical company had been charging him twenty thousand a month. Can you believe it?"

"You certainly have learned a lot in a few days."

"It's a hot case, as you can well imagine. I'm lucky the FBI got into it big-time. They have been carrying the ball. The lobbyist organization is in Washington, D.C., as you might imagine."

"So, in a very real way, Angels Healthcare has been subverted for the last number of months."

"That's a good way to describe it. But they

have not been lily-white by any stretch of the imagination."

"I should say!" Laurie agreed. "Even if they didn't know the MRSA was being deliberately spread, they kept on doing surgery, even though people kept dying."

"They are guilty of a little more than that in these days of Sarbanes-Oxley. This part of the case is being handled by the SEC investigators. Once Angels Healthcare got into financial difficulty with their cash flow, they were required by law to have conveyed the information to the SEC so investors could protect themselves, especially if there was an imminent IPO. And this isn't the kind of thing you get slapped on the wrist for and told you are bad. Nowadays, this kind of oversight means big fines and stiff prison sentences. The government is intent on making examples of these white-collar criminals, because it is the little guy who is always hurt."

"We've all heard of some notorious cases over the last couple of years," Laurie said.

"That's an understatement," Lou said. "I'm ninety-nine-point-nine percent sure that all the Angels Healthcare principals will be able to spend some time with those more famous brethren. The CEO, CFO, and COO have all been arrested and arraigned. Two posted very high bail, but the third couldn't."

"What if they didn't know they were supposed to file when their cash flow fell?"

"Ignorance of the law is not an excuse," Lou said. "At the same time, they knew. Except for the CEO, they are experienced businesspeople, and the CEO had recently been through business school. They all knew what they should have done. In fact, the reason Paul Yang and his secretary, Amy Lucas, were killed, as near as we can tell, is because Paul wanted to file the necessary paperwork and the others put pressure on him not to do it. That's serious business."

"Have the Angels Healthcare executives also been charged with murder?" Laurie asked with shock.

"No. We were able to learn through Freddie Capuso, who has copped a plea, that the two killings and your being put in jeopardy was from the civilian guy on the boat, Michael Calabrese."

"I remember your mentioning him. What was his role?"

"He used to be married to the CEO, Angela Dawson, and even had a child with her. In the past, he was an investment banker with Morgan Stanley but left because of the opportunity to invest all the racketeering and drug money Vinnie Dominick controlled. He was, in essence, a professional money launderer. On top of that, he's going to be tried for murder."

"God, what a mess," Laurie said.

"In a very real way, we owe you for breaking the case or, more accurately, breaking the cases. If it hadn't been for you, all these people would be still carrying on."

"I don't think I deserve the credit," Laurie said. "I'm afraid my motivations were to get Jack to postpone his surgery, so the rest is fallout."

Lou smiled. He didn't agree but wasn't going to argue.

"What has Walter Osgood been charged with?" Laurie asked.

"Haven't you heard?"

"Heard what?"

"Walter Osgood committed suicide yesterday."

"Good grief," Laurie said.

"His son, whom he'd been trying to raise the money for, died on Saturday. Osgood had a lot of reasons to be depressed."

"It's a multilayered tragedy for everyone involved."

"I'll tell you what it is," Jack said, speaking up for the first time. "It's equivalent to the adage in politics that power corrupts, and absolute power corrupts absolutely. The difference is that with medicine it's money, not power."

Chet McGovern pressed his nose against the bus's window and looked across the East River at LaGuardia Airport. He was close enough to see individual windows on the jetliners as they waited to take off. He was close, but in another way he was far because Chet was on a New York City bus heading across a long two-lane bridge that not only had he never seen but he never knew even existed. Having lived in the city for fifteen years, he thought he was familiar with it, but here he was on a bridge every bit as long as the mighty George Washington, and it was his first contact, and he hoped his last. The bridge led from the borough of Queens to Rikers Island, the largest penal institution in the world. As a metaphor for incarceration, Rikers Island was a long way from its neighbor, LaGuardia Airport, which, like any airport, was a contrasting icon for freedom.

Chet's morning had started early in the courthouse. Although he had had significant experience testifying during many trials involving all manner of death, he'd had little other contact with the courts, and that morning, he'd had to face a steep learning curve. Over the Easter weekend, he'd fretted over the news that had been in the *Times* concerning Angels Healthcare and its CEO and founder, Angela Dawson. She, her chief financial officer, and her chief operating officer had been arrested for an astounding array of charges, including various conspiracies, a number of different categories of fraud, money laundering, violations of the Patriot Act, and violation of Sarbanes-Oxley. An even more serious charge of accessory to depraved-heart murder had been quickly dropped.

Chet had first been angry. Here was a woman who'd impressed and charmed him into going to frivolous lengths to spend a little time with her and to get to know her, not to mention the money he'd spent on her, and now, after all the effort, he learns from a newspaper that she's a criminal. For him, it had been yet another reminder that women, like his old college girlfriend, cannot be trusted, and keeping them at arm's length represented an act of self-preservation.

Yet by late Easter Sunday, Chet's initial response had mellowed enough for him to question the charges, since they hardly fit the mental and emotional image he'd begun to construct of Angela Dawson. He also reminded himself of a basic tenet of American jurisprudence: namely, that people are innocent until proven guilty. It was at that point that another fact had begun to bother him: All three individuals had been offered bail, but only two had posted it. Angela Dawson had not done so, and the reason given was that she'd consumed all her equity in trying to prop up her floundering company.

From there on it had been downhill, as far as Chet's sense of well-being was concerned. He'd been unable to get two images out of his mind. One was Angela chained to a bare stone wall in a damp, dungeonlike cell with rats and cockroaches running around. The second was a ten-year-old daughter crying incessantly. By Monday, Chet had made a decision, which he assumed was irrational and surely had more to do with his own needs than with chivalry. And by that morning, Tuesday, he'd started the process by calling a bail bondsman and arranging for a quick meeting.

It had been at that point that Chet's learning curve about criminal law had had to begin. He'd always had a rather simplified view of posting bail. A person brought the money, handed it over, and that was it. But, particularly in high-profile cases, such as Angela's, especially when the bail amount was high, as it was, there was a bit more involved.

In fact, it took all morning for Chet and the bail bondsman to arrange for a court surety hearing to make sure Chet's twenty-five thousand cash and his collateral for the other two hundred thousand were coming from legitimate sources and not drug money or something similar. Forced to wait even over a court adjournment for lunch, Chet had not gotten the final determination that the bail had been met until one-thirty. It was for that reason that it was now almost three as he was at last approaching Rikers Island.

Chet looked around the bus's interior. The other riders were mostly female and appeared to reside mostly on the south side of the poverty line. Although it was abundantly clear that rich people were as capable as anyone else of committing crime, the lion's share of the burden of paying for it fell on the poor.

After what seemed like an exceptionally long drive, the bus drove onto Rikers Island proper and presently came to a stop at the Rikers Island Visitors Center. As Chet climbed down from the bus, he got the immediate impression the complex was generally dirty and run-down. It was not a happy place.

Unsure of where to go, Chet followed the crowd into the scarred and scuffed building.

The atmosphere was repressive. As the others who'd come on the bus with Chet filed off to their respective destinations, Chet stopped. He didn't know where to go. He'd not realized how large the place was. Spotting an official-appearing person, Chet started in his direction for advice, but he didn't need it. He saw Angela sitting among a crowd who plainly had more in common with one another than with her.

Angela had been staring ahead blankly until she caught sight of Chet. Her first reaction was confusion, as if she recognized him but couldn't quite remember who he was. Chet walked directly up to her and looked down into her eyes, which suddenly reflected recognition. She stood up with confusion.

"Chet," she said, as much a question as a statement.

"What a coincidence meeting you here," Chet said spontaneously. He'd not planned on what he should say.

Angela laughed uneasily. "I had no idea it would be you. Suddenly, I was told my bail had been posted and that I was to be picked up. I thought maybe by my CFO or my COO, but never you."

"I hope I'm not a disappointment."

"Hardly," Angela said. She reached out and gave him a hug, pinning his arms to his sides. For a moment, she wouldn't let go. When she did, he saw her eyes had become significantly wetter. "Thank you, and my daughter thanks you. I don't know what else to say."

"Thanks is fine," Chet said. "And you're welcome." Then he hooked a thumb over his shoulder. "Maybe we should try to catch the bus I came out here on. Otherwise, I don't know how long we will have to wait."

"Let's for sure!" Angela said eagerly. She wanted to put as much distance between herself and Rikers Island as possible, and as quickly as possible. She picked up her small bag. Together, they headed for the exit. Both were self-conscious. They didn't touch.

"Why did you do it?" Angela asked when they got outside.

"To be honest, I don't know."

Angela stopped for a moment and glanced around. "When you are locked up, you realize how much you take freedom for granted. This has been the worst experience of my life."

"I think we better hurry," Chet said. The bus was still standing where Chet had gotten off, but the line to board was down to three people.

Chet and Angela ran and climbed on. The first empty double seat was close to the very rear.

"I guess I posted your bail because I don't think you could have done the things you are charged with."

"I'm sorry to disabuse you of that belief," Angela said, turning to Chet. "I did do some of them, but hardly as charged. I have had a number of miserable hours thinking about everything. The main thing is that I knowingly did not file an eight-K. It's a required SEC form. But do you know something? There was never a precise moment when it should have been filed. I mean, at first there was no cash-flow problem. It happened over time, and we thought the MRSA would be easily handled. We never suspected it was being deliberately spread."

"I spoke to a lawyer friend of mine," Chet said. "He told me in cases like this, the judge has a lot of discretion."

"I hope so," Angela said. "My biggest worry right now is the threat of losing my medical license, which is a very real possibility. For me, that will be the worst punishment, because I've finally seen the light. As a businesswoman, I don't like the person I've become. It's like I've had blinders on. I've come to realize that money is a seductive but illusionary goal, and it's addictive. The problem is one's never satisfied, and no matter how much money is made, it can't shake a stick at how I remember feeling after helping an office full of patients. What I'm saying is I want to go back to medicine."

"Come again?" Chet said with surprise.

"I want to go back to the practice of medicine," Angela repeated. "My immediate goal is going to be to solve my legal problems, so I can do it. It's been a hard lesson, but I know now that mixing medicine and business is great for business, with the huge amount of money available, but an unmitigated disaster for medicine and the doctors who allow themselves to be caught up in it."

"Interesting," Chet said.

"Interesting?" Angela repeated questioningly. "Are you humoring me? I've really been thinking about this nonstop. I'm being very serious."

"I'm not humoring you at all," Chet said. "Quite the contrary. I'm realizing that you are telling me why I was willing to post your bail."